OZY AND MILLIE

Also by Dana Simpson

***Phoebe and Her Unicorn* Collections**

Phoebe and Her Unicorn

Unicorn on a Roll

Unicorn vs. Goblins

Razzle Dazzle Unicorn

Unicorn Crossing

Phoebe and Her Unicorn in the Magic Storm

Unicorn of Many Hats

Activity Books

Rainy Day Unicorn Fun

For Young Children

Today I'll Be a Unicorn

Dana Simpson

Andrews McMeel
PUBLISHING®

INTRODUCTION

A lot of artists kind of wince when they look at their old work.

If you draw a lot, you tend to improve a lot, and one result is looking at things you drew in the past and seeing all the mistakes you wouldn't make now. Because mistakes are how you learn.

Long before I ever imagined Phoebe, or her unicorn, *Ozy and Millie* was where I learned how to make comics. I was nineteen years old when I decided I wanted to be a comic strip artist and plunged into it head first. Webcomics were still a pretty new thing then, and there weren't that many, so mine got some attention. I kept doing it.

I had dreams of getting the strip into newspapers, making tons of money, and hanging out with movie stars or whatever syndicated cartoonists get to do. (Usually not that, it turns out.) It wasn't to be; *Ozy and Millie* would run on the Internet for ten whole years before I made the difficult decision to move on to other things.

There's no easy "elevator pitch" for the strip. Ozy and Millie are fifth graders and also foxes because everyone's an animal. Millie is a troublemaker who enjoys trying to be unsettling. Ozy is serene and centered to a fault, and he also wears a top hat for some reason. They're best friends. Ozy's adopted, and his father is a dragon who is either wise or messing with everyone. Their fair-weather raccoon friend, Avery, is openly only hanging around until he can get someone cooler to hang out with him. Ozy is bullied by a rabbit jock, and Millie is tormented by a mean-girl sheep.

These are the creatures who ran amok inside my head for ten years.

I look at *Ozy and Millie* now and see its flaws, but I also see a thousand little lessons learned. About writing, and drawing, and trying to say what's on your mind while also being funny and keeping your characters consistent. I've often described *Ozy and Millie* as my graduate thesis in cartooning.

I also see the story of that part of my life. It still means a lot to me, and, it seems, not just me. Even now, years after I drew the last strip, people often come up to me at conventions, or send me e-mails, telling me they miss Ozy and Millie and hope to see them again.

These are vintage strips, not new ones, although they were never in color before now. I tried to pick strips that represented what the comic was, who the main characters were (I'm sorry if I left out your favorite secondary character), and what the strip was generally about. I also went for strips that don't have a bunch of dated references in them, that are a bit more ageless. (It's a bit late now for jokes about George W. Bush, late '90s boy bands, or early 2000s reality TV.)

I picked strips from a few years in the middle because the art style evolved a lot over the years, and I wanted to keep it semi-consistent.

Most of all, though, I wanted to pick strips that make me laugh. And a lot of these do. That surprised me. I had forgotten how funny a lot of this stuff is. Well done, younger me.

If you've met Ozy and Millie before, welcome back. If you haven't, welcome. I hope you have fun!

Dana Simpson
March 2018

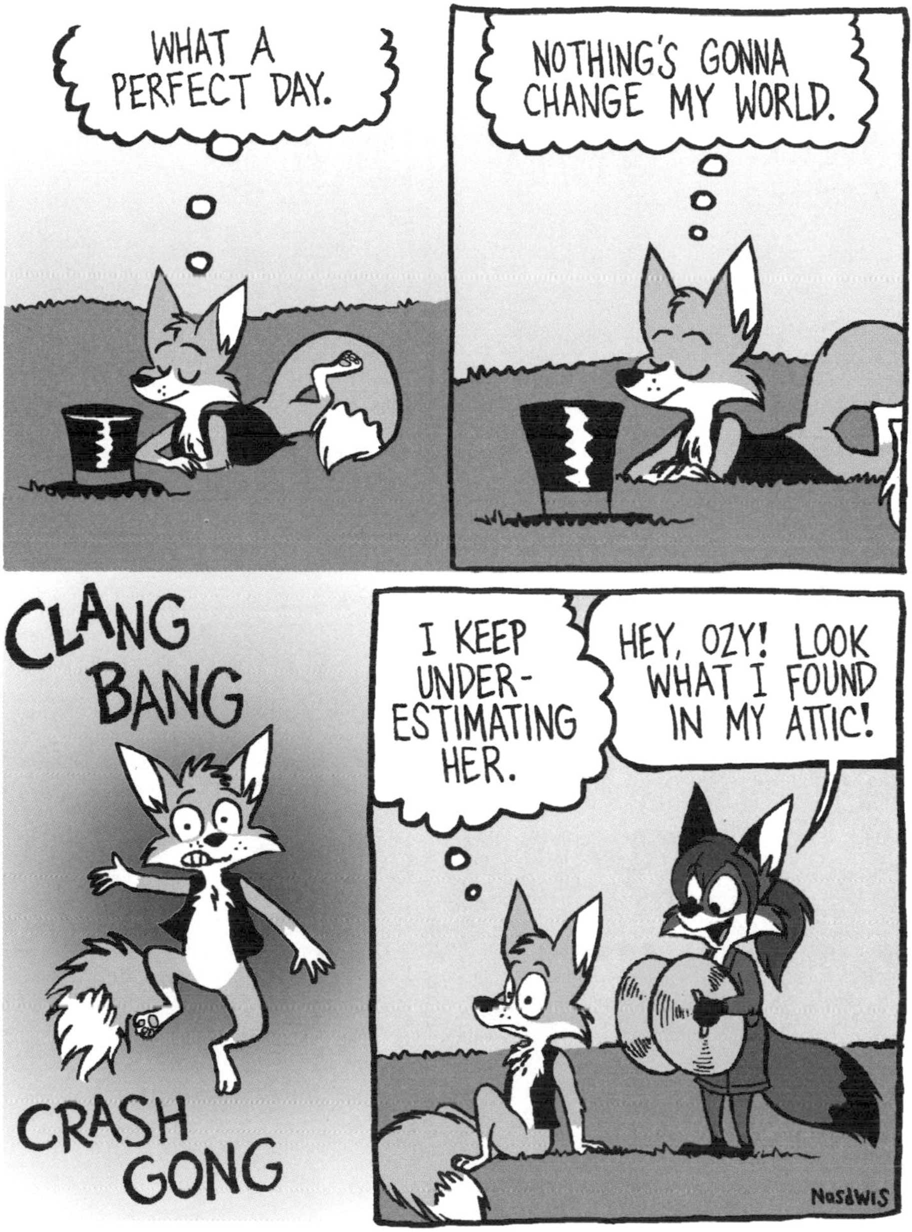
WHAT A PERFECT DAY.
NOTHING'S GONNA CHANGE MY WORLD.
CLANG
BANG
CRASH
GONG
I KEEP UNDER-ESTIMATING HER.
HEY, OZY! LOOK WHAT I FOUND IN MY ATTIC!
NASDWIS

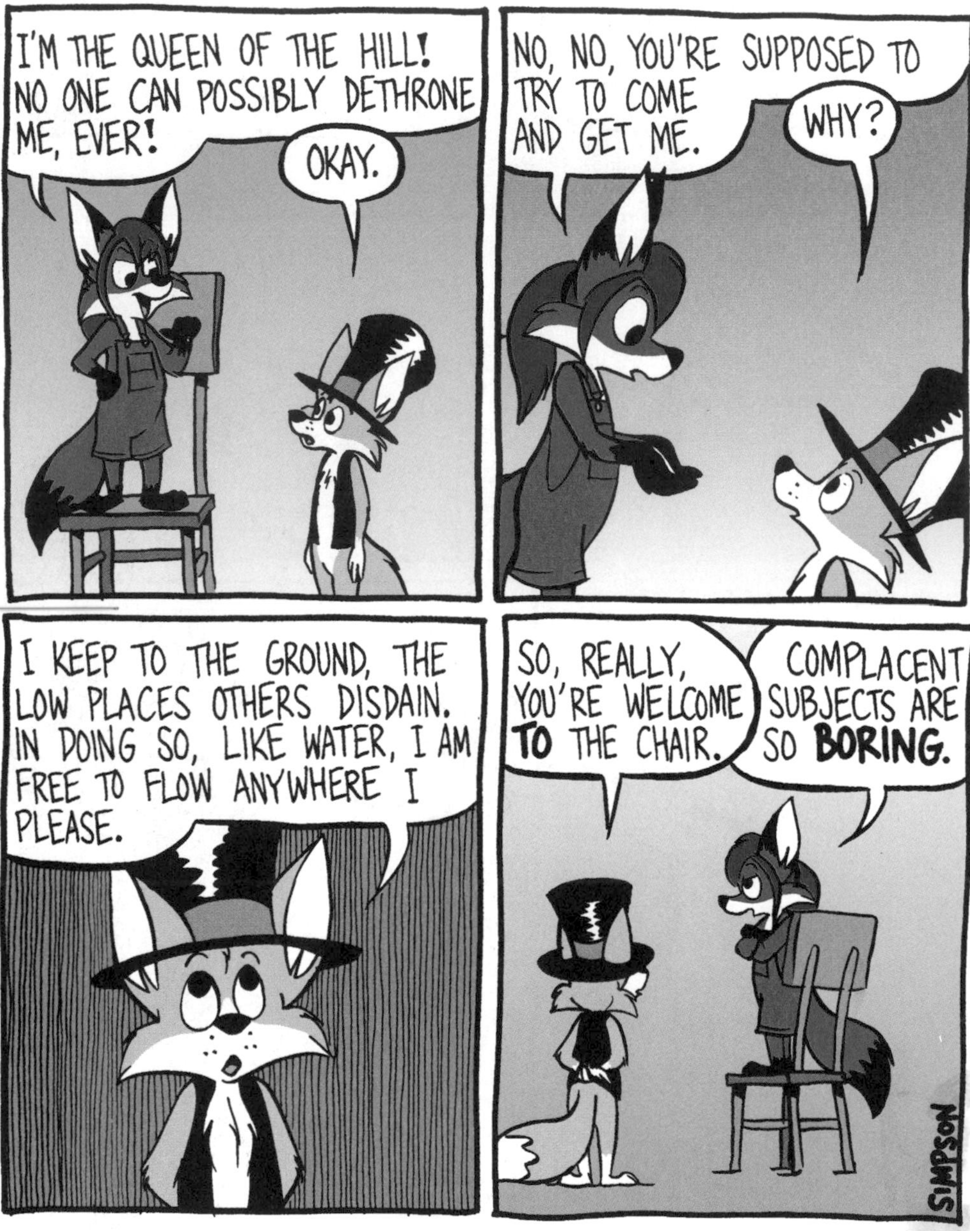
I'M THE QUEEN OF THE HILL! NO ONE CAN POSSIBLY DETHRONE ME, EVER!
OKAY.
NO, NO, YOU'RE SUPPOSED TO TRY TO COME AND GET ME.
WHY?
I KEEP TO THE GROUND, THE LOW PLACES OTHERS DISDAIN. IN DOING SO, LIKE WATER, I AM FREE TO FLOW ANYWHERE I PLEASE.
SO, REALLY, YOU'RE WELCOME **TO** THE CHAIR.
COMPLACENT SUBJECTS ARE SO **BORING.**
SIMPSON

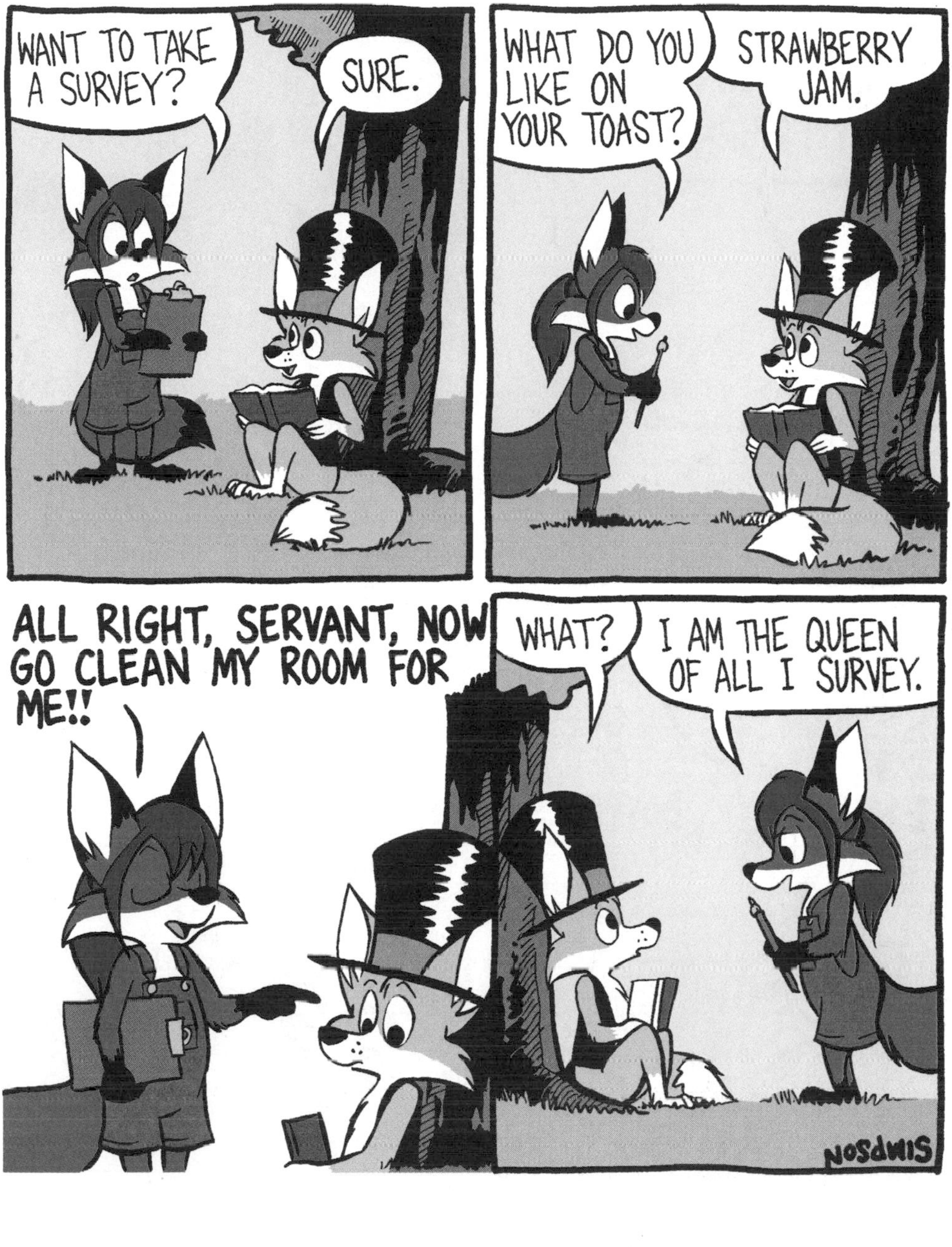
WANT TO TAKE A SURVEY?
SURE.
WHAT DO YOU LIKE ON YOUR TOAST?
STRAWBERRY JAM.
ALL RIGHT, SERVANT, NOW GO CLEAN MY ROOM FOR ME!!
WHAT?
I AM THE QUEEN OF ALL I SURVEY.
SIMPSON

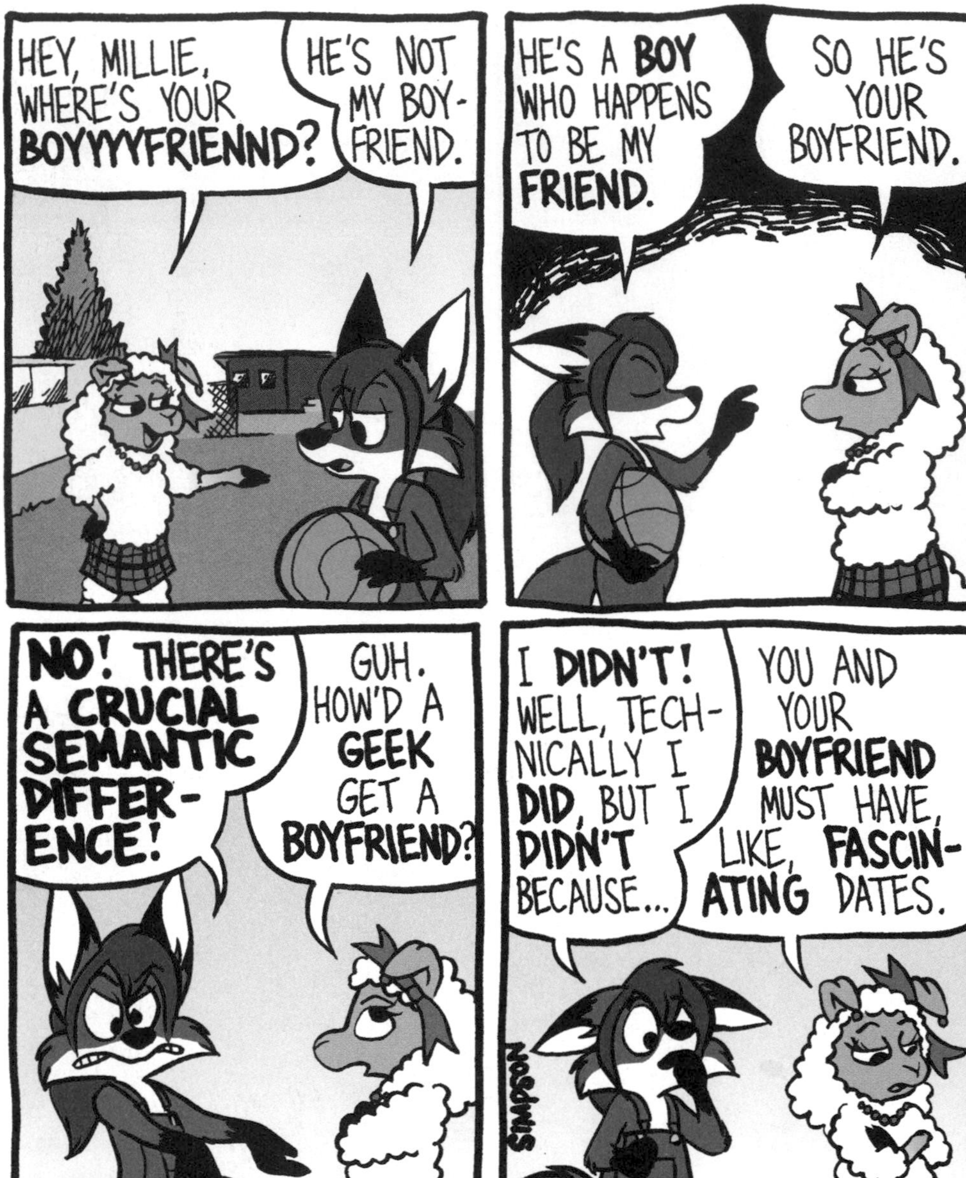
HEY, MILLIE, WHERE'S YOUR **BOYYYYFRIENND?**
HE'S NOT MY BOY-FRIEND.
HE'S A **BOY** WHO HAPPENS TO BE MY **FRIEND.**
SO HE'S YOUR BOYFRIEND.
NO! THERE'S A **CRUCIAL SEMANTIC DIFFER-ENCE!**
GUH. HOW'D A **GEEK** GET A **BOYFRIEND?**
I **DIDN'T!** WELL, TECH-NICALLY I **DID**, BUT I **DIDN'T** BECAUSE...
YOU AND YOUR **BOYFRIEND** MUST HAVE, LIKE, **FASCIN-ATING** DATES.
SIMPSON

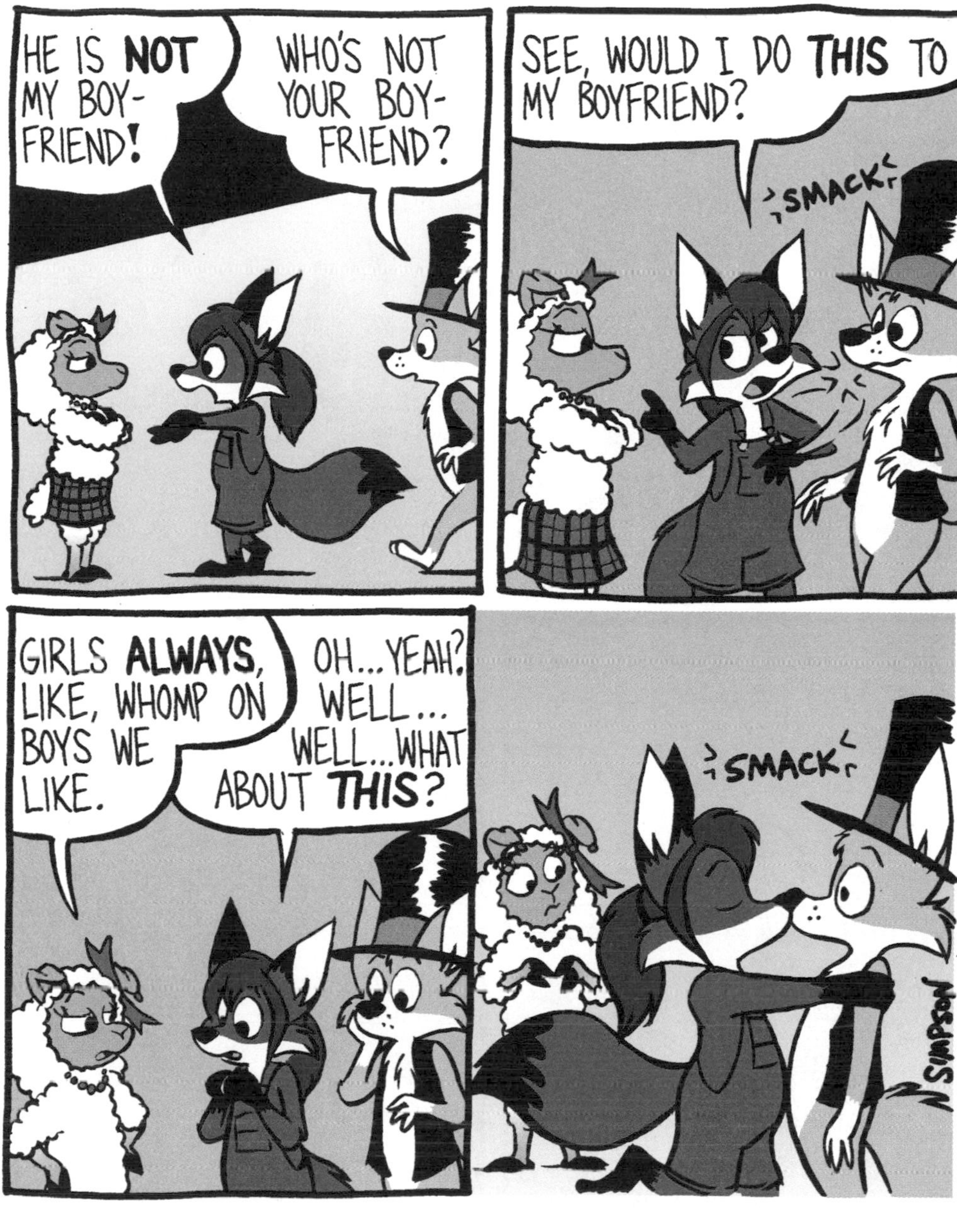

HE IS **NOT** MY BOY-FRIEND!
WHO'S NOT YOUR BOY-FRIEND?
SEE, WOULD I DO **THIS** TO MY BOYFRIEND?
SMACK
GIRLS **ALWAYS**, LIKE, WHOMP ON BOYS WE LIKE.
OH... YEAH? WELL... WELL... WHAT ABOUT **THIS**?
SMACK
SIMPSON

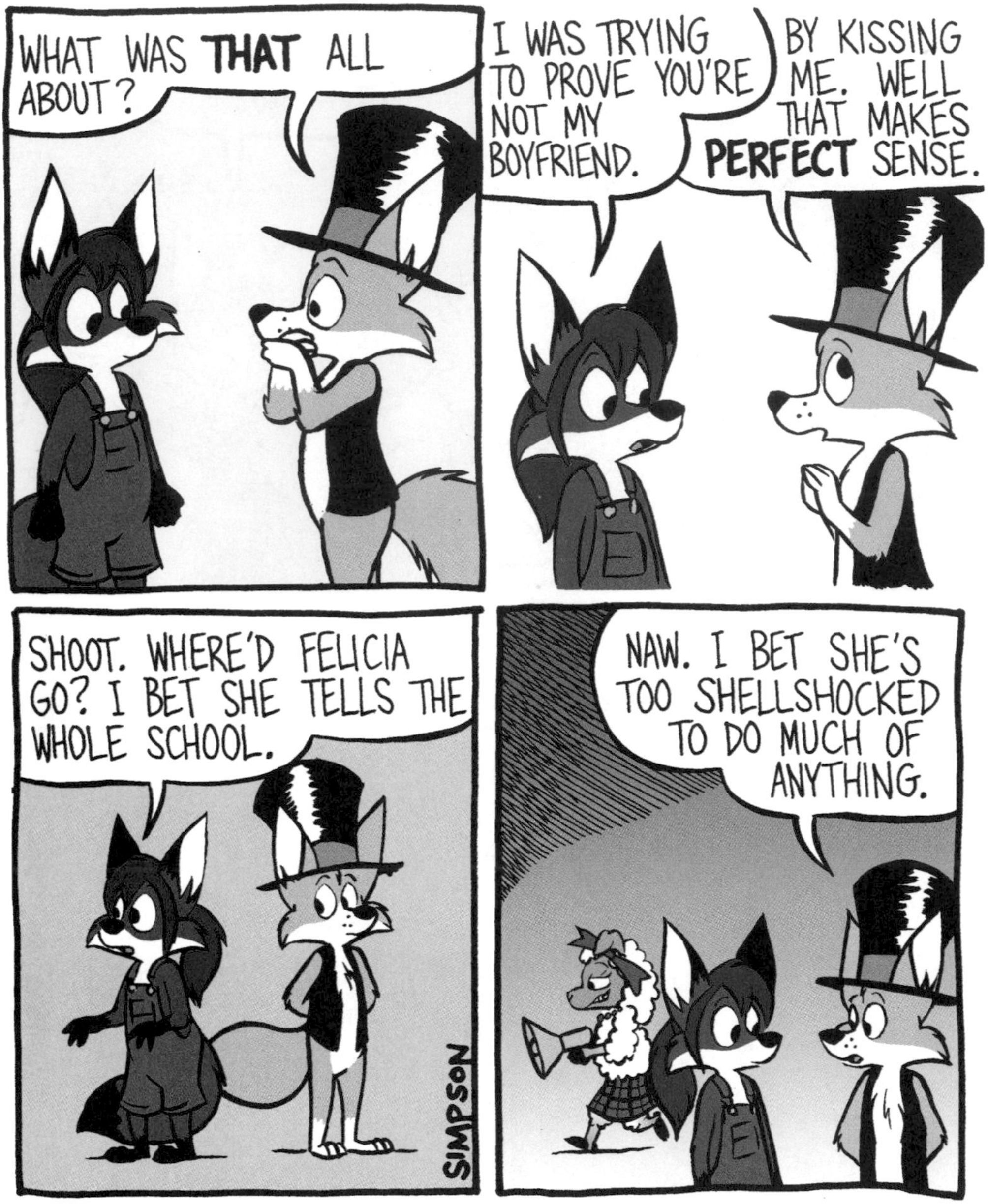
WHAT WAS **THAT** ALL ABOUT?
I WAS TRYING TO PROVE YOU'RE NOT MY BOYFRIEND.
BY KISSING ME. WELL THAT MAKES **PERFECT** SENSE.
SHOOT. WHERE'D FELICIA GO? I BET SHE TELLS THE WHOLE SCHOOL.
SIMPSON
NAW. I BET SHE'S TOO SHELLSHOCKED TO DO MUCH OF ANYTHING.

MOM, THERE'S A RUMOR **ALL OVER THE SCHOOL** THAT OZY AND I ARE, LIKE, ENGAGED.
OZY'S LUCKY. BOYS DON'T GOSSIP THE WAY GIRLS DO. ...DO THEY?
NOT QUITE THE SAME WAY, NO.
OZY, IT SAYS IN THIS COMMENTS SECTION THAT YOU HAVE TERMINAL GIRL GERMS.
UH-HUH.

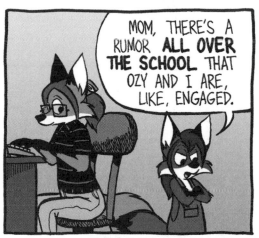

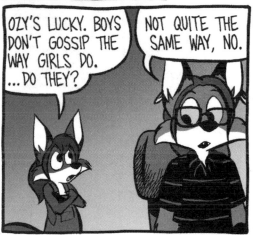

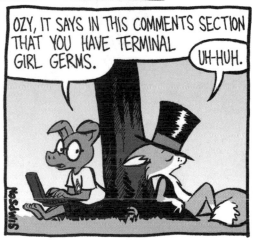

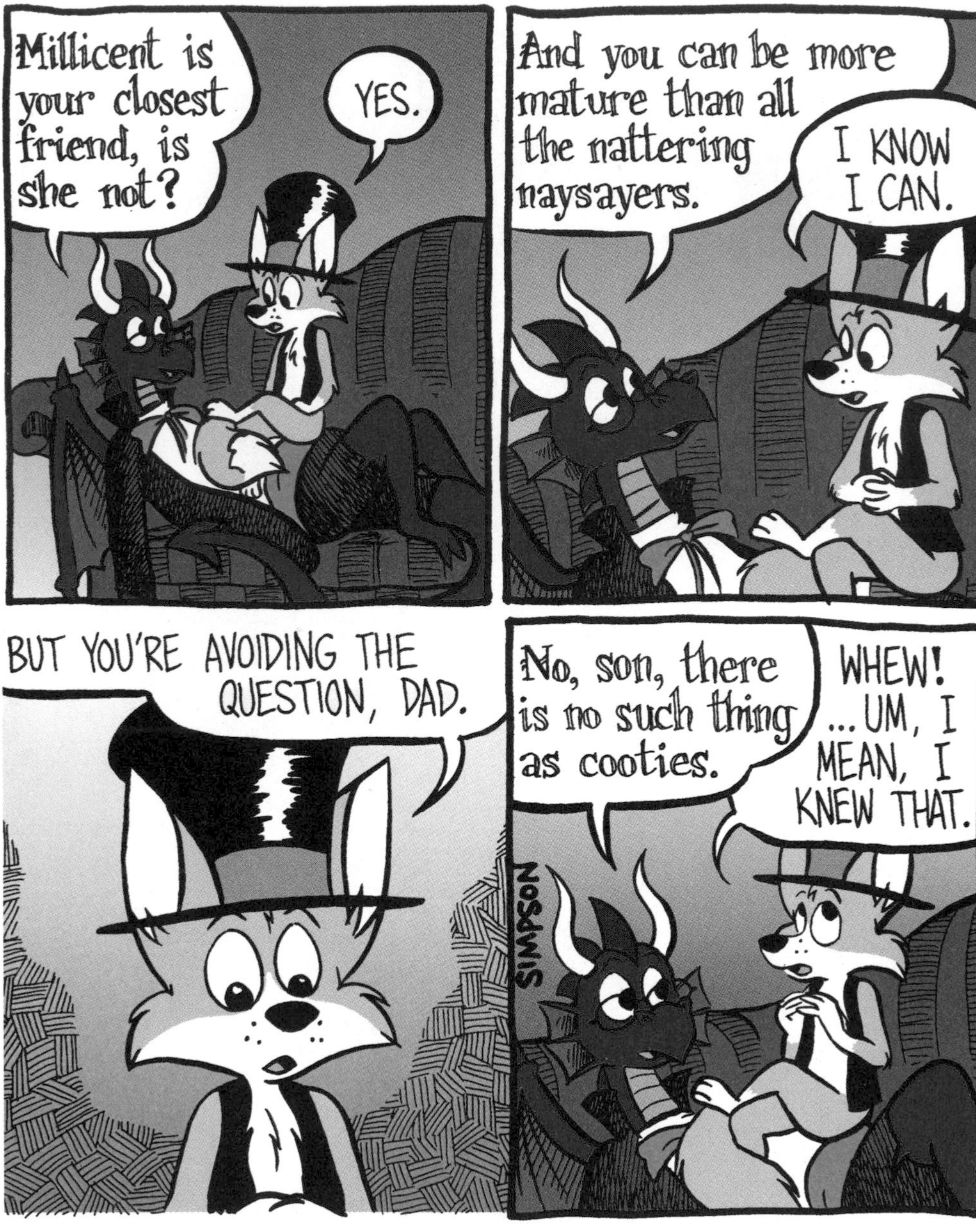
Millicent is your closest friend, is she not?
YES.
And you can be more mature than all the nattering naysayers.
I KNOW I CAN.
BUT YOU'RE AVOIDING THE QUESTION, DAD.
No, son, there is no such thing as cooties.
WHEW! ...UM, I MEAN, I KNEW THAT.
SIMPSON

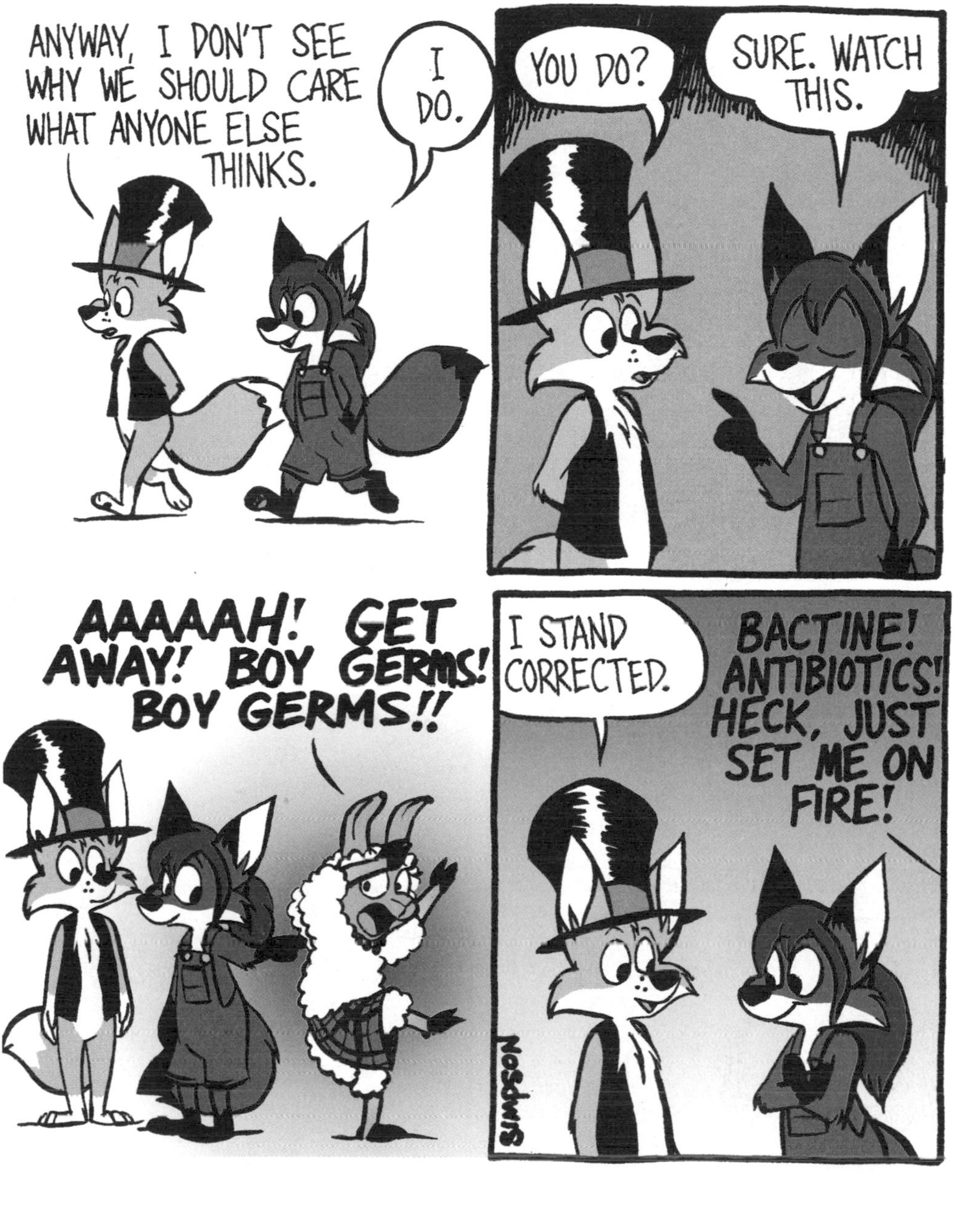
ANYWAY, I DON'T SEE WHY WE SHOULD CARE WHAT ANYONE ELSE THINKS.
I DO.
YOU DO?
SURE. WATCH THIS.
AAAAAH! GET AWAY! BOY GERMS! BOY GERMS!!
I STAND CORRECTED.
BACTINE! ANTIBIOTICS! HECK, JUST SET ME ON FIRE!
SIMPSON

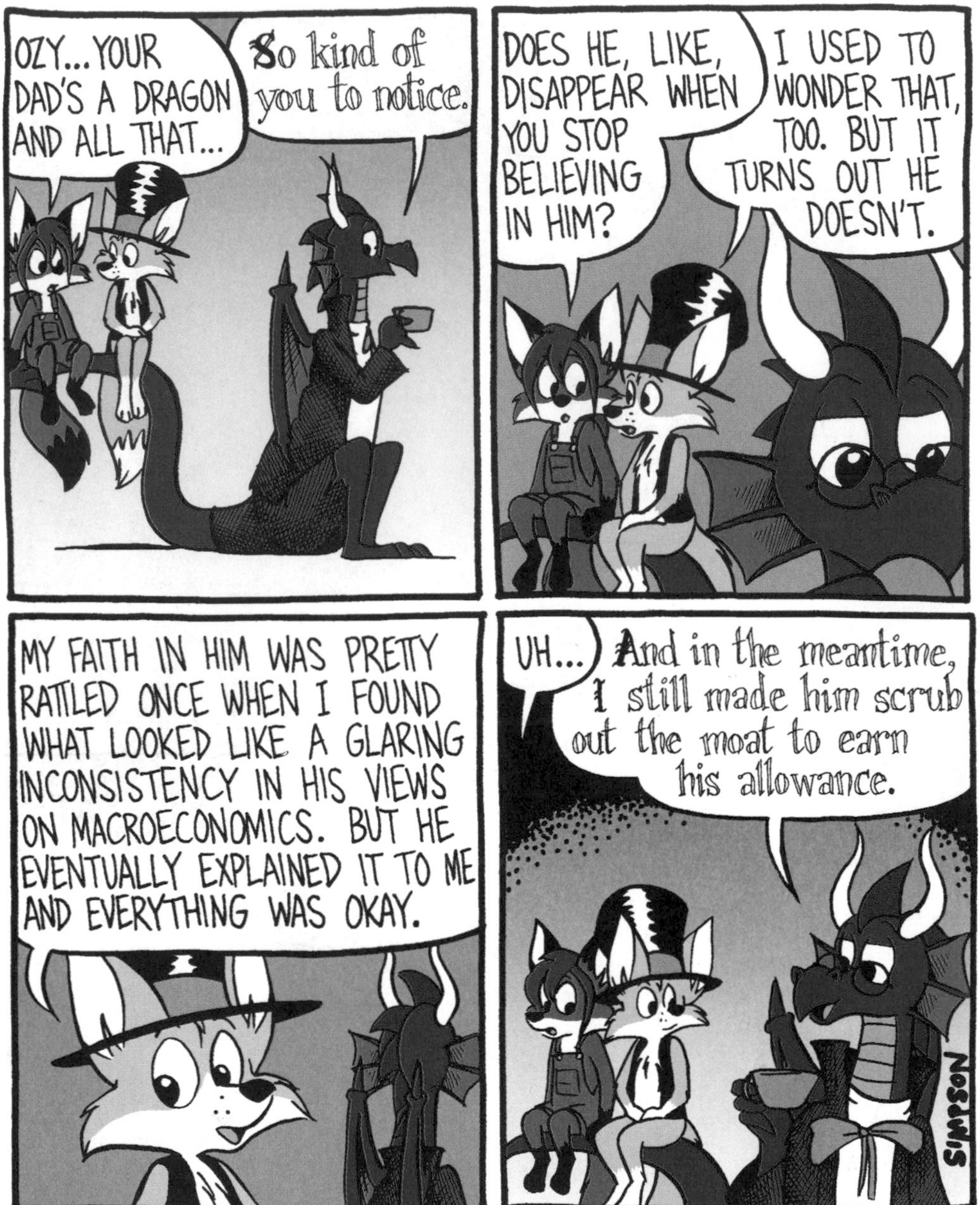
OZY... YOUR DAD'S A DRAGON AND ALL THAT...
So kind of you to notice.
DOES HE, LIKE, DISAPPEAR WHEN YOU STOP BELIEVING IN HIM?
I USED TO WONDER THAT, TOO. BUT IT TURNS OUT HE DOESN'T.
MY FAITH IN HIM WAS PRETTY RATTLED ONCE WHEN I FOUND WHAT LOOKED LIKE A GLARING INCONSISTENCY IN HIS VIEWS ON MACROECONOMICS. BUT HE EVENTUALLY EXPLAINED IT TO ME AND EVERYTHING WAS OKAY.
UH...
And in the meantime, I still made him scrub out the moat to earn his allowance.
SIMPSON

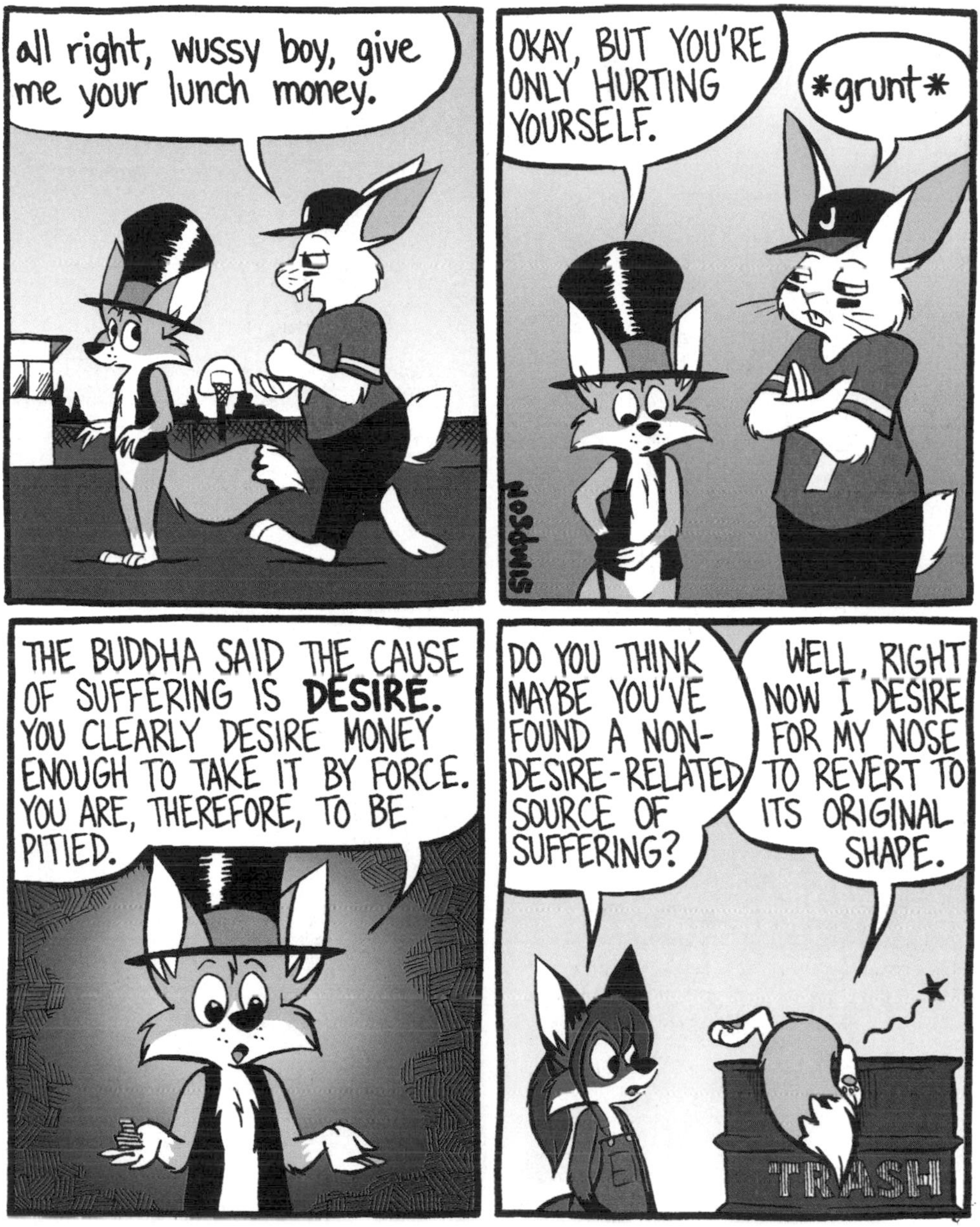
all right, wussy boy, give me your lunch money.
OKAY, BUT YOU'RE ONLY HURTING YOURSELF.
grunt
SIMPSON
THE BUDDHA SAID THE CAUSE OF SUFFERING IS **DESIRE.** YOU CLEARLY DESIRE MONEY ENOUGH TO TAKE IT BY FORCE. YOU ARE, THEREFORE, TO BE PITIED.
DO YOU THINK MAYBE YOU'VE FOUND A NON-DESIRE-RELATED SOURCE OF SUFFERING?
WELL, RIGHT NOW I DESIRE FOR MY NOSE TO REVERT TO ITS ORIGINAL SHAPE.
TRASH

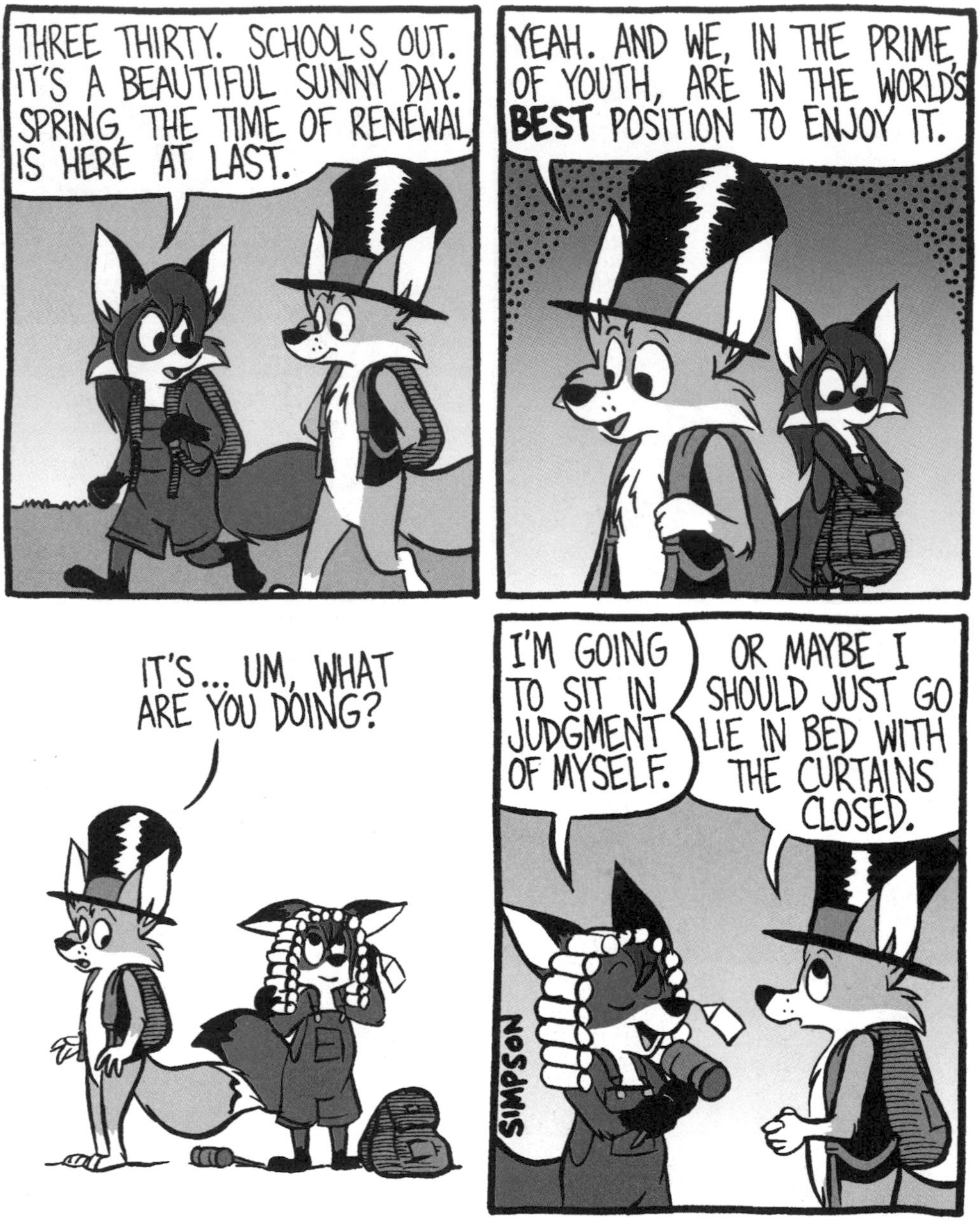
THREE THIRTY. SCHOOL'S OUT. IT'S A BEAUTIFUL SUNNY DAY. SPRING, THE TIME OF RENEWAL, IS HERE AT LAST.
YEAH. AND WE, IN THE PRIME OF YOUTH, ARE IN THE WORLD'S **BEST** POSITION TO ENJOY IT.
IT'S... UM, WHAT ARE YOU DOING?
I'M GOING TO SIT IN JUDGMENT OF MYSELF.
OR MAYBE I SHOULD JUST GO LIE IN BED WITH THE CURTAINS CLOSED.
SIMPSON

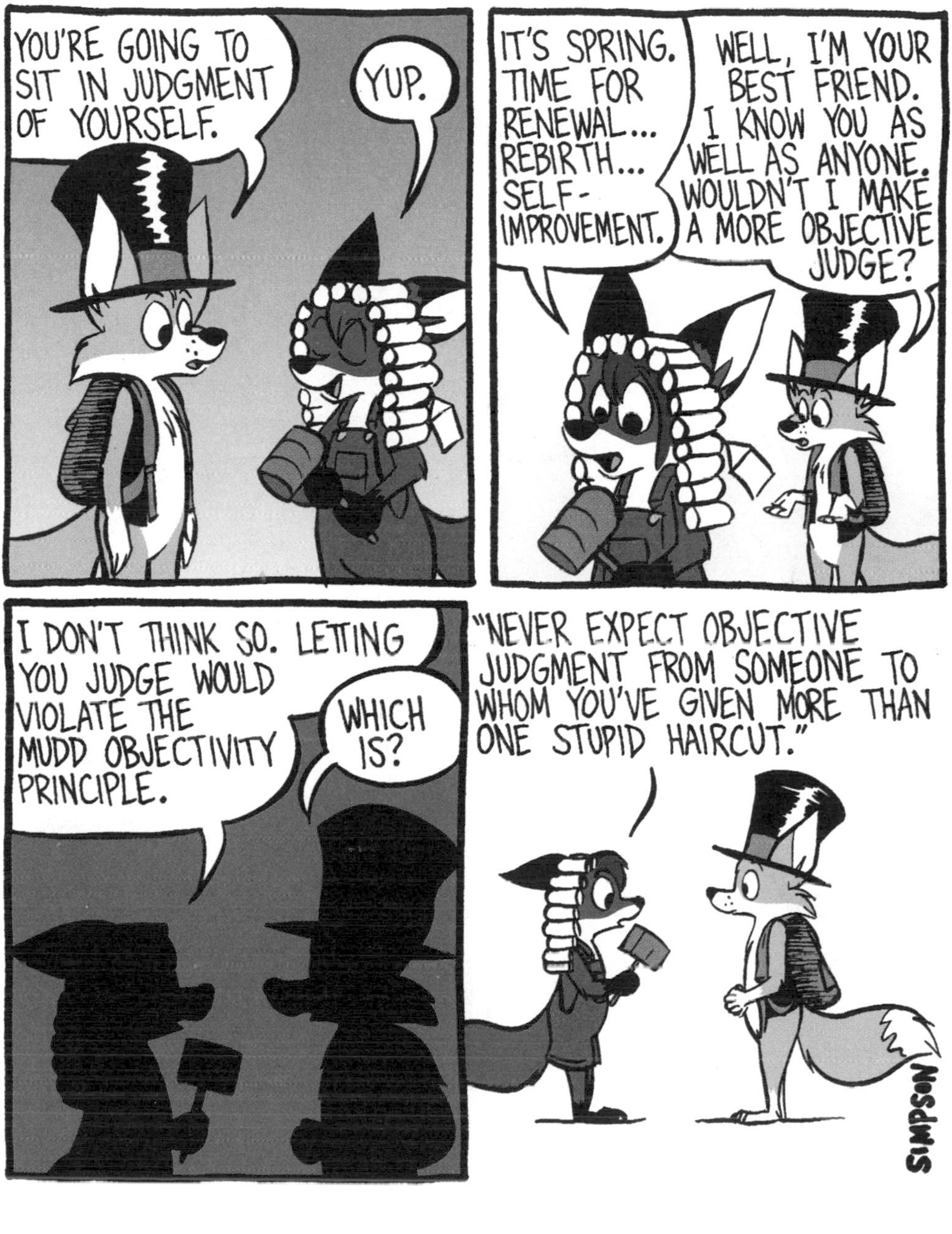
YOU'RE GOING TO SIT IN JUDGMENT OF YOURSELF.
YUP.
IT'S SPRING. TIME FOR RENEWAL... REBIRTH... SELF-IMPROVEMENT.
WELL, I'M YOUR BEST FRIEND. I KNOW YOU AS WELL AS ANYONE. WOULDN'T I MAKE A MORE OBJECTIVE JUDGE?
I DON'T THINK SO. LETTING YOU JUDGE WOULD VIOLATE THE MUDD OBJECTIVITY PRINCIPLE.
WHICH IS?
"NEVER EXPECT OBJECTIVE JUDGMENT FROM SOMEONE TO WHOM YOU'VE GIVEN MORE THAN ONE STUPID HAIRCUT."
SIMPSON

SO FEW PEOPLE TAKE THE TIME TO ACTUALLY EVALUATE THEMSELVES.
BUT THE UNEXAMINED LIFE IS NOT WORTH LIVING! I INTEND TO PUT MYSELF ON TRIAL AND REALLY GET TO THE BOTTOM OF MYSELF.
I FIGURE A **TRULY** OBJECTIVE SELF-TRIAL SHOULD TAKE ABOUT TWENTY MINUTES.
WHY SO LITTLE?
WELL, BECAUSE I'M **GREAT**.
AH.
NOSdWIS

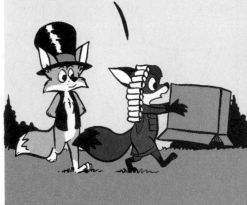

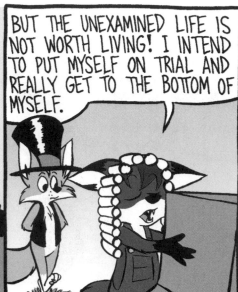

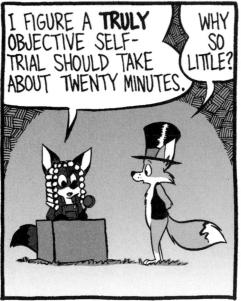

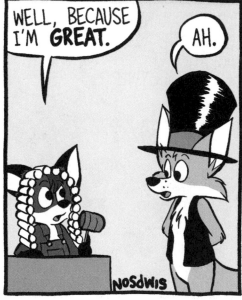

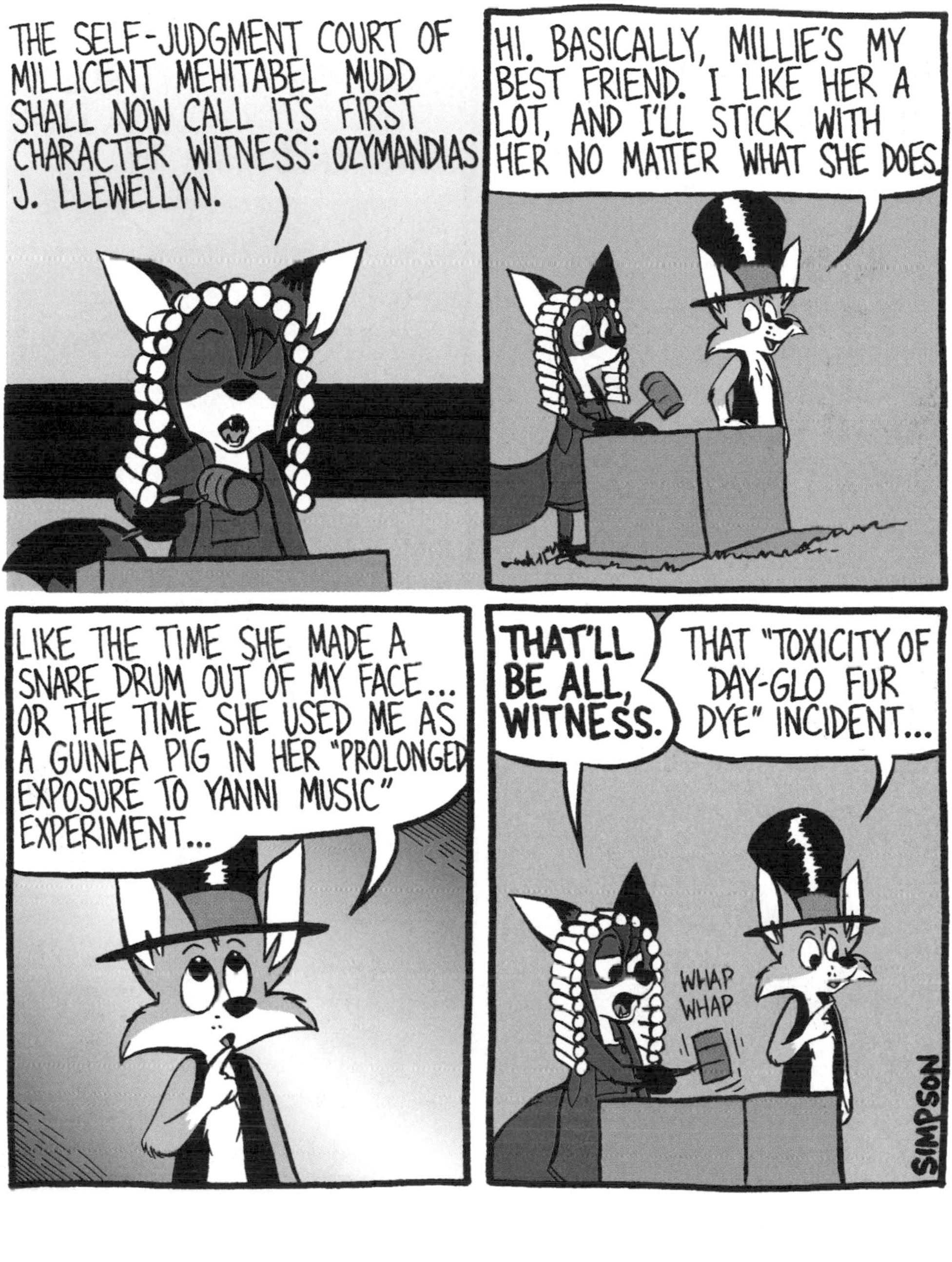
THE SELF-JUDGMENT COURT OF MILLICENT MEHITABEL MUDD SHALL NOW CALL ITS FIRST CHARACTER WITNESS: OZYMANDIAS J. LLEWELLYN.
HI. BASICALLY, MILLIE'S MY BEST FRIEND. I LIKE HER A LOT, AND I'LL STICK WITH HER NO MATTER WHAT SHE DOES.
LIKE THE TIME SHE MADE A SNARE DRUM OUT OF MY FACE... OR THE TIME SHE USED ME AS A GUINEA PIG IN HER "PROLONGED EXPOSURE TO YANNI MUSIC" EXPERIMENT...
THAT "TOXICITY OF DAY-GLO FUR DYE" INCIDENT...
THAT'LL BE ALL, WITNESS.
WHAP WHAP
SIMPSON

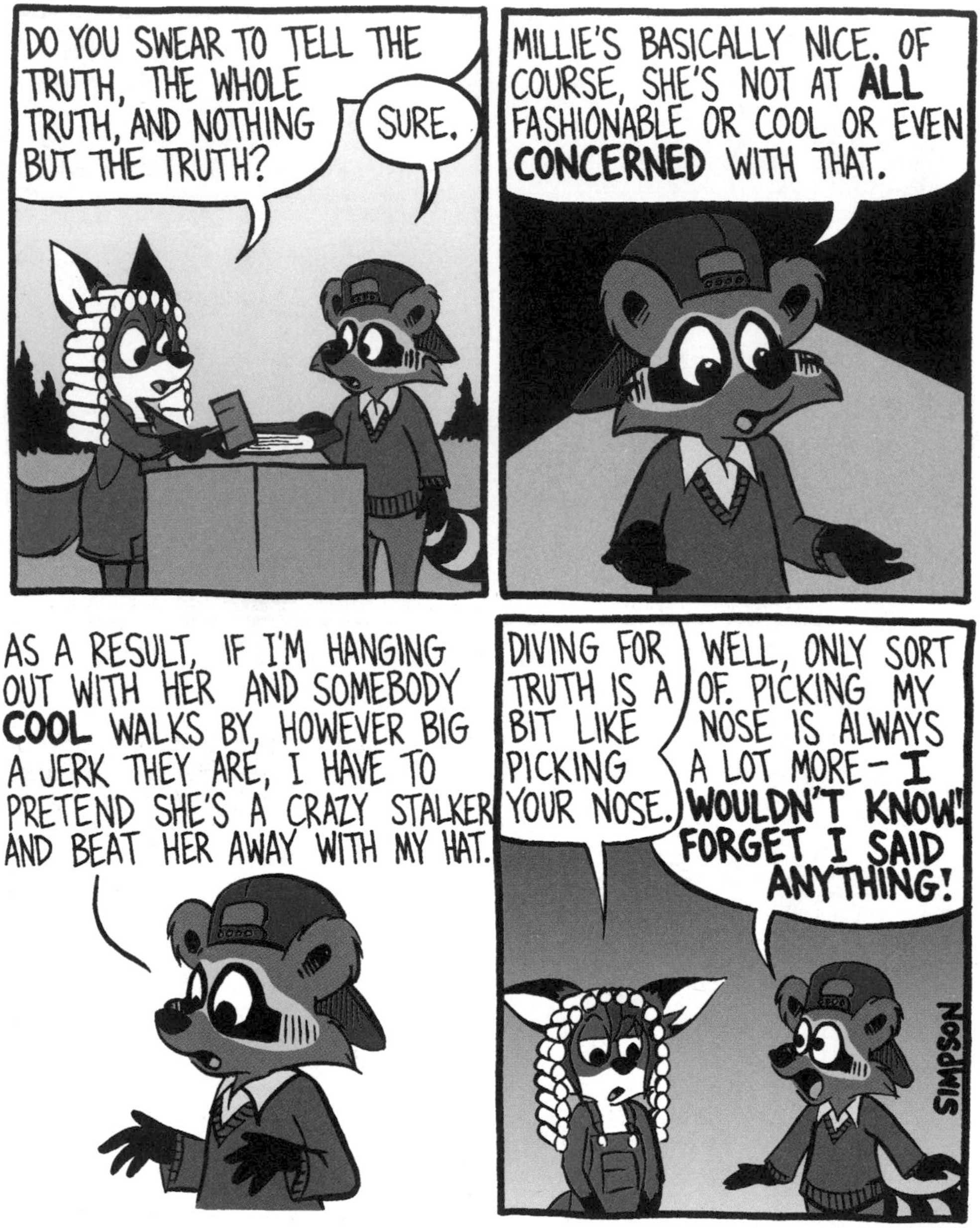
DO YOU SWEAR TO TELL THE TRUTH, THE WHOLE TRUTH, AND NOTHING BUT THE TRUTH?
SURE.
MILLIE'S BASICALLY NICE. OF COURSE, SHE'S NOT AT **ALL** FASHIONABLE OR COOL OR EVEN **CONCERNED** WITH THAT.
AS A RESULT, IF I'M HANGING OUT WITH HER AND SOMEBODY **COOL** WALKS BY, HOWEVER BIG A JERK THEY ARE, I HAVE TO PRETEND SHE'S A CRAZY STALKER AND BEAT HER AWAY WITH MY HAT.
DIVING FOR TRUTH IS A BIT LIKE PICKING YOUR NOSE.
WELL, ONLY SORT OF. PICKING MY NOSE IS ALWAYS A LOT MORE– **I WOULDN'T KNOW! FORGET I SAID ANYTHING!**
SIMPSON

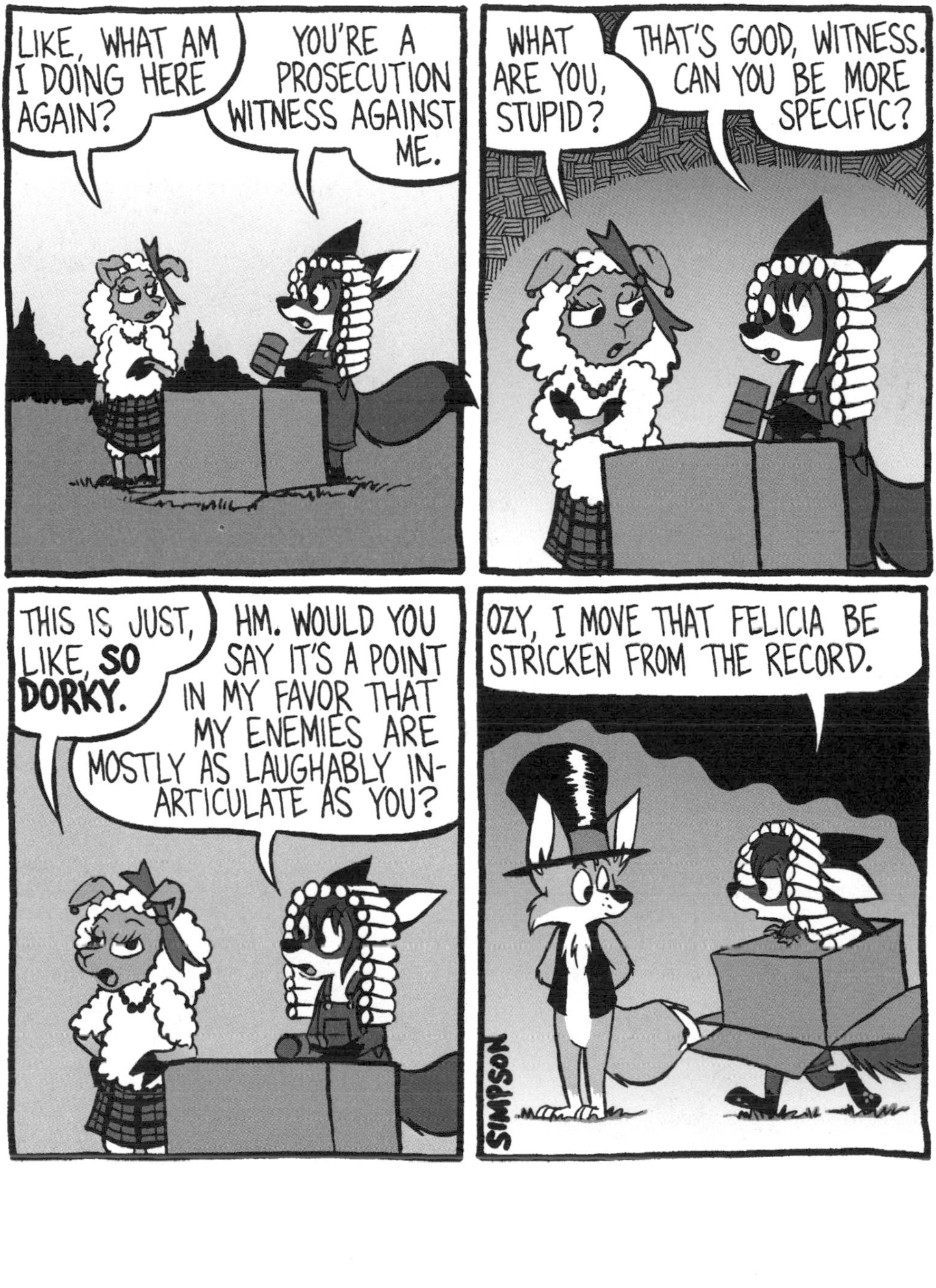
LIKE, WHAT AM I DOING HERE AGAIN?
YOU'RE A PROSECUTION WITNESS AGAINST ME.
WHAT ARE YOU, STUPID?
THAT'S GOOD, WITNESS. CAN YOU BE MORE SPECIFIC?
THIS IS JUST, LIKE, **SO DORKY.**
HM. WOULD YOU SAY IT'S A POINT IN MY FAVOR THAT MY ENEMIES ARE MOSTLY AS LAUGHABLY INARTICULATE AS YOU?
OZY, I MOVE THAT FELICIA BE STRICKEN FROM THE RECORD.
SIMPSON

Panel 1:

SO NOW YOU'VE—

CALLED MY RUBBER DUCKIE ERNEST AS MY FINAL CHARACTER WITNESS.

Panel 2:

MY GOAL HERE HAS BEEN TO GET TO KNOW MYSELF. SOMETIMES THAT'S NOT BEST ACHIEVED BY LISTENING TO PEOPLE TALK.

Panel 3:

YOU ARE WHAT YOU HEAR WHEN YOU FINALLY SHUT UP AND ALLOW YOURSELF TO HEAR THE THINGS INSIDE YOU! THE TIME FOR TALK IS PAST; WORDS HAVE EXHAUSTED THEIR USEFULNESS. ALL THAT REMAINS FOR ME TO DO IS LISTEN.

SIMPSON

Panel 4:

IT'S AWFULLY HARD TO HEAR THE WISDOM IN T... INNERMOST SE... IF YOU ALWAYS... JUST KEEP *JABBERING* ON LIKE A COMPLETE *MORON* W... JUST DOESN'T UNDER... ...HE VA...E OF INNER SIL...AND PE... ...EREN... OH ...D SI... ALR... BUT I... ...RE ...A... ...POINT... I'M GE... WAY FRO... ...HE YO... YOUR FAC... ...E...

LET'S GIVE HER A HAND, FOLKS.

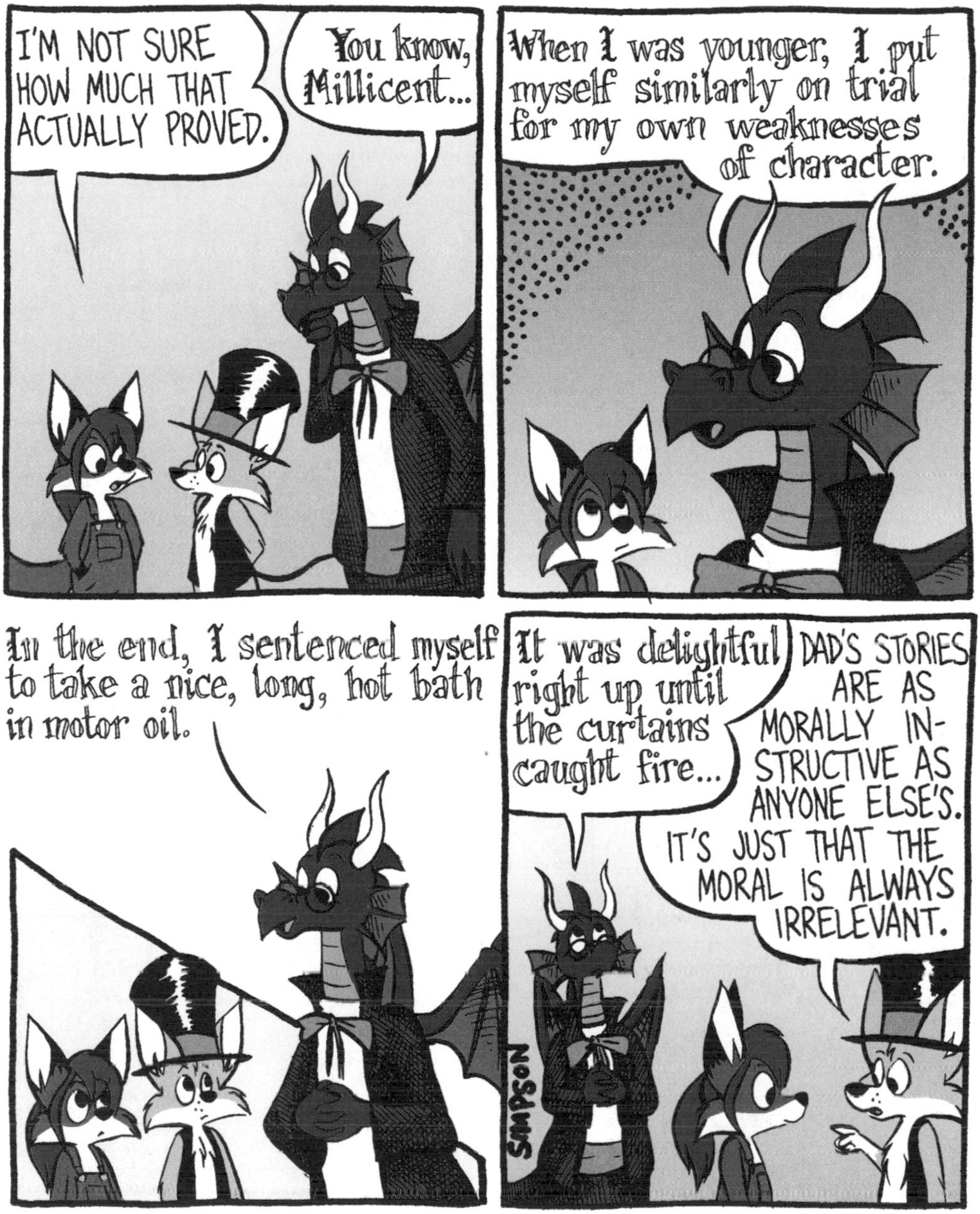
I'M NOT SURE HOW MUCH THAT ACTUALLY PROVED.
You know, Millicent...
When I was younger, I put myself similarly on trial for my own weaknesses of character.
In the end, I sentenced myself to take a nice, long, hot bath in motor oil.
It was delightful right up until the curtains caught fire...
DAD'S STORIES ARE AS MORALLY INSTRUCTIVE AS ANYONE ELSE'S. IT'S JUST THAT THE MORAL IS ALWAYS IRRELEVANT.
SAMPSON

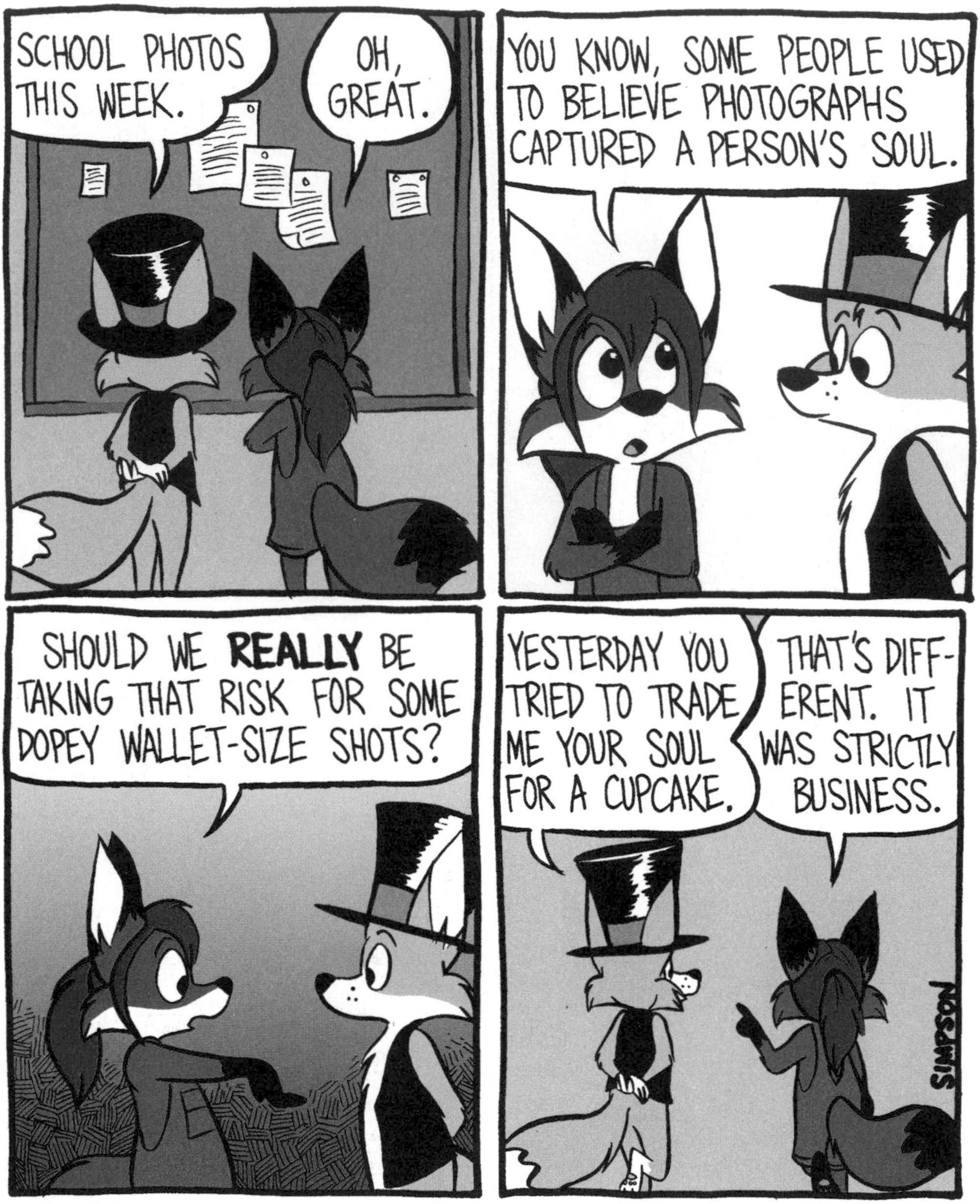
SCHOOL PHOTOS THIS WEEK.
OH, GREAT.
YOU KNOW, SOME PEOPLE USED TO BELIEVE PHOTOGRAPHS CAPTURED A PERSON'S SOUL.
SHOULD WE **REALLY** BE TAKING THAT RISK FOR SOME DOPEY WALLET-SIZE SHOTS?
YESTERDAY YOU TRIED TO TRADE ME YOUR SOUL FOR A CUPCAKE.
THAT'S DIFF-ERENT. IT WAS STRICTLY BUSINESS.
SIMPSON

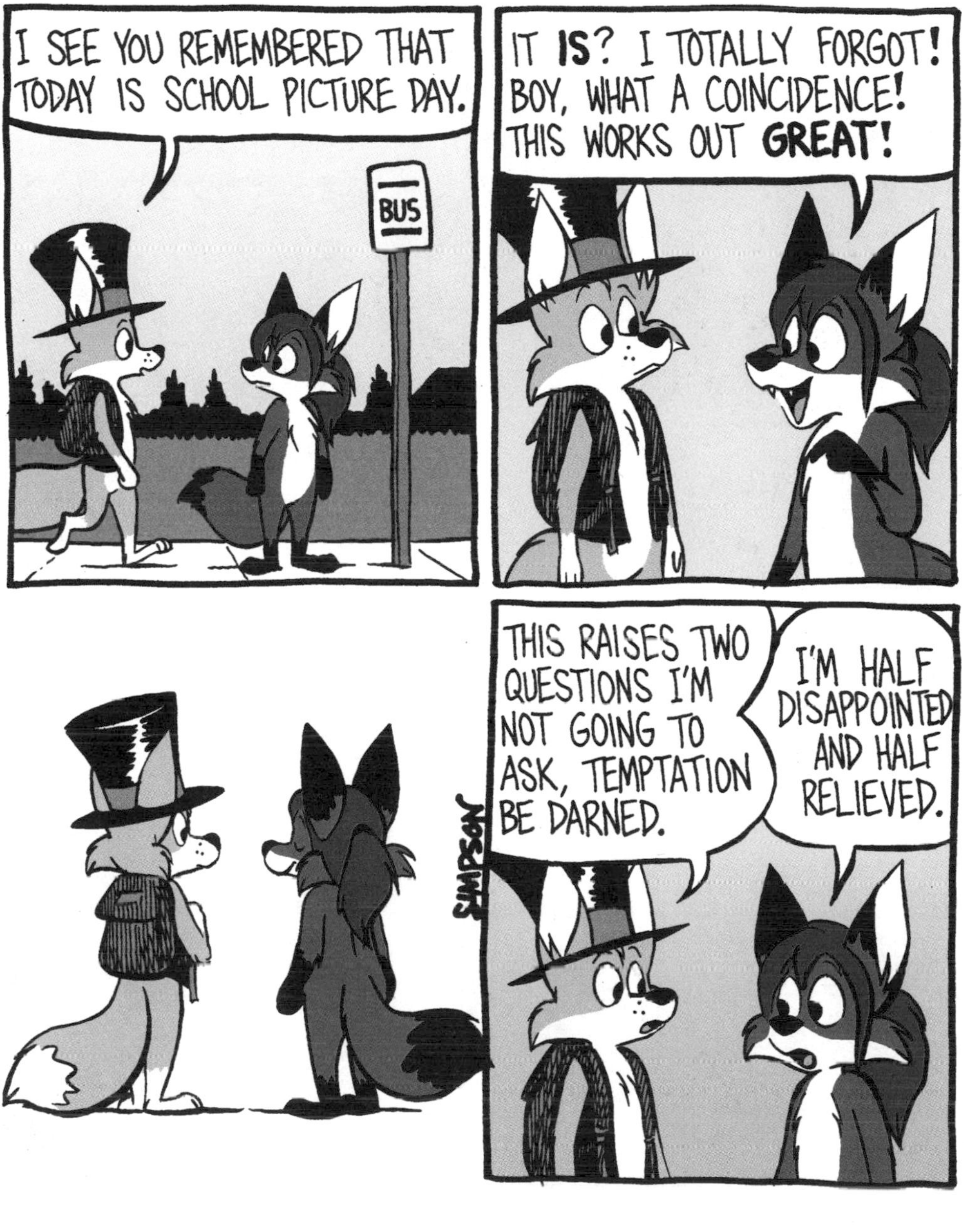
I SEE YOU REMEMBERED THAT TODAY IS SCHOOL PICTURE DAY.
BUS
IT **IS**? I TOTALLY FORGOT! BOY, WHAT A COINCIDENCE! THIS WORKS OUT **GREAT**!
SIMPSON
THIS RAISES TWO QUESTIONS I'M NOT GOING TO ASK, TEMPTATION BE DARNED.
I'M HALF DISAPPOINTED AND HALF RELIEVED.

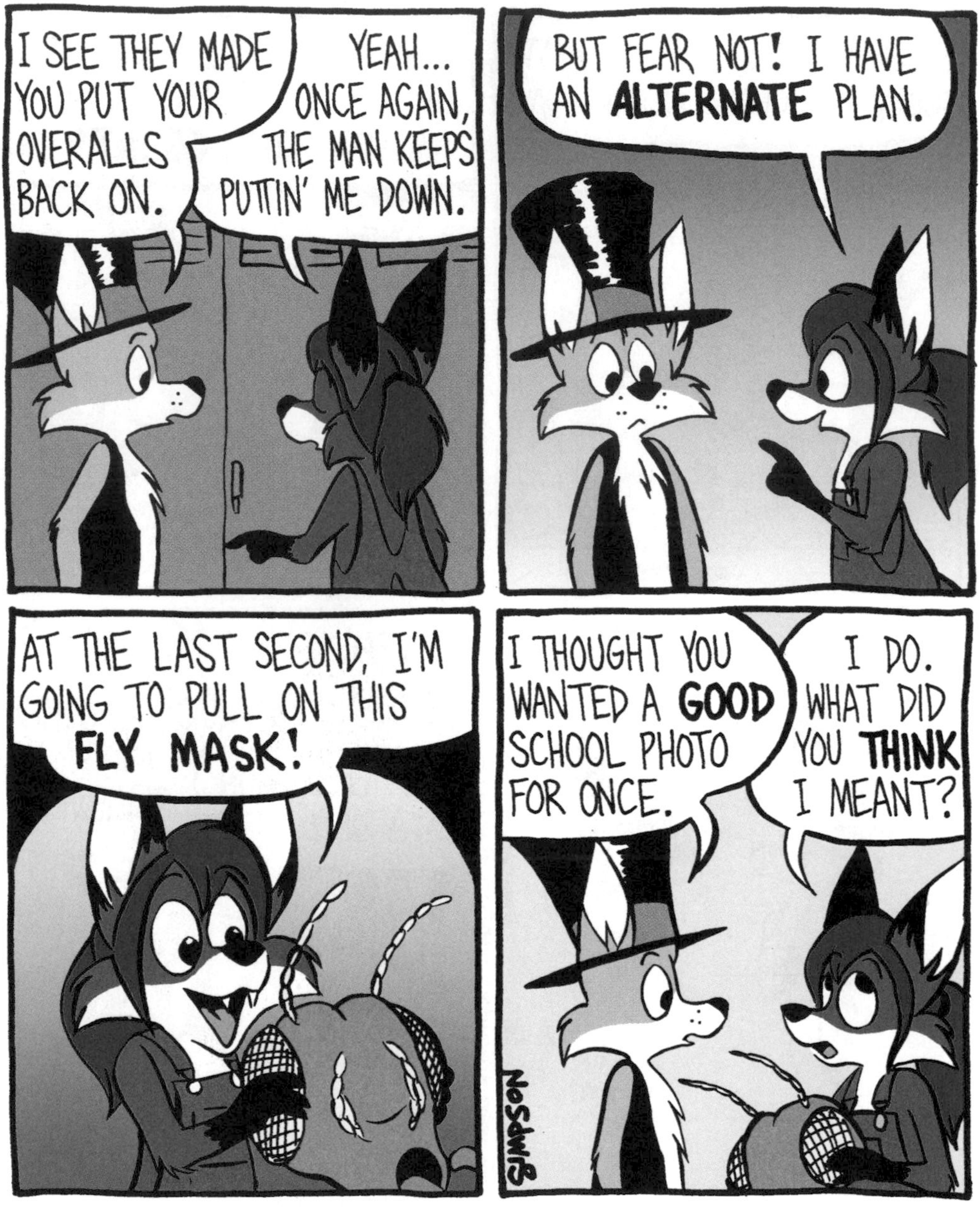
I SEE THEY MADE YOU PUT YOUR OVERALLS BACK ON.
YEAH... ONCE AGAIN, THE MAN KEEPS PUTTIN' ME DOWN.
BUT FEAR NOT! I HAVE AN **ALTERNATE** PLAN.
AT THE LAST SECOND, I'M GOING TO PULL ON THIS **FLY MASK!**
I THOUGHT YOU WANTED A **GOOD** SCHOOL PHOTO FOR ONCE.
I DO. WHAT DID YOU **THINK** I MEANT?
SIMPSON

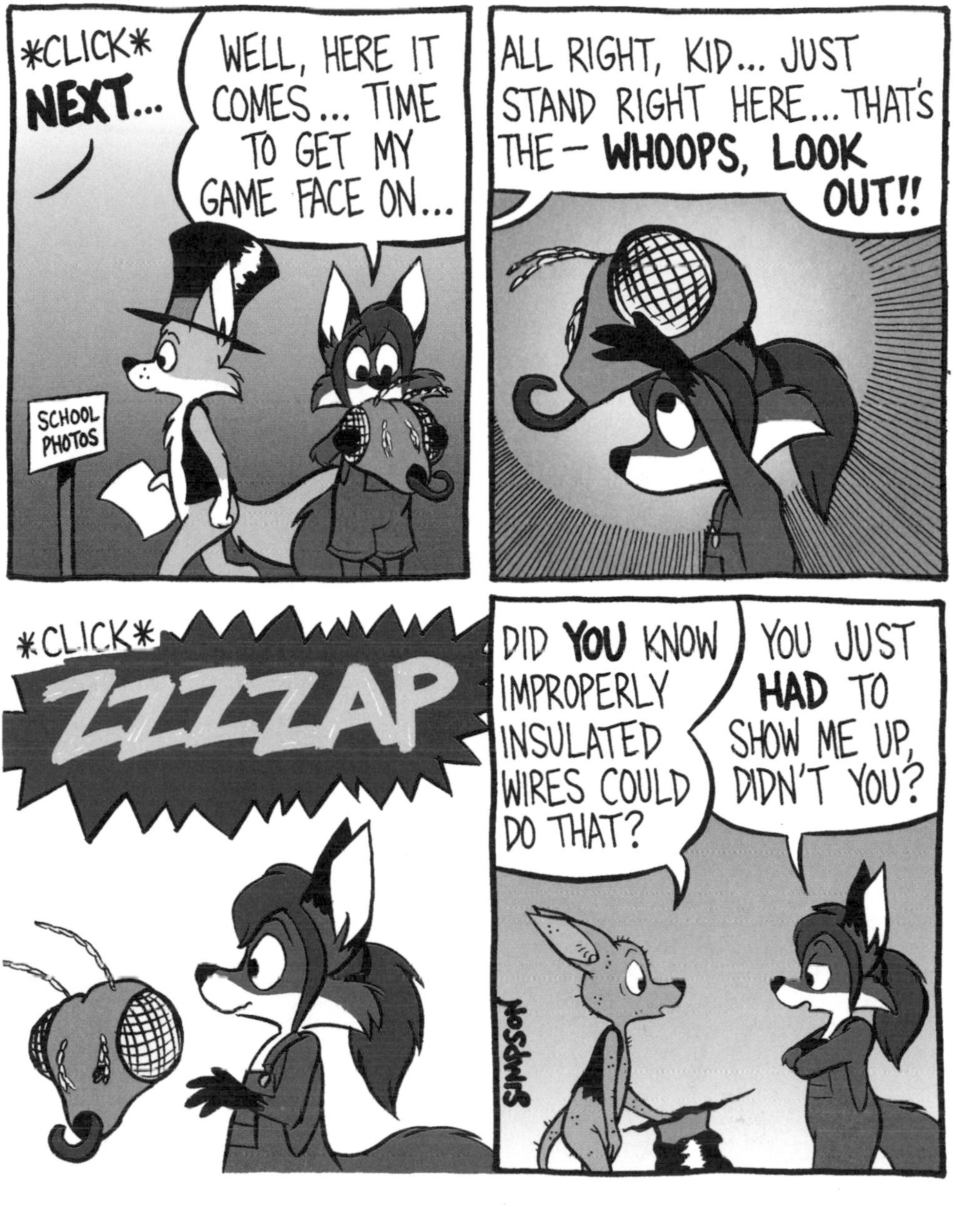
CLICK
NEXT...
WELL, HERE IT COMES... TIME TO GET MY GAME FACE ON...
SCHOOL PHOTOS
ALL RIGHT, KID... JUST STAND RIGHT HERE... THAT'S THE– WHOOPS, LOOK OUT!!
CLICK
ZZZZAP
DID YOU KNOW IMPROPERLY INSULATED WIRES COULD DO THAT?
YOU JUST HAD TO SHOW ME UP, DIDN'T YOU?
SIMPSON

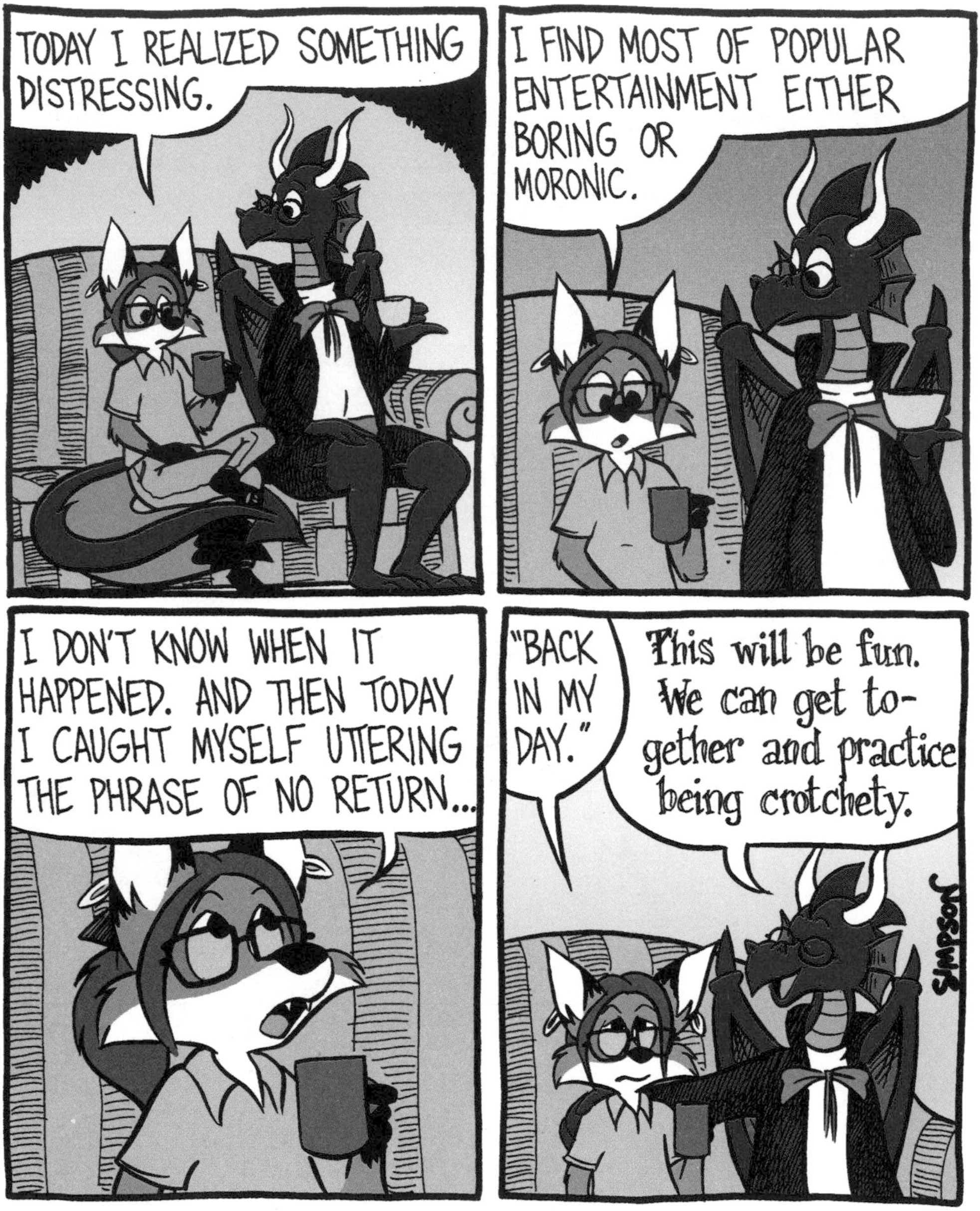
TODAY I REALIZED SOMETHING DISTRESSING.
I FIND MOST OF POPULAR ENTERTAINMENT EITHER BORING OR MORONIC.
I DON'T KNOW WHEN IT HAPPENED. AND THEN TODAY I CAUGHT MYSELF UTTERING THE PHRASE OF NO RETURN...
"BACK IN MY DAY."
This will be fun. We can get together and practice being crotchety.
SIMPSON

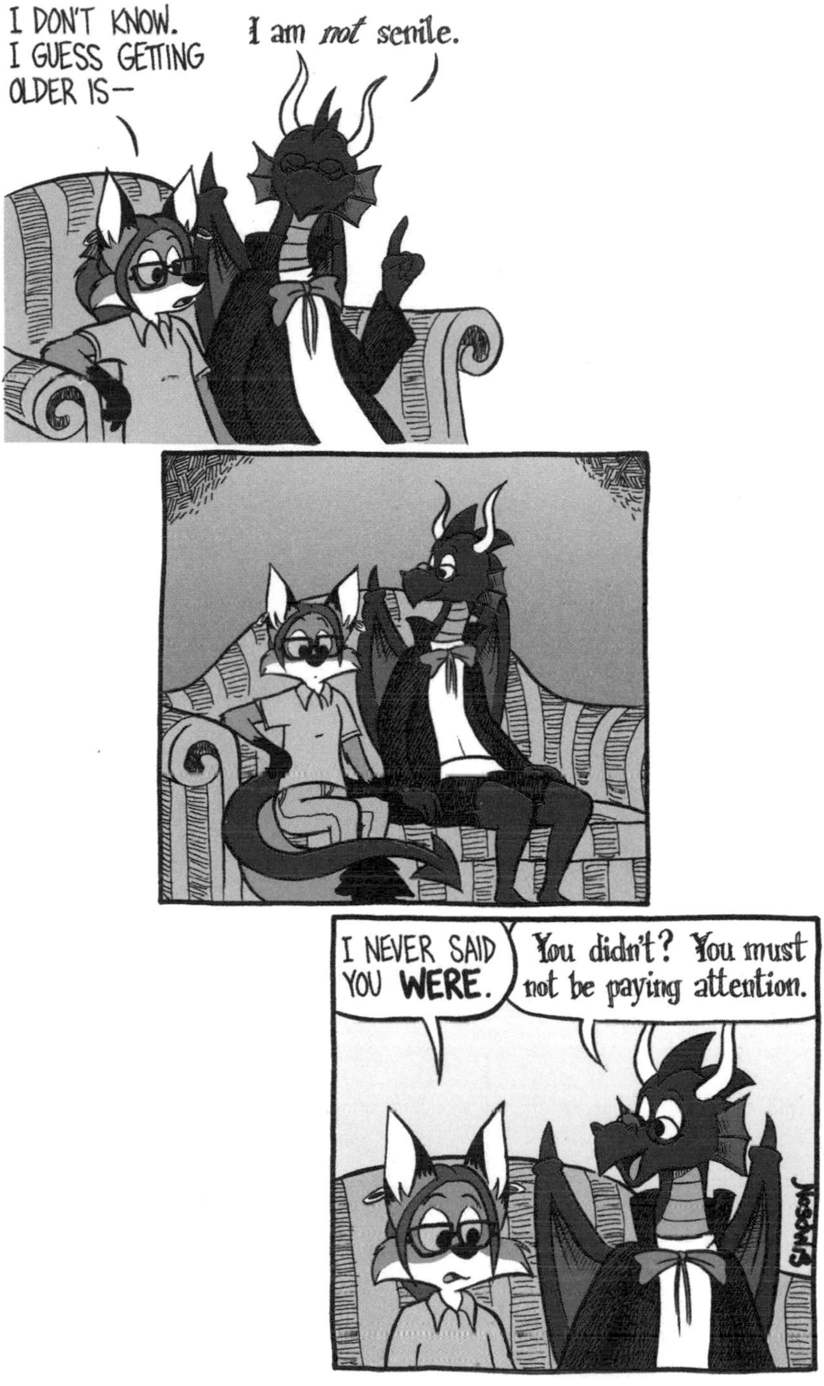

I DON'T KNOW. I GUESS GETTING OLDER IS—
I am *not* senile.
I NEVER SAID YOU **WERE**.
You didn't? You must not be paying attention.

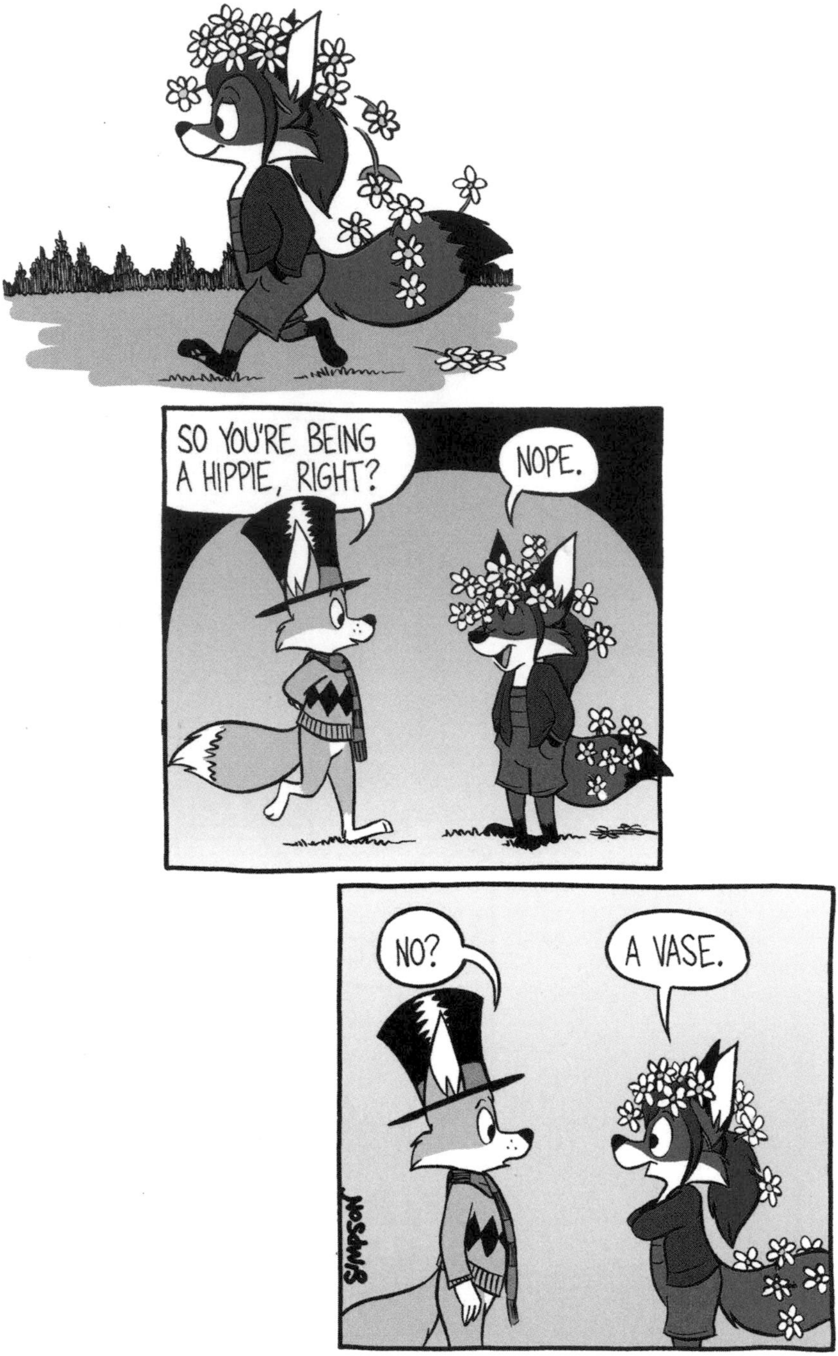
SO YOU'RE BEING A HIPPIE, RIGHT?
NOPE.
NO?
A VASE.
SIMPSON

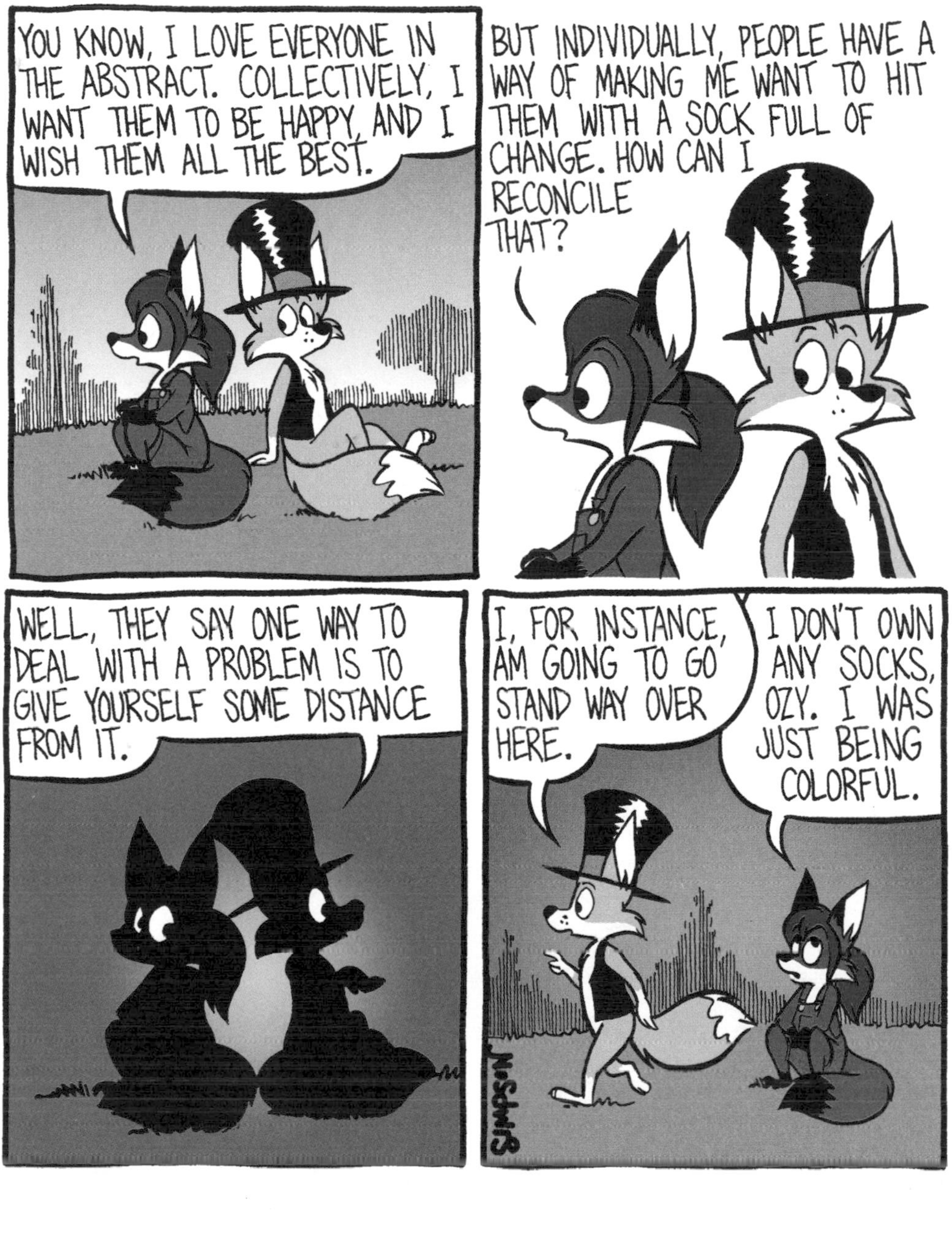
YOU KNOW, I LOVE EVERYONE IN THE ABSTRACT. COLLECTIVELY, I WANT THEM TO BE HAPPY, AND I WISH THEM ALL THE BEST.
BUT INDIVIDUALLY, PEOPLE HAVE A WAY OF MAKING ME WANT TO HIT THEM WITH A SOCK FULL OF CHANGE. HOW CAN I RECONCILE THAT?
WELL, THEY SAY ONE WAY TO DEAL WITH A PROBLEM IS TO GIVE YOURSELF SOME DISTANCE FROM IT.
I, FOR INSTANCE, AM GOING TO GO STAND WAY OVER HERE.
I DON'T OWN ANY SOCKS, OZY. I WAS JUST BEING COLORFUL.
SIMPSON

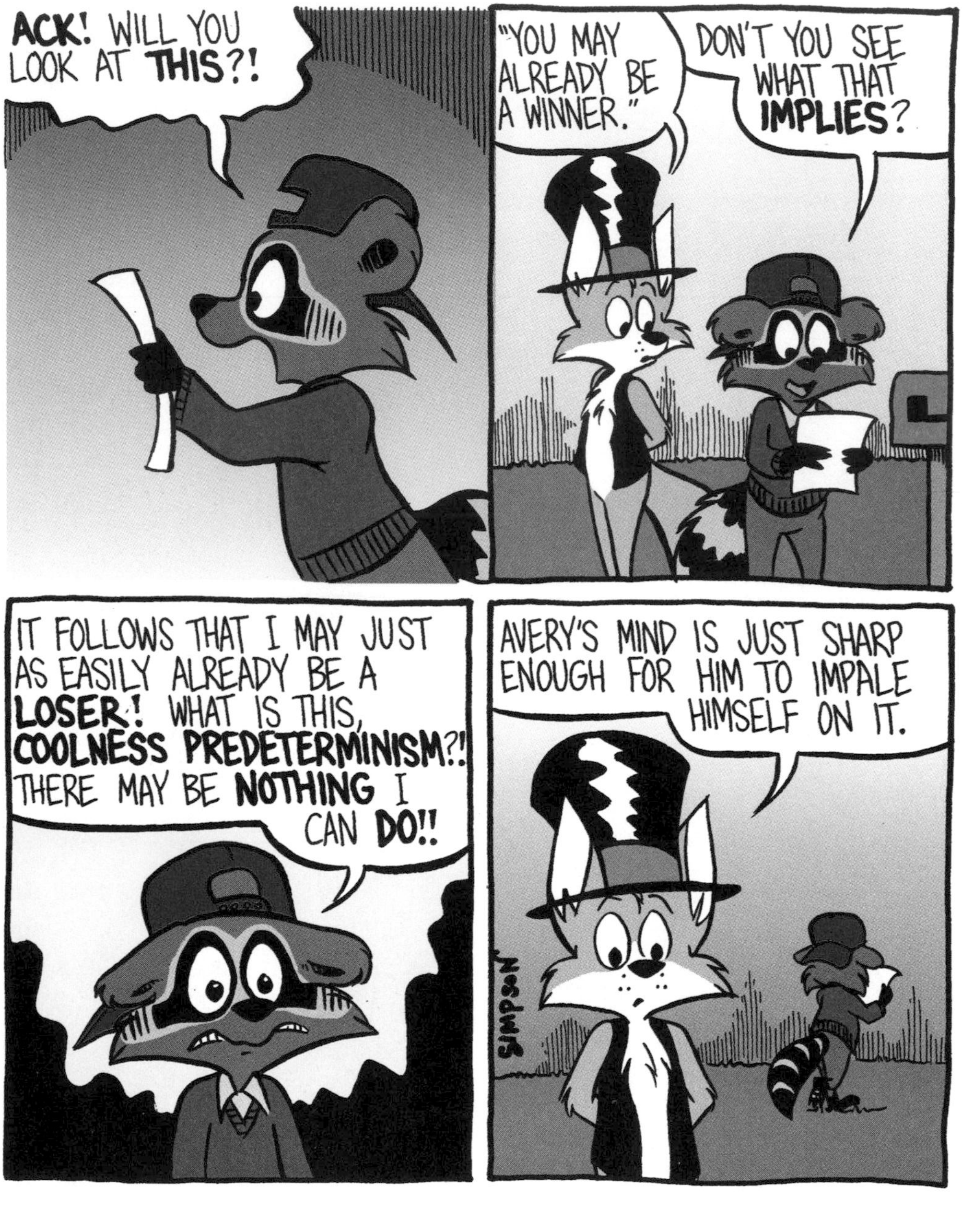
ACK! WILL YOU LOOK AT THIS?!
"YOU MAY ALREADY BE A WINNER."
DON'T YOU SEE WHAT THAT IMPLIES?
IT FOLLOWS THAT I MAY JUST AS EASILY ALREADY BE A LOSER! WHAT IS THIS, COOLNESS PREDETERMINISM?! THERE MAY BE NOTHING I CAN DO!!
AVERY'S MIND IS JUST SHARP ENOUGH FOR HIM TO IMPALE HIMSELF ON IT.
SIMPSON

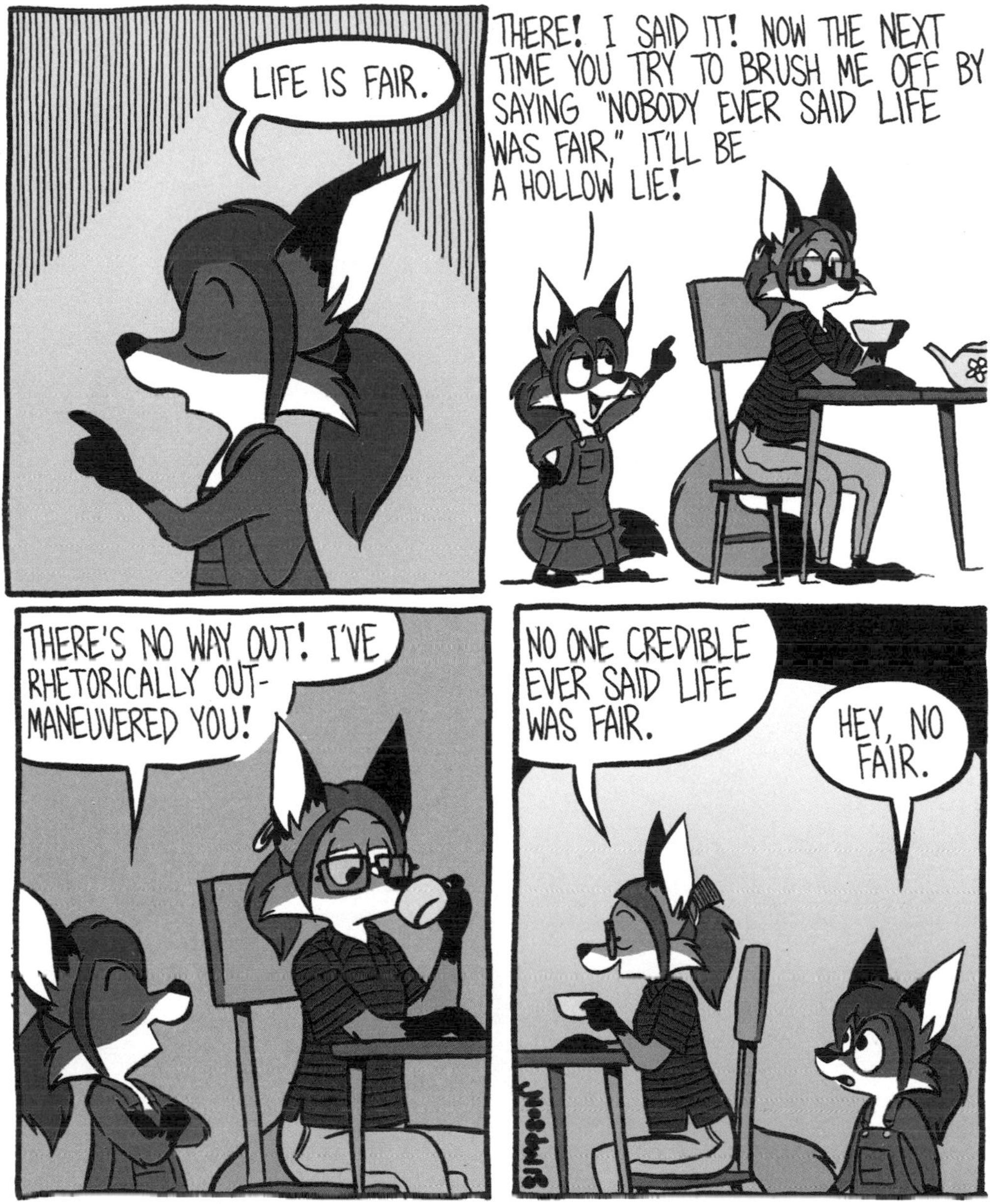
LIFE IS FAIR.
THERE! I SAID IT! NOW THE NEXT TIME YOU TRY TO BRUSH ME OFF BY SAYING "NOBODY EVER SAID LIFE WAS FAIR," IT'LL BE A HOLLOW LIE!
THERE'S NO WAY OUT! I'VE RHETORICALLY OUT-MANEUVERED YOU!
NO ONE CREDIBLE EVER SAID LIFE WAS FAIR.
HEY, NO FAIR.

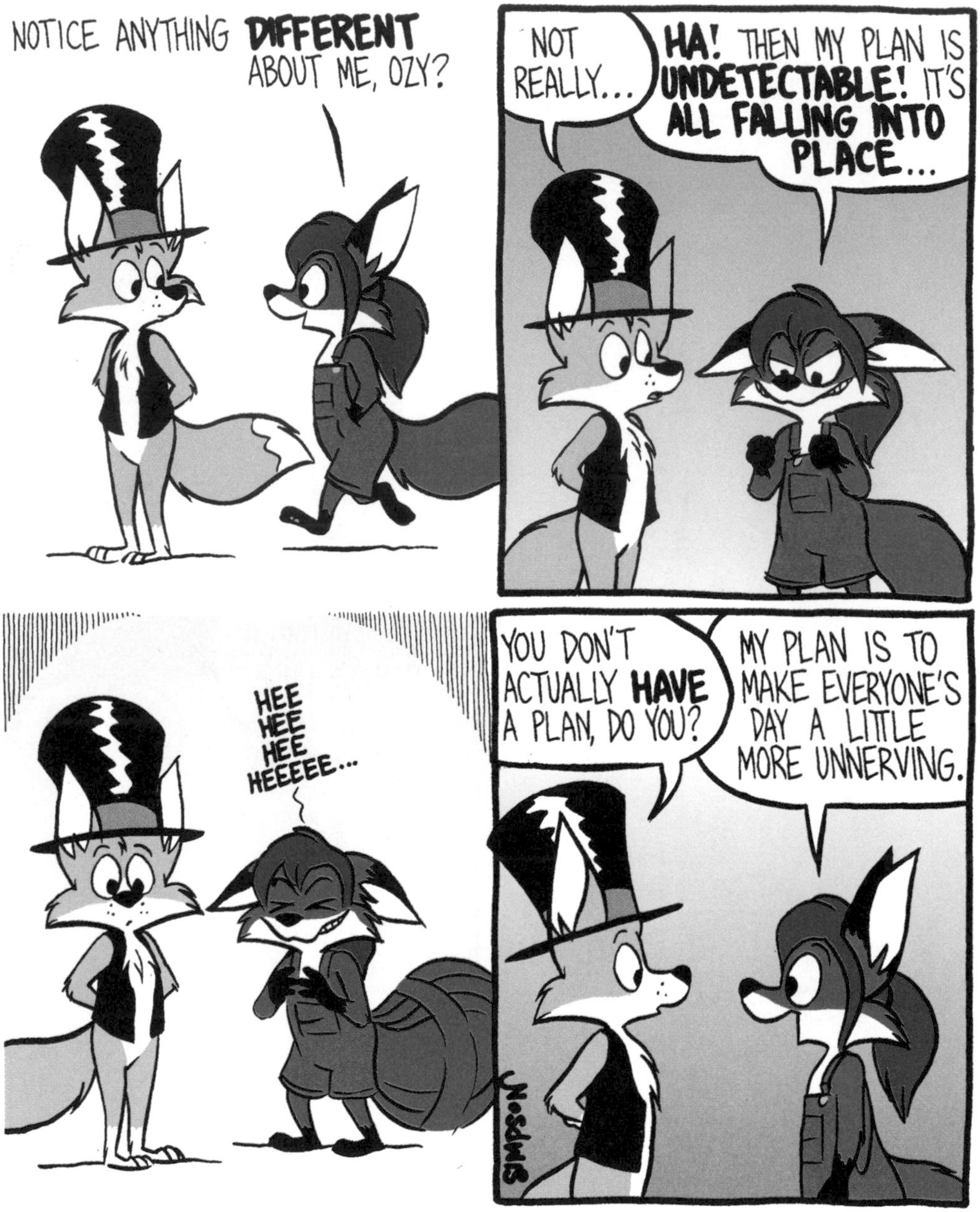
NOTICE ANYTHING **DIFFERENT** ABOUT ME, OZY?
NOT REALLY...
HA! THEN MY PLAN IS **UNDETECTABLE!** IT'S **ALL FALLING INTO PLACE...**
HEE HEE HEE HEEEEE...
YOU DON'T ACTUALLY **HAVE** A PLAN, DO YOU?
MY PLAN IS TO MAKE EVERYONE'S DAY A LITTLE MORE UNNERVING.

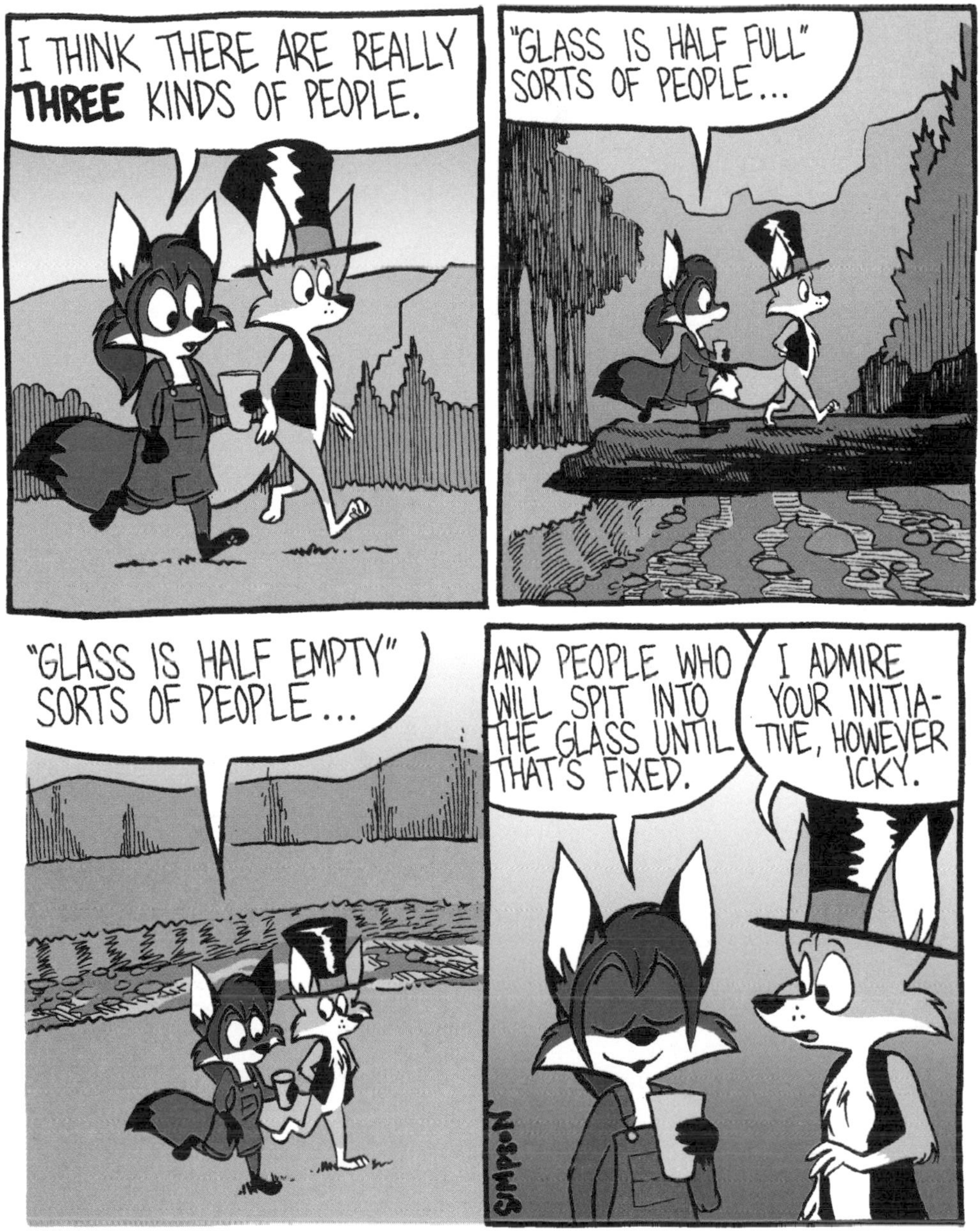
I THINK THERE ARE REALLY **THREE** KINDS OF PEOPLE.
"GLASS IS HALF FULL" SORTS OF PEOPLE...
"GLASS IS HALF EMPTY" SORTS OF PEOPLE...
AND PEOPLE WHO WILL SPIT INTO THE GLASS UNTIL THAT'S FIXED.
I ADMIRE YOUR INITIATIVE, HOWEVER ICKY.
SIMPSON

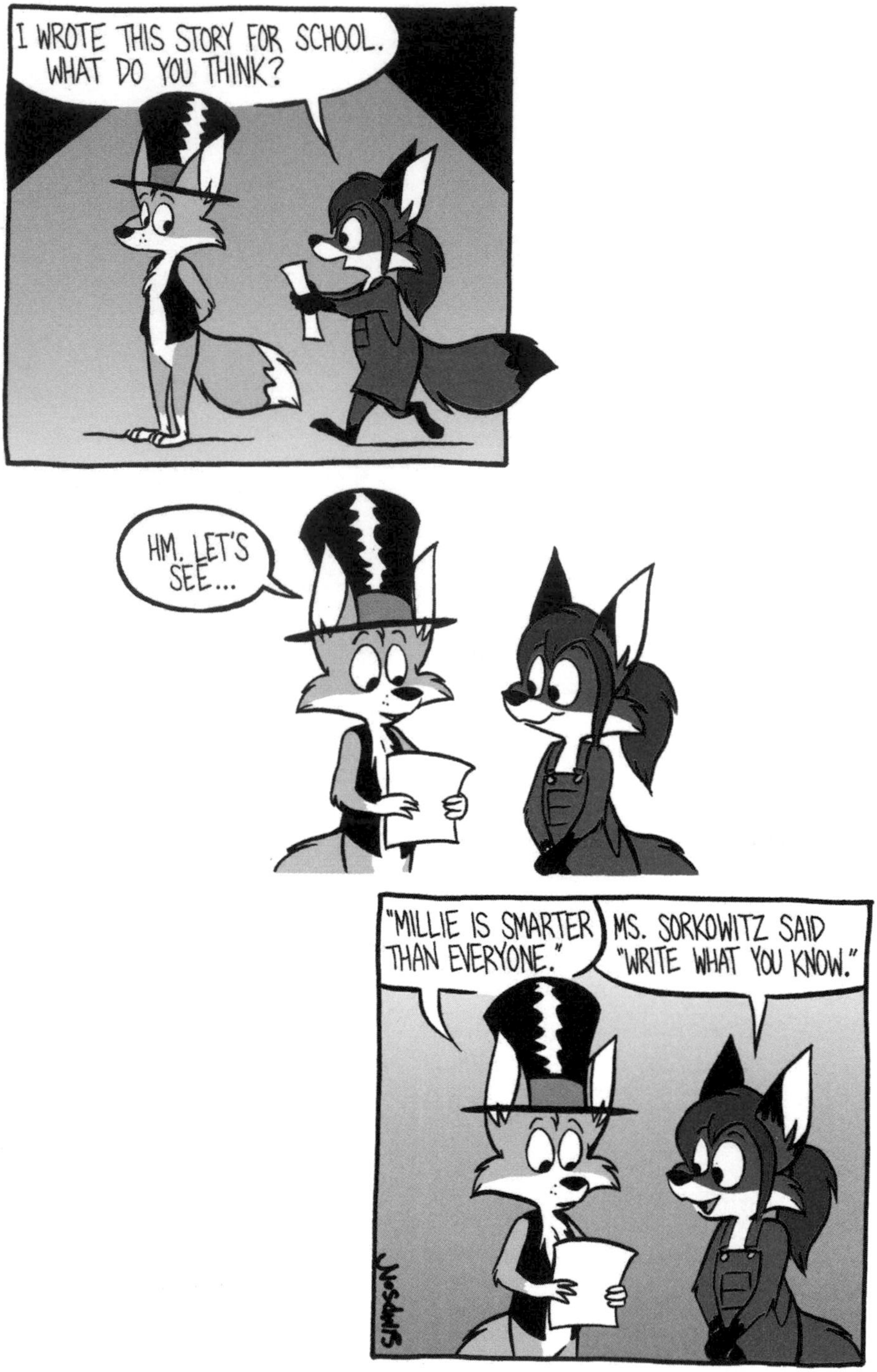
I WROTE THIS STORY FOR SCHOOL. WHAT DO YOU THINK?
HM. LET'S SEE...
"MILLIE IS SMARTER THAN EVERYONE."
MS. SORKOWITZ SAID "WRITE WHAT YOU KNOW."

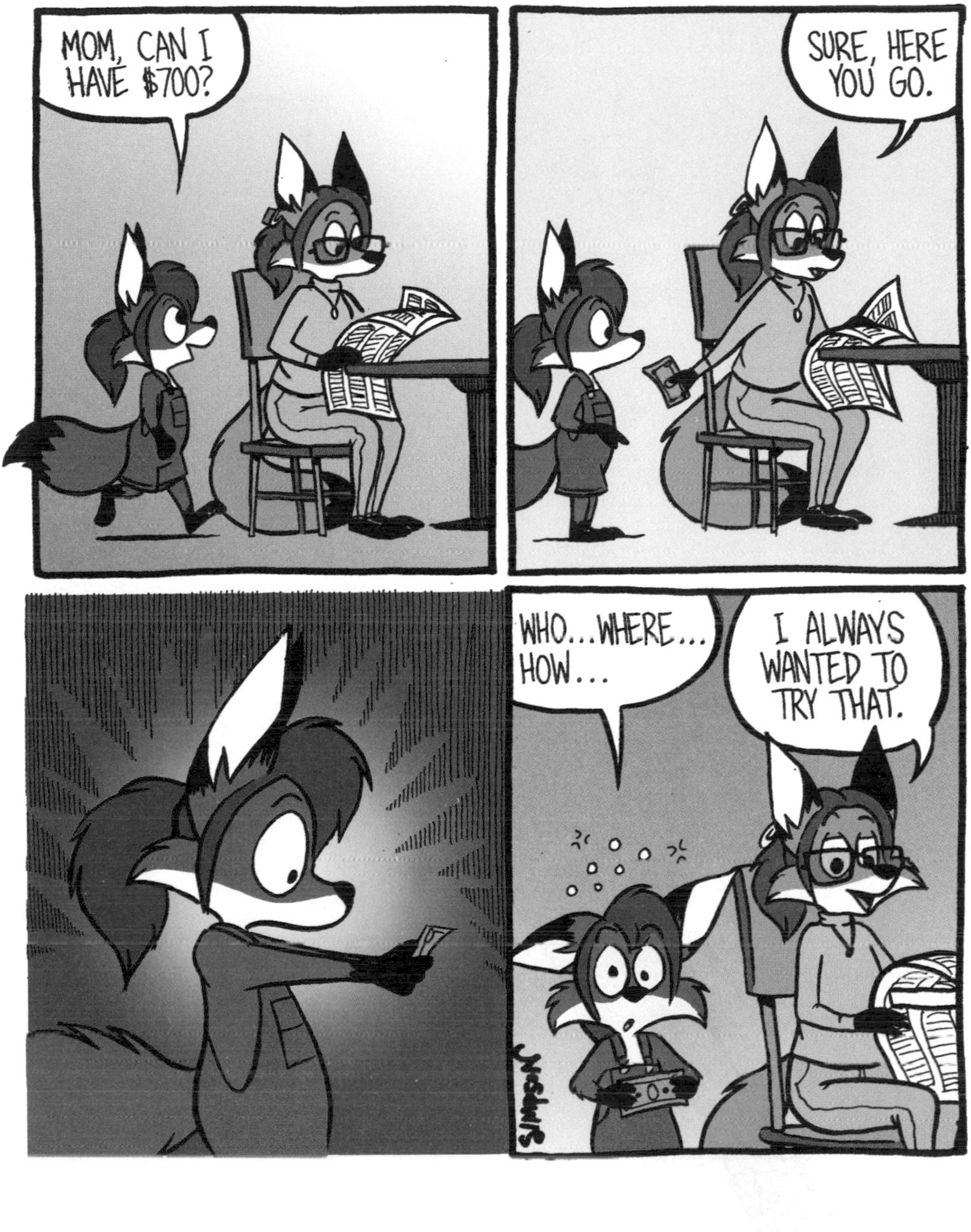
MOM, CAN I HAVE $700?
SURE, HERE YOU GO.
WHO...WHERE... HOW...
I ALWAYS WANTED TO TRY THAT.

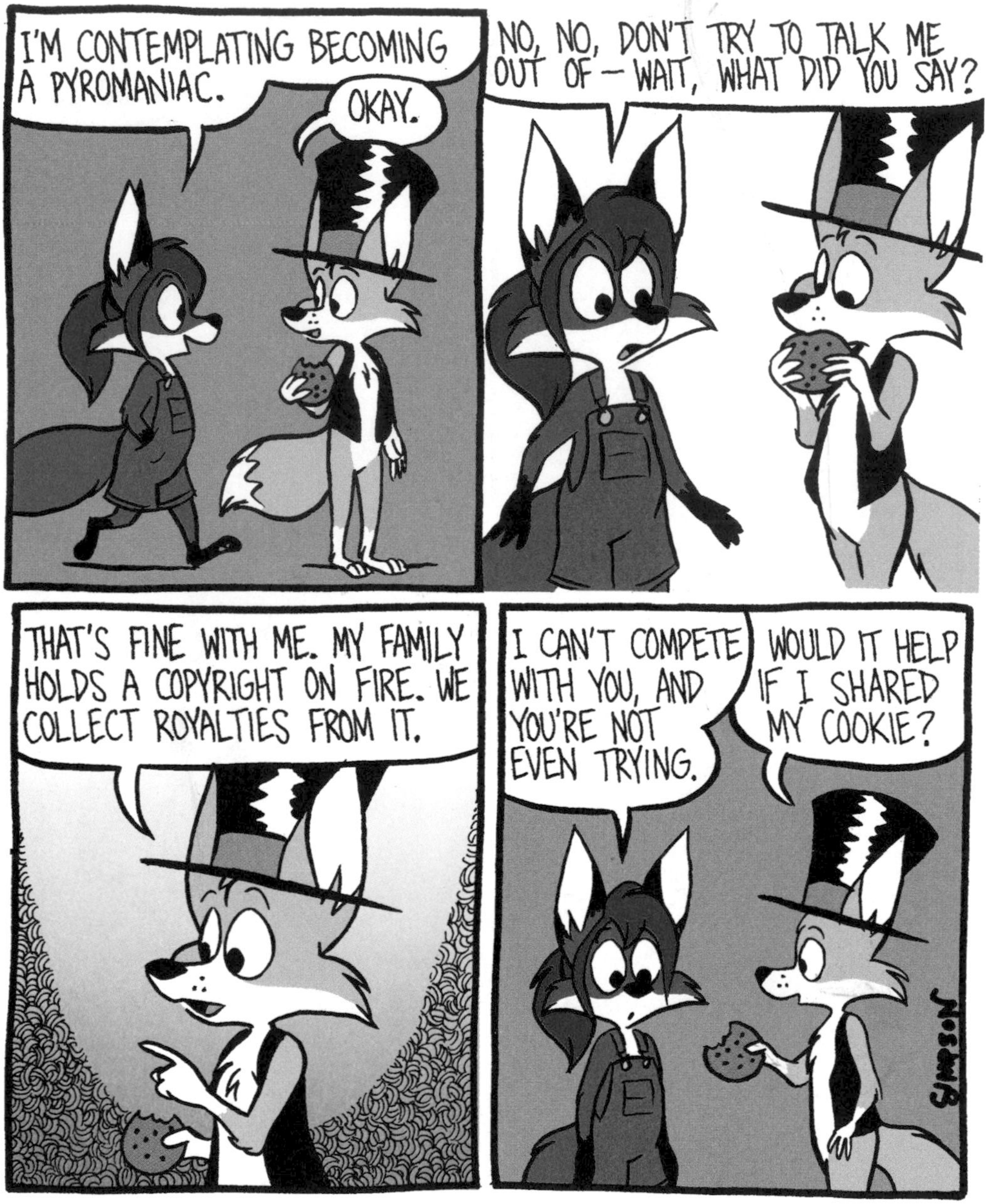
I'M CONTEMPLATING BECOMING A PYROMANIAC.
OKAY.
NO, NO, DON'T TRY TO TALK ME OUT OF — WAIT, WHAT DID YOU SAY?
THAT'S FINE WITH ME. MY FAMILY HOLDS A COPYRIGHT ON FIRE. WE COLLECT ROYALTIES FROM IT.
I CAN'T COMPETE WITH YOU, AND YOU'RE NOT EVEN TRYING.
WOULD IT HELP IF I SHARED MY COOKIE?
SIMPSON

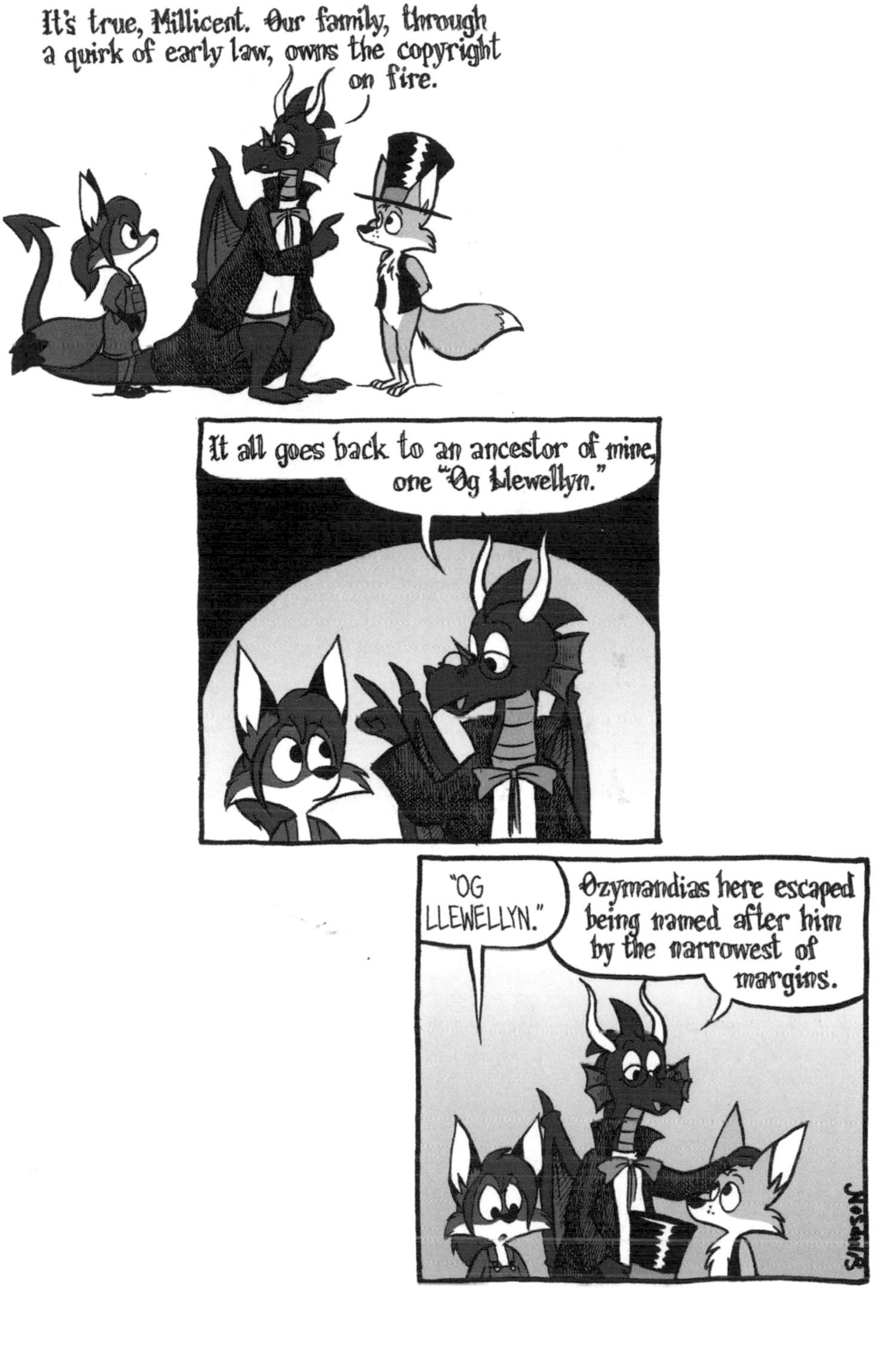
It's true, Millicent. Our family, through a quirk of early law, owns the copyright on fire.
It all goes back to an ancestor of mine, one "Og Llewellyn."
"OG LLEWELLYN."
Ozymandias here escaped being named after him by the narrowest of margins.

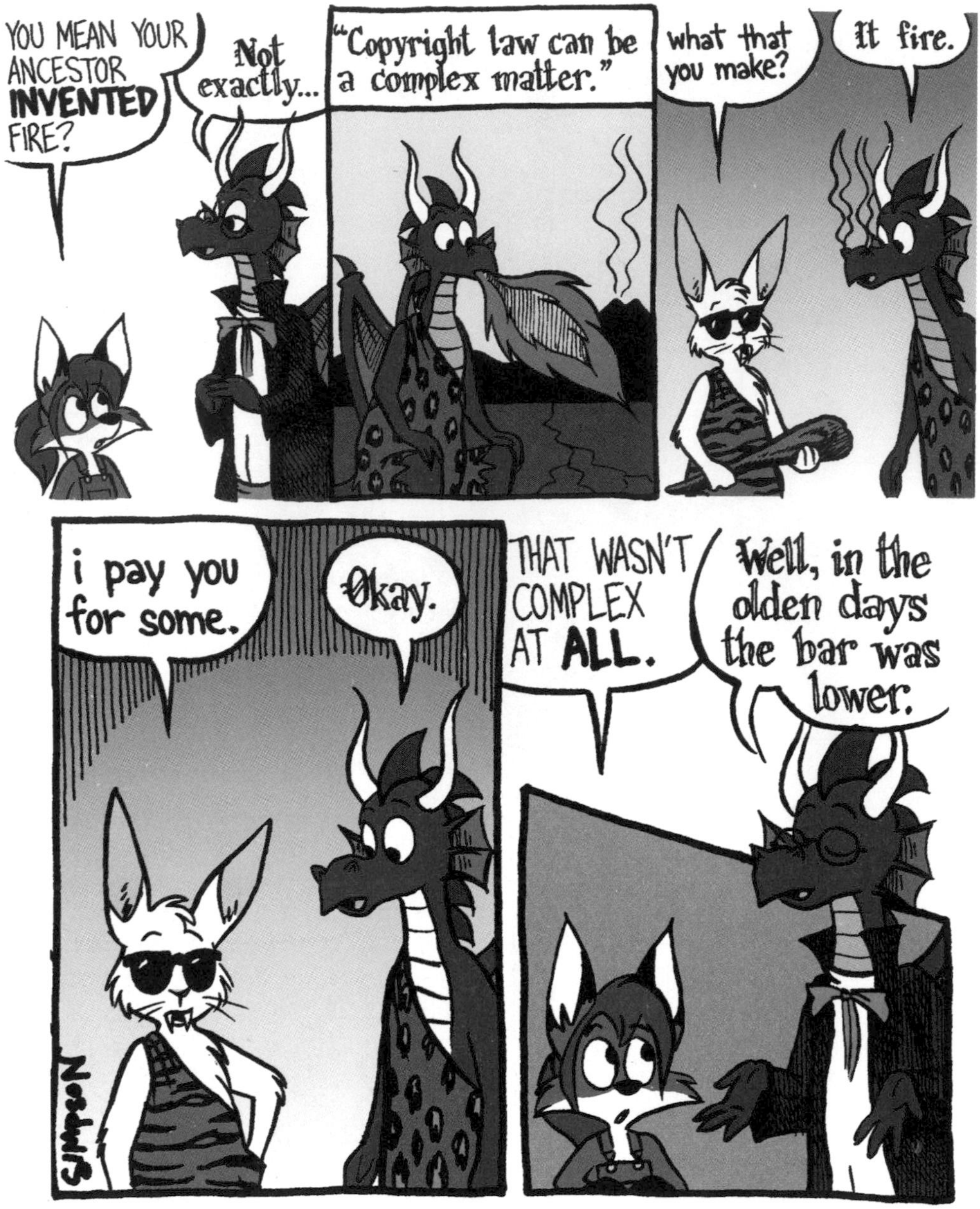
YOU MEAN YOUR ANCESTOR **INVENTED** FIRE?
Not exactly...
"Copyright law can be a complex matter."
what that you make?
It fire.
i pay you for some.
Okay.
THAT WASN'T COMPLEX AT **ALL**.
Well, in the olden days the bar was lower.
SIMPSON

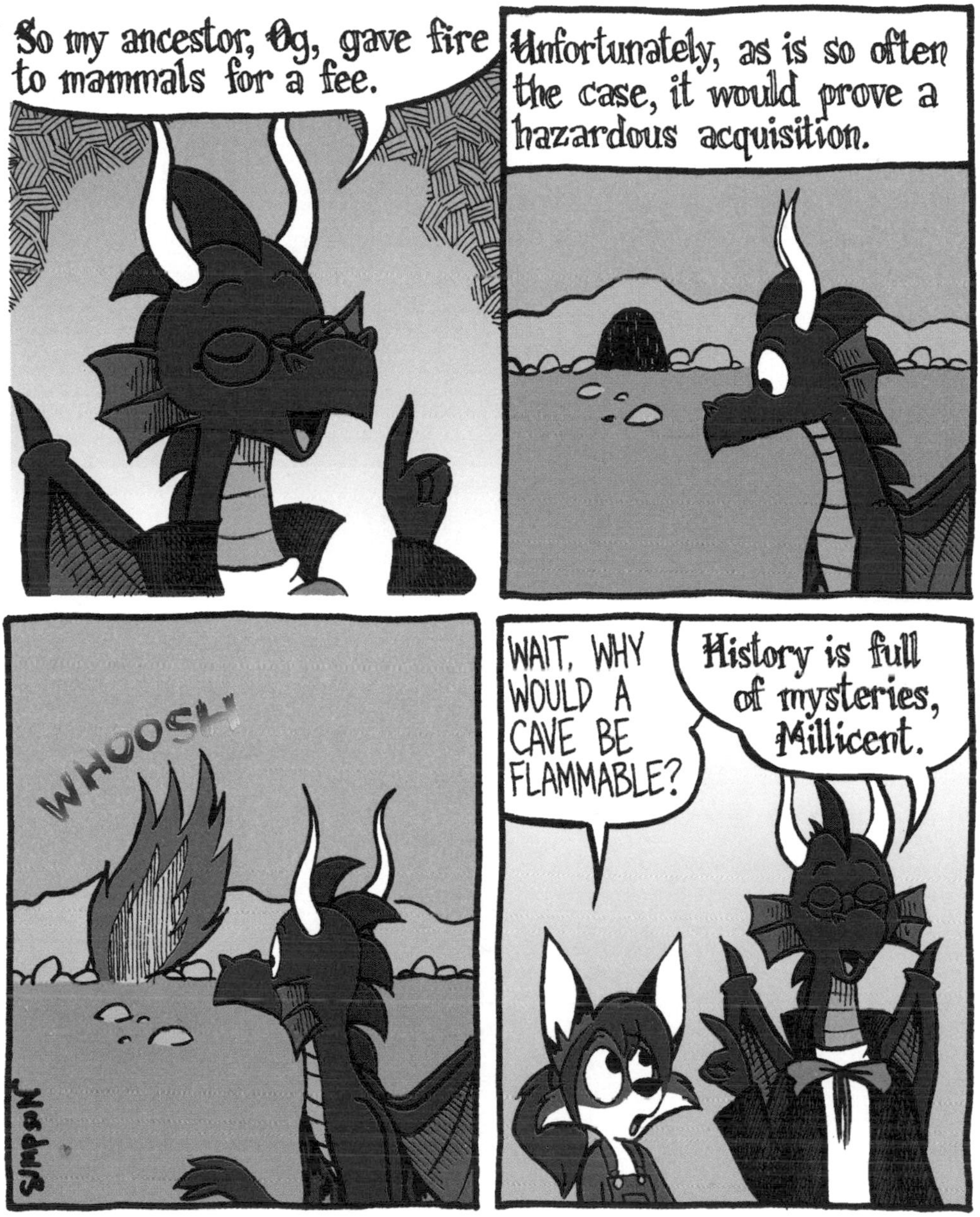
So my ancestor, Og, gave fire to mammals for a fee.
Unfortunately, as is so often the case, it would prove a hazardous acquisition.
WHOOSH
SIMPSON
WAIT, WHY WOULD A CAVE BE FLAMMABLE?
History is full of mysteries, Millicent.

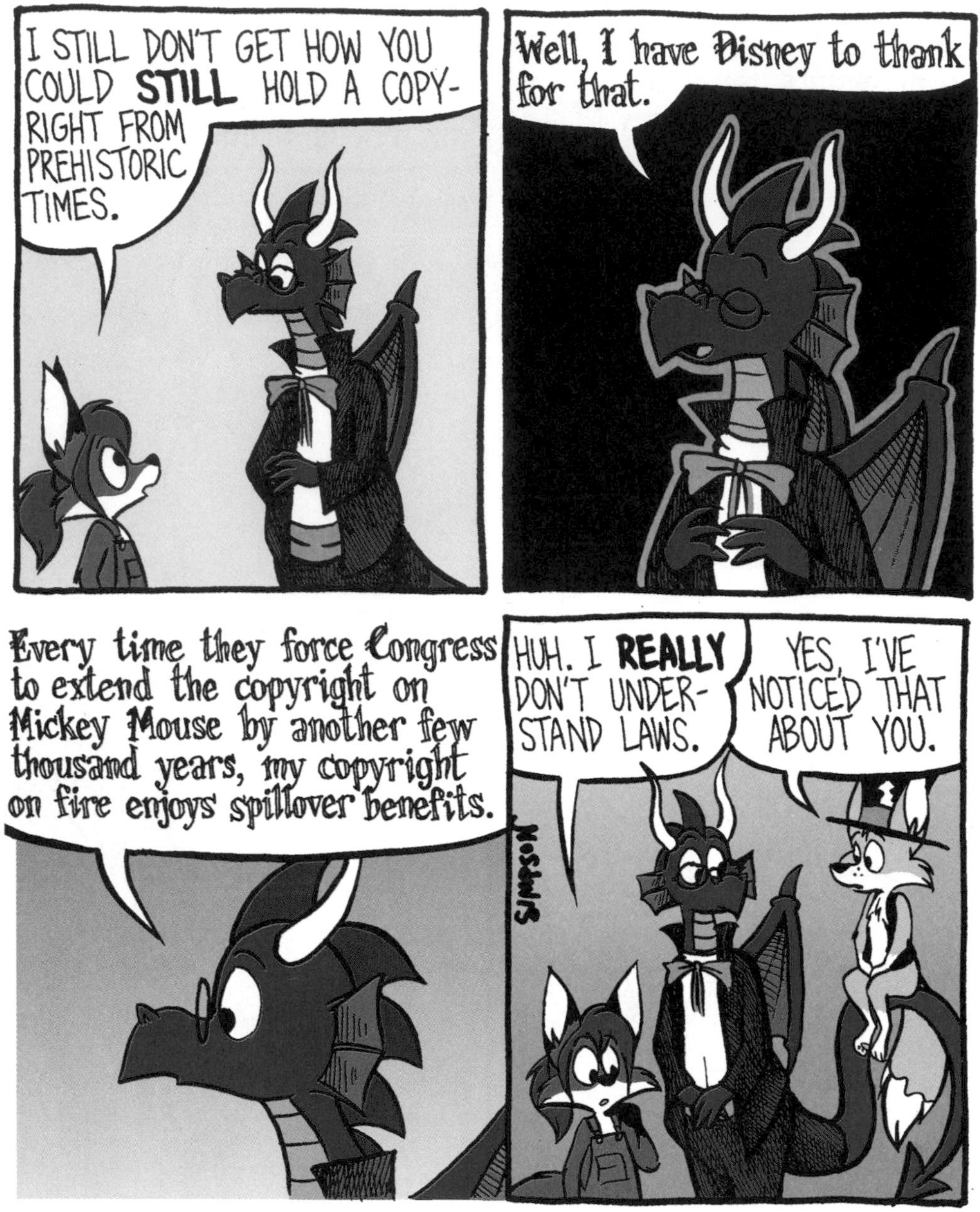
I STILL DON'T GET HOW YOU COULD **STILL** HOLD A COPY-RIGHT FROM PREHISTORIC TIMES.
Well, I have Disney to thank for that.
Every time they force Congress to extend the copyright on Mickey Mouse by another few thousand years, my copyright on fire enjoys spillover benefits.
HUH. I **REALLY** DON'T UNDER-STAND LAWS.
YES, I'VE NOTICED THAT ABOUT YOU.

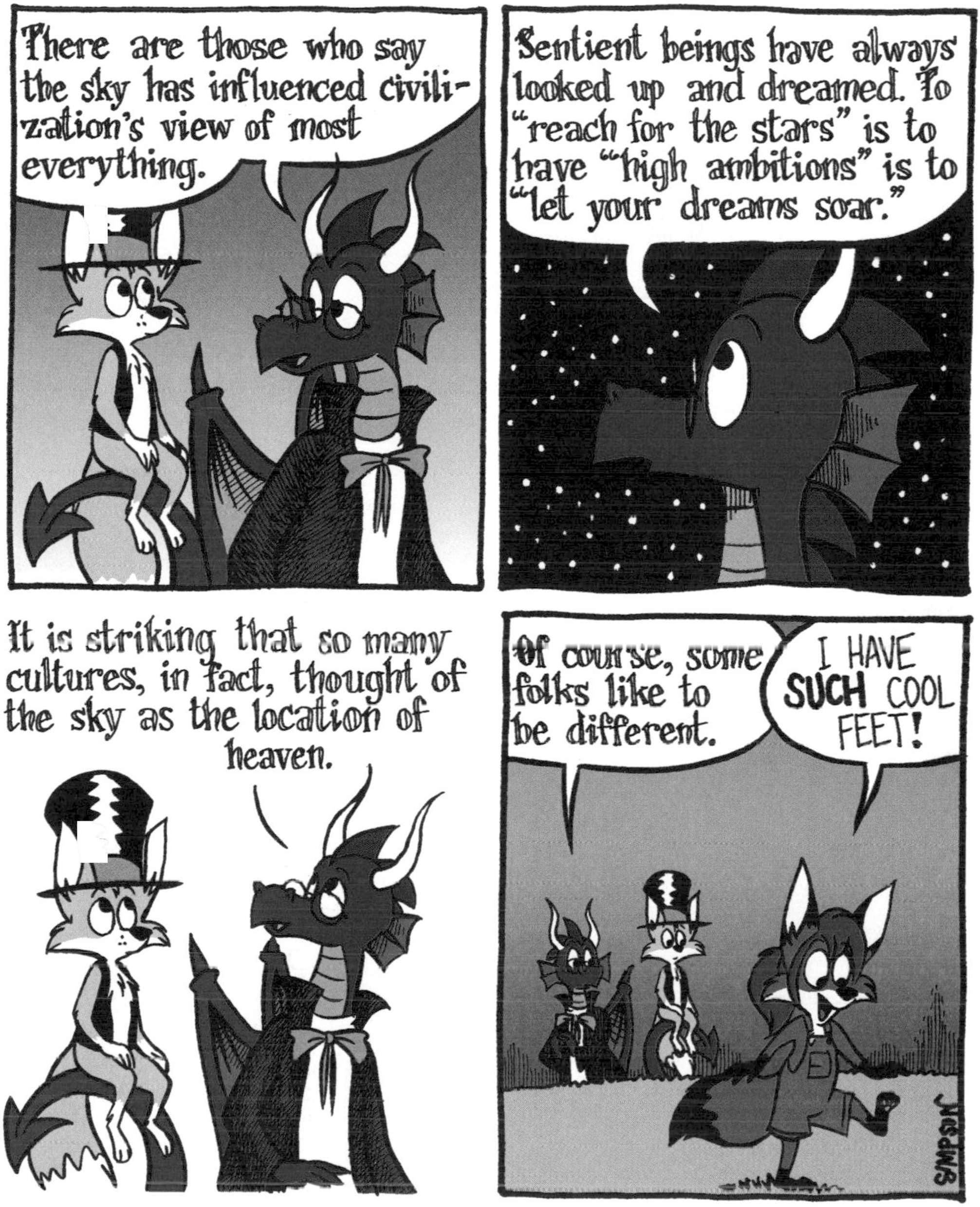
There are those who say the sky has influenced civilization's view of most everything.
Sentient beings have always looked up and dreamed. To "reach for the stars" is to have "high ambitions" is to "let your dreams soar."
It is striking that so many cultures, in fact, thought of the sky as the location of heaven.
Of course, some folks like to be different.
I HAVE SUCH COOL FEET!
SIMPSON

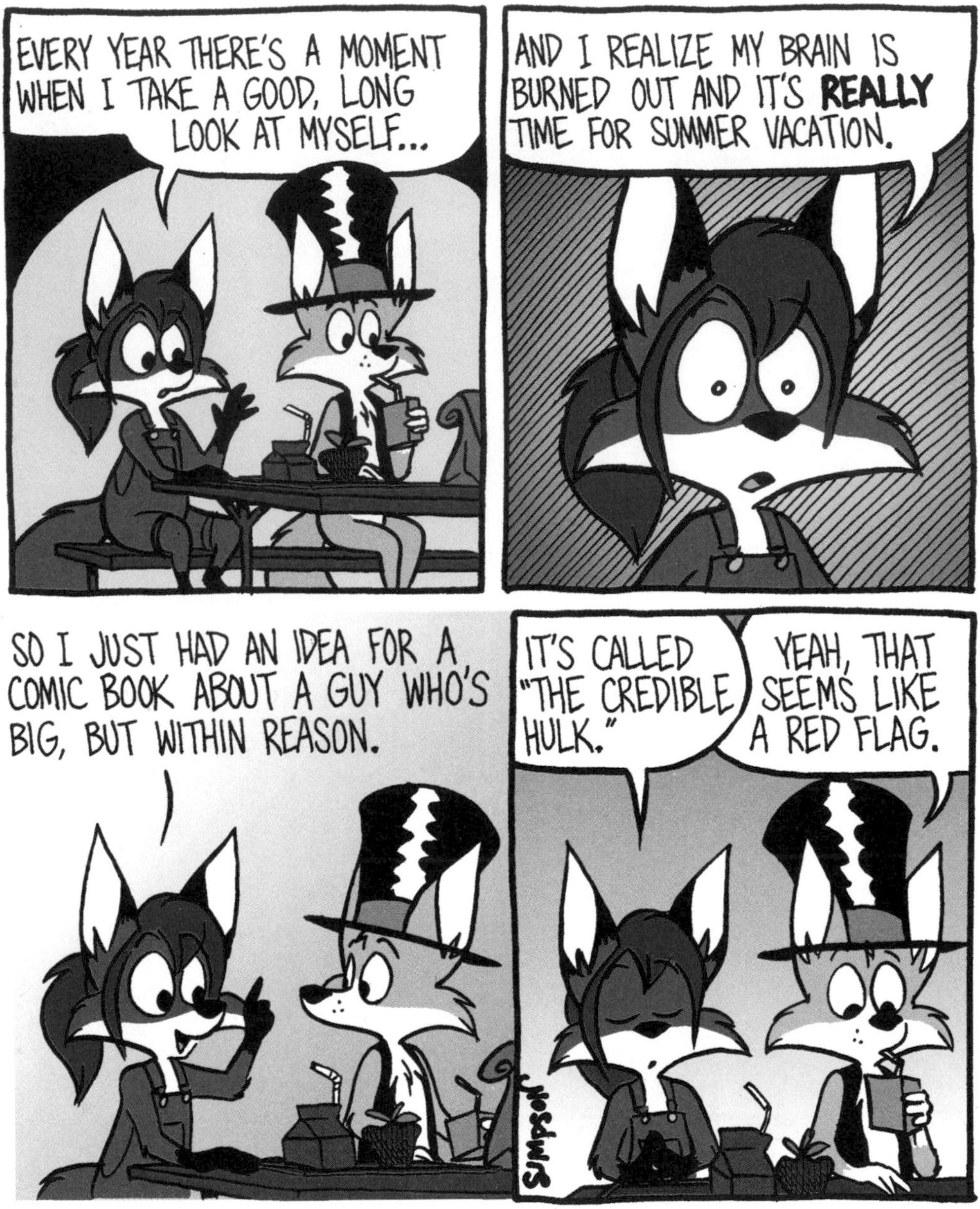
EVERY YEAR THERE'S A MOMENT WHEN I TAKE A GOOD, LONG LOOK AT MYSELF...
AND I REALIZE MY BRAIN IS BURNED OUT AND IT'S **REALLY** TIME FOR SUMMER VACATION.
SO I JUST HAD AN IDEA FOR A COMIC BOOK ABOUT A GUY WHO'S BIG, BUT WITHIN REASON.
IT'S CALLED "THE CREDIBLE HULK."
YEAH, THAT SEEMS LIKE A RED FLAG.
SIMPSON

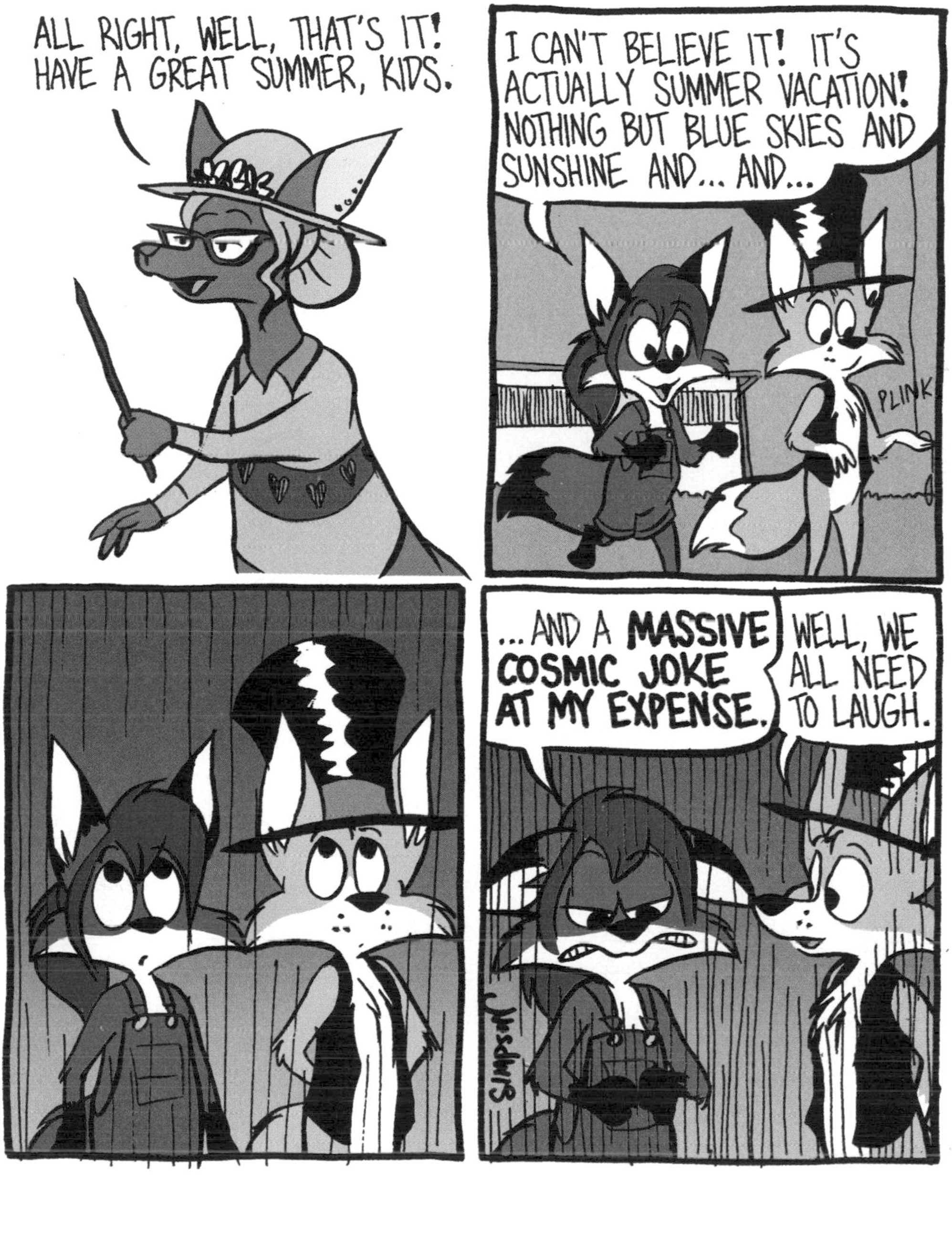
ALL RIGHT, WELL, THAT'S IT! HAVE A GREAT SUMMER, KIDS.
I CAN'T BELIEVE IT! IT'S ACTUALLY SUMMER VACATION! NOTHING BUT BLUE SKIES AND SUNSHINE AND... AND...
PLINK
...AND A MASSIVE COSMIC JOKE AT MY EXPENSE.
WELL, WE ALL NEED TO LAUGH.
SIMPSON

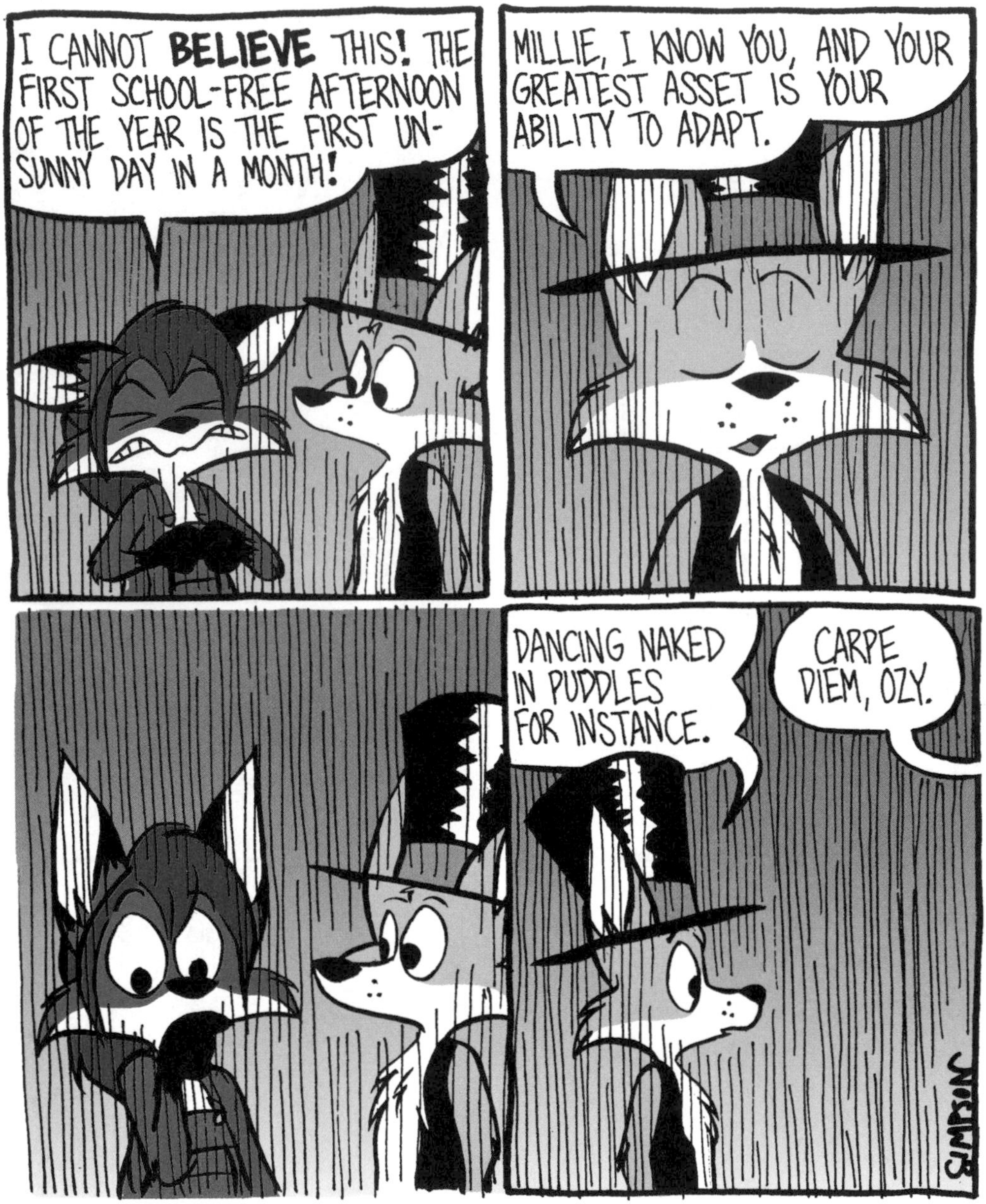
I CANNOT **BELIEVE** THIS! THE FIRST SCHOOL-FREE AFTERNOON OF THE YEAR IS THE FIRST UN-SUNNY DAY IN A MONTH!
MILLIE, I KNOW YOU, AND YOUR GREATEST ASSET IS YOUR ABILITY TO ADAPT.
DANCING NAKED IN PUDDLES FOR INSTANCE.
CARPE DIEM, OZY.
SIMPSON

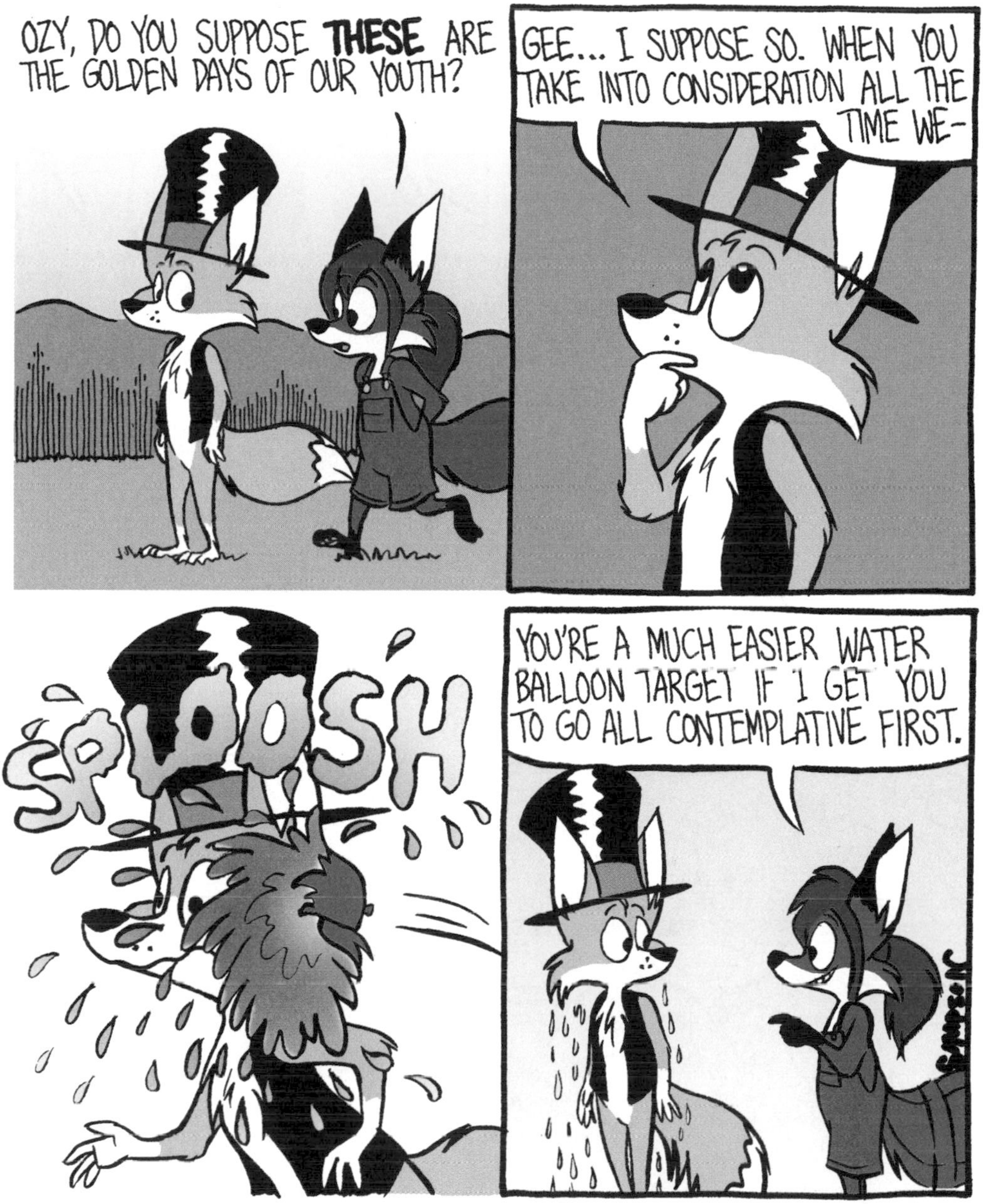
OZY, DO YOU SUPPOSE **THESE** ARE THE GOLDEN DAYS OF OUR YOUTH?
GEE... I SUPPOSE SO. WHEN YOU TAKE INTO CONSIDERATION ALL THE TIME WE-
SPLOOSH
YOU'RE A MUCH EASIER WATER BALLOON TARGET IF I GET YOU TO GO ALL CONTEMPLATIVE FIRST.

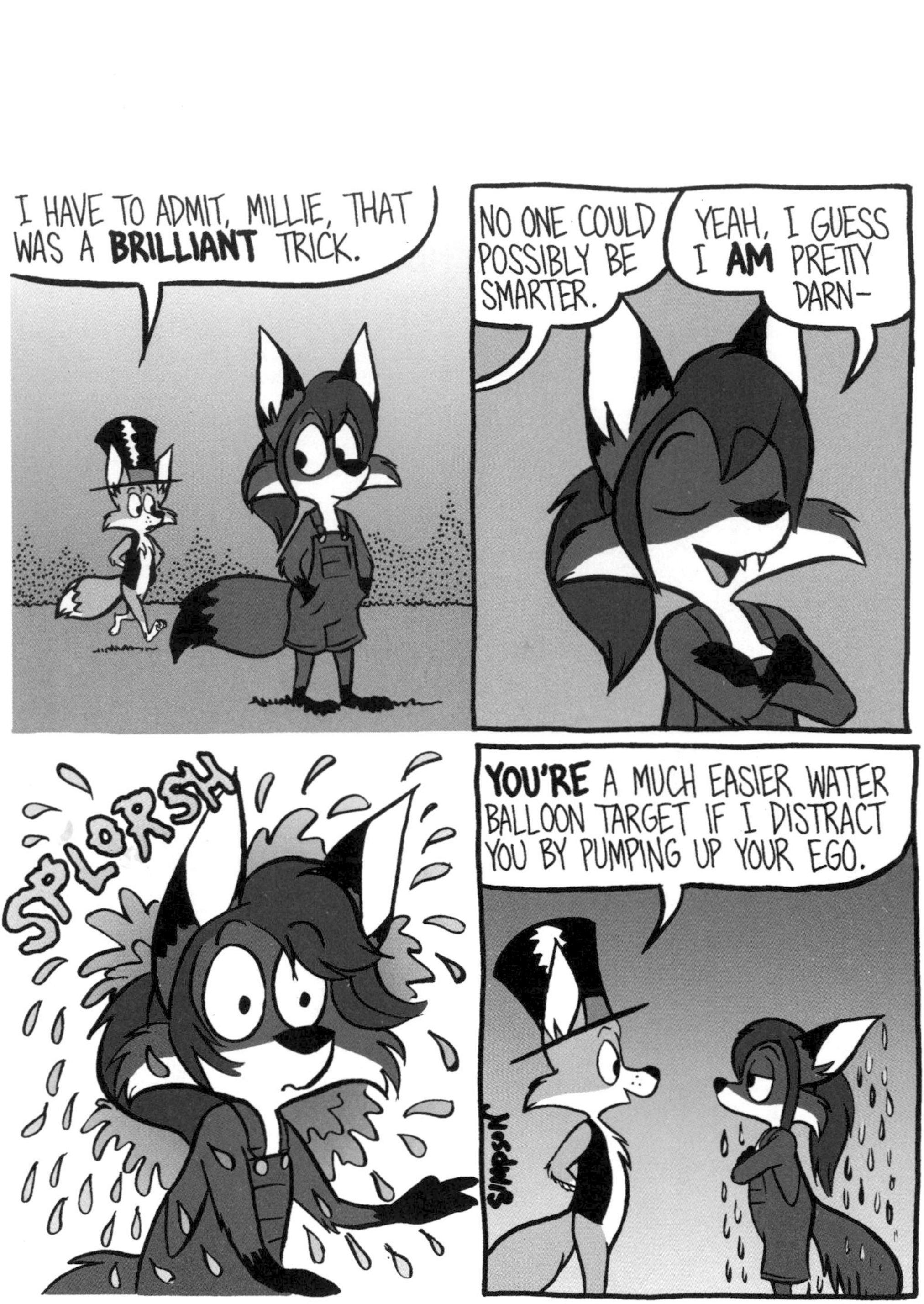
I HAVE TO ADMIT, MILLIE, THAT WAS A **BRILLIANT** TRICK.
NO ONE COULD POSSIBLY BE SMARTER.
YEAH, I GUESS I **AM** PRETTY DARN-
SPLORSH
YOU'RE A MUCH EASIER WATER BALLOON TARGET IF I DISTRACT YOU BY PUMPING UP YOUR EGO.
SIMPSON

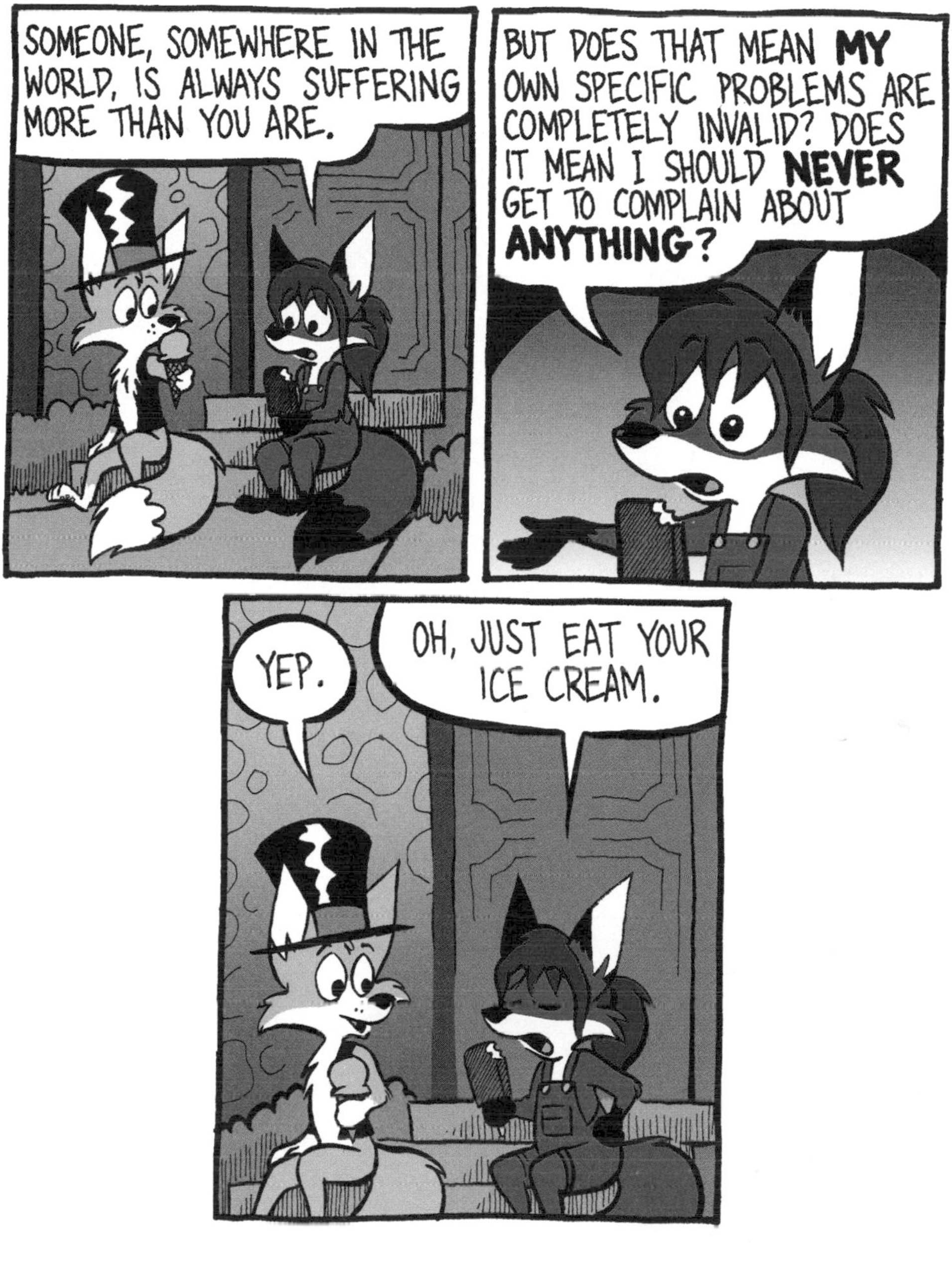
SOMEONE, SOMEWHERE IN THE WORLD, IS ALWAYS SUFFERING MORE THAN YOU ARE.
BUT DOES THAT MEAN **MY** OWN SPECIFIC PROBLEMS ARE COMPLETELY INVALID? DOES IT MEAN I SHOULD **NEVER** GET TO COMPLAIN ABOUT **ANYTHING**?
YEP.
OH, JUST EAT YOUR ICE CREAM.

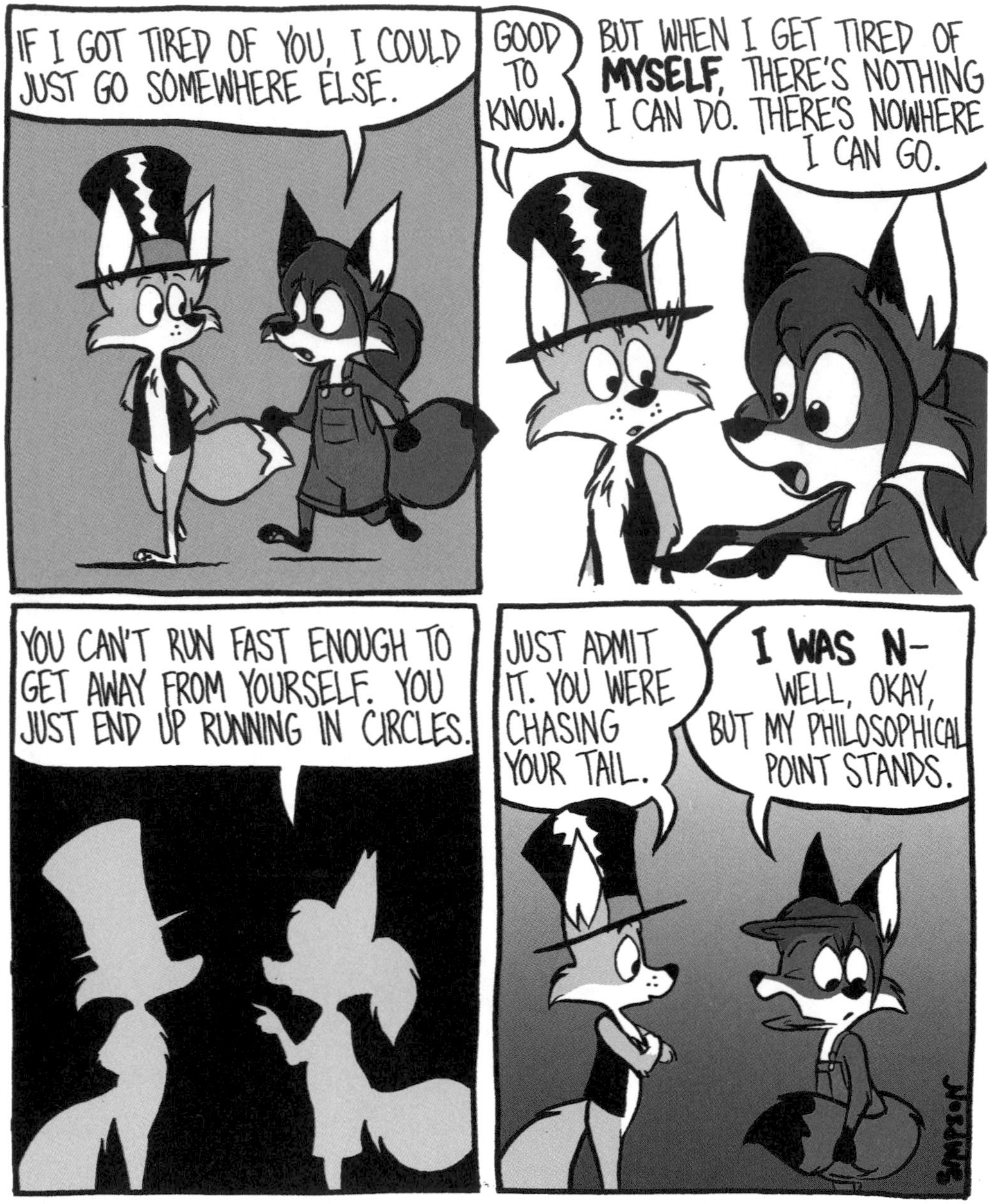
IF I GOT TIRED OF YOU, I COULD JUST GO SOMEWHERE ELSE.
GOOD TO KNOW.
BUT WHEN I GET TIRED OF **MYSELF**, THERE'S NOTHING I CAN DO. THERE'S NOWHERE I CAN GO.
YOU CAN'T RUN FAST ENOUGH TO GET AWAY FROM YOURSELF. YOU JUST END UP RUNNING IN CIRCLES.
JUST ADMIT IT. YOU WERE CHASING YOUR TAIL.
I WAS N- WELL, OKAY, BUT MY PHILOSOPHICAL POINT STANDS.
SAMPSON

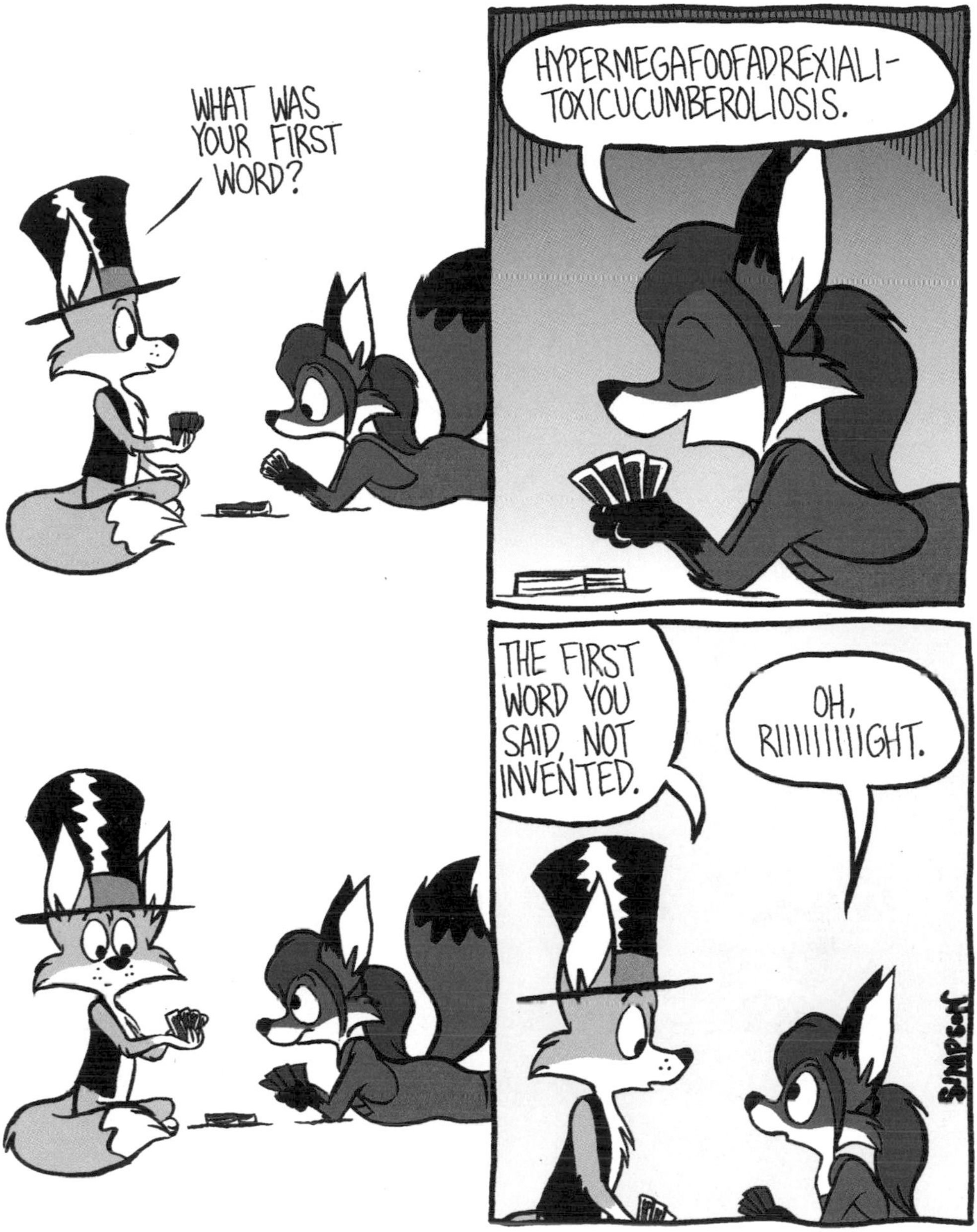
WHAT WAS YOUR FIRST WORD?
HYPERMEGAFOOFADREXIALI-TOXICUCUMBEROLIOSIS.
THE FIRST WORD YOU SAID, NOT INVENTED.
OH, RIIIIIIIIIGHT.
SIMPSON

BLAAAAAAAAP!
COOL
AAAAAAAAA
GREAT MUSIC SHOULD MOVE PEOPLE.
SIMPSON

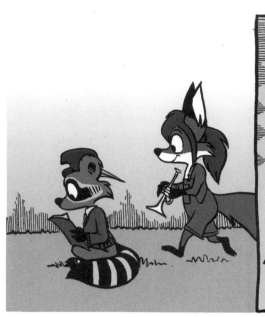

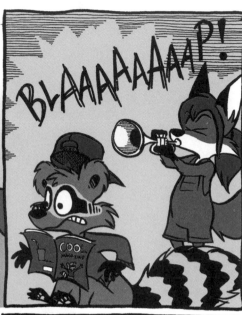

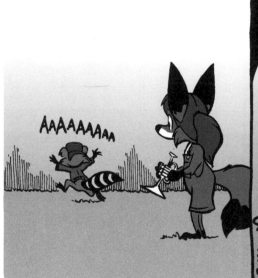

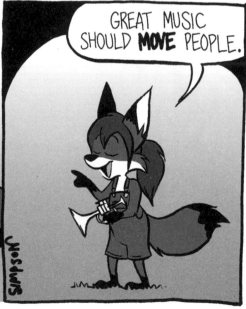

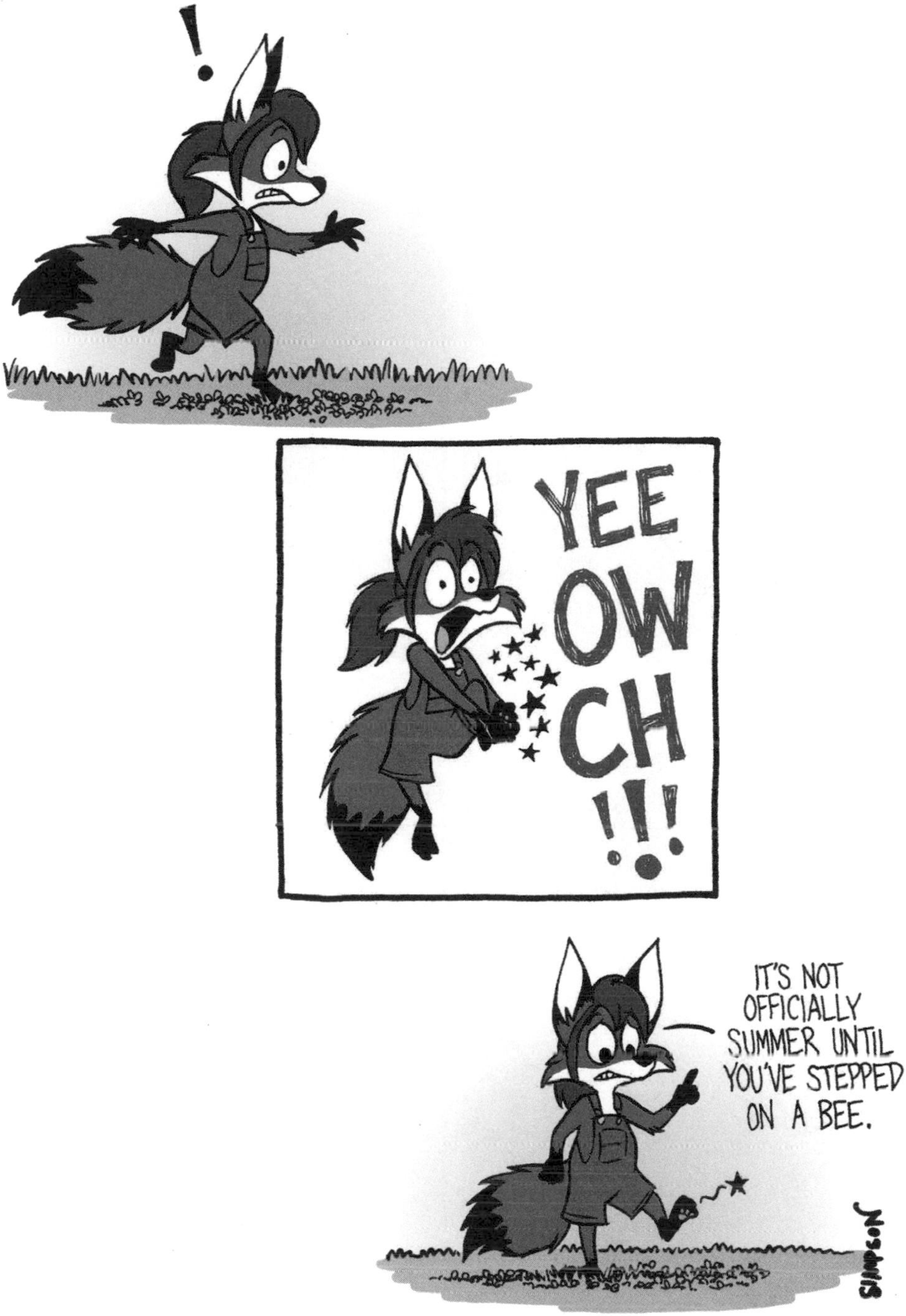
!
YEE OW CH !!!
IT'S NOT OFFICIALLY SUMMER UNTIL YOU'VE STEPPED ON A BEE.
SIMPSON

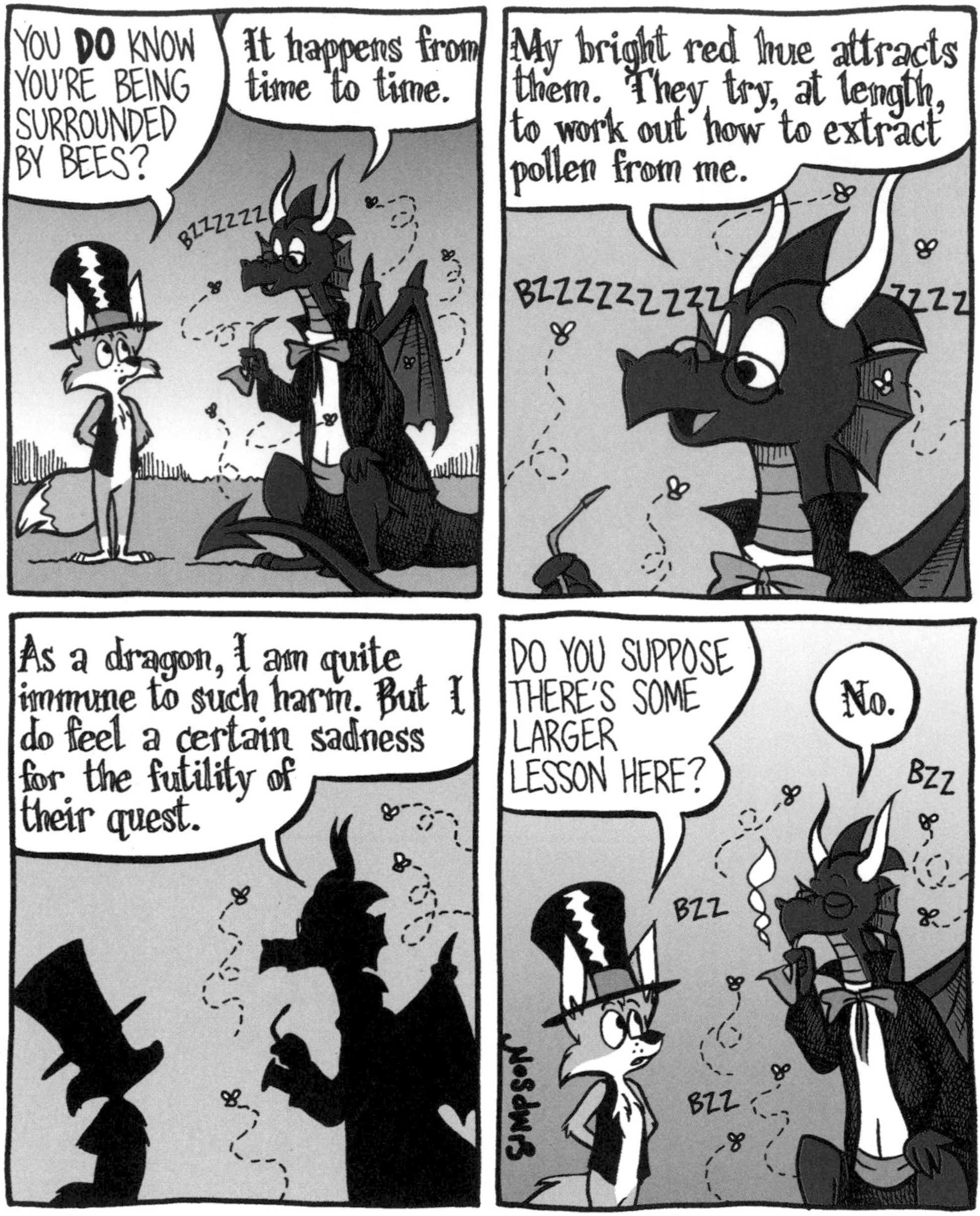
YOU **DO** KNOW YOU'RE BEING SURROUNDED BY BEES?
It happens from time to time.
BZZZZZZ
My bright red hue attracts them. They try, at length, to work out how to extract pollen from me.
BZZZZZZZZZ
ZZZZ
As a dragon, I am quite immune to such harm. But I do feel a certain sadness for the futility of their quest.
DO YOU SUPPOSE THERE'S SOME LARGER LESSON HERE?
No.
BZZ
BZZ
BZZ
SIMPSON

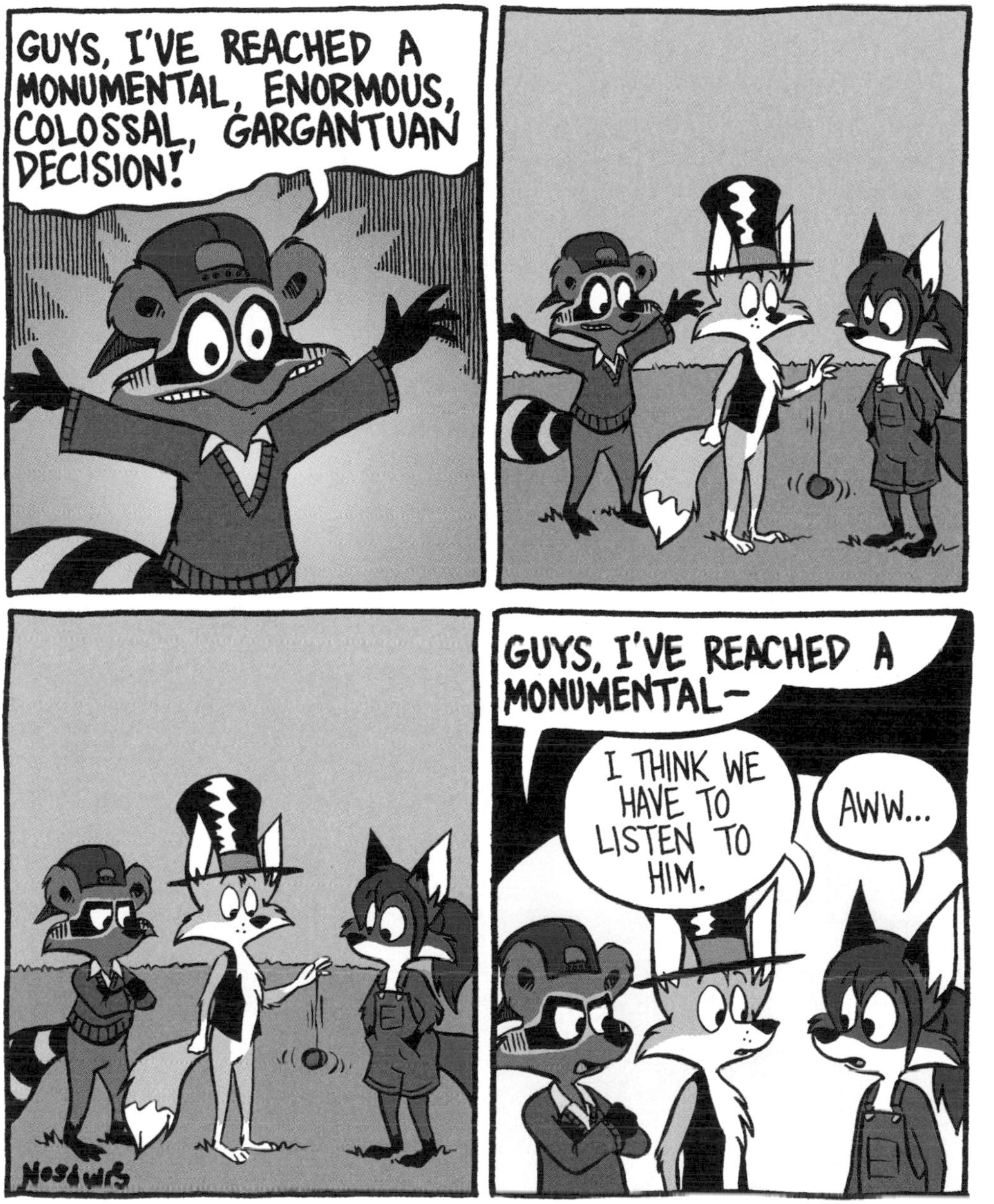
GUYS, I'VE REACHED A MONUMENTAL, ENORMOUS, COLOSSAL, GARGANTUAN DECISION!
NOSDAWG
GUYS, I'VE REACHED A MONUMENTAL–
I THINK WE HAVE TO LISTEN TO HIM.
AWW...

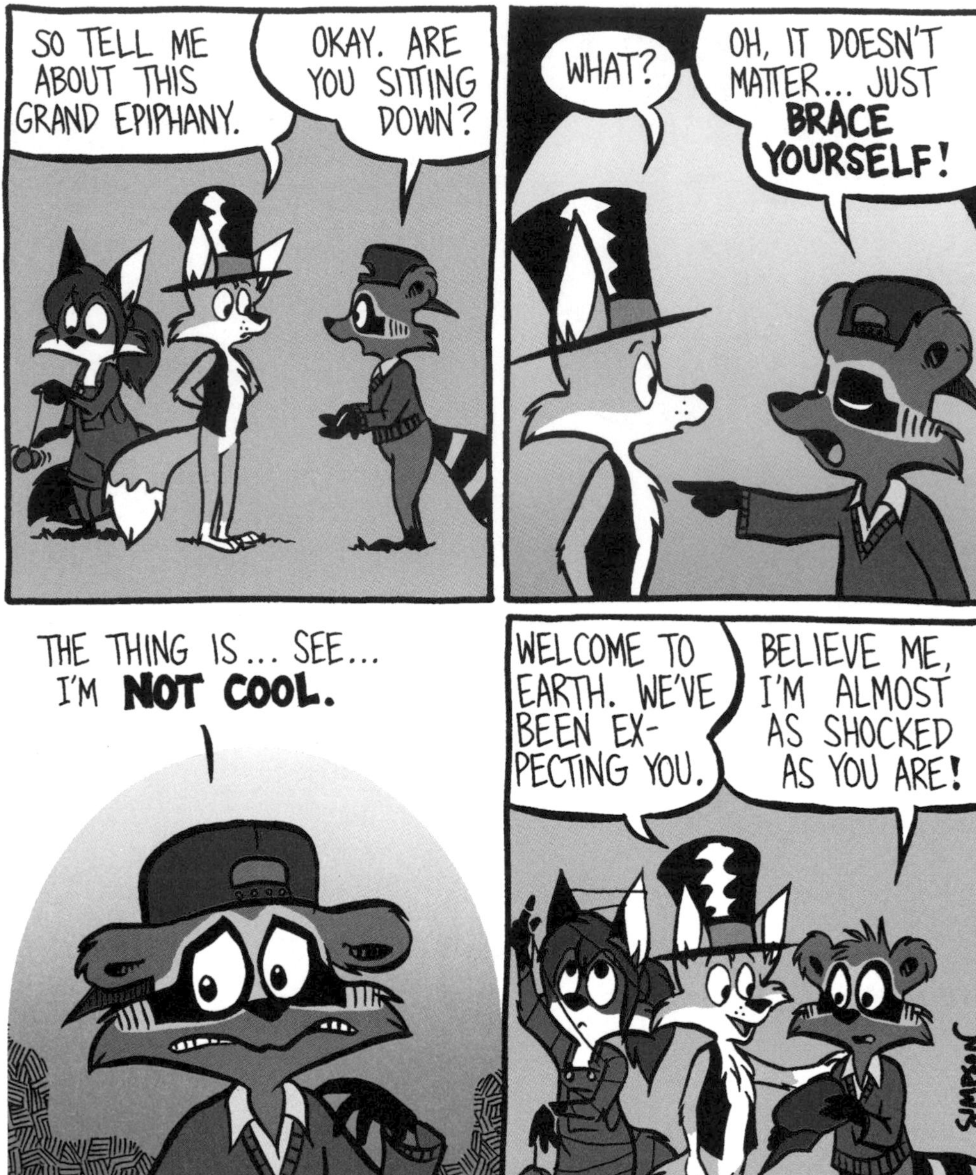
SO TELL ME ABOUT THIS GRAND EPIPHANY.
OKAY. ARE YOU SITTING DOWN?
WHAT?
OH, IT DOESN'T MATTER... JUST **BRACE YOURSELF!**
THE THING IS... SEE... I'M **NOT COOL.**
WELCOME TO EARTH. WE'VE BEEN EX-PECTING YOU.
BELIEVE ME, I'M ALMOST AS SHOCKED AS YOU ARE!
SIMPSON

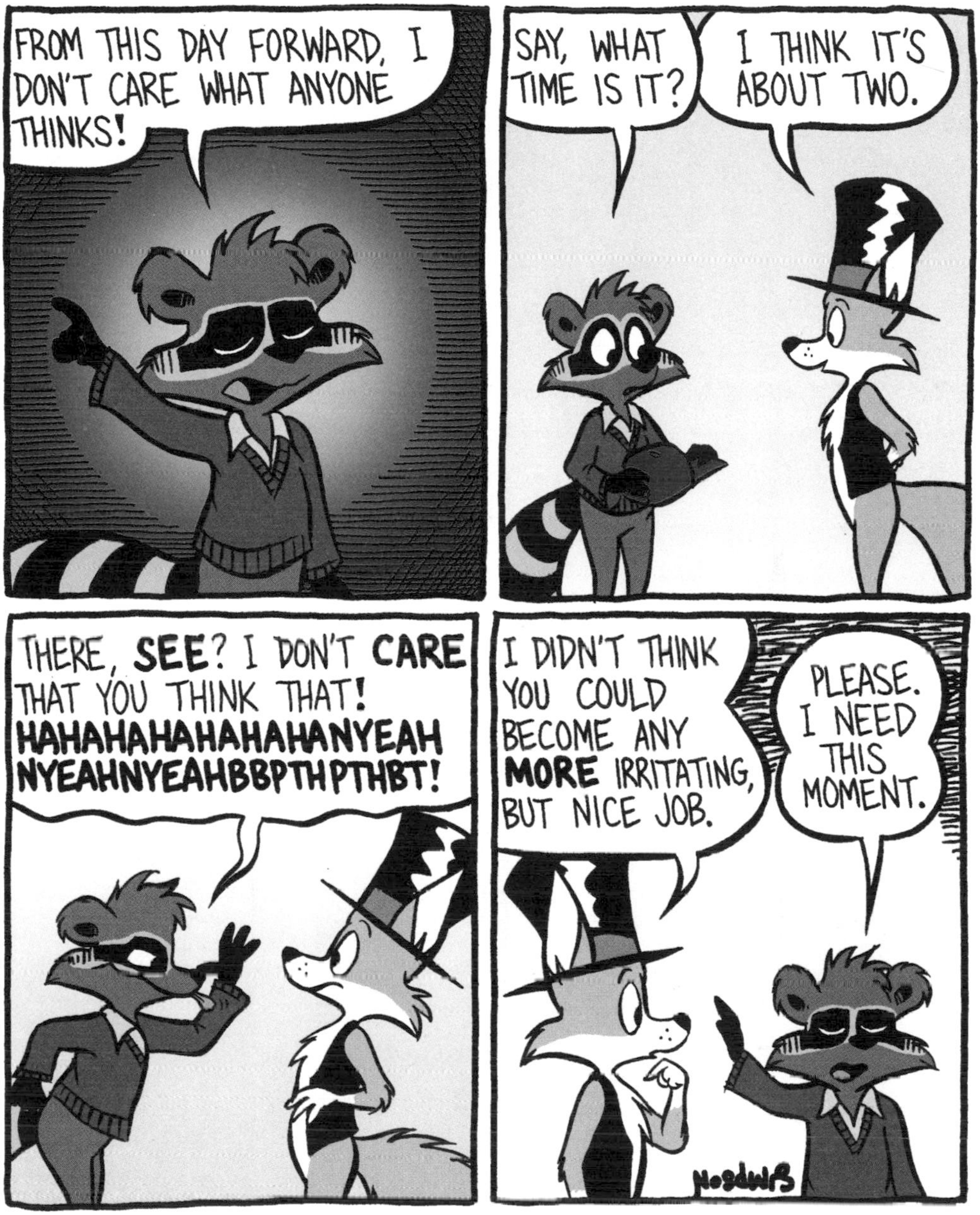
FROM THIS DAY FORWARD, I DON'T CARE WHAT ANYONE THINKS!
SAY, WHAT TIME IS IT?
I THINK IT'S ABOUT TWO.
THERE, SEE? I DON'T CARE THAT YOU THINK THAT! HAHAHAHAHAHAHANYEAH NYEAHNYEAHBBPTHPTHBT!
I DIDN'T THINK YOU COULD BECOME ANY MORE IRRITATING, BUT NICE JOB.
PLEASE. I NEED THIS MOMENT.

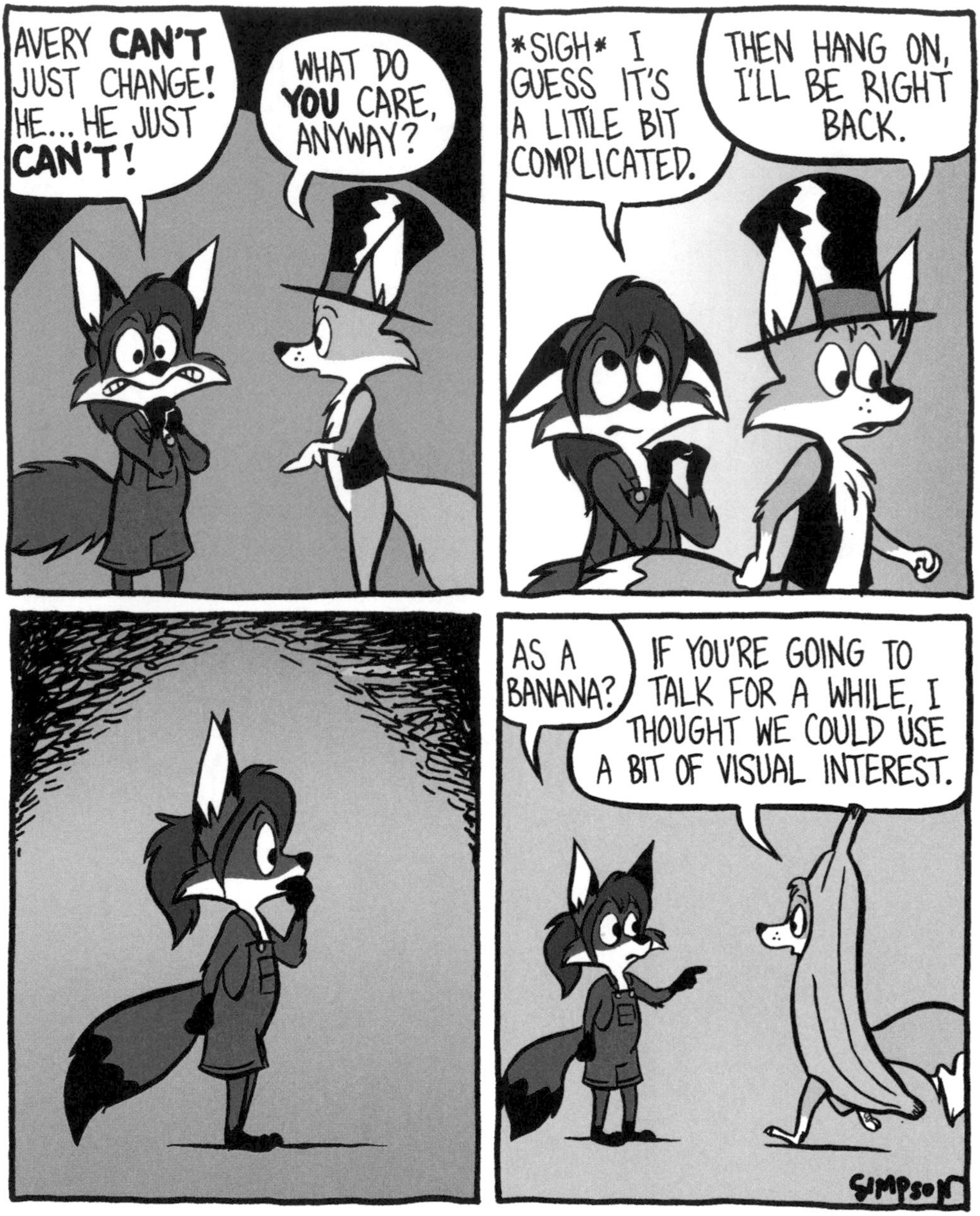
AVERY CAN'T JUST CHANGE! HE... HE JUST CAN'T!
WHAT DO YOU CARE, ANYWAY?
SIGH I GUESS IT'S A LITTLE BIT COMPLICATED.
THEN HANG ON, I'LL BE RIGHT BACK.
AS A BANANA?
IF YOU'RE GOING TO TALK FOR A WHILE, I THOUGHT WE COULD USE A BIT OF VISUAL INTEREST.
SIMPSON

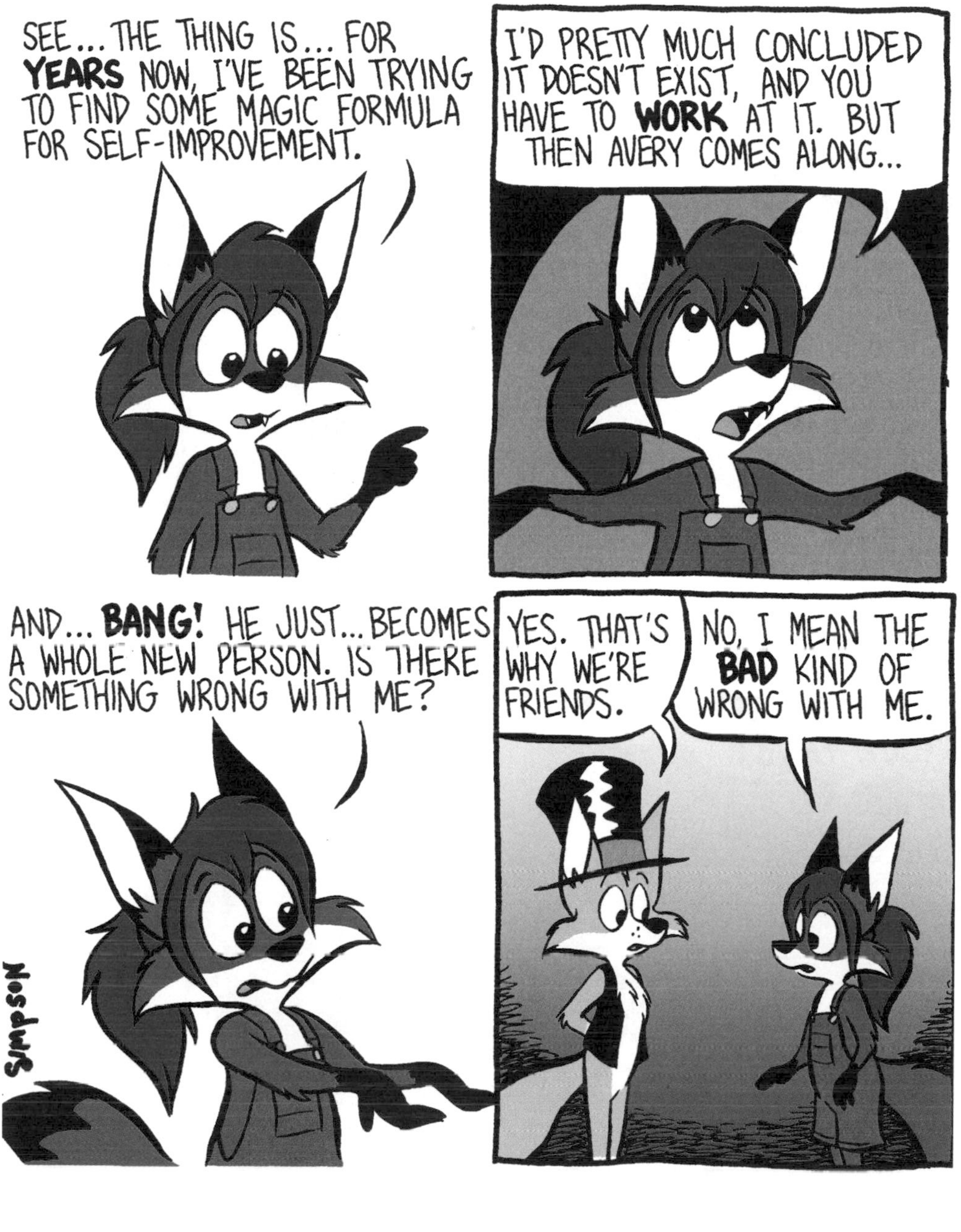
SEE... THE THING IS... FOR YEARS NOW, I'VE BEEN TRYING TO FIND SOME MAGIC FORMULA FOR SELF-IMPROVEMENT.
I'D PRETTY MUCH CONCLUDED IT DOESN'T EXIST, AND YOU HAVE TO WORK AT IT. BUT THEN AVERY COMES ALONG...
AND... BANG! HE JUST... BECOMES A WHOLE NEW PERSON. IS THERE SOMETHING WRONG WITH ME?
YES. THAT'S WHY WE'RE FRIENDS.
NO, I MEAN THE BAD KIND OF WRONG WITH ME.
SIMPSON

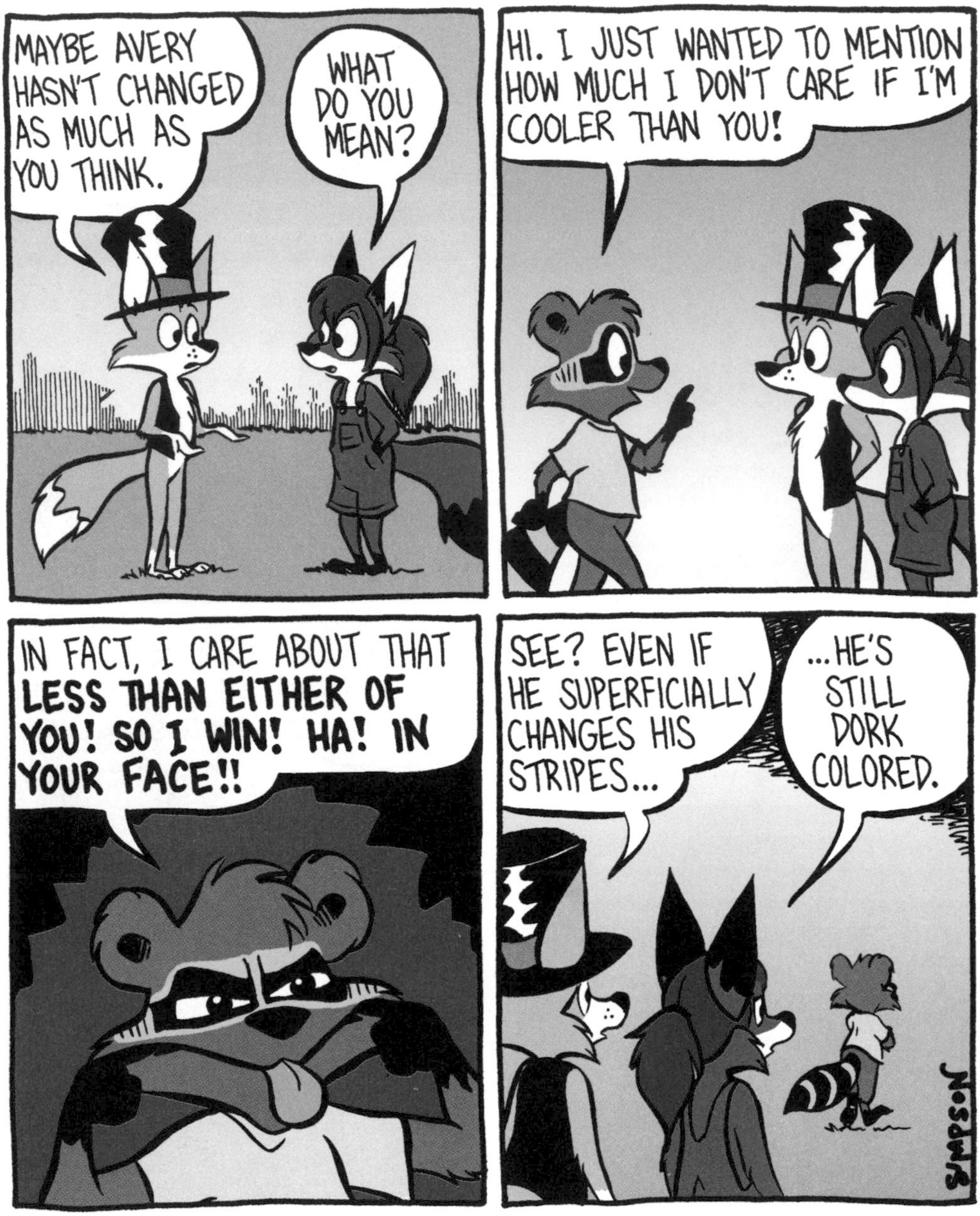
MAYBE AVERY HASN'T CHANGED AS MUCH AS YOU THINK.
WHAT DO YOU MEAN?
HI. I JUST WANTED TO MENTION HOW MUCH I DON'T CARE IF I'M COOLER THAN YOU!
IN FACT, I CARE ABOUT THAT LESS THAN EITHER OF YOU! SO I WIN! HA! IN YOUR FACE!!
SEE? EVEN IF HE SUPERFICIALLY CHANGES HIS STRIPES...
...HE'S STILL DORK COLORED.
SIMPSON

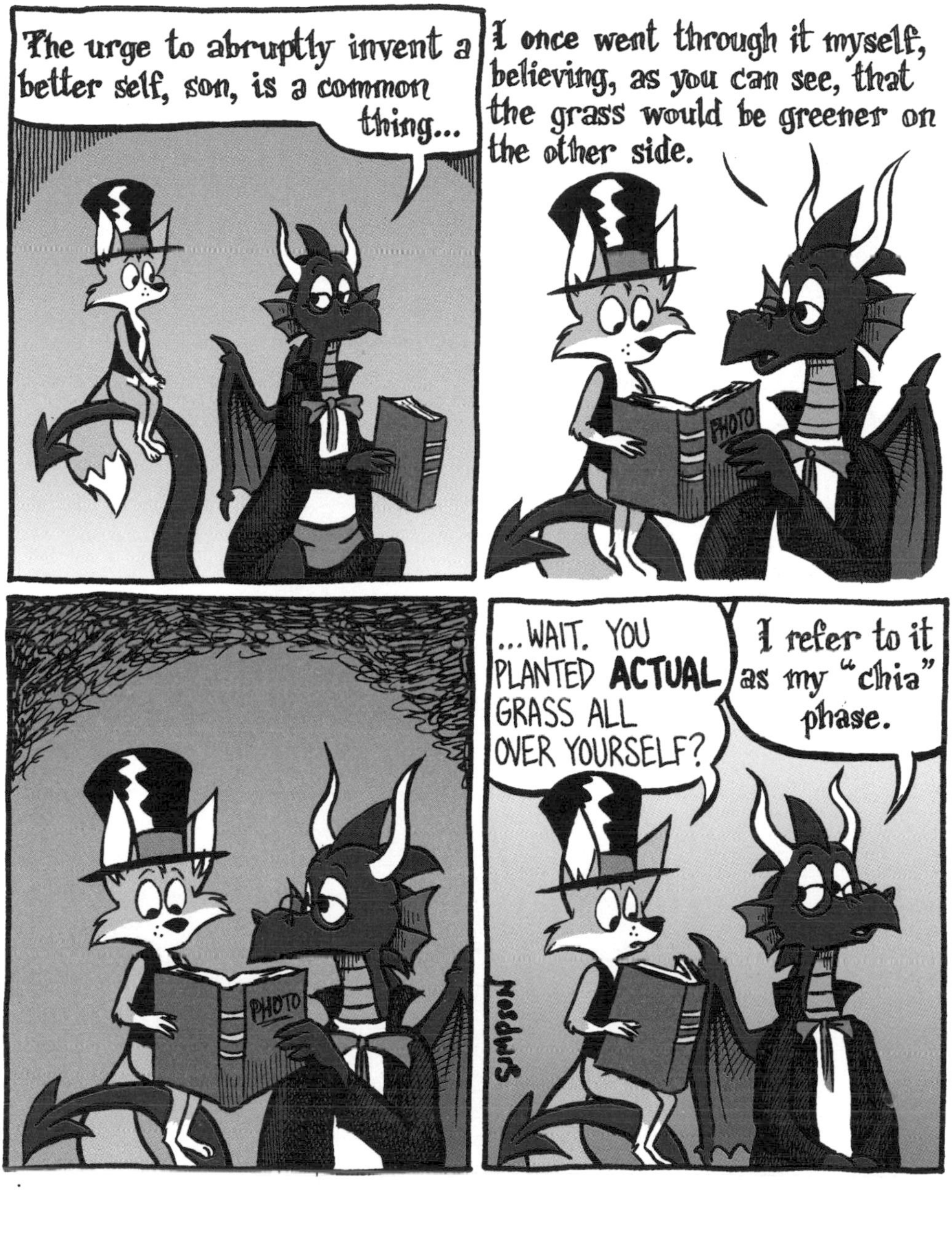
The urge to abruptly invent a better self, son, is a common thing...
I once went through it myself, believing, as you can see, that the grass would be greener on the other side.
PHOTO
PHOTO
SIMPSON
...WAIT. YOU PLANTED ACTUAL GRASS ALL OVER YOURSELF?
I refer to it as my "chia" phase.

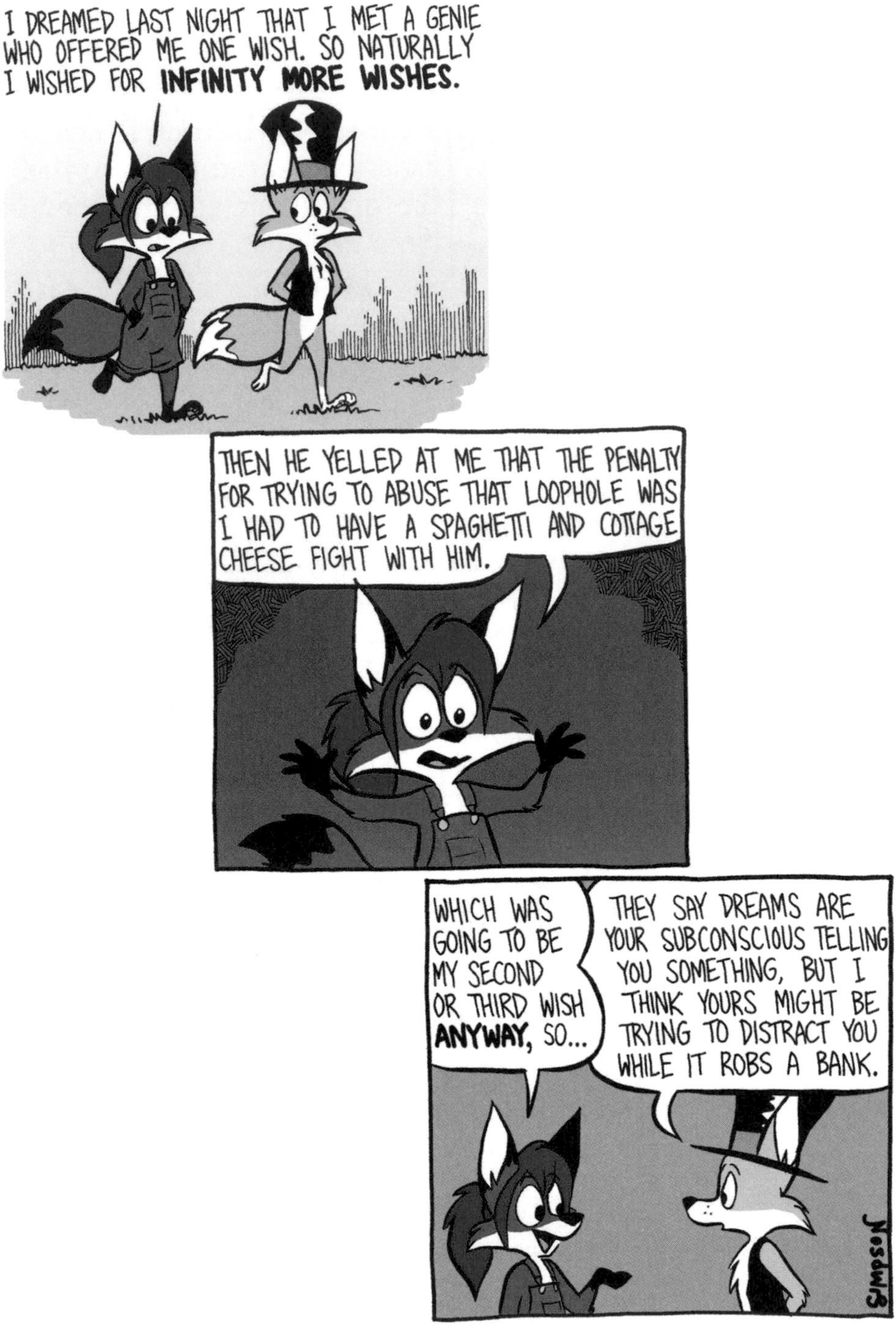
I DREAMED LAST NIGHT THAT I MET A GENIE WHO OFFERED ME ONE WISH. SO NATURALLY I WISHED FOR **INFINITY MORE WISHES.**
THEN HE YELLED AT ME THAT THE PENALTY FOR TRYING TO ABUSE THAT LOOPHOLE WAS I HAD TO HAVE A SPAGHETTI AND COTTAGE CHEESE FIGHT WITH HIM.
WHICH WAS GOING TO BE MY SECOND OR THIRD WISH **ANYWAY**, SO...
THEY SAY DREAMS ARE YOUR SUBCONSCIOUS TELLING YOU SOMETHING, BUT I THINK YOURS MIGHT BE TRYING TO DISTRACT YOU WHILE IT ROBS A BANK.
Simpson

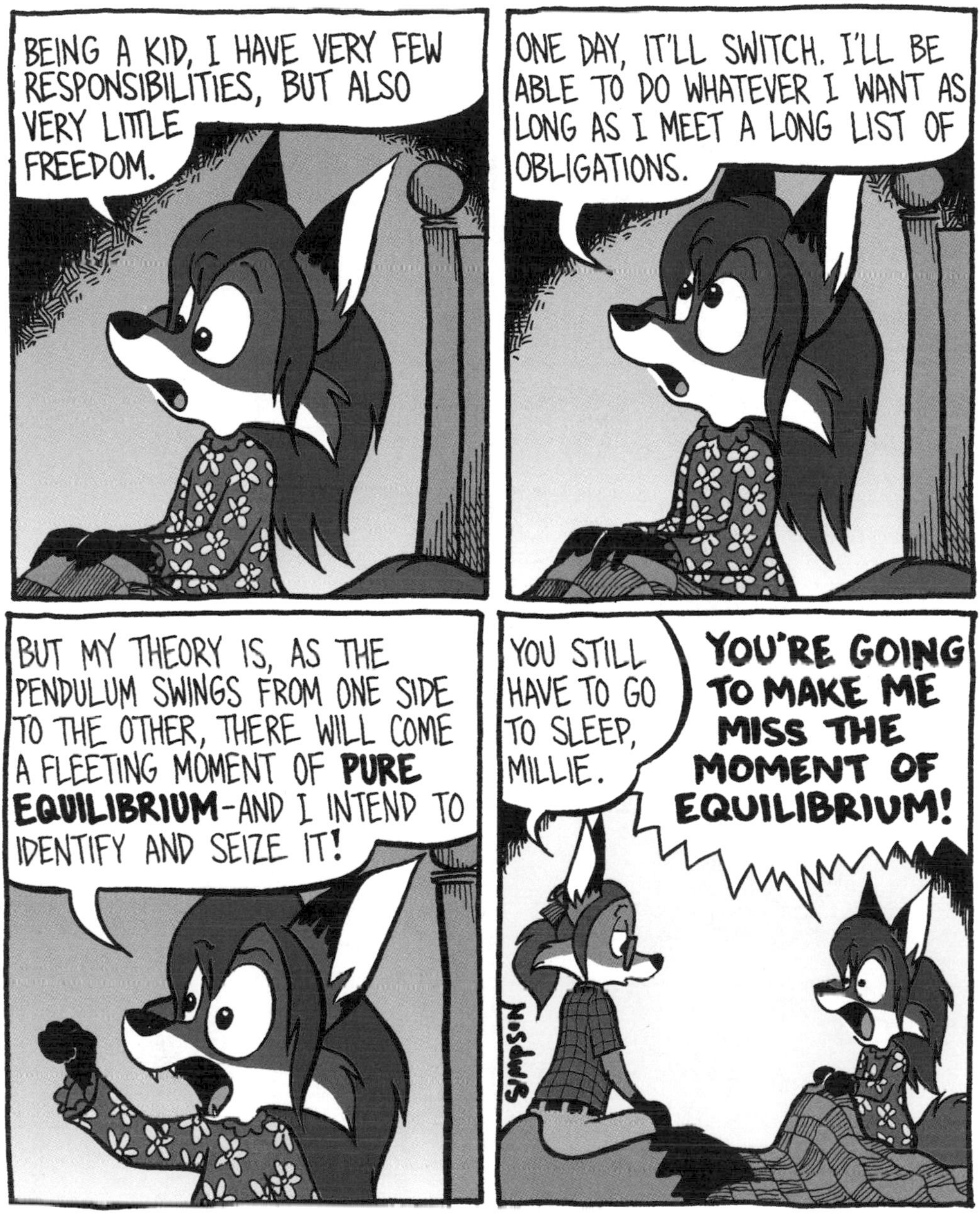
BEING A KID, I HAVE VERY FEW RESPONSIBILITIES, BUT ALSO VERY LITTLE FREEDOM.
ONE DAY, IT'LL SWITCH. I'LL BE ABLE TO DO WHATEVER I WANT AS LONG AS I MEET A LONG LIST OF OBLIGATIONS.
BUT MY THEORY IS, AS THE PENDULUM SWINGS FROM ONE SIDE TO THE OTHER, THERE WILL COME A FLEETING MOMENT OF PURE EQUILIBRIUM-AND I INTEND TO IDENTIFY AND SEIZE IT!
YOU STILL HAVE TO GO TO SLEEP, MILLIE.
YOU'RE GOING TO MAKE ME MISS THE MOMENT OF EQUILIBRIUM!
SIMPSON

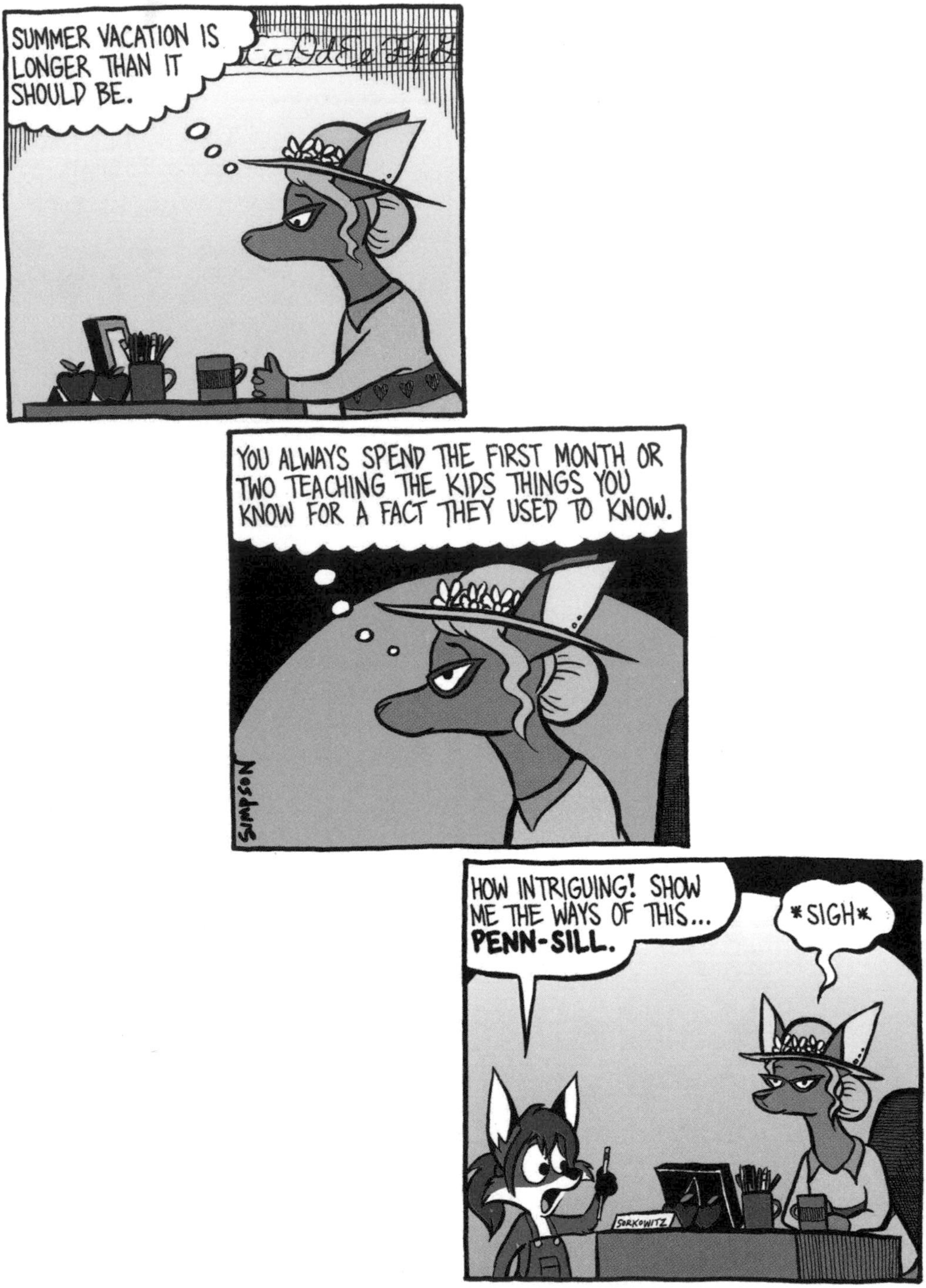
SUMMER VACATION IS LONGER THAN IT SHOULD BE.
YOU ALWAYS SPEND THE FIRST MONTH OR TWO TEACHING THE KIDS THINGS YOU KNOW FOR A FACT THEY USED TO KNOW.
SIMPSON
HOW INTRIGUING! SHOW ME THE WAYS OF THIS... **PENN-SILL.**
SIGH
SORKOWITZ

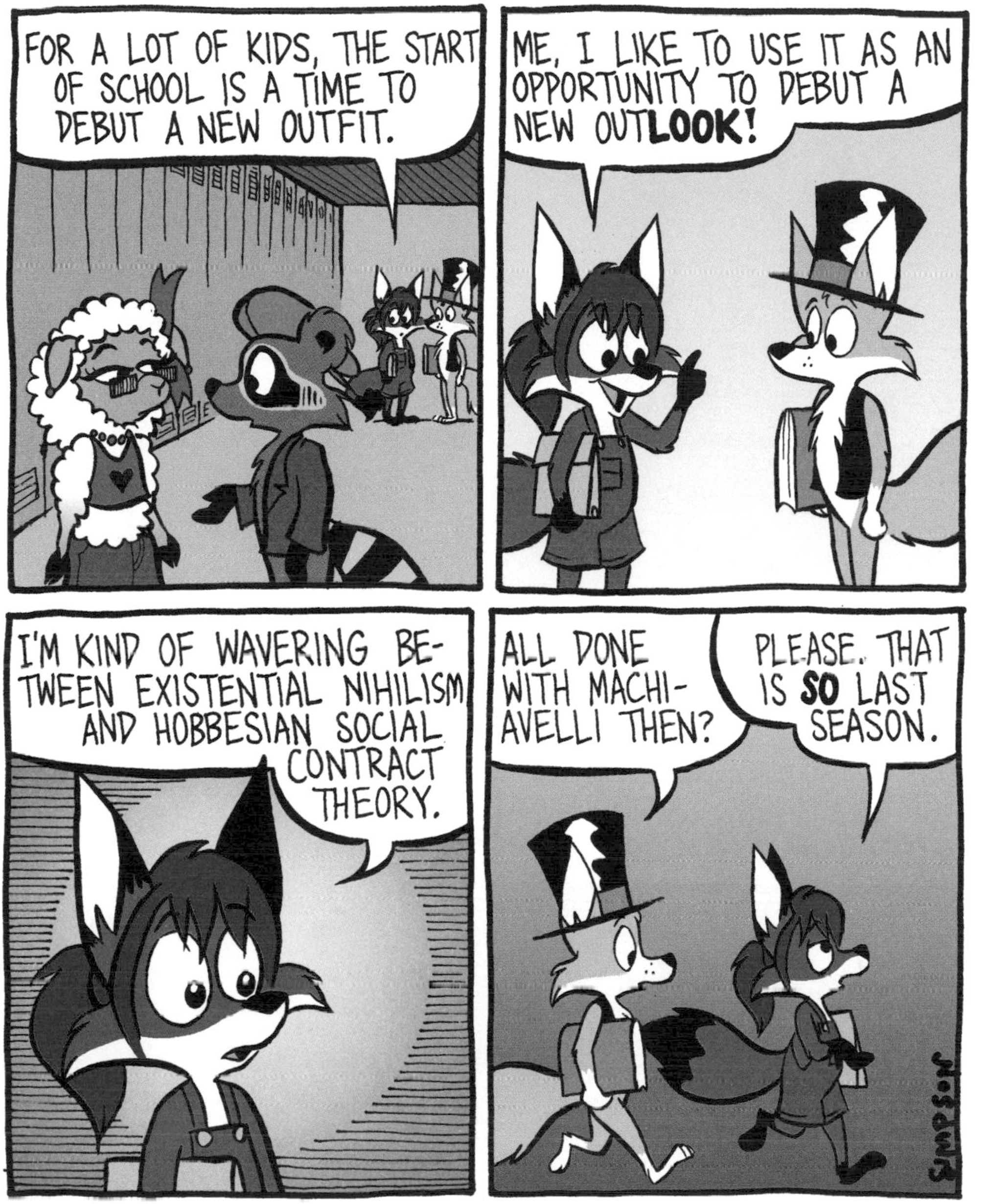
FOR A LOT OF KIDS, THE START OF SCHOOL IS A TIME TO DEBUT A NEW OUTFIT.
ME, I LIKE TO USE IT AS AN OPPORTUNITY TO DEBUT A NEW OUTLOOK!
I'M KIND OF WAVERING BETWEEN EXISTENTIAL NIHILISM AND HOBBESIAN SOCIAL CONTRACT THEORY.
ALL DONE WITH MACHIAVELLI THEN?
PLEASE. THAT IS SO LAST SEASON.
SIMPSON

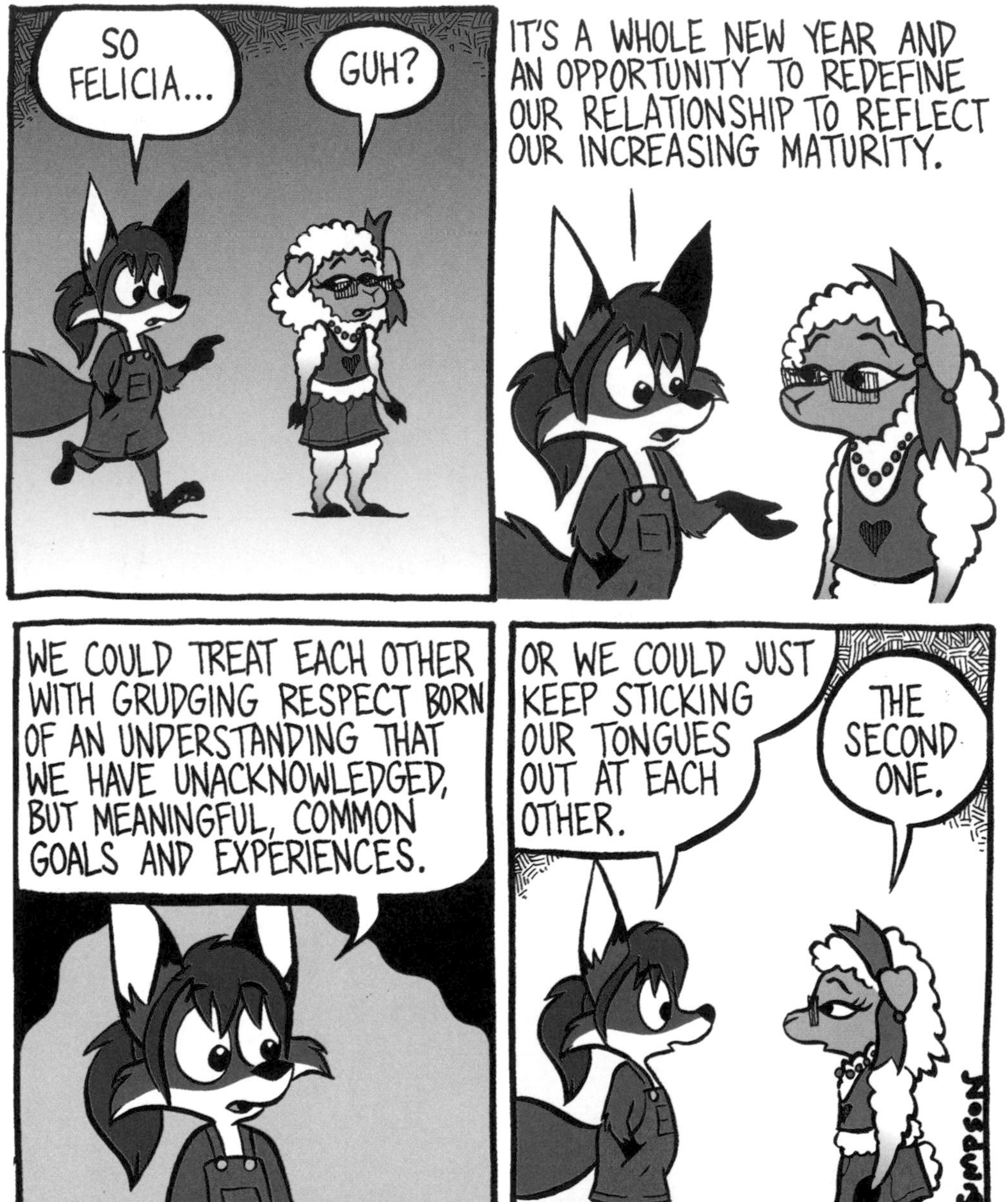
SO FELICIA...
GUH?
IT'S A WHOLE NEW YEAR AND AN OPPORTUNITY TO REDEFINE OUR RELATIONSHIP TO REFLECT OUR INCREASING MATURITY.
WE COULD TREAT EACH OTHER WITH GRUDGING RESPECT BORN OF AN UNDERSTANDING THAT WE HAVE UNACKNOWLEDGED, BUT MEANINGFUL, COMMON GOALS AND EXPERIENCES.
OR WE COULD JUST KEEP STICKING OUR TONGUES OUT AT EACH OTHER.
THE SECOND ONE.
SIMPSON

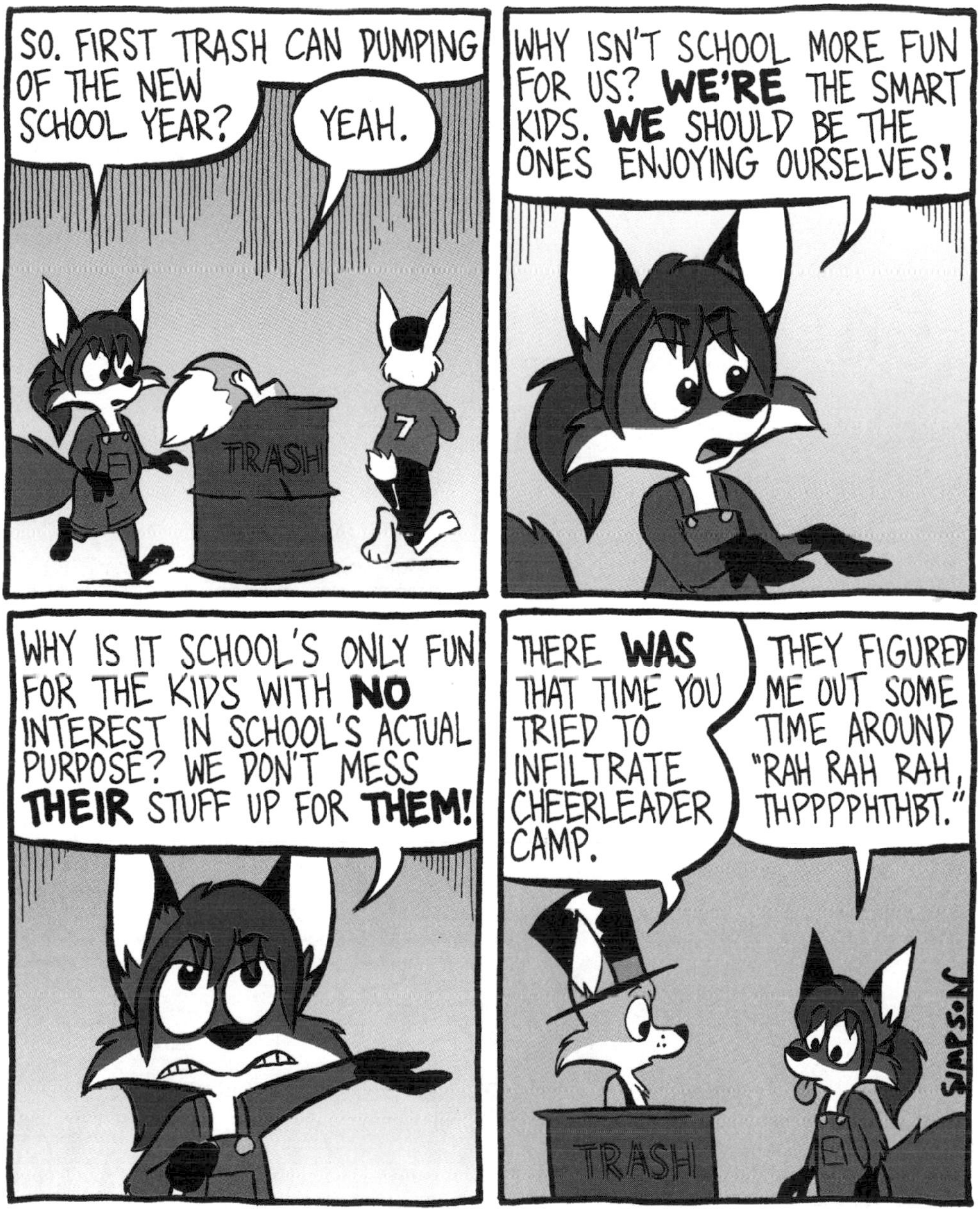
SO. FIRST TRASH CAN DUMPING OF THE NEW SCHOOL YEAR?
YEAH.
TRASH
7
WHY ISN'T SCHOOL MORE FUN FOR US? WE'RE THE SMART KIDS. WE SHOULD BE THE ONES ENJOYING OURSELVES!
WHY IS IT SCHOOL'S ONLY FUN FOR THE KIDS WITH NO INTEREST IN SCHOOL'S ACTUAL PURPOSE? WE DON'T MESS THEIR STUFF UP FOR THEM!
THERE WAS THAT TIME YOU TRIED TO INFILTRATE CHEERLEADER CAMP.
THEY FIGURED ME OUT SOME TIME AROUND "RAH RAH RAH, THPPPPHTHBT."
SIMPSON
TRASH

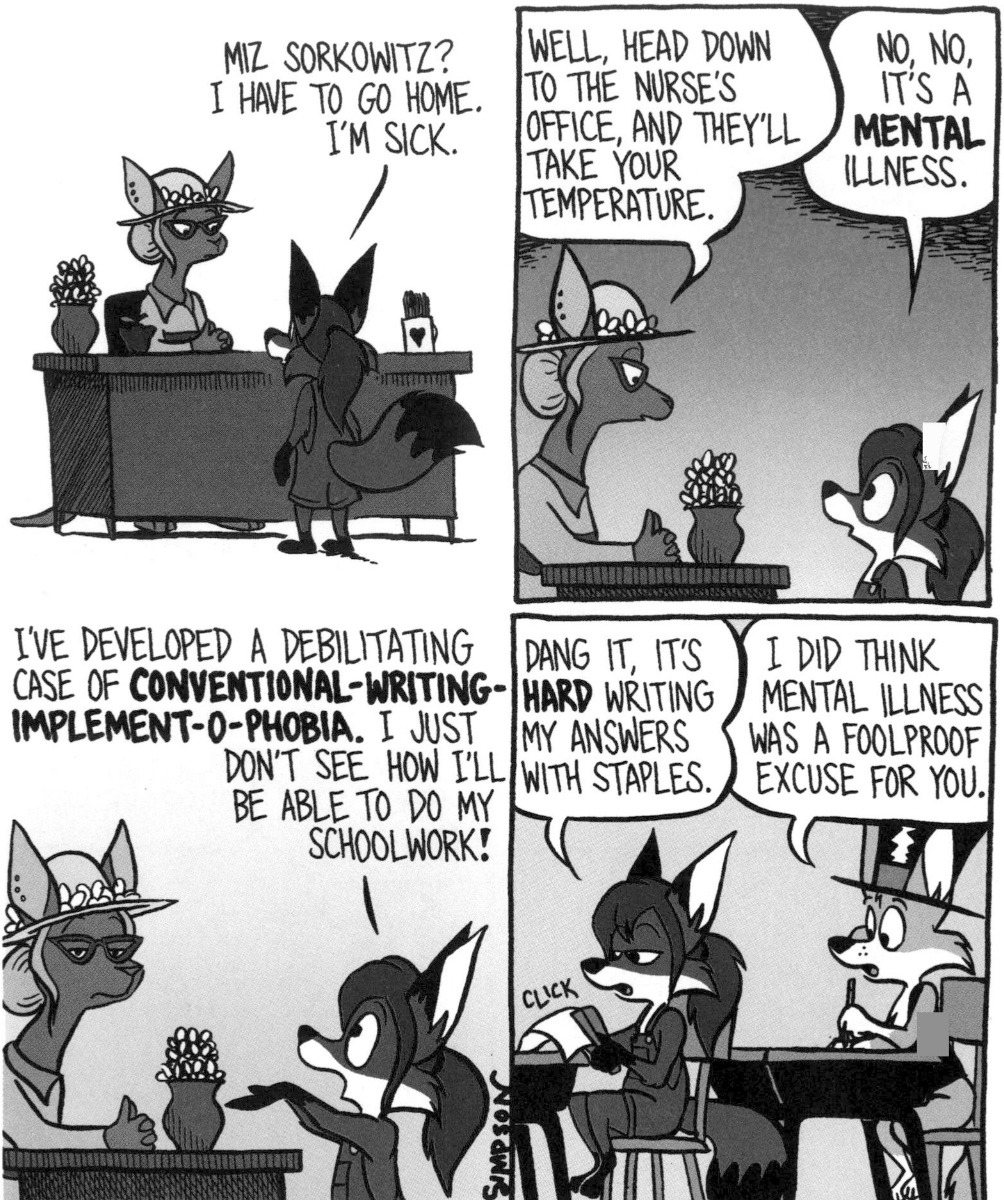
MIZ SORKOWITZ? I HAVE TO GO HOME. I'M SICK.
WELL, HEAD DOWN TO THE NURSE'S OFFICE, AND THEY'LL TAKE YOUR TEMPERATURE.
NO, NO, IT'S A **MENTAL** ILLNESS.
I'VE DEVELOPED A DEBILITATING CASE OF **CONVENTIONAL-WRITING-IMPLEMENT-O-PHOBIA.** I JUST DON'T SEE HOW I'LL BE ABLE TO DO MY SCHOOLWORK!
SIMPSON
DANG IT, IT'S **HARD** WRITING MY ANSWERS WITH STAPLES.
I DID THINK MENTAL ILLNESS WAS A FOOLPROOF EXCUSE FOR YOU.
CLICK

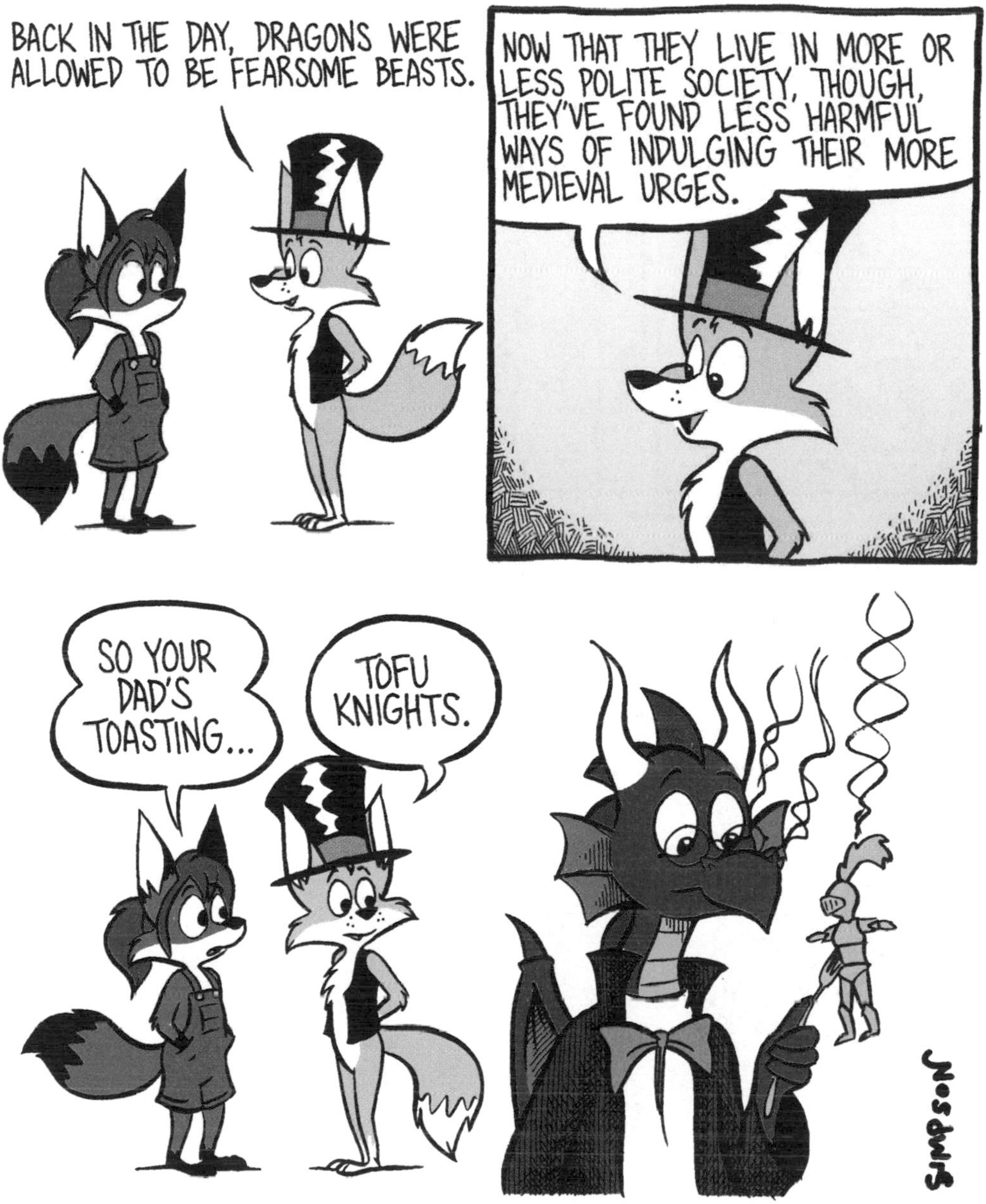
BACK IN THE DAY, DRAGONS WERE ALLOWED TO BE FEARSOME BEASTS.
NOW THAT THEY LIVE IN MORE OR LESS POLITE SOCIETY, THOUGH, THEY'VE FOUND LESS HARMFUL WAYS OF INDULGING THEIR MORE MEDIEVAL URGES.
SO YOUR DAD'S TOASTING...
TOFU KNIGHTS.
Simpson

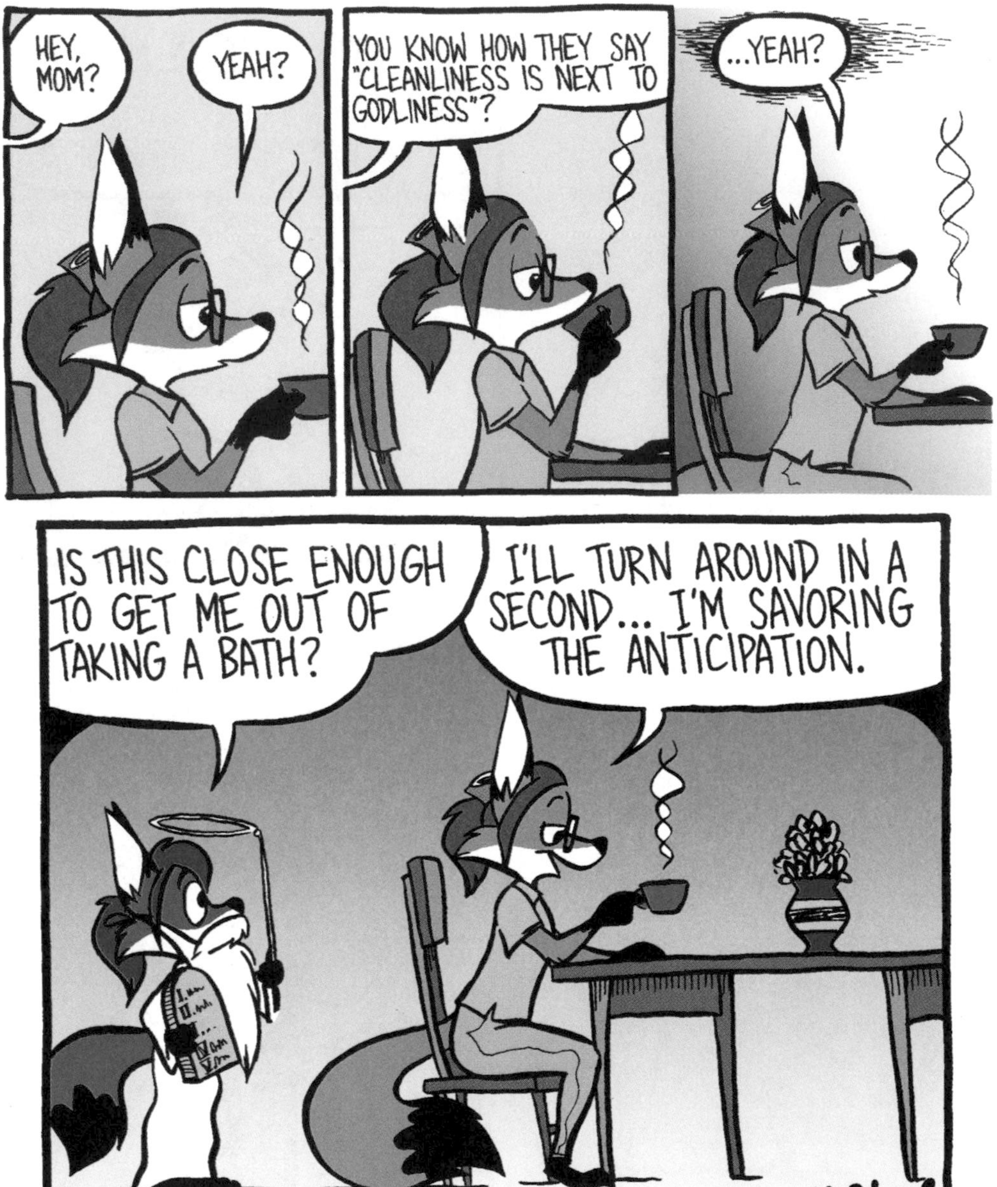
HEY, MOM?
YEAH?
YOU KNOW HOW THEY SAY "CLEANLINESS IS NEXT TO GODLINESS"?
...YEAH?
IS THIS CLOSE ENOUGH TO GET ME OUT OF TAKING A BATH?
I'LL TURN AROUND IN A SECOND... I'M SAVORING THE ANTICIPATION.

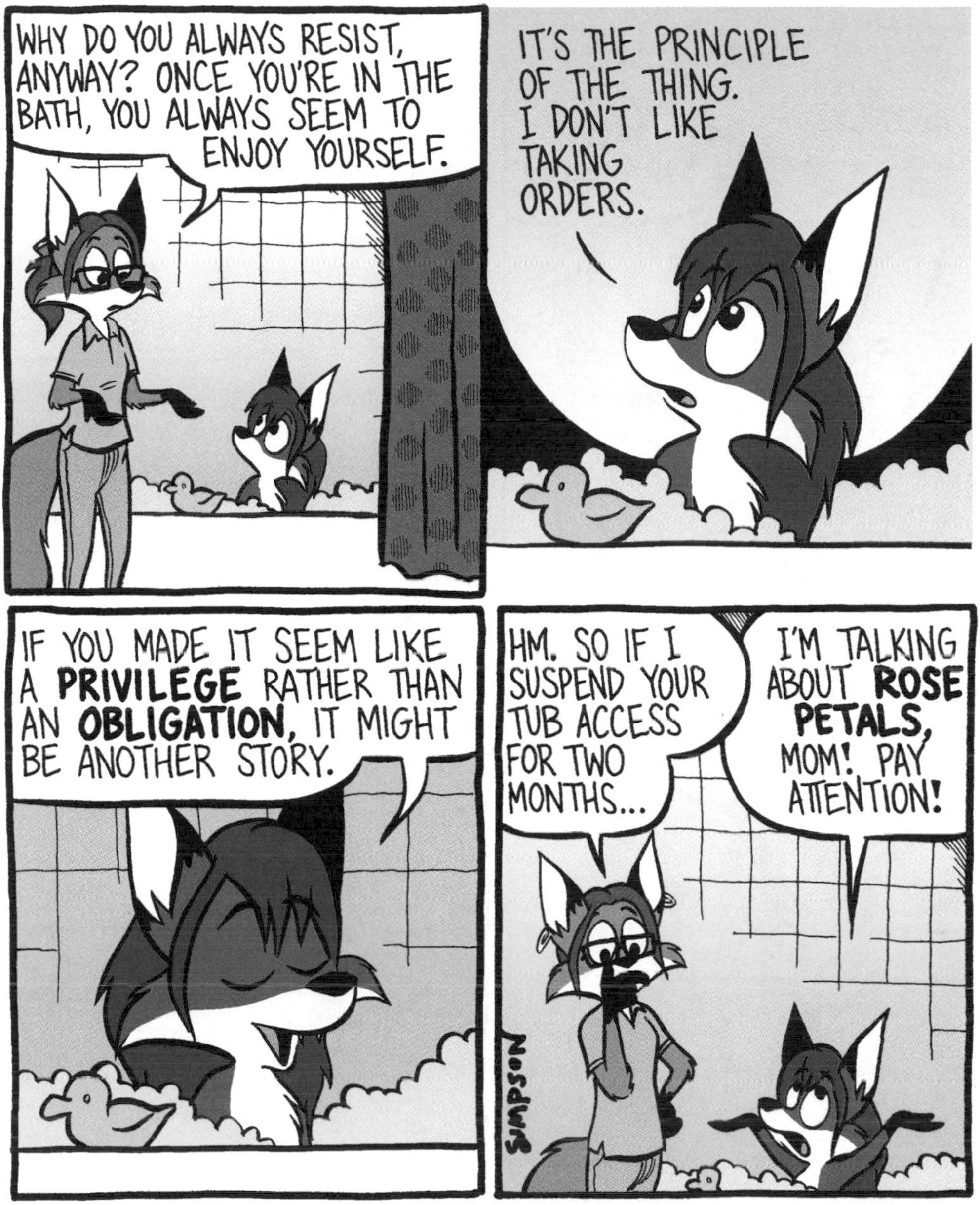
WHY DO YOU ALWAYS RESIST, ANYWAY? ONCE YOU'RE IN THE BATH, YOU ALWAYS SEEM TO ENJOY YOURSELF.
IT'S THE PRINCIPLE OF THE THING. I DON'T LIKE TAKING ORDERS.
IF YOU MADE IT SEEM LIKE A PRIVILEGE RATHER THAN AN OBLIGATION, IT MIGHT BE ANOTHER STORY.
HM. SO IF I SUSPEND YOUR TUB ACCESS FOR TWO MONTHS...
I'M TALKING ABOUT ROSE PETALS, MOM! PAY ATTENTION!
SIMPSON

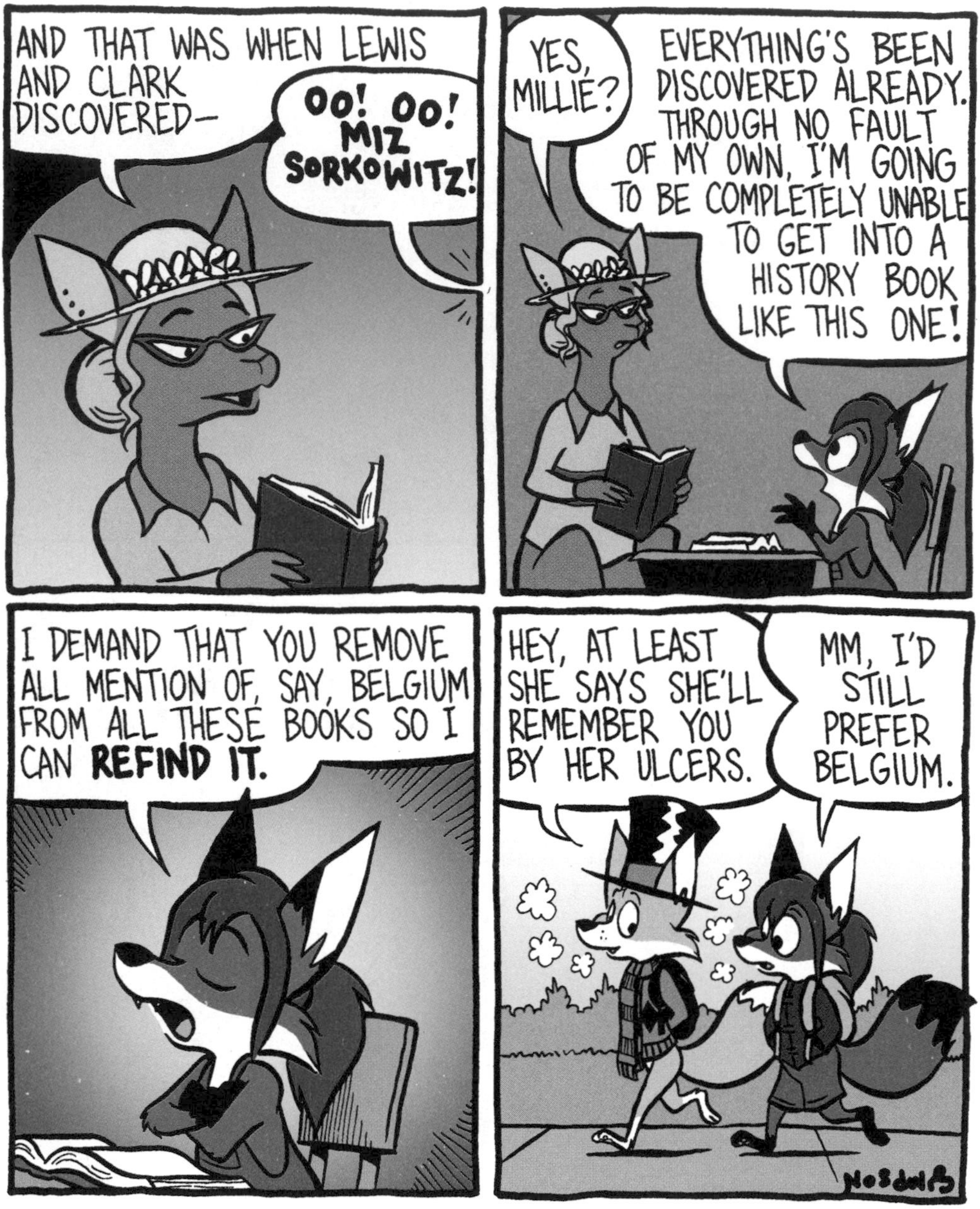
AND THAT WAS WHEN LEWIS AND CLARK DISCOVERED—
OO! OO! MIZ SORKOWITZ!
YES, MILLIE?
EVERYTHING'S BEEN DISCOVERED ALREADY. THROUGH NO FAULT OF MY OWN, I'M GOING TO BE COMPLETELY UNABLE TO GET INTO A HISTORY BOOK LIKE THIS ONE!
I DEMAND THAT YOU REMOVE ALL MENTION OF, SAY, BELGIUM FROM ALL THESE BOOKS SO I CAN **REFIND IT.**
HEY, AT LEAST SHE SAYS SHE'LL REMEMBER YOU BY HER ULCERS.
MM, I'D STILL PREFER BELGIUM.

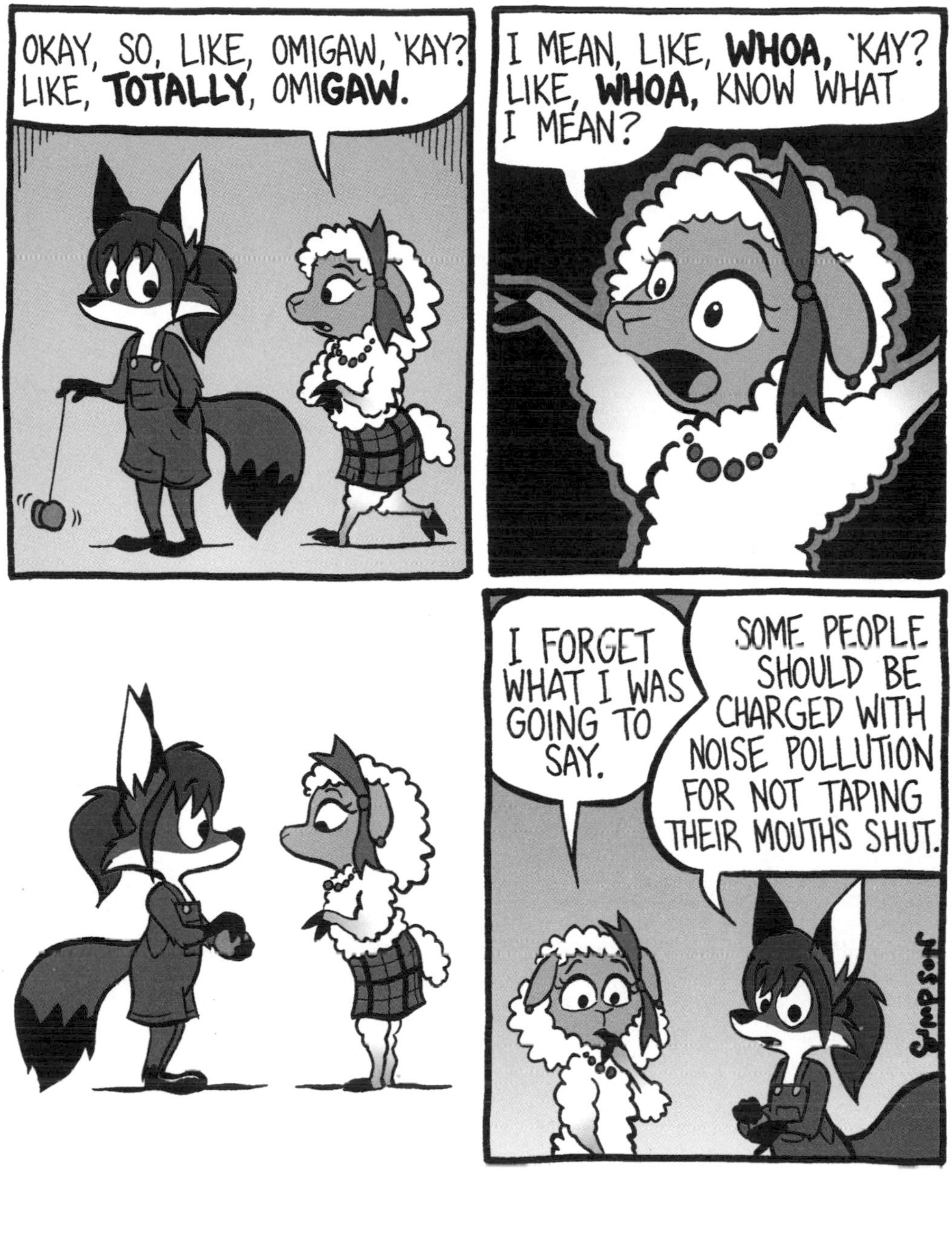
OKAY, SO, LIKE, OMIGAW, 'KAY? LIKE, TOTALLY, OMIGAW.
I MEAN, LIKE, WHOA, 'KAY? LIKE, WHOA, KNOW WHAT I MEAN?
I FORGET WHAT I WAS GOING TO SAY.
SOME PEOPLE SHOULD BE CHARGED WITH NOISE POLLUTION FOR NOT TAPING THEIR MOUTHS SHUT.
SIMPSON

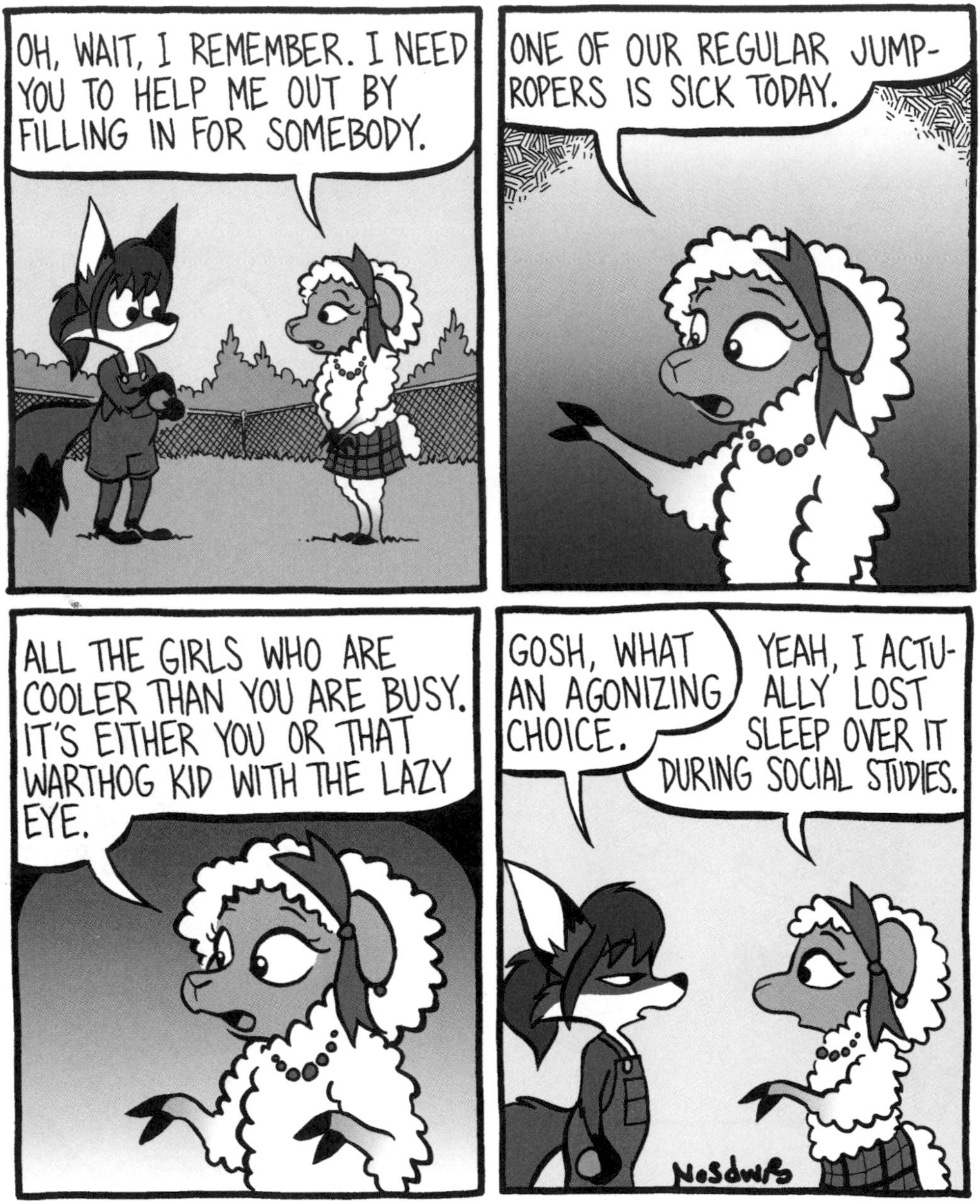
OH, WAIT, I REMEMBER. I NEED YOU TO HELP ME OUT BY FILLING IN FOR SOMEBODY.
ONE OF OUR REGULAR JUMP-ROPERS IS SICK TODAY.
ALL THE GIRLS WHO ARE COOLER THAN YOU ARE BUSY. IT'S EITHER YOU OR THAT WARTHOG KID WITH THE LAZY EYE.
GOSH, WHAT AN AGONIZING CHOICE.
YEAH, I ACTU-ALLY LOST SLEEP OVER IT DURING SOCIAL STUDIES.
NOSDWRS

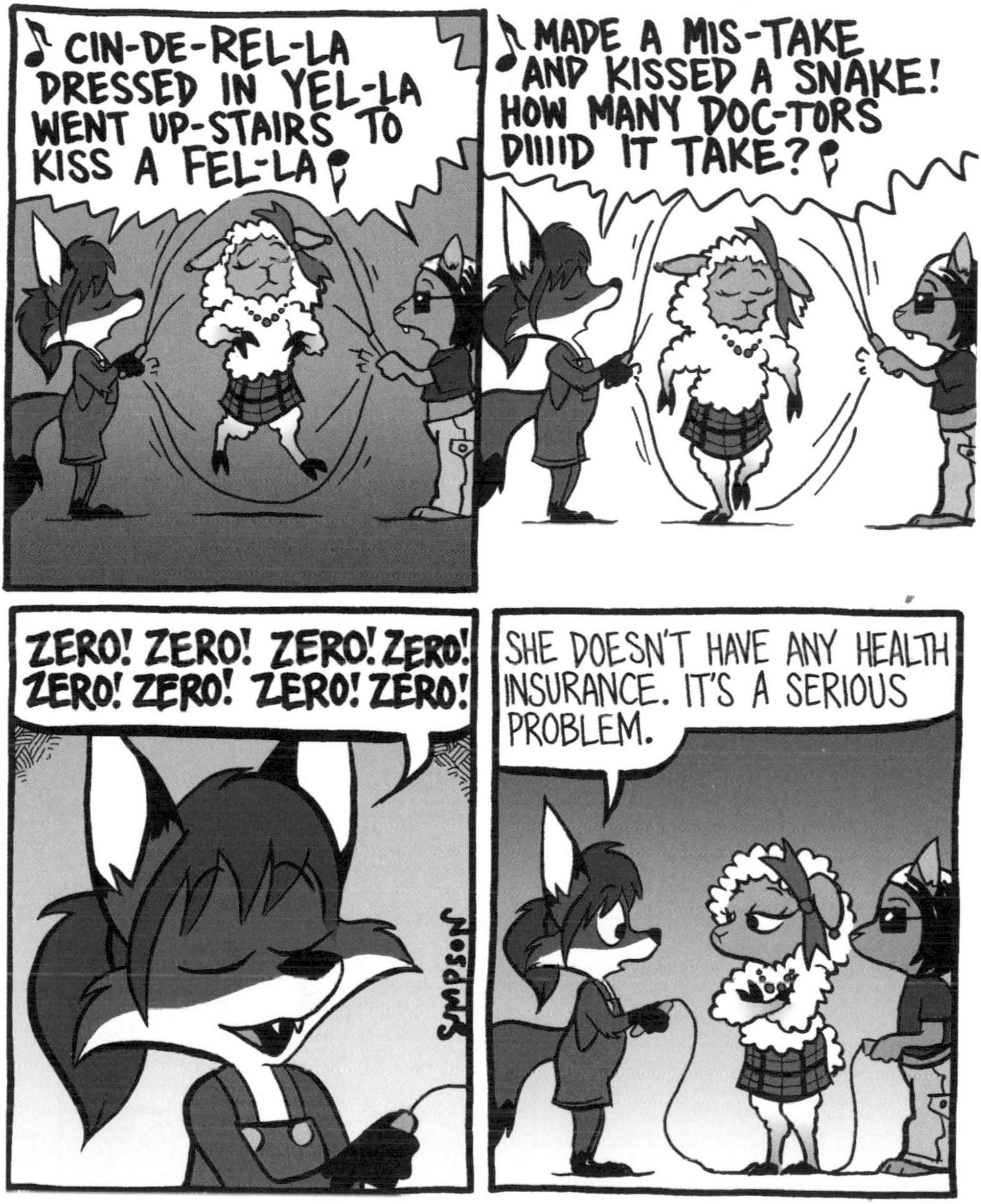

♪ CIN-DE-REL-LA DRESSED IN YEL-LA WENT UP-STAIRS TO KISS A FEL-LA ♪
♪ MADE A MIS-TAKE AND KISSED A SNAKE! HOW MANY DOC-TORS DIIIID IT TAKE? ♪
ZERO! ZERO! ZERO! ZERO! ZERO! ZERO! ZERO! ZERO!
SIMPSON
SHE DOESN'T HAVE ANY HEALTH INSURANCE. IT'S A SERIOUS PROBLEM.

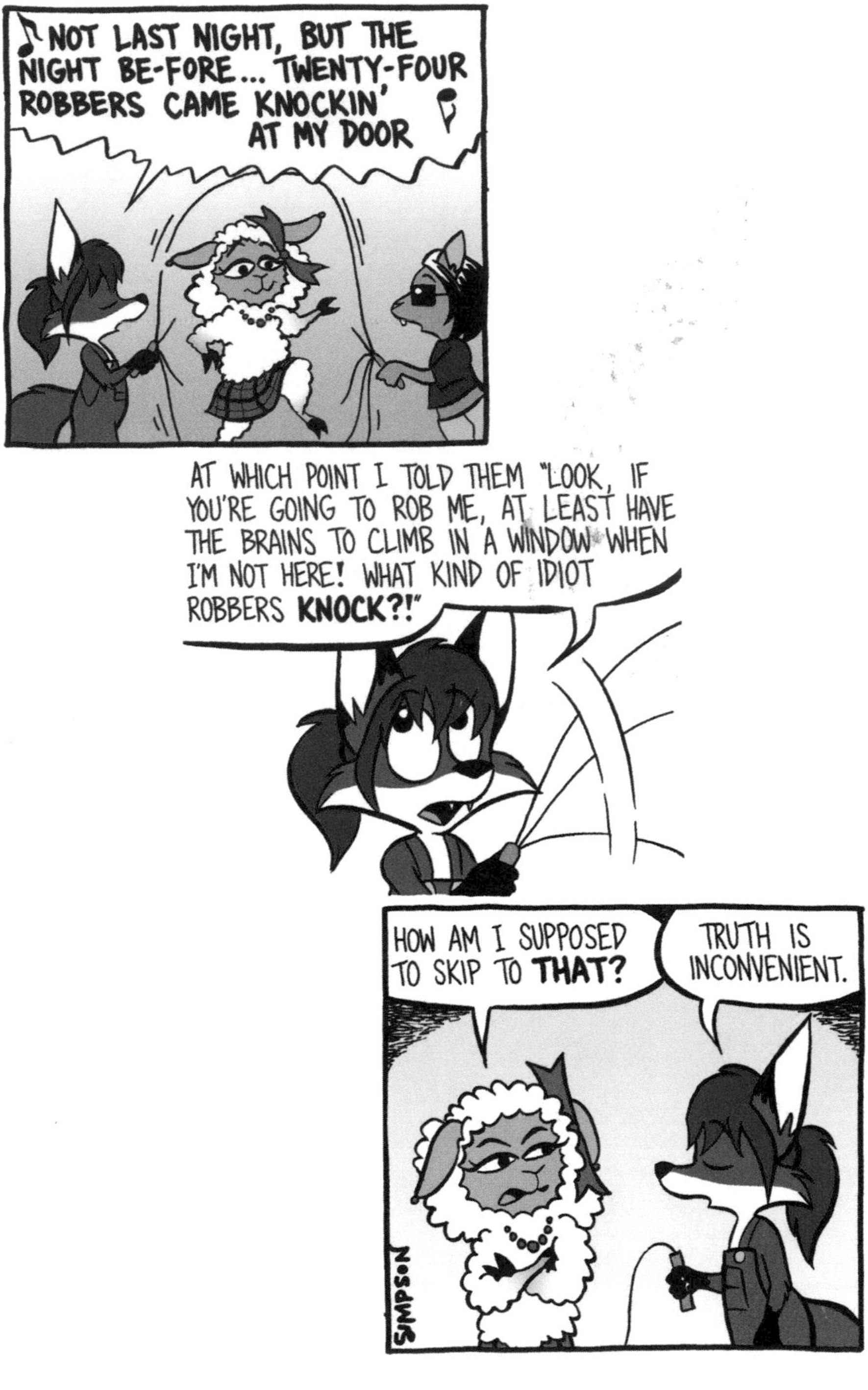
NOT LAST NIGHT, BUT THE NIGHT BE-FORE... TWENTY-FOUR ROBBERS CAME KNOCKIN' AT MY DOOR
AT WHICH POINT I TOLD THEM "LOOK, IF YOU'RE GOING TO ROB ME, AT LEAST HAVE THE BRAINS TO CLIMB IN A WINDOW WHEN I'M NOT HERE! WHAT KIND OF IDIOT ROBBERS KNOCK?!"
HOW AM I SUPPOSED TO SKIP TO THAT?
TRUTH IS INCONVENIENT.
SIMPSON

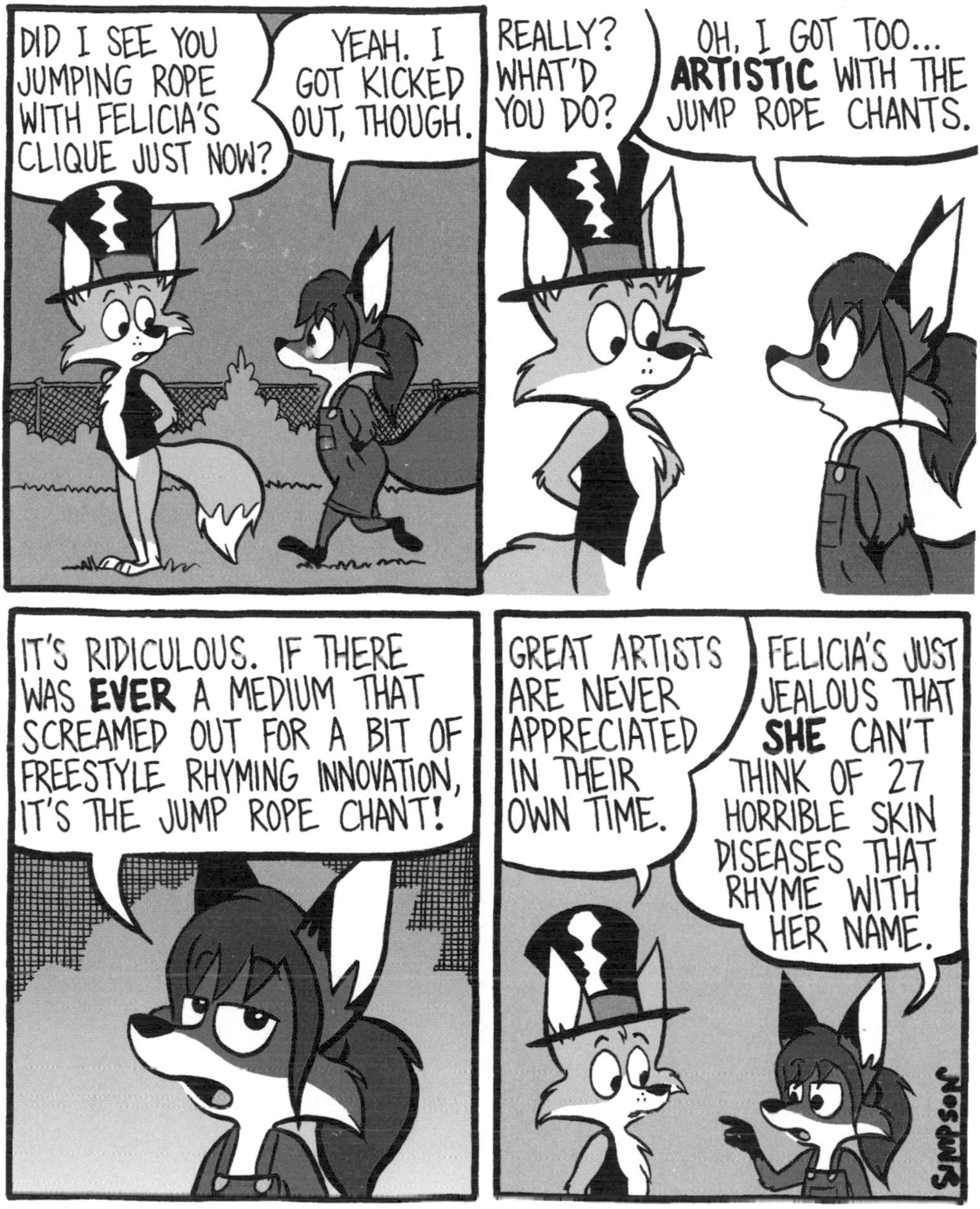
DID I SEE YOU JUMPING ROPE WITH FELICIA'S CLIQUE JUST NOW?
YEAH. I GOT KICKED OUT, THOUGH.
REALLY? WHAT'D YOU DO?
OH, I GOT TOO... **ARTISTIC** WITH THE JUMP ROPE CHANTS.
IT'S RIDICULOUS. IF THERE WAS **EVER** A MEDIUM THAT SCREAMED OUT FOR A BIT OF FREESTYLE RHYMING INNOVATION, IT'S THE JUMP ROPE CHANT!
GREAT ARTISTS ARE NEVER APPRECIATED IN THEIR OWN TIME.
FELICIA'S JUST JEALOUS THAT **SHE** CAN'T THINK OF 27 HORRIBLE SKIN DISEASES THAT RHYME WITH HER NAME.
SIMPSON

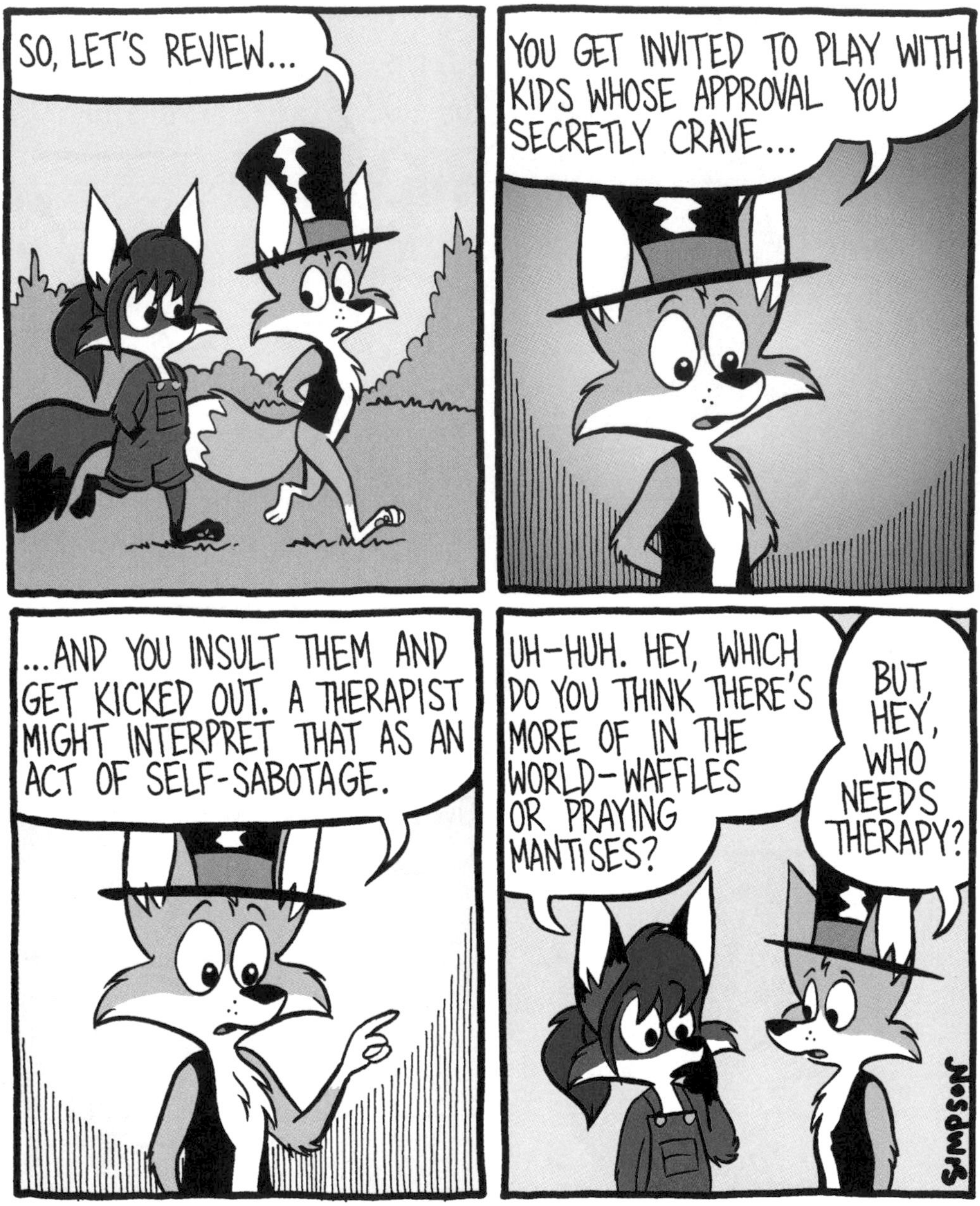
SO, LET'S REVIEW...
YOU GET INVITED TO PLAY WITH KIDS WHOSE APPROVAL YOU SECRETLY CRAVE...
...AND YOU INSULT THEM AND GET KICKED OUT. A THERAPIST MIGHT INTERPRET THAT AS AN ACT OF SELF-SABOTAGE.
UH-HUH. HEY, WHICH DO YOU THINK THERE'S MORE OF IN THE WORLD–WAFFLES OR PRAYING MANTISES?
BUT, HEY, WHO NEEDS THERAPY?
SIMPSON

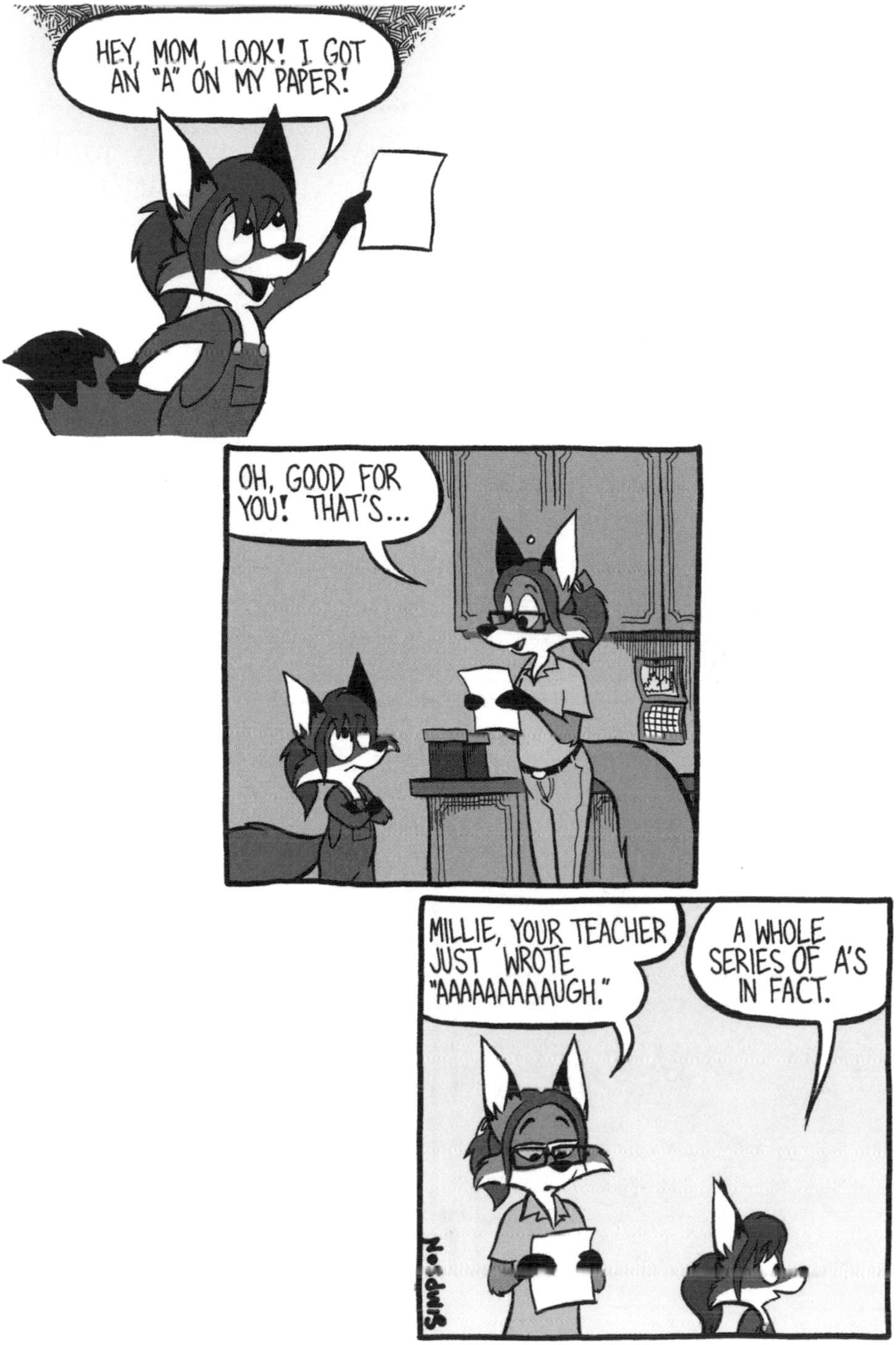

HEY, MOM, LOOK! I GOT AN "A" ON MY PAPER!
OH, GOOD FOR YOU! THAT'S...
MILLIE, YOUR TEACHER JUST WROTE "AAAAAAAAAUGH."
A WHOLE SERIES OF A'S IN FACT.
SIMPSON

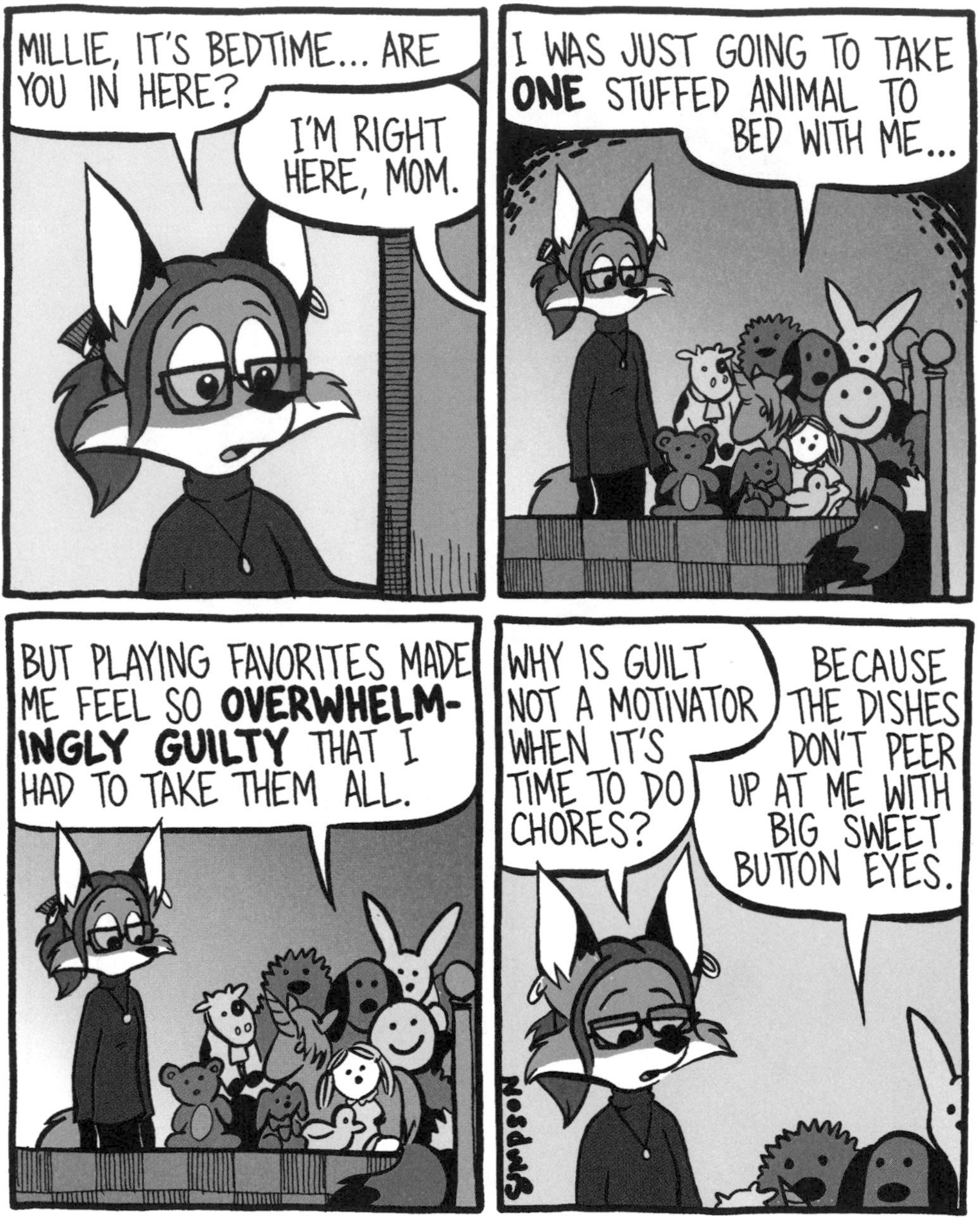
MILLIE, IT'S BEDTIME... ARE YOU IN HERE?
I'M RIGHT HERE, MOM.
I WAS JUST GOING TO TAKE **ONE** STUFFED ANIMAL TO BED WITH ME...
BUT PLAYING FAVORITES MADE ME FEEL SO **OVERWHELMINGLY GUILTY** THAT I HAD TO TAKE THEM ALL.
WHY IS GUILT NOT A MOTIVATOR WHEN IT'S TIME TO DO CHORES?
BECAUSE THE DISHES DON'T PEER UP AT ME WITH BIG SWEET BUTTON EYES.

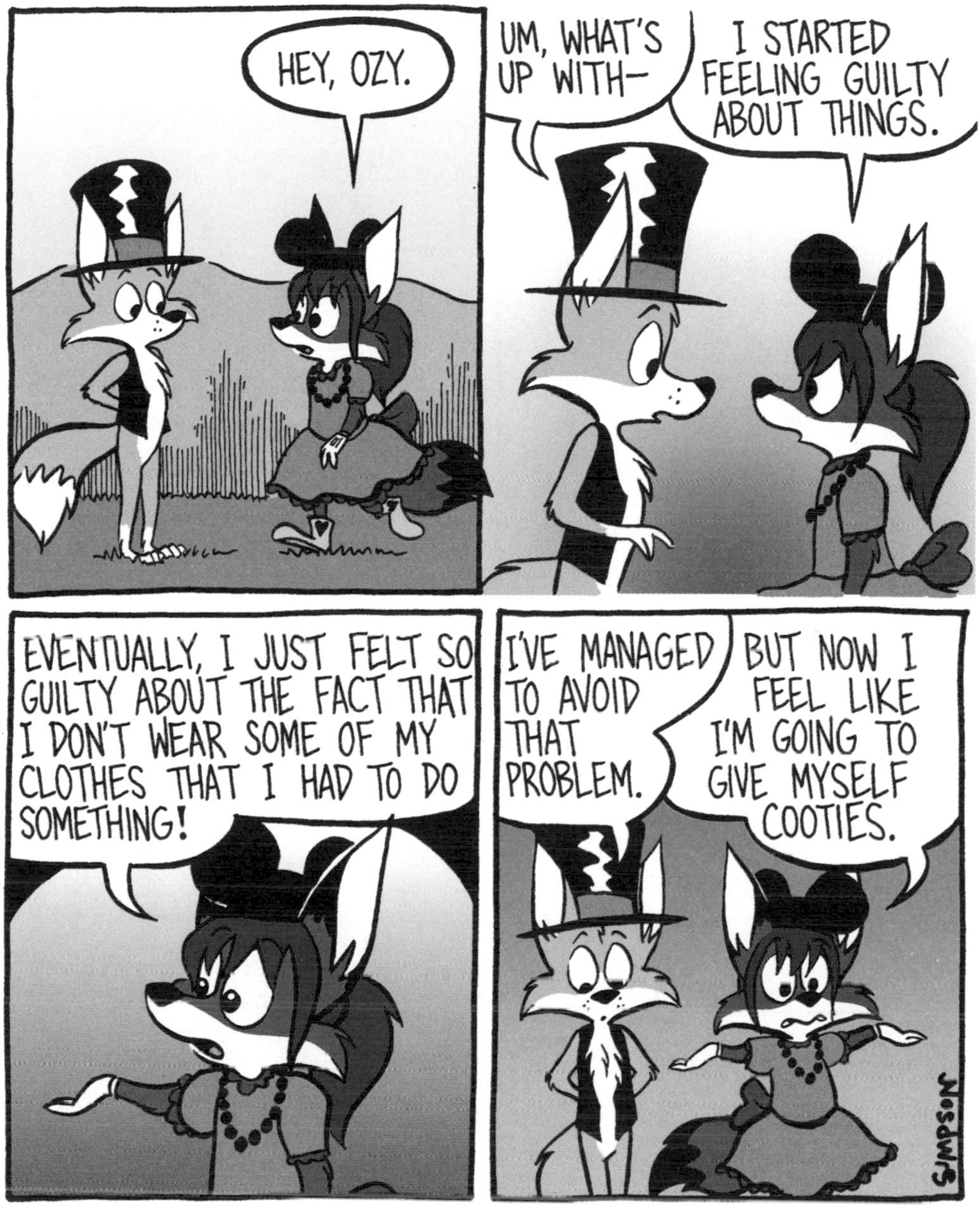
HEY, OZY.
UM, WHAT'S UP WITH–
I STARTED FEELING GUILTY ABOUT THINGS.
EVENTUALLY, I JUST FELT SO GUILTY ABOUT THE FACT THAT I DON'T WEAR SOME OF MY CLOTHES THAT I HAD TO DO SOMETHING!
I'VE MANAGED TO AVOID THAT PROBLEM.
BUT NOW I FEEL LIKE I'M GOING TO GIVE MYSELF COOTIES.
SIMPSON

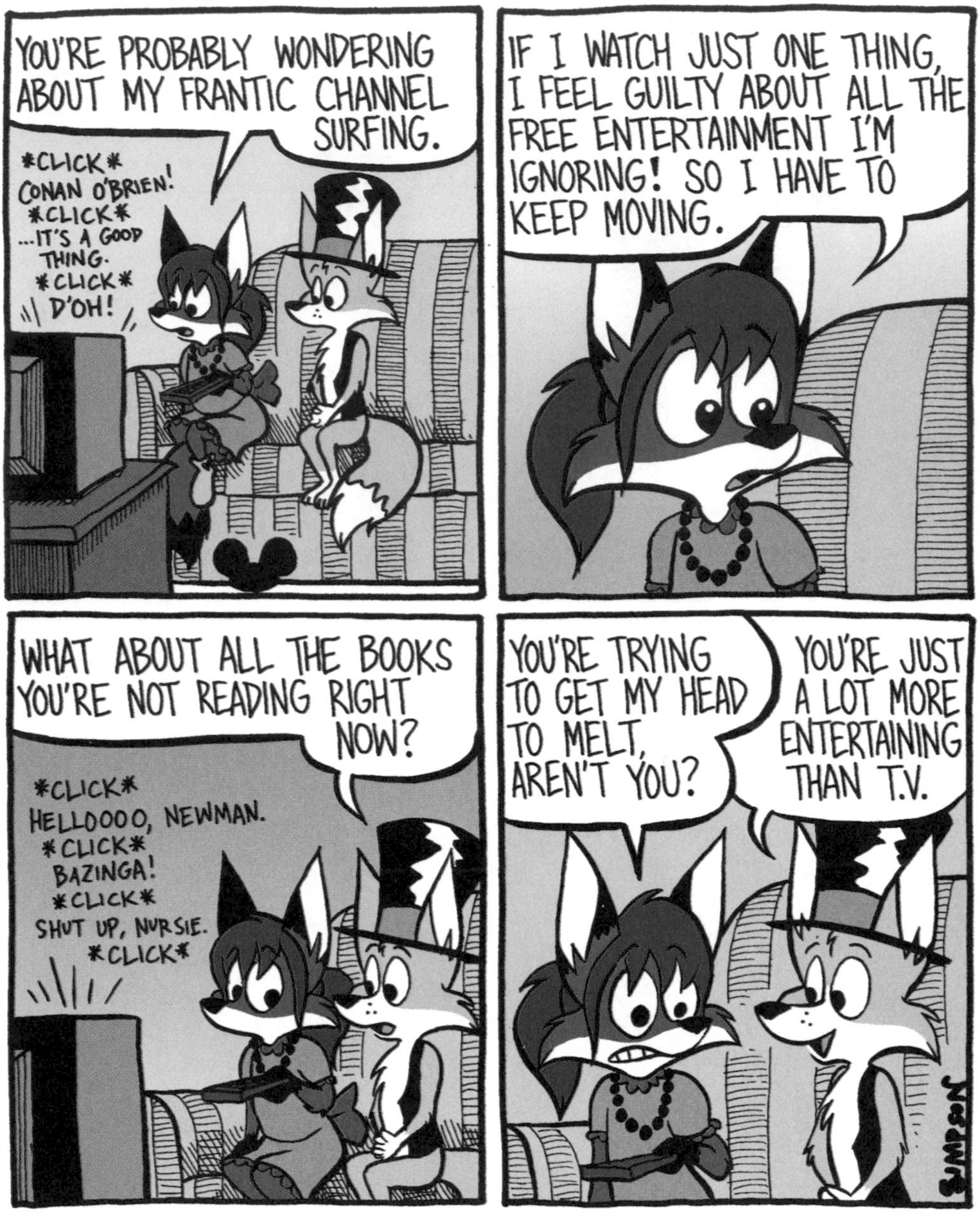

YOU'RE PROBABLY WONDERING ABOUT MY FRANTIC CHANNEL SURFING.
CLICK CONAN O'BRIEN! *CLICK* ...IT'S A GOOD THING. *CLICK* D'OH!
IF I WATCH JUST ONE THING, I FEEL GUILTY ABOUT ALL THE FREE ENTERTAINMENT I'M IGNORING! SO I HAVE TO KEEP MOVING.
WHAT ABOUT ALL THE BOOKS YOU'RE NOT READING RIGHT NOW?
CLICK HELLOOOO, NEWMAN. *CLICK* BAZINGA! *CLICK* SHUT UP, NURSIE. *CLICK*
YOU'RE TRYING TO GET MY HEAD TO MELT, AREN'T YOU?
YOU'RE JUST A LOT MORE ENTERTAINING THAN T.V.
SIMPSON

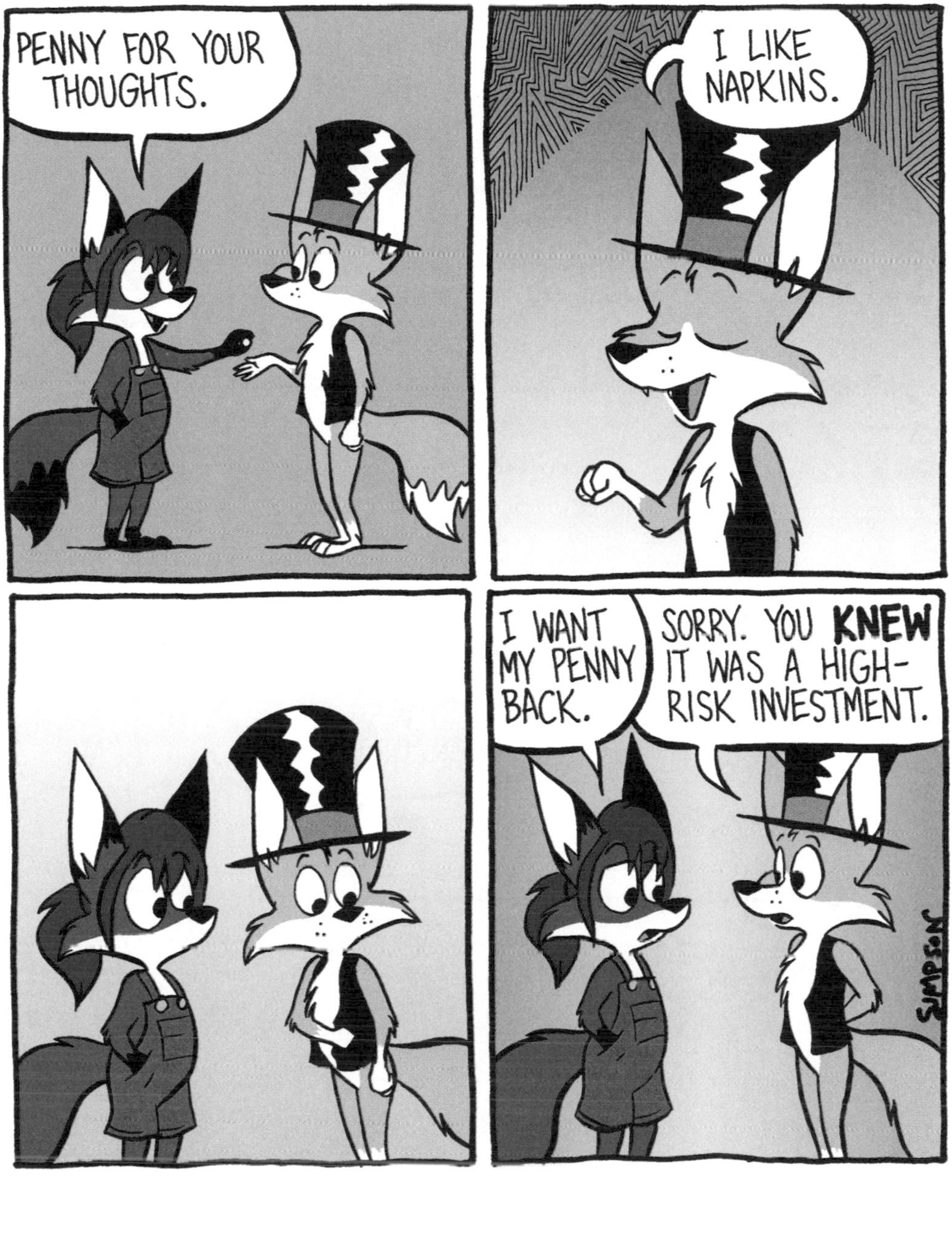
PENNY FOR YOUR THOUGHTS.
I LIKE NAPKINS.
I WANT MY PENNY BACK.
SORRY. YOU **KNEW** IT WAS A HIGH-RISK INVESTMENT.
SIMPSON

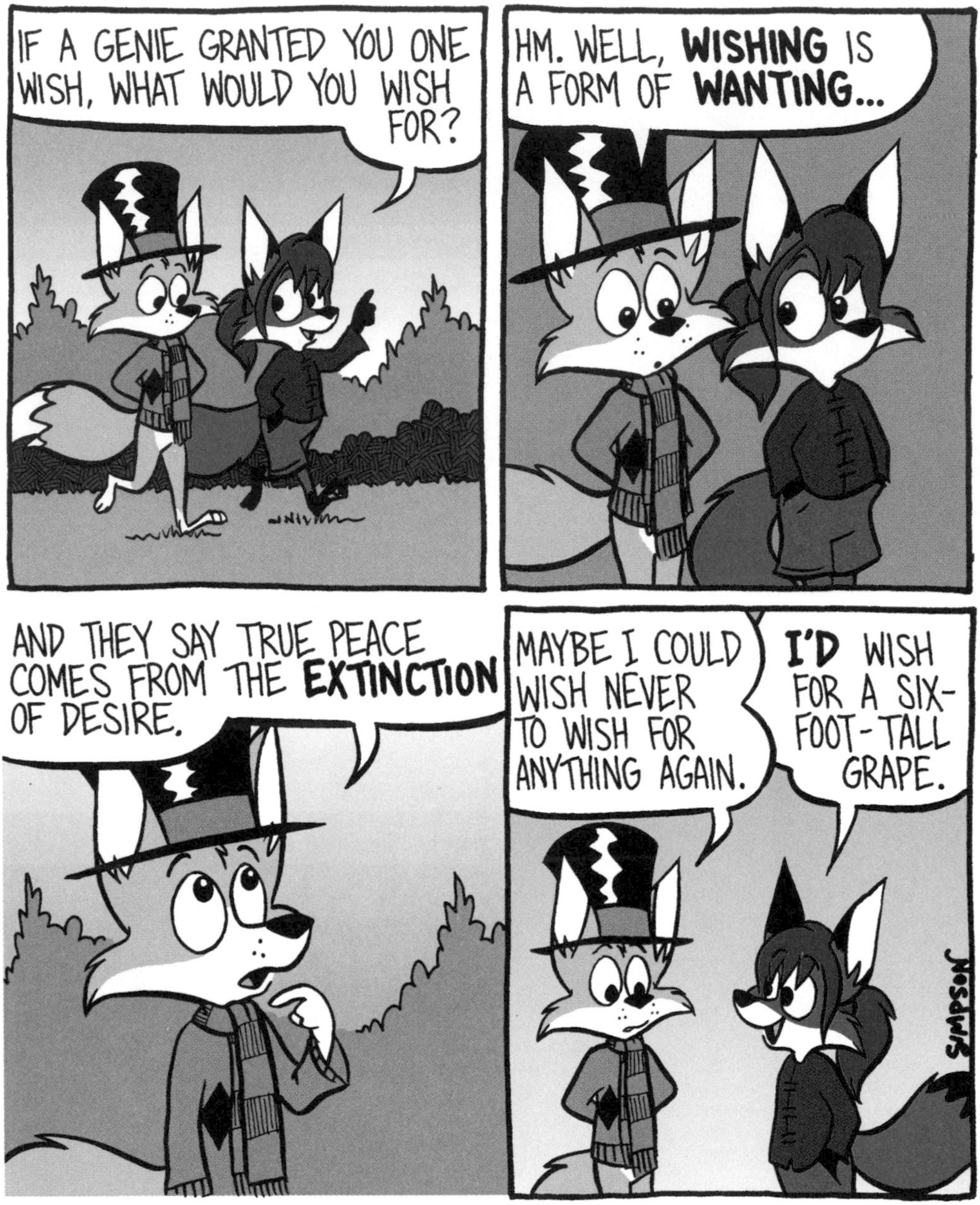
IF A GENIE GRANTED YOU ONE WISH, WHAT WOULD YOU WISH FOR?
HM. WELL, **WISHING** IS A FORM OF **WANTING...**
AND THEY SAY TRUE PEACE COMES FROM THE **EXTINCTION** OF DESIRE.
MAYBE I COULD WISH NEVER TO WISH FOR ANYTHING AGAIN.
I'D WISH FOR A SIX-FOOT-TALL GRAPE.
SIMPSON

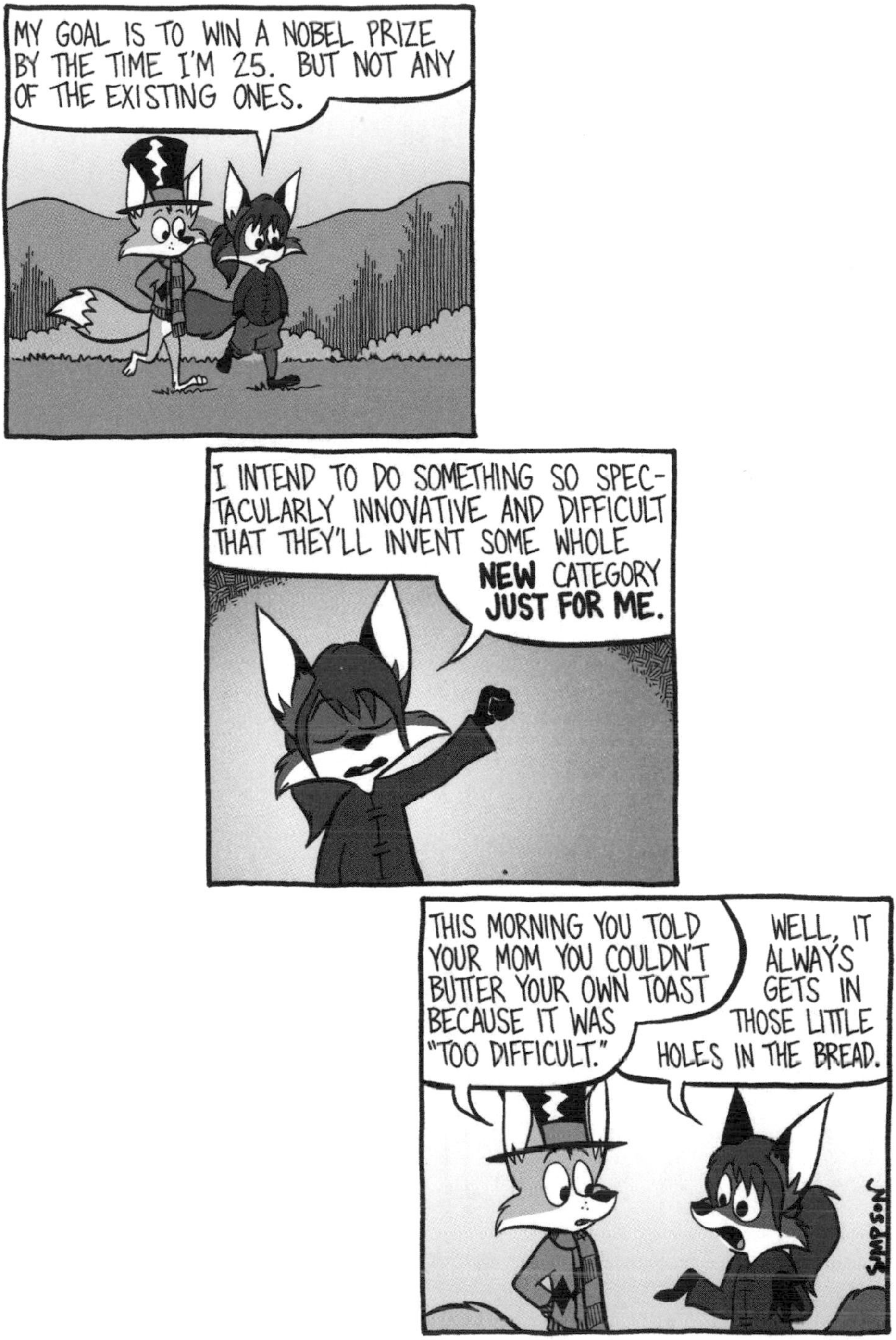
MY GOAL IS TO WIN A NOBEL PRIZE BY THE TIME I'M 25. BUT NOT ANY OF THE EXISTING ONES.
I INTEND TO DO SOMETHING SO SPECTACULARLY INNOVATIVE AND DIFFICULT THAT THEY'LL INVENT SOME WHOLE **NEW** CATEGORY **JUST FOR ME.**
THIS MORNING YOU TOLD YOUR MOM YOU COULDN'T BUTTER YOUR OWN TOAST BECAUSE IT WAS "TOO DIFFICULT."
WELL, IT ALWAYS GETS IN THOSE LITTLE HOLES IN THE BREAD.
SIMPSON

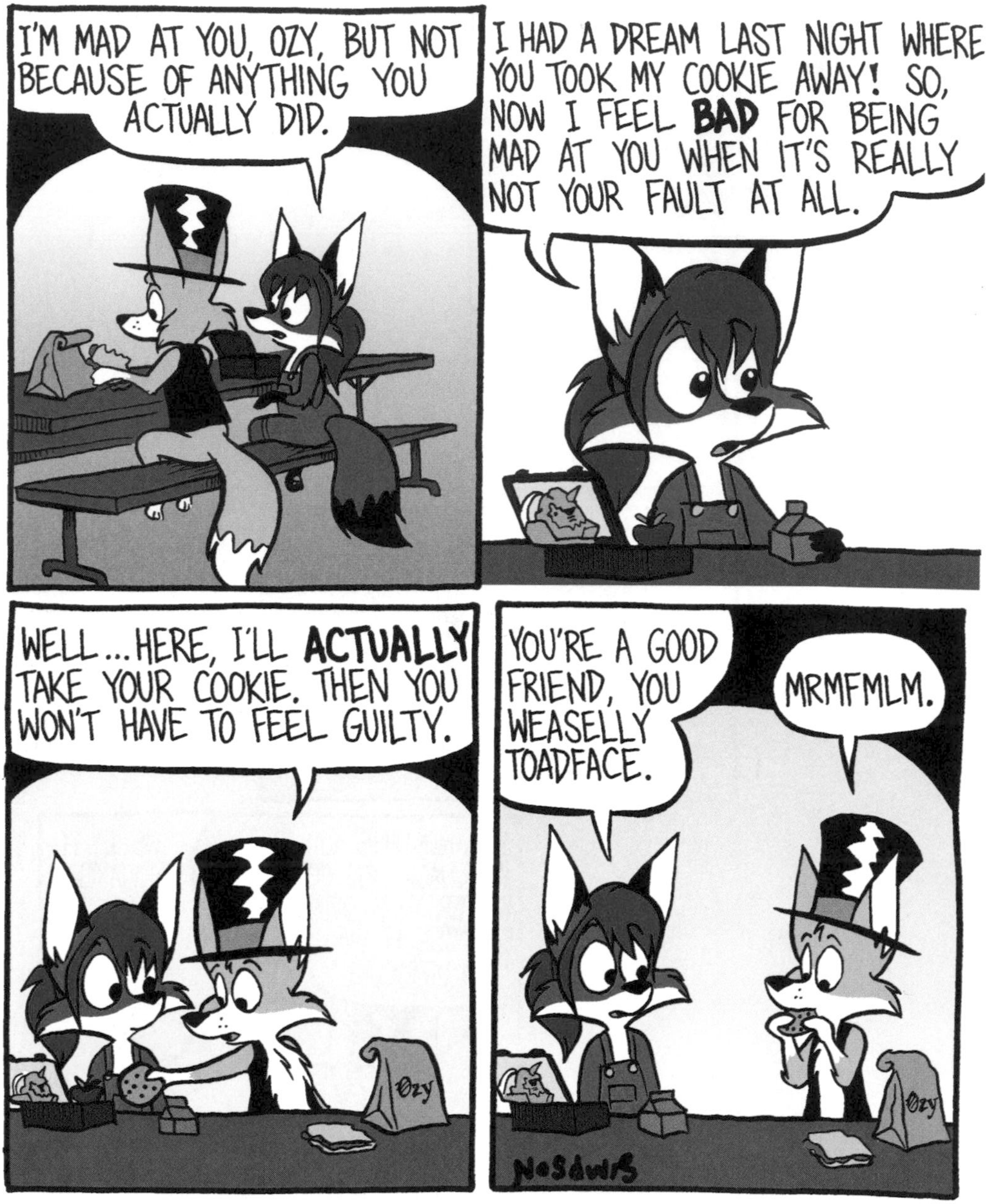
I'M MAD AT YOU, OZY, BUT NOT BECAUSE OF ANYTHING YOU ACTUALLY DID.
I HAD A DREAM LAST NIGHT WHERE YOU TOOK MY COOKIE AWAY! SO, NOW I FEEL BAD FOR BEING MAD AT YOU WHEN IT'S REALLY NOT YOUR FAULT AT ALL.
WELL ... HERE, I'LL ACTUALLY TAKE YOUR COOKIE. THEN YOU WON'T HAVE TO FEEL GUILTY.
Ozy
YOU'RE A GOOD FRIEND, YOU WEASELLY TOADFACE.
MRMFMLM.
Ozy
NOSAWIS

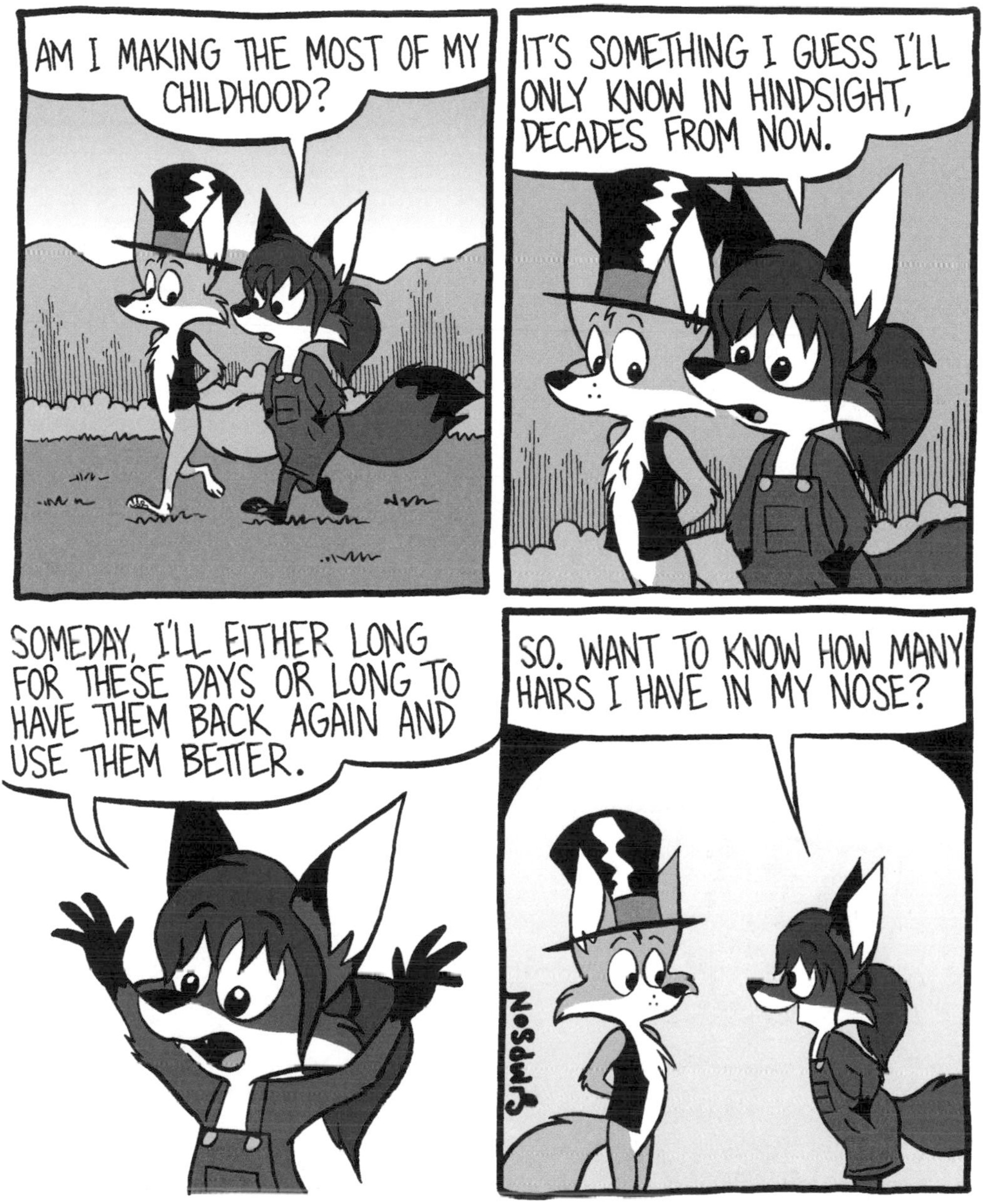
AM I MAKING THE MOST OF MY CHILDHOOD?
IT'S SOMETHING I GUESS I'LL ONLY KNOW IN HINDSIGHT, DECADES FROM NOW.
SOMEDAY, I'LL EITHER LONG FOR THESE DAYS OR LONG TO HAVE THEM BACK AGAIN AND USE THEM BETTER.
SO. WANT TO KNOW HOW MANY HAIRS I HAVE IN MY NOSE?
SIMPSON

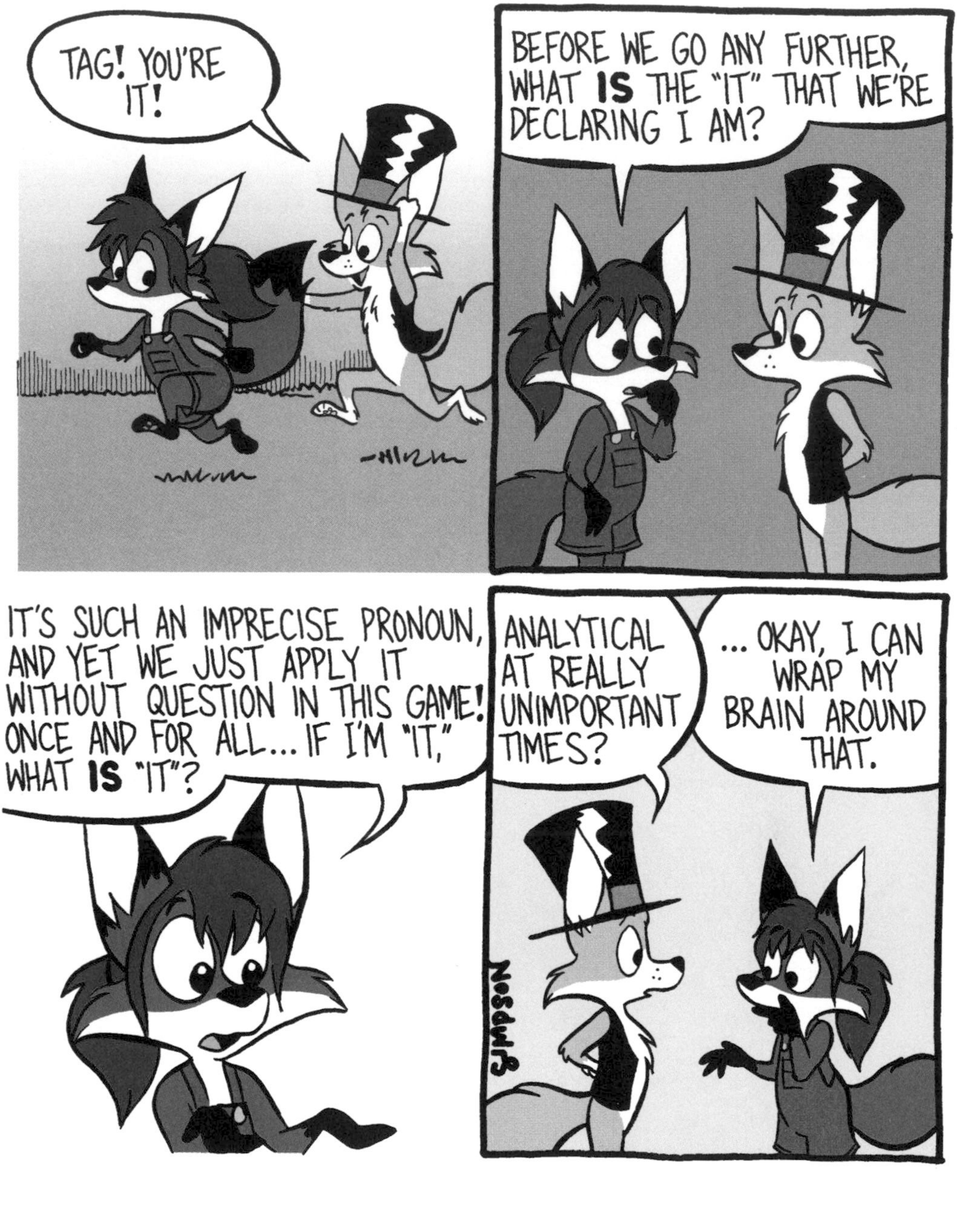
TAG! YOU'RE IT!
BEFORE WE GO ANY FURTHER, WHAT IS THE "IT" THAT WE'RE DECLARING I AM?
IT'S SUCH AN IMPRECISE PRONOUN, AND YET WE JUST APPLY IT WITHOUT QUESTION IN THIS GAME! ONCE AND FOR ALL... IF I'M "IT," WHAT IS "IT"?
ANALYTICAL AT REALLY UNIMPORTANT TIMES?
... OKAY, I CAN WRAP MY BRAIN AROUND THAT.
SIMPSON

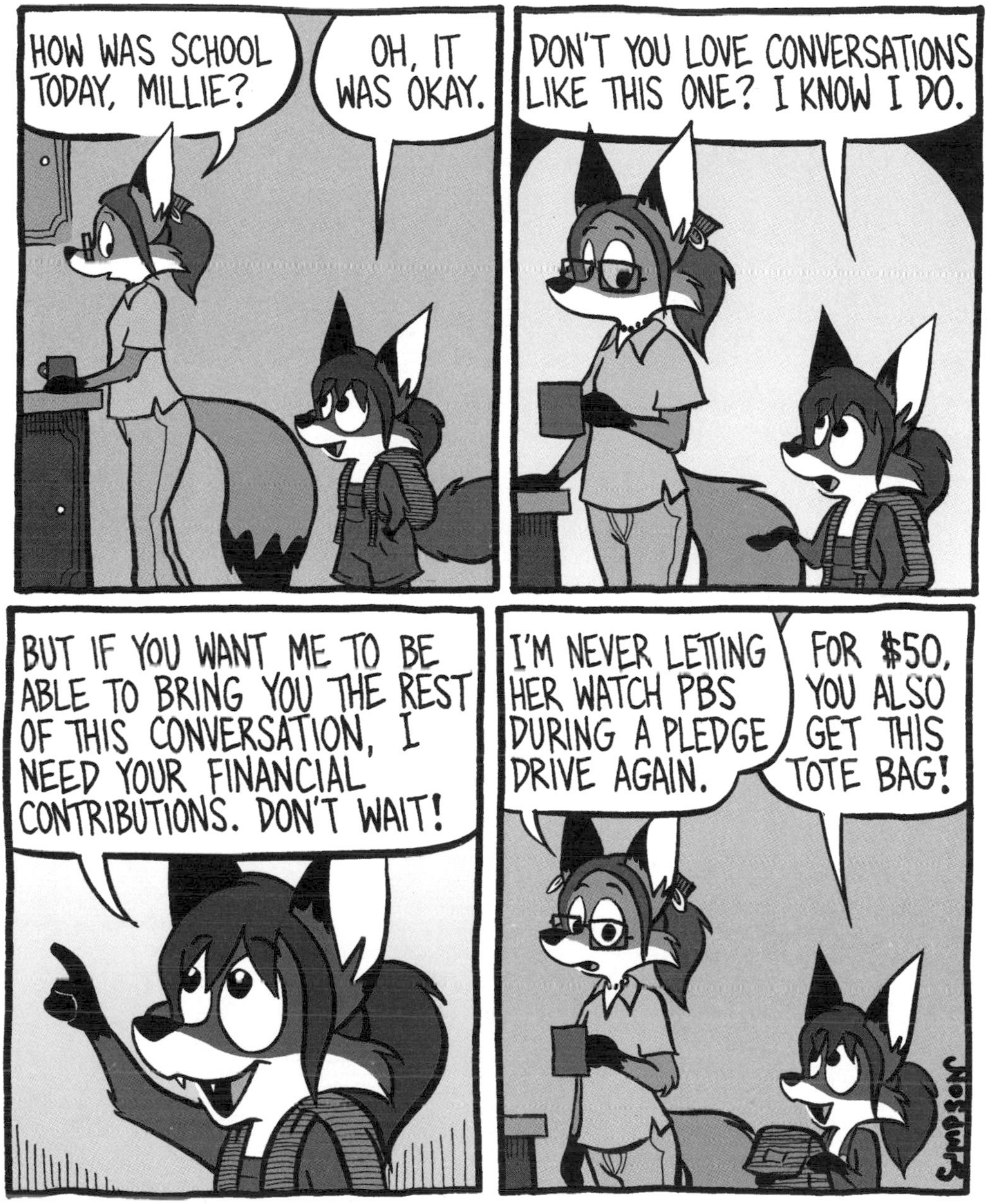
HOW WAS SCHOOL TODAY, MILLIE?
OH, IT WAS OKAY.
DON'T YOU LOVE CONVERSATIONS LIKE THIS ONE? I KNOW I DO.
BUT IF YOU WANT ME TO BE ABLE TO BRING YOU THE REST OF THIS CONVERSATION, I NEED YOUR FINANCIAL CONTRIBUTIONS. DON'T WAIT!
I'M NEVER LETTING HER WATCH PBS DURING A PLEDGE DRIVE AGAIN.
FOR $50, YOU ALSO GET THIS TOTE BAG!
SIMPSON

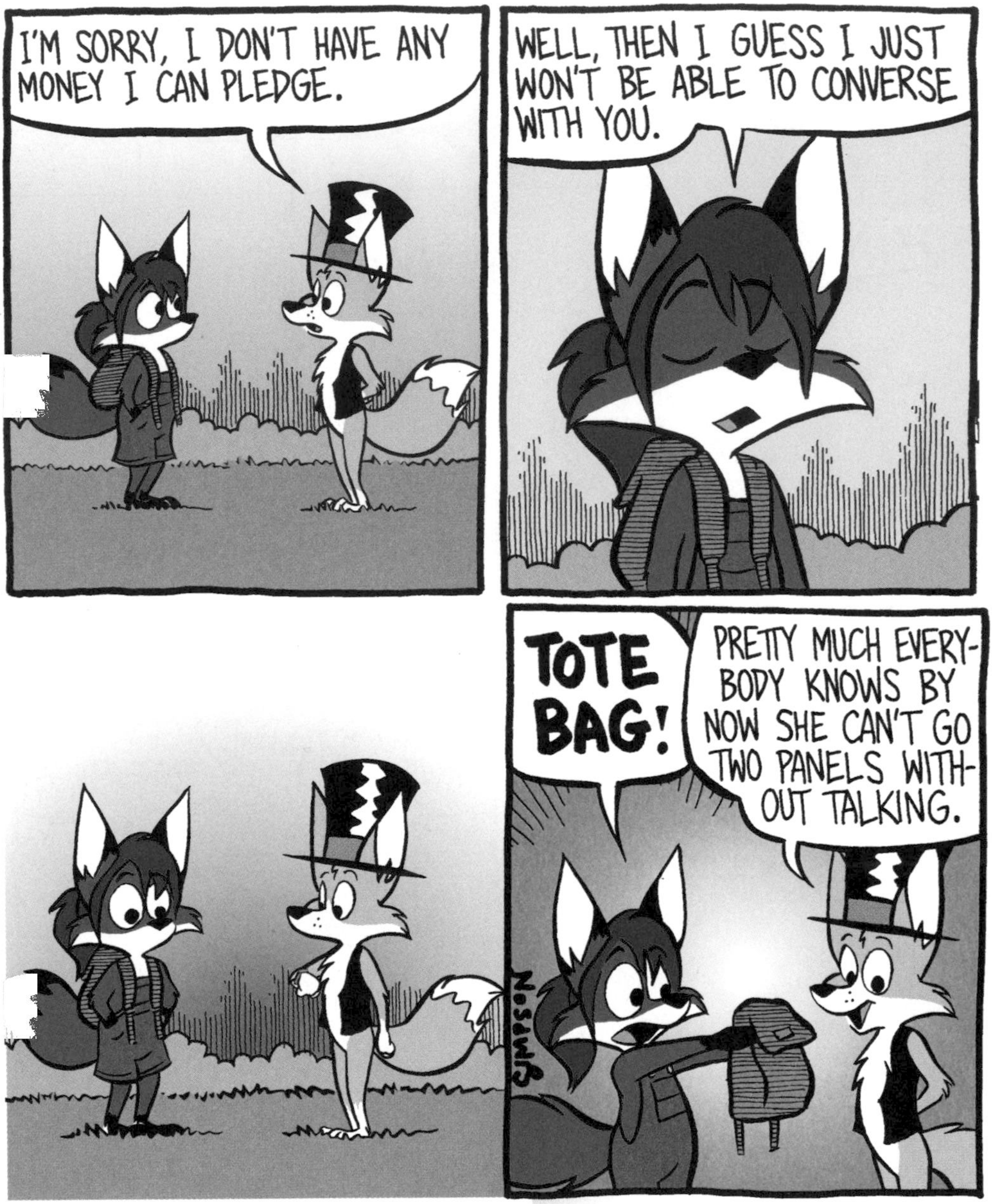
I'M SORRY, I DON'T HAVE ANY MONEY I CAN PLEDGE.
WELL, THEN I GUESS I JUST WON'T BE ABLE TO CONVERSE WITH YOU.
TOTE BAG!
PRETTY MUCH EVERY-BODY KNOWS BY NOW SHE CAN'T GO TWO PANELS WITH-OUT TALKING.
SIMPSON

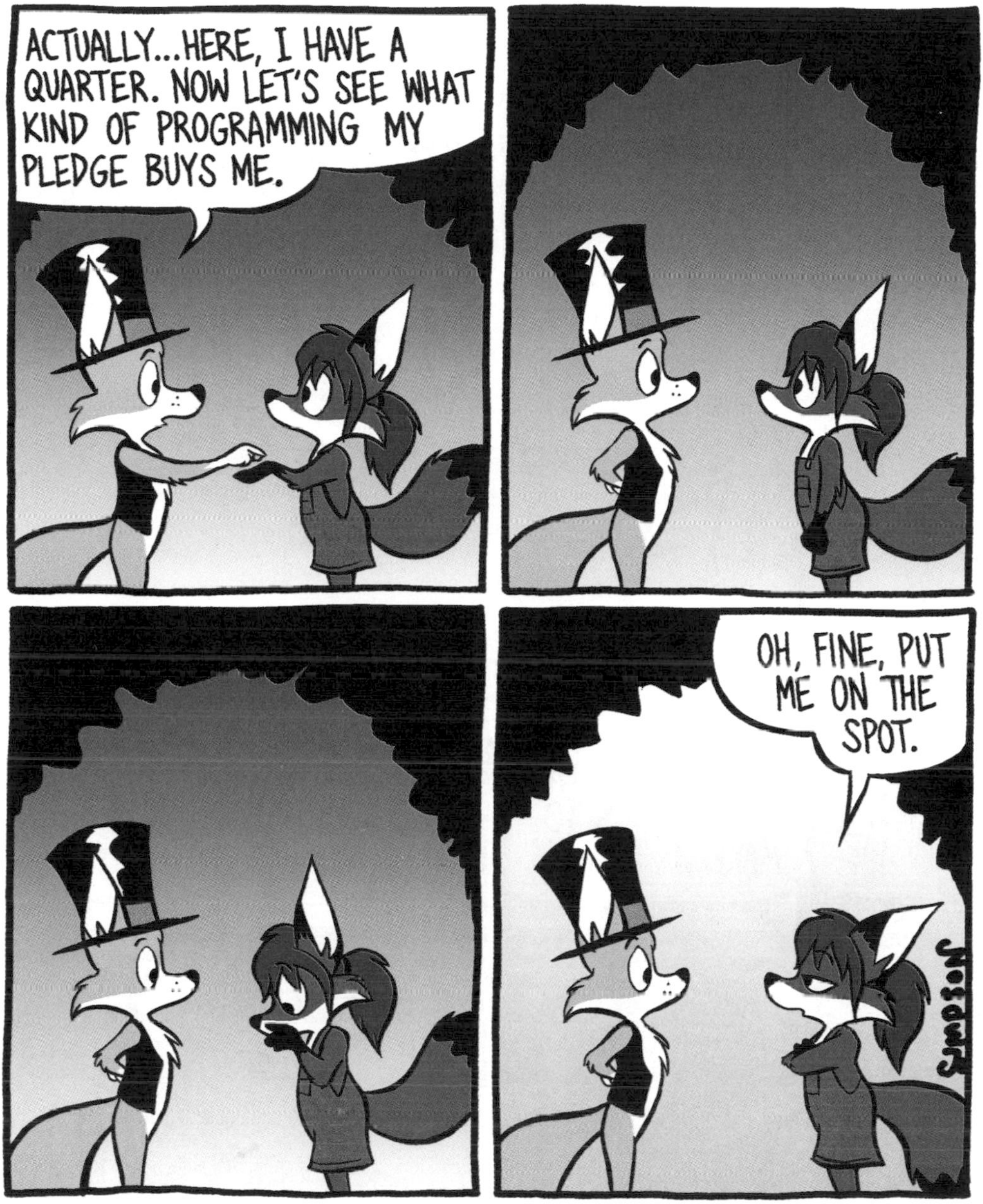
ACTUALLY...HERE, I HAVE A QUARTER. NOW LET'S SEE WHAT KIND OF PROGRAMMING MY PLEDGE BUYS ME.
OH, FINE, PUT ME ON THE SPOT.
SIMPSON

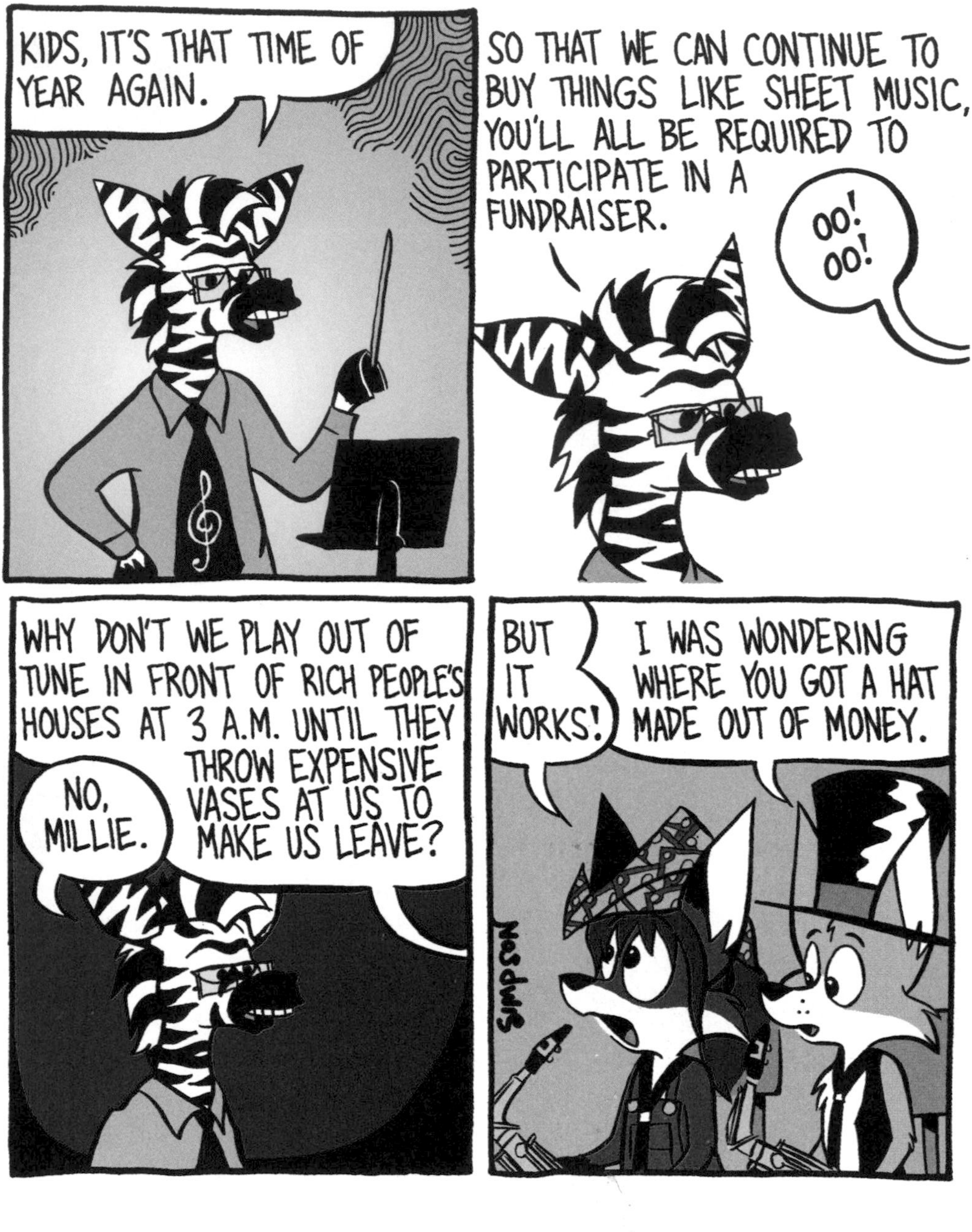
KIDS, IT'S THAT TIME OF YEAR AGAIN.
SO THAT WE CAN CONTINUE TO BUY THINGS LIKE SHEET MUSIC, YOU'LL ALL BE REQUIRED TO PARTICIPATE IN A FUNDRAISER.
OO! OO!
WHY DON'T WE PLAY OUT OF TUNE IN FRONT OF RICH PEOPLE'S HOUSES AT 3 A.M. UNTIL THEY THROW EXPENSIVE VASES AT US TO MAKE US LEAVE?
NO, MILLIE.
BUT IT WORKS!
I WAS WONDERING WHERE YOU GOT A HAT MADE OUT OF MONEY.
SIMPSON

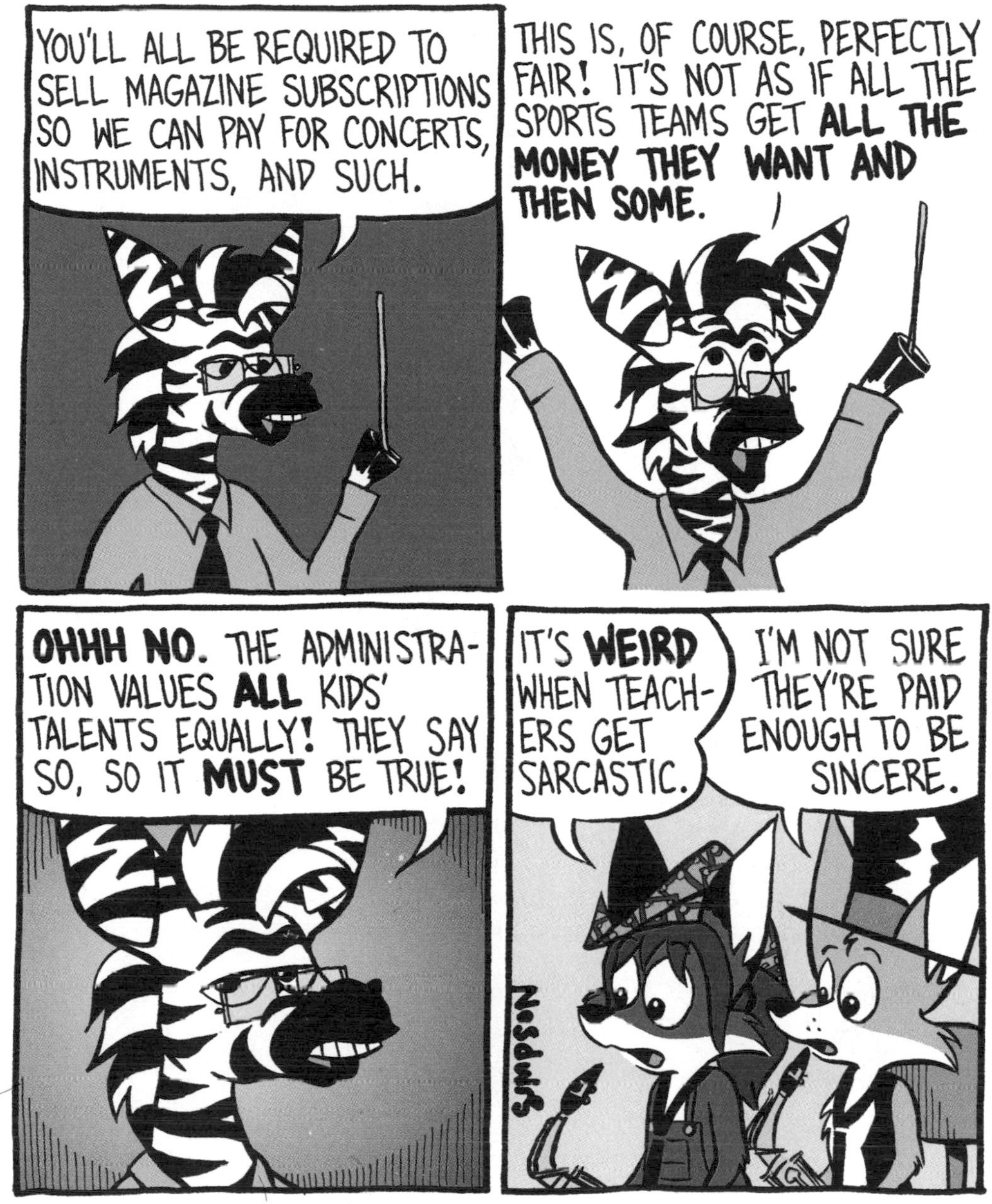

YOU'LL ALL BE REQUIRED TO SELL MAGAZINE SUBSCRIPTIONS SO WE CAN PAY FOR CONCERTS, INSTRUMENTS, AND SUCH.
THIS IS, OF COURSE, PERFECTLY FAIR! IT'S NOT AS IF ALL THE SPORTS TEAMS GET **ALL THE MONEY THEY WANT AND THEN SOME.**
OHHH NO. THE ADMINISTRATION VALUES **ALL** KIDS' TALENTS EQUALLY! THEY SAY SO, SO IT **MUST** BE TRUE!
IT'S **WEIRD** WHEN TEACHERS GET SARCASTIC.
I'M NOT SURE THEY'RE PAID ENOUGH TO BE SINCERE.

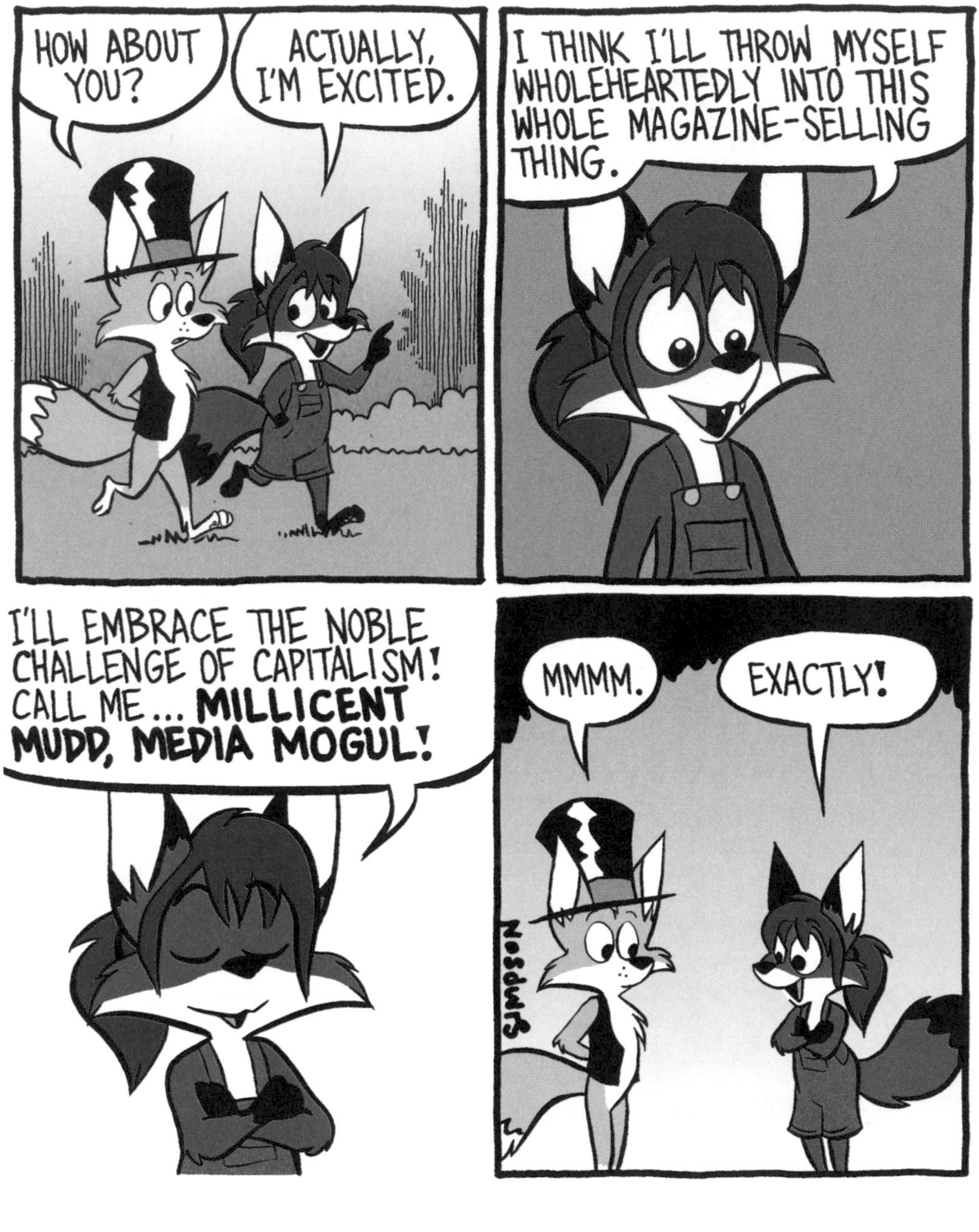
HOW ABOUT YOU?
ACTUALLY, I'M EXCITED.
I THINK I'LL THROW MYSELF WHOLEHEARTEDLY INTO THIS WHOLE MAGAZINE-SELLING THING.
I'LL EMBRACE THE NOBLE CHALLENGE OF CAPITALISM! CALL ME... **MILLICENT MUDD, MEDIA MOGUL!**
MMMM.
EXACTLY!
Simpson

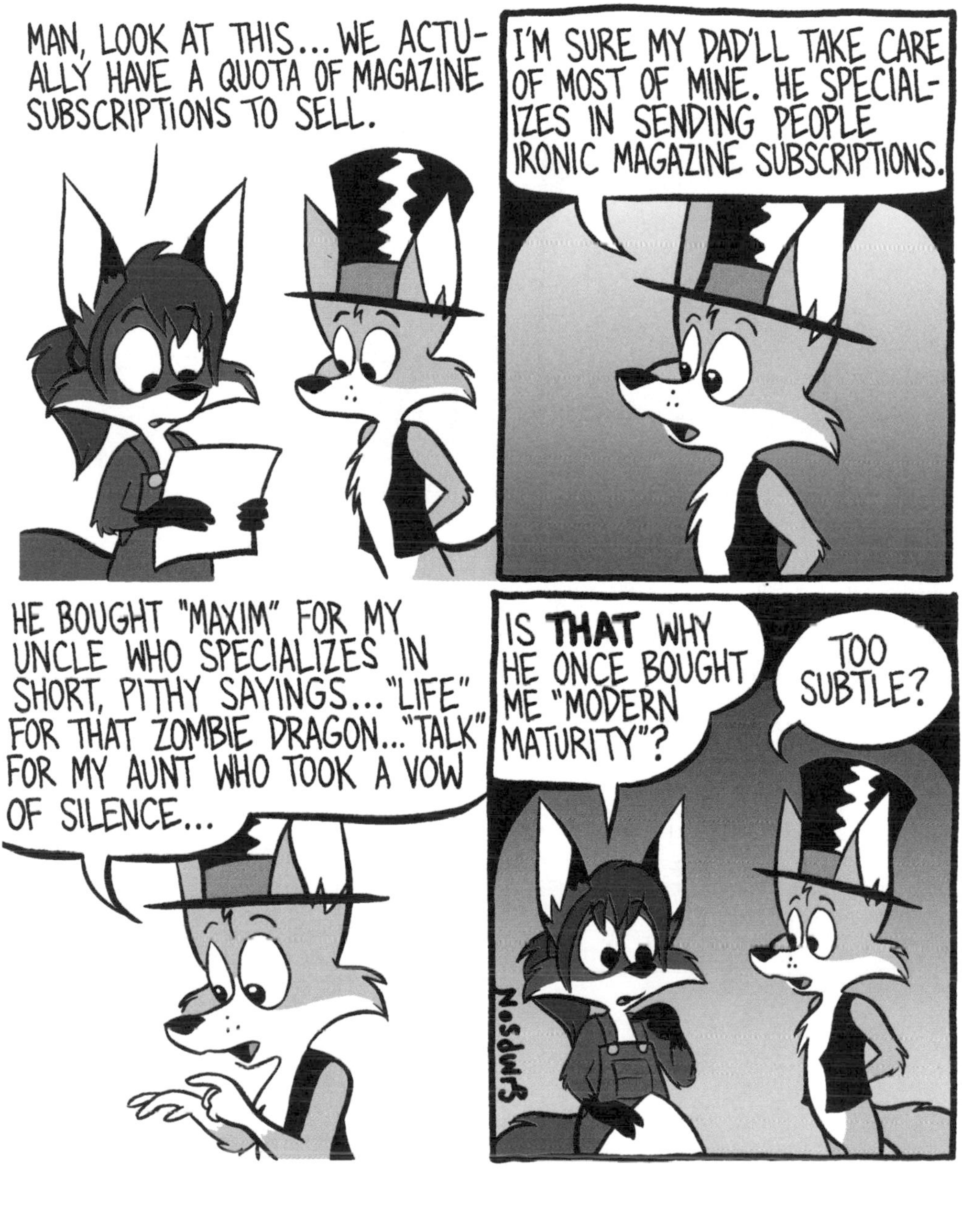
MAN, LOOK AT THIS... WE ACTUALLY HAVE A QUOTA OF MAGAZINE SUBSCRIPTIONS TO SELL.
I'M SURE MY DAD'LL TAKE CARE OF MOST OF MINE. HE SPECIALIZES IN SENDING PEOPLE IRONIC MAGAZINE SUBSCRIPTIONS.
HE BOUGHT "MAXIM" FOR MY UNCLE WHO SPECIALIZES IN SHORT, PITHY SAYINGS... "LIFE" FOR THAT ZOMBIE DRAGON... "TALK" FOR MY AUNT WHO TOOK A VOW OF SILENCE...
IS **THAT** WHY HE ONCE BOUGHT ME "MODERN MATURITY"?
TOO SUBTLE?
Simpson

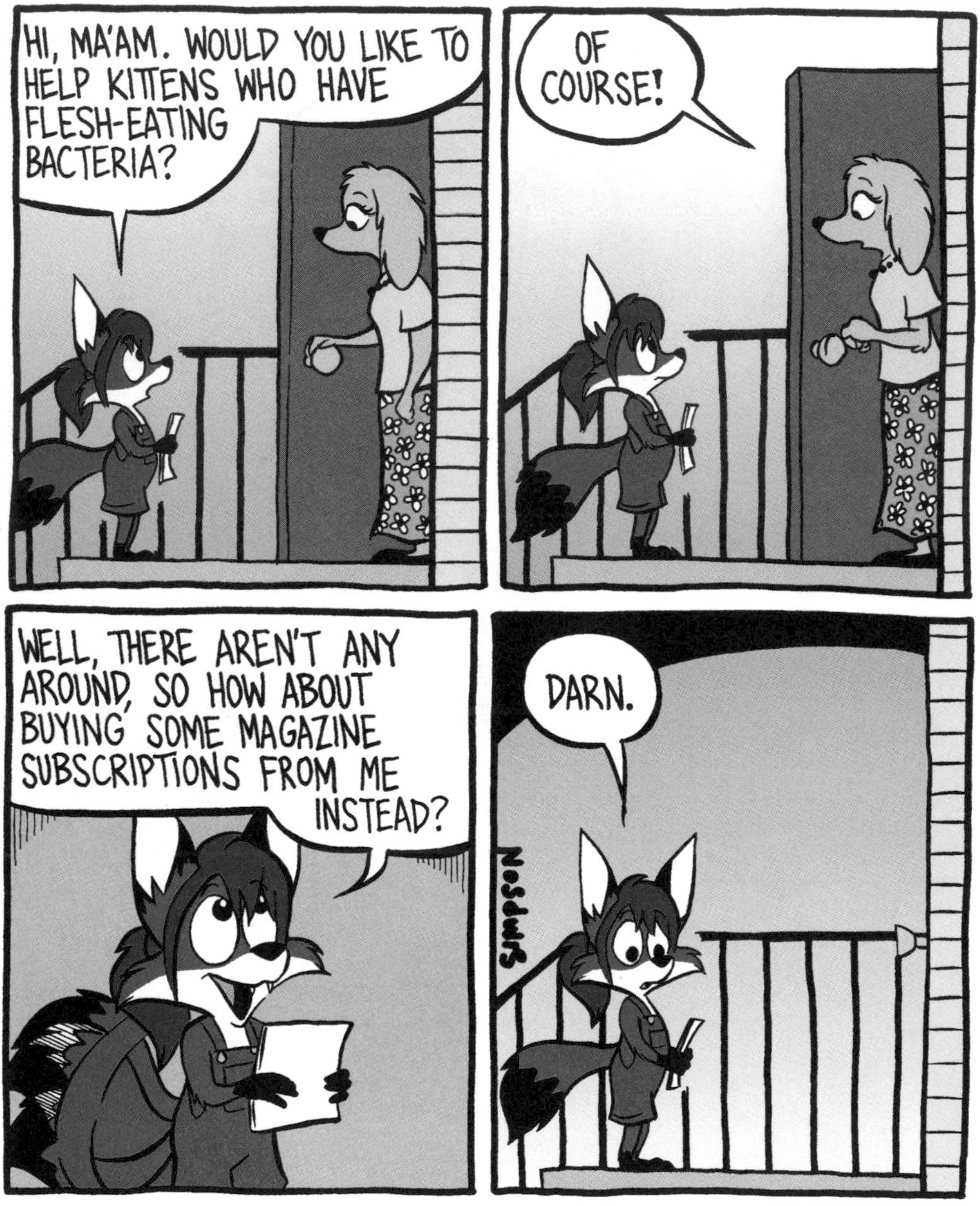
HI, MA'AM. WOULD YOU LIKE TO HELP KITTENS WHO HAVE FLESH-EATING BACTERIA?
OF COURSE!
WELL, THERE AREN'T ANY AROUND, SO HOW ABOUT BUYING SOME MAGAZINE SUBSCRIPTIONS FROM ME INSTEAD?
DARN.
SIMPSON

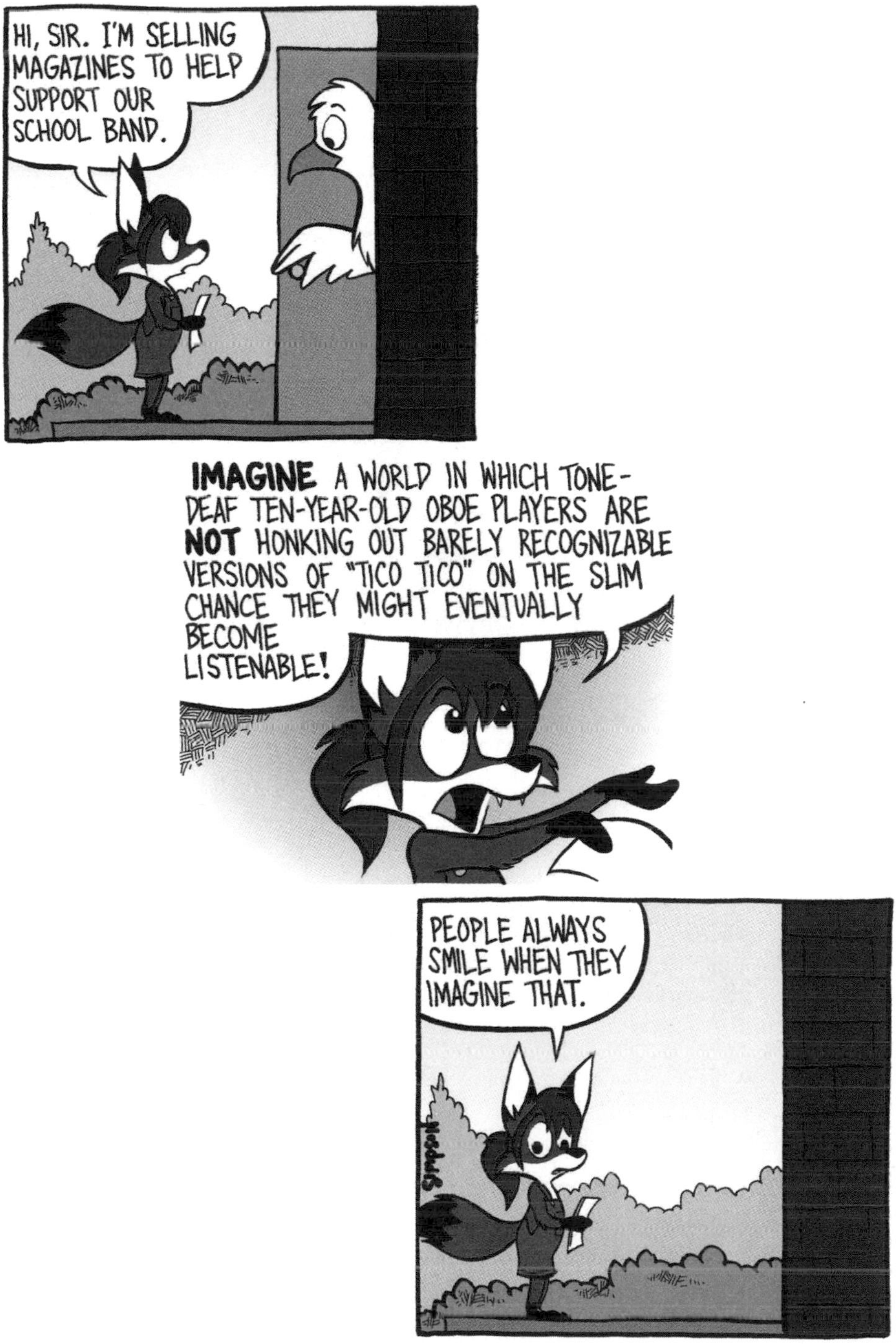
HI, SIR. I'M SELLING MAGAZINES TO HELP SUPPORT OUR SCHOOL BAND.
IMAGINE A WORLD IN WHICH TONE-DEAF TEN-YEAR-OLD OBOE PLAYERS ARE **NOT** HONKING OUT BARELY RECOGNIZABLE VERSIONS OF "TICO TICO" ON THE SLIM CHANCE THEY MIGHT EVENTUALLY BECOME LISTENABLE!
PEOPLE ALWAYS SMILE WHEN THEY IMAGINE THAT.

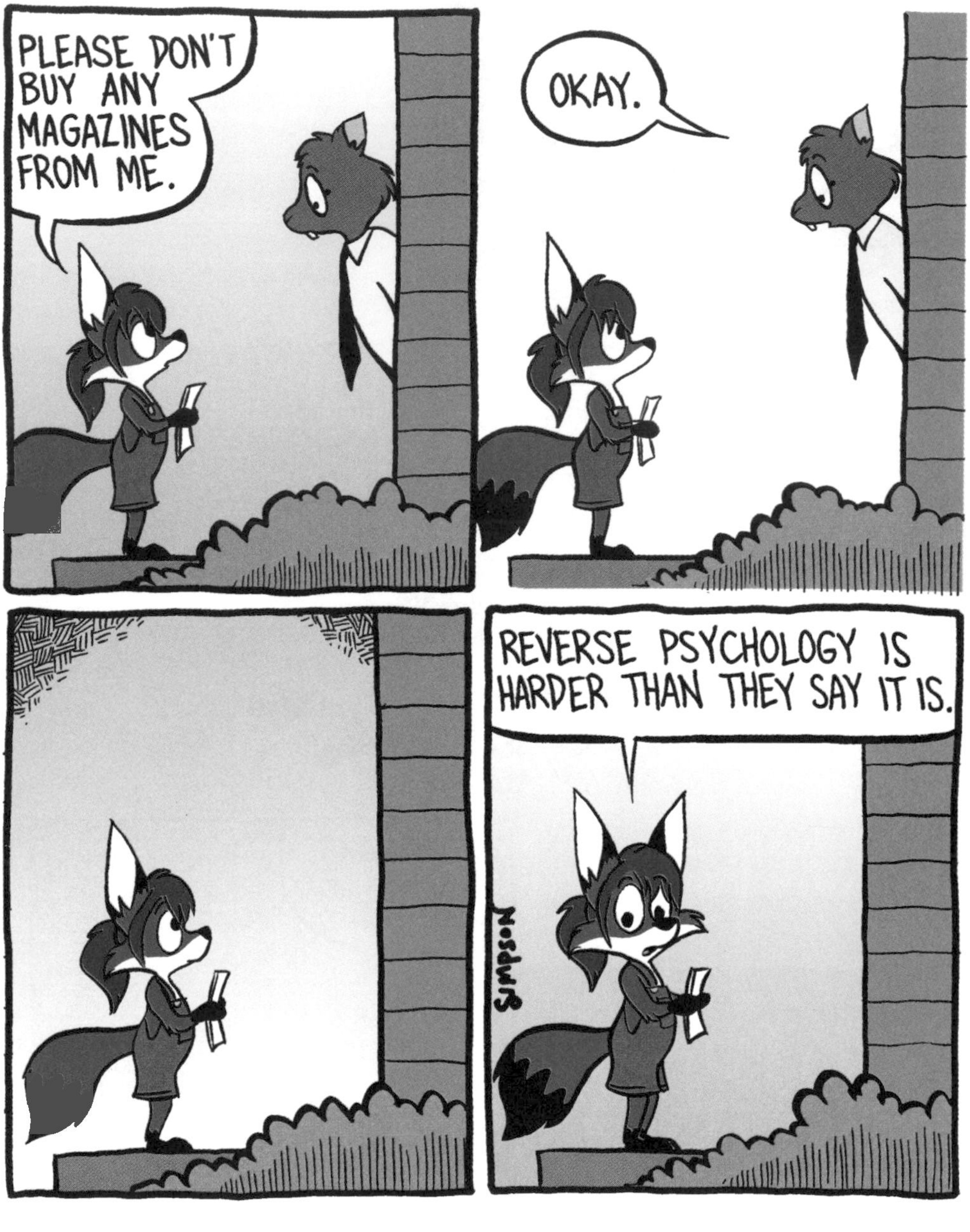
PLEASE DON'T BUY ANY MAGAZINES FROM ME.
OKAY.
REVERSE PSYCHOLOGY IS HARDER THAN THEY SAY IT IS.
SIMPSON

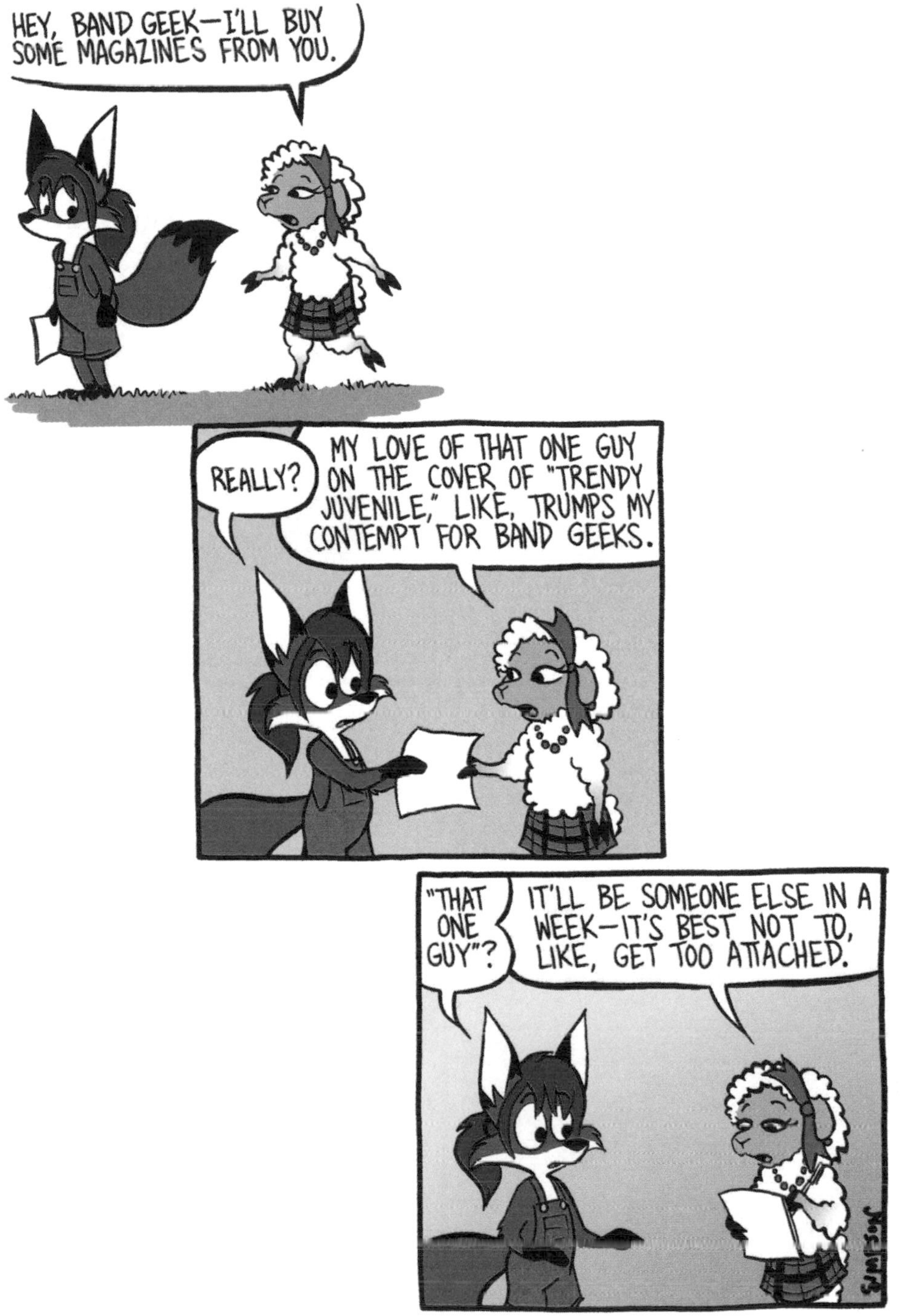
HEY, BAND GEEK—I'LL BUY SOME MAGAZINES FROM YOU.
REALLY?
MY LOVE OF THAT ONE GUY ON THE COVER OF "TRENDY JUVENILE," LIKE, TRUMPS MY CONTEMPT FOR BAND GEEKS.
"THAT ONE GUY"?
IT'LL BE SOMEONE ELSE IN A WEEK—IT'S BEST NOT TO, LIKE, GET TOO ATTACHED.

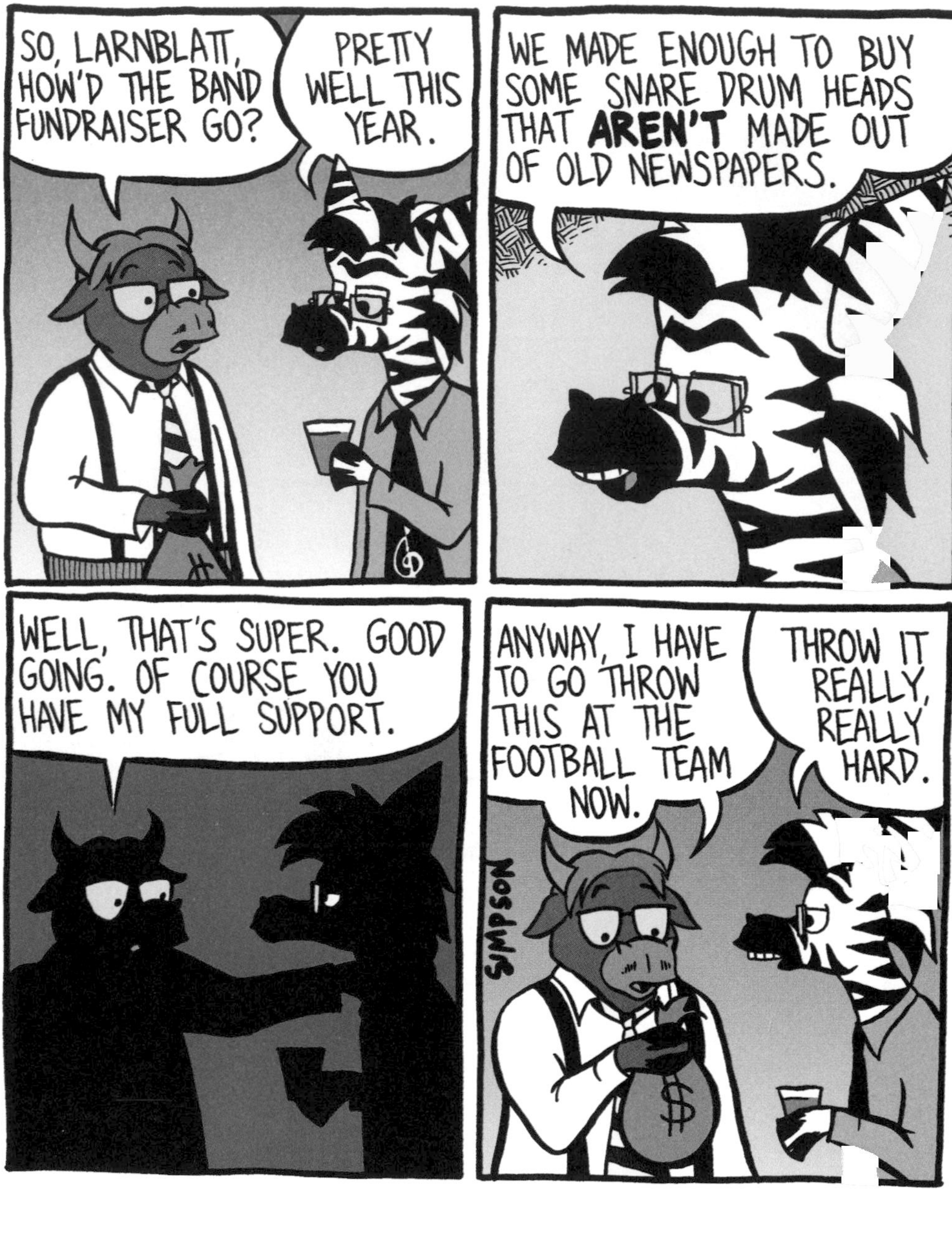

SO, LARNBLATT, HOW'D THE BAND FUNDRAISER GO?
PRETTY WELL THIS YEAR.
WE MADE ENOUGH TO BUY SOME SNARE DRUM HEADS THAT **AREN'T** MADE OUT OF OLD NEWSPAPERS.
WELL, THAT'S SUPER. GOOD GOING. OF COURSE YOU HAVE MY FULL SUPPORT.
ANYWAY, I HAVE TO GO THROW THIS AT THE FOOTBALL TEAM NOW.
THROW IT REALLY, REALLY HARD.
SIMPSON

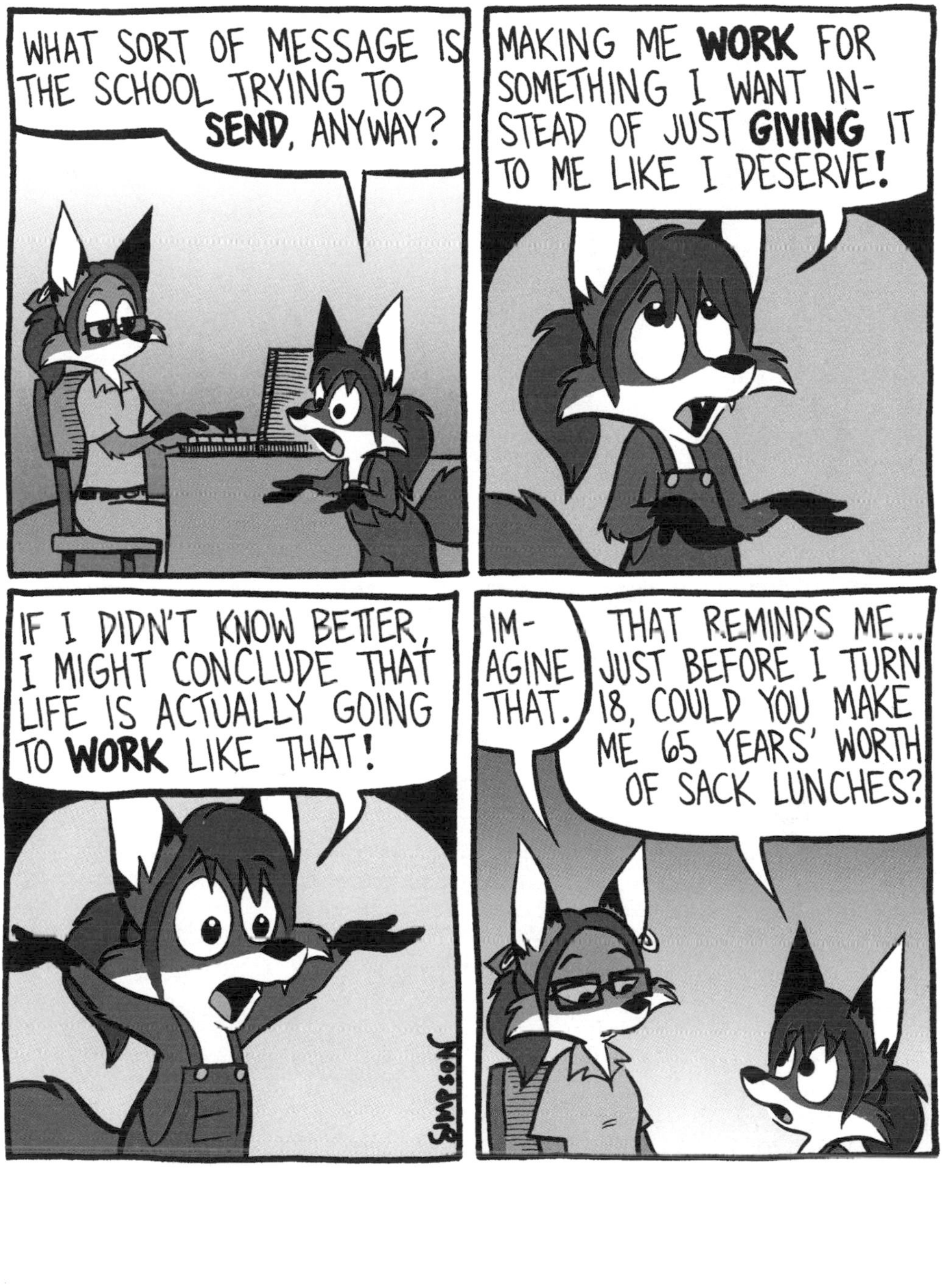
WHAT SORT OF MESSAGE IS THE SCHOOL TRYING TO **SEND**, ANYWAY?
MAKING ME **WORK** FOR SOMETHING I WANT IN-STEAD OF JUST **GIVING** IT TO ME LIKE I DESERVE!
IF I DIDN'T KNOW BETTER, I MIGHT CONCLUDE THAT LIFE IS ACTUALLY GOING TO **WORK** LIKE THAT!
SIMPSON
IM-AGINE THAT.
THAT REMINDS ME... JUST BEFORE I TURN 18, COULD YOU MAKE ME 65 YEARS' WORTH OF SACK LUNCHES?

HM. WE'RE MISSING THE DICE FOR THIS GAME.
WELL, INSTEAD OF ROLLING DICE, WE COULD BATTLE TO THE DEATH WITH HANDFULS OF UNCOOKED SPAGHETTI.
NO.
OKAY, LET'S FIND SOME DICE.

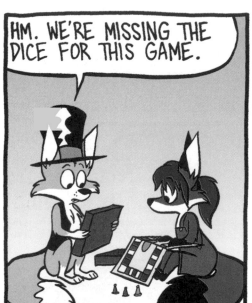

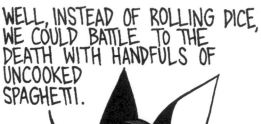

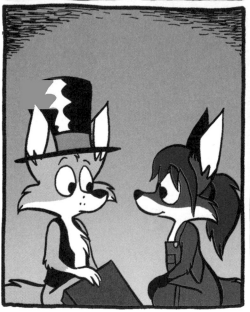

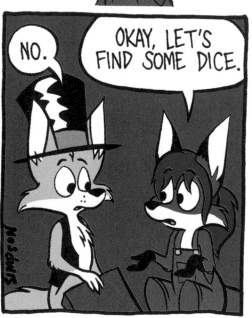

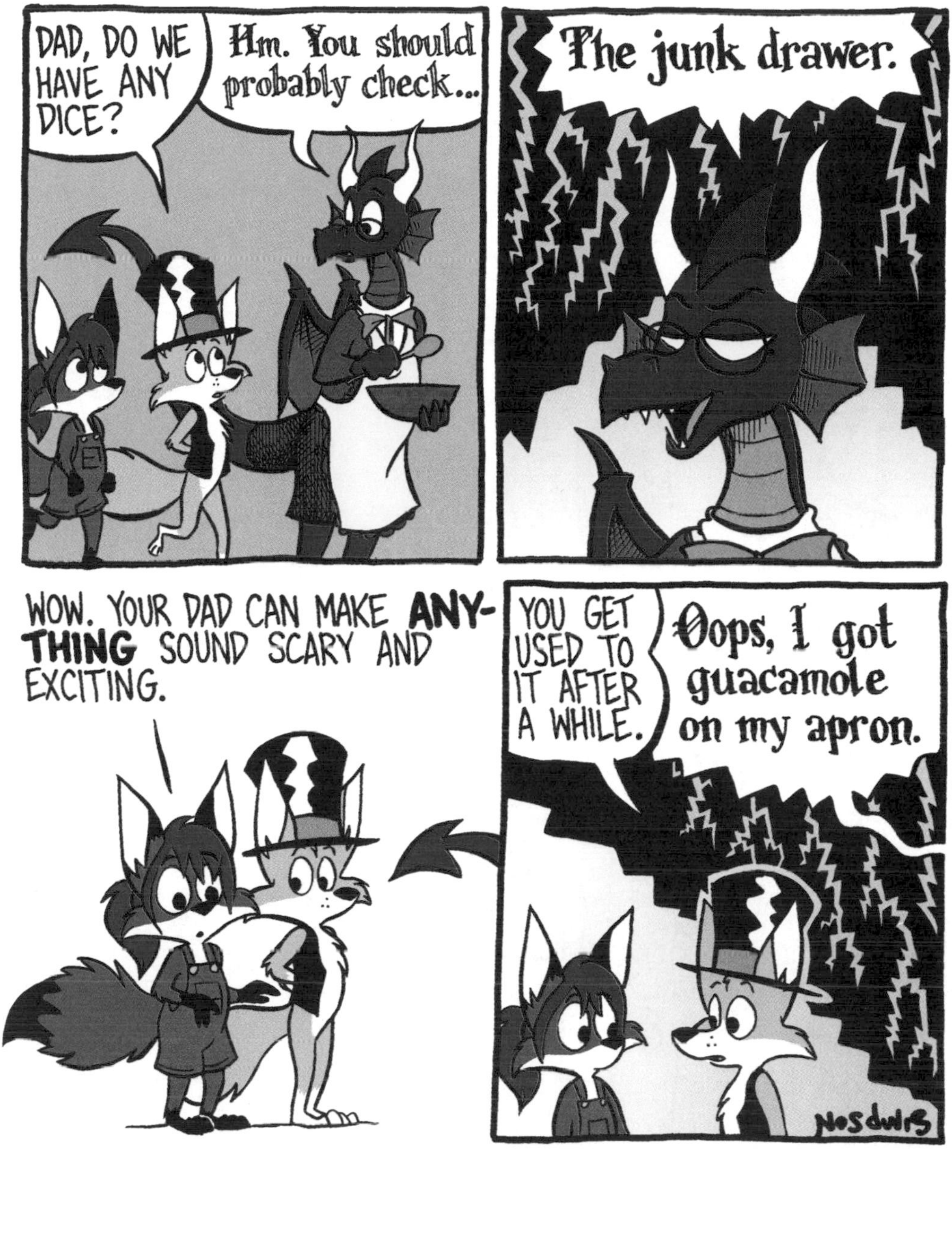
DAD, DO WE HAVE ANY DICE?
Hm. You should probably check...
The junk drawer.
WOW. YOUR DAD CAN MAKE **ANY-THING** SOUND SCARY AND EXCITING.
YOU GET USED TO IT AFTER A WHILE.
Oops, I got guacamole on my apron.
Nosdulrs

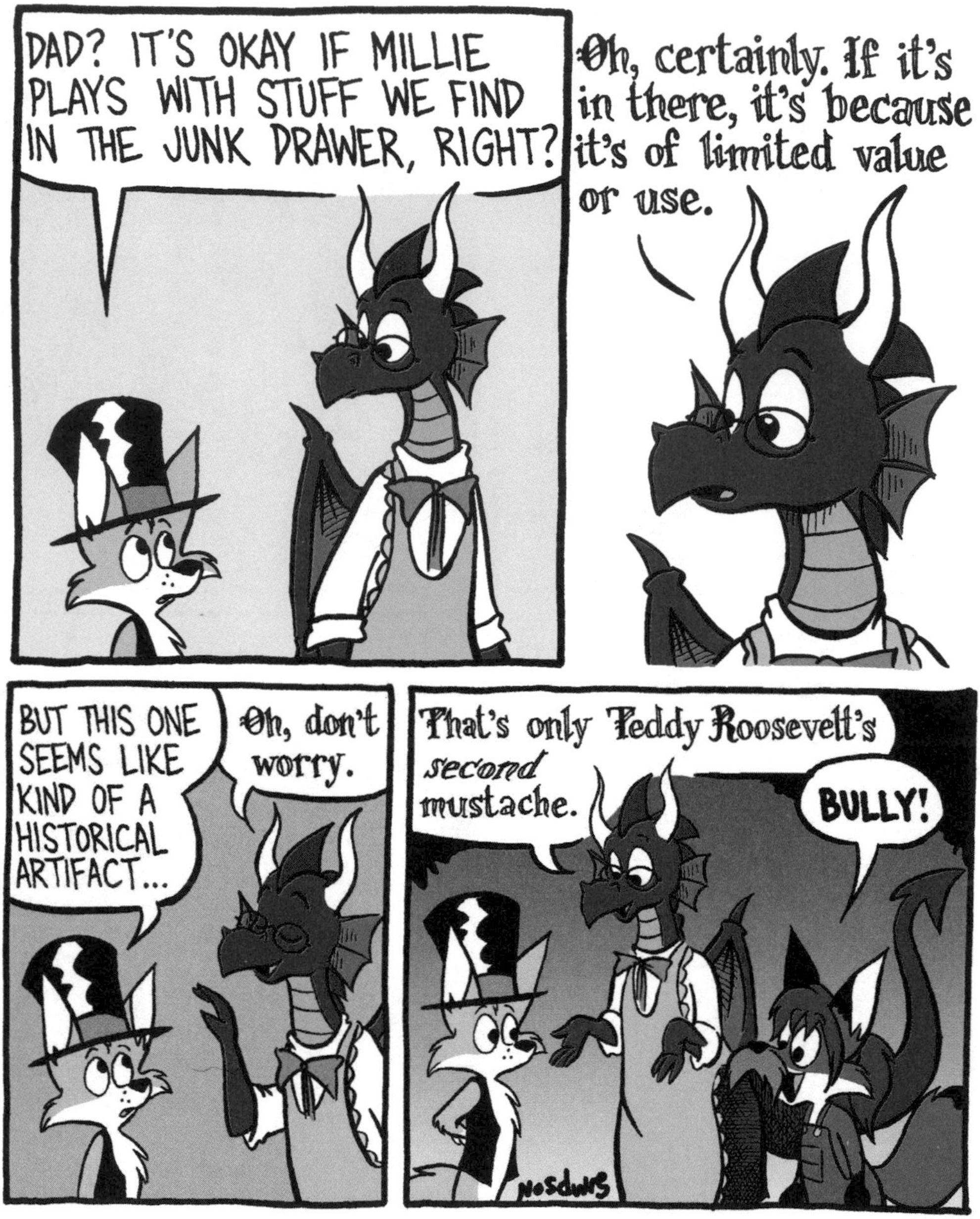
DAD? IT'S OKAY IF MILLIE PLAYS WITH STUFF WE FIND IN THE JUNK DRAWER, RIGHT?
Oh, certainly. If it's in there, it's because it's of limited value or use.
BUT THIS ONE SEEMS LIKE KIND OF A HISTORICAL ARTIFACT...
Oh, don't worry.
That's only Teddy Roosevelt's *second* mustache.
BULLY!
NOSDUMS

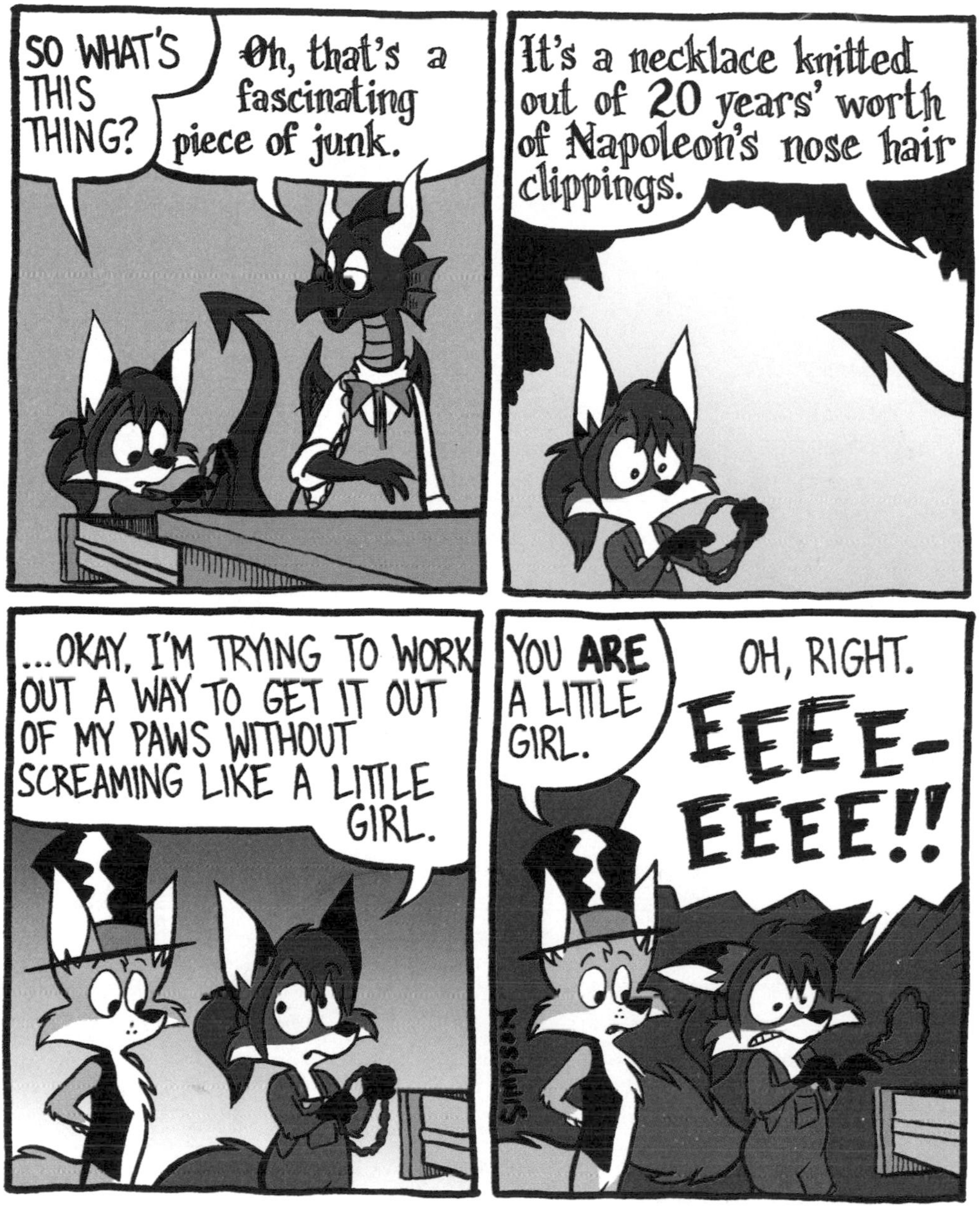
SO WHAT'S THIS THING?
Oh, that's a fascinating piece of junk.
It's a necklace knitted out of 20 years' worth of Napoleon's nose hair clippings.
...OKAY, I'M TRYING TO WORK OUT A WAY TO GET IT OUT OF MY PAWS WITHOUT SCREAMING LIKE A LITTLE GIRL.
YOU **ARE** A LITTLE GIRL.
OH, RIGHT.
EEEE-EEEE!!
SIMPSON

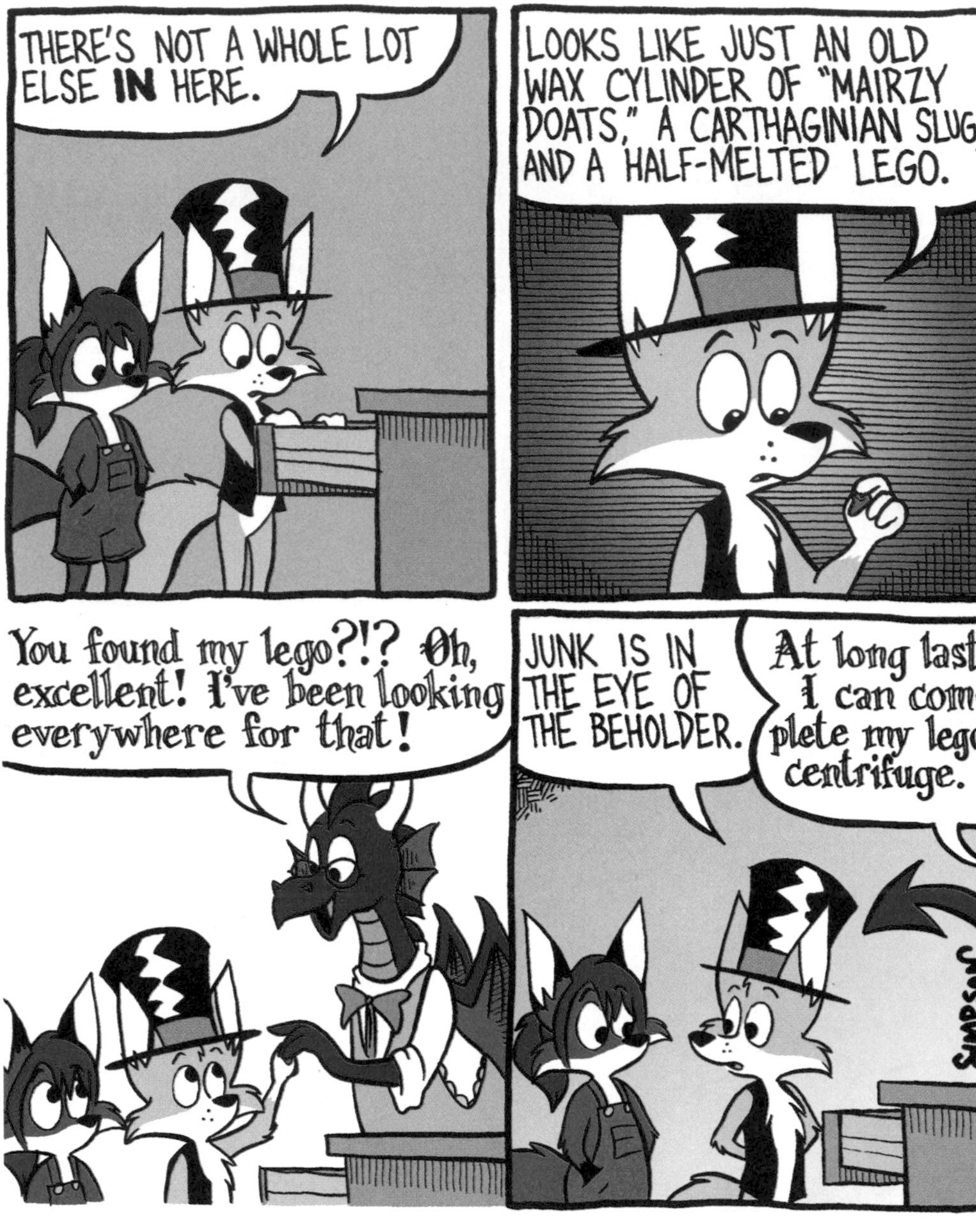
THERE'S NOT A WHOLE LOT ELSE **IN** HERE.
LOOKS LIKE JUST AN OLD WAX CYLINDER OF "MAIRZY DOATS," A CARTHAGINIAN SLUG, AND A HALF-MELTED LEGO.
You found my lego?!? Oh, excellent! I've been looking everywhere for that!
JUNK IS IN THE EYE OF THE BEHOLDER.
At long last, I can complete my lego centrifuge.
SIMPSON

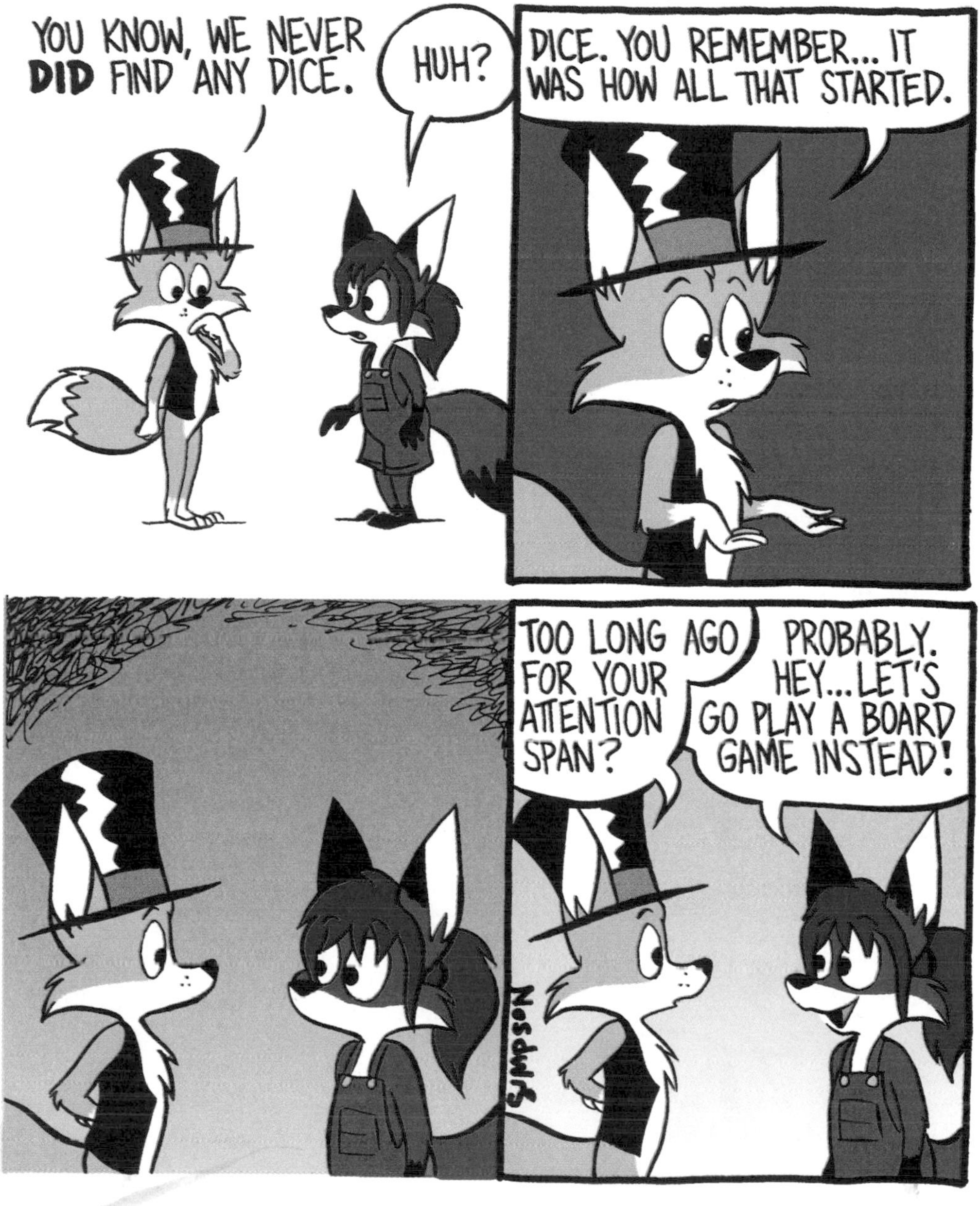
YOU KNOW, WE NEVER **DID** FIND ANY DICE.
HUH?
DICE. YOU REMEMBER... IT WAS HOW ALL THAT STARTED.
TOO LONG AGO FOR YOUR ATTENTION SPAN?
PROBABLY. HEY...LET'S GO PLAY A BOARD GAME INSTEAD!
Nosdwlf

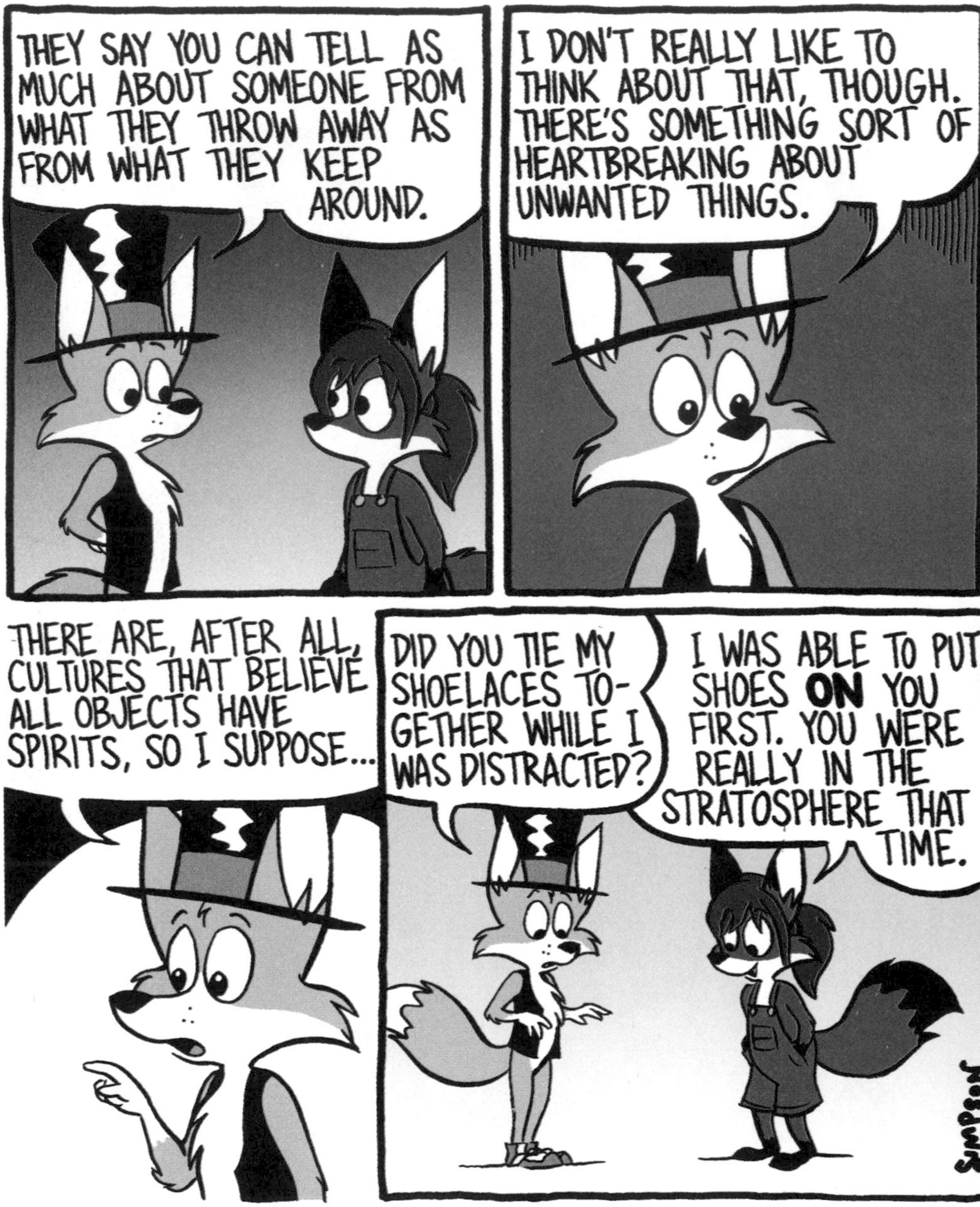
THEY SAY YOU CAN TELL AS MUCH ABOUT SOMEONE FROM WHAT THEY THROW AWAY AS FROM WHAT THEY KEEP AROUND.
I DON'T REALLY LIKE TO THINK ABOUT THAT, THOUGH. THERE'S SOMETHING SORT OF HEARTBREAKING ABOUT UNWANTED THINGS.
THERE ARE, AFTER ALL, CULTURES THAT BELIEVE ALL OBJECTS HAVE SPIRITS, SO I SUPPOSE...
DID YOU TIE MY SHOELACES TOGETHER WHILE I WAS DISTRACTED?
I WAS ABLE TO PUT SHOES **ON** YOU FIRST. YOU WERE REALLY IN THE STRATOSPHERE THAT TIME.
SIMPSON

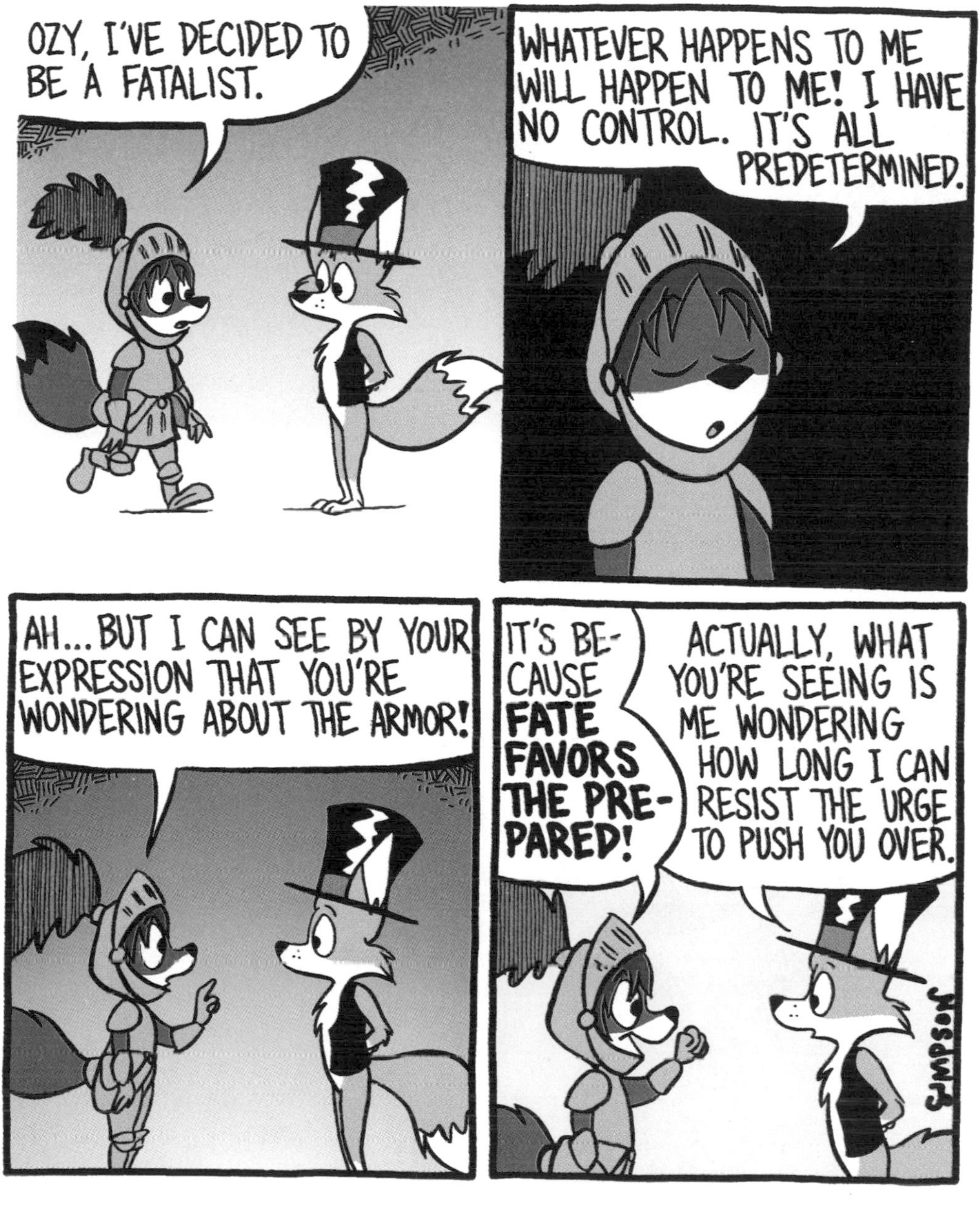
OZY, I'VE DECIDED TO BE A FATALIST.
WHATEVER HAPPENS TO ME WILL HAPPEN TO ME! I HAVE NO CONTROL. IT'S ALL PREDETERMINED.
AH... BUT I CAN SEE BY YOUR EXPRESSION THAT YOU'RE WONDERING ABOUT THE ARMOR!
IT'S BE-CAUSE FATE FAVORS THE PRE-PARED!
ACTUALLY, WHAT YOU'RE SEEING IS ME WONDERING HOW LONG I CAN RESIST THE URGE TO PUSH YOU OVER.
SIMPSON

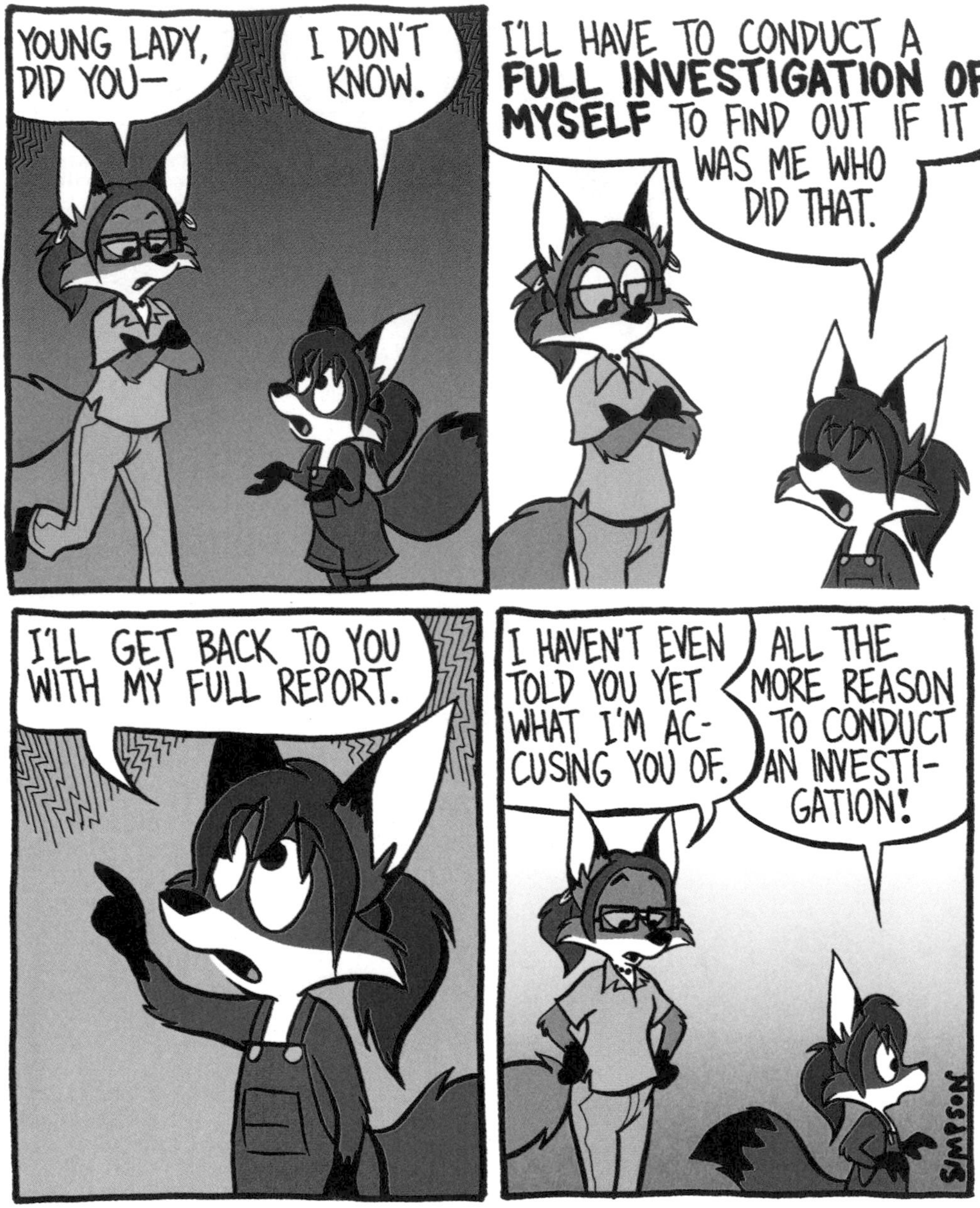
YOUNG LADY, DID YOU—
I DON'T KNOW.
I'LL HAVE TO CONDUCT A **FULL INVESTIGATION OF MYSELF** TO FIND OUT IF IT WAS ME WHO DID THAT.
I'LL GET BACK TO YOU WITH MY FULL REPORT.
I HAVEN'T EVEN TOLD YOU YET WHAT I'M ACCUSING YOU OF.
ALL THE MORE REASON TO CONDUCT AN INVESTIGATION!
SIMPSON

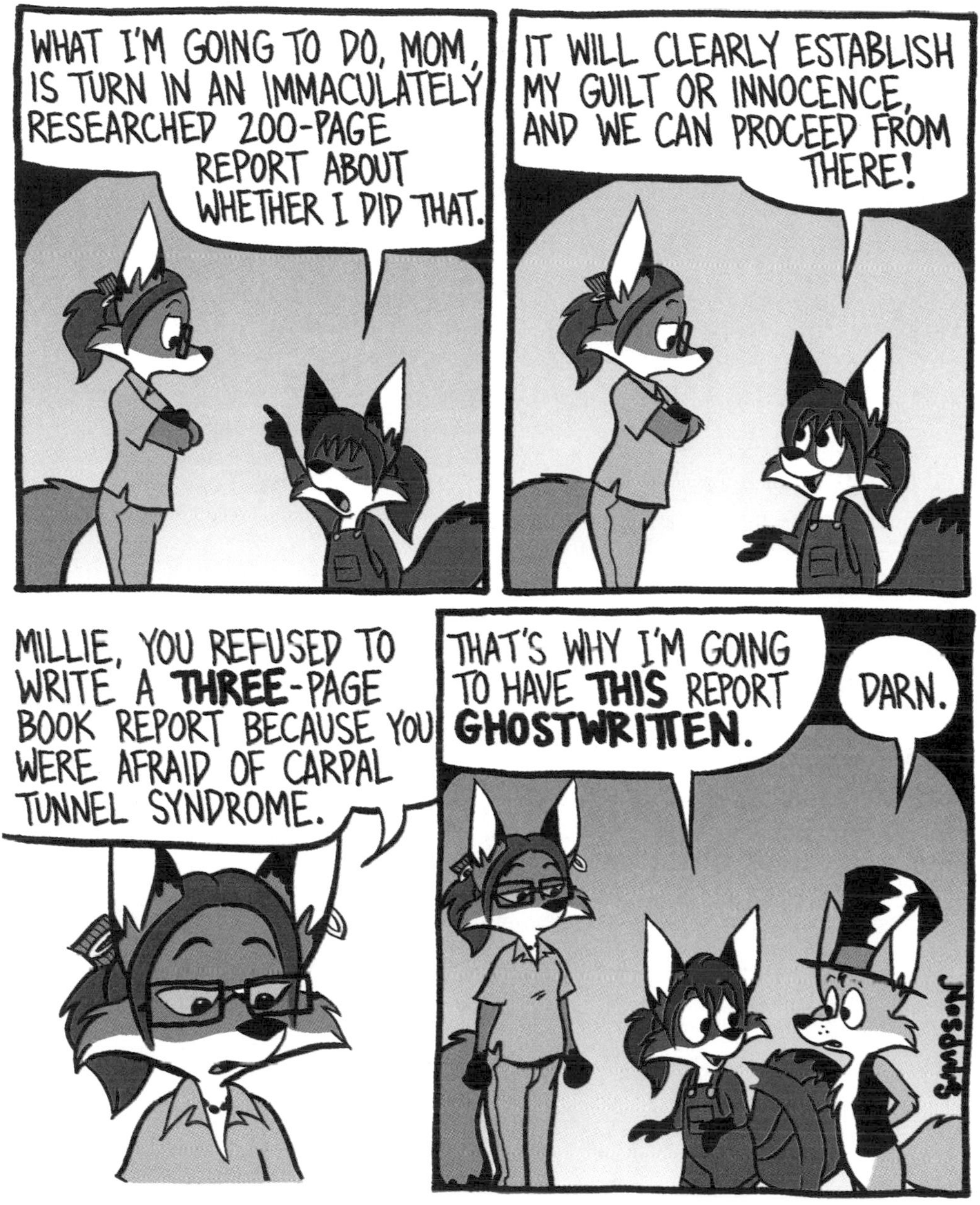
WHAT I'M GOING TO DO, MOM, IS TURN IN AN IMMACULATELY RESEARCHED 200-PAGE REPORT ABOUT WHETHER I DID THAT.
IT WILL CLEARLY ESTABLISH MY GUILT OR INNOCENCE, AND WE CAN PROCEED FROM THERE!
MILLIE, YOU REFUSED TO WRITE A **THREE**-PAGE BOOK REPORT BECAUSE YOU WERE AFRAID OF CARPAL TUNNEL SYNDROME.
THAT'S WHY I'M GOING TO HAVE **THIS** REPORT **GHOSTWRITTEN**.
DARN.
SIMPSON

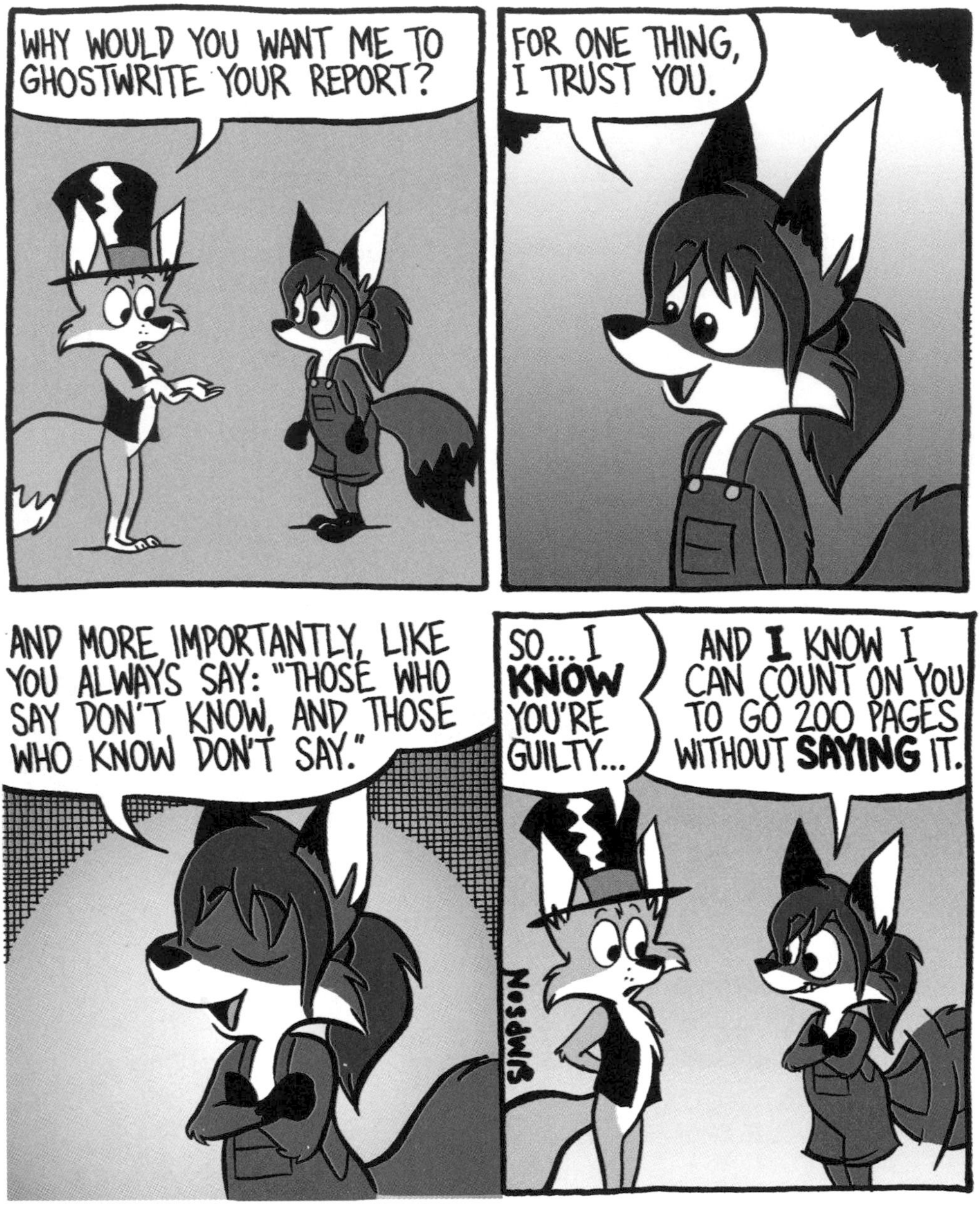
WHY WOULD YOU WANT ME TO GHOSTWRITE YOUR REPORT?
FOR ONE THING, I TRUST YOU.
AND MORE IMPORTANTLY, LIKE YOU ALWAYS SAY: "THOSE WHO SAY DON'T KNOW, AND THOSE WHO KNOW DON'T SAY."
SO... I **KNOW** YOU'RE GUILTY...
AND **I** KNOW I CAN COUNT ON YOU TO GO 200 PAGES WITHOUT **SAYING** IT.
SIMPSON

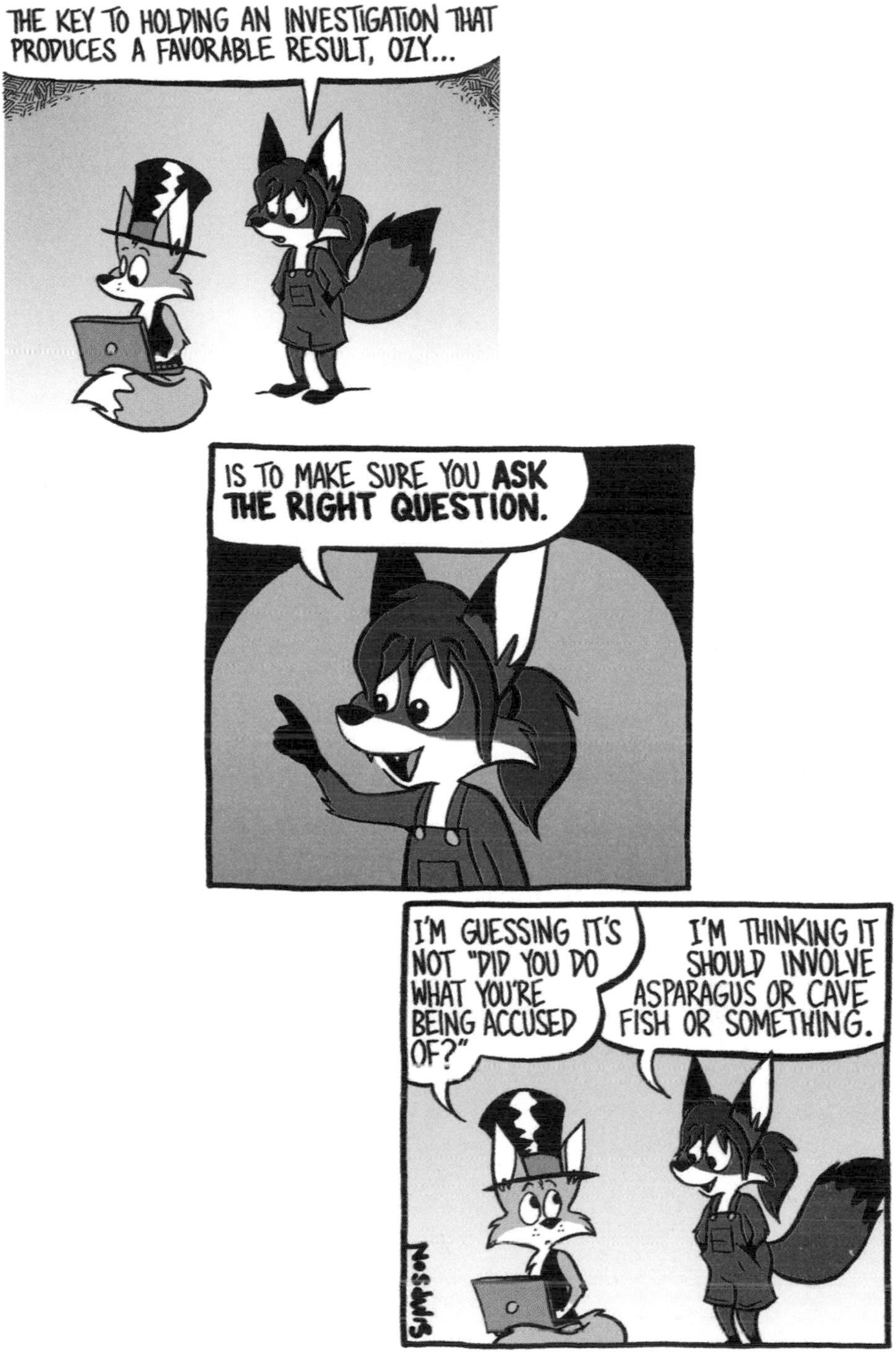
THE KEY TO HOLDING AN INVESTIGATION THAT PRODUCES A FAVORABLE RESULT, OZY...
IS TO MAKE SURE YOU **ASK THE RIGHT QUESTION.**
I'M GUESSING IT'S NOT "DID YOU DO WHAT YOU'RE BEING ACCUSED OF?"
I'M THINKING IT SHOULD INVOLVE ASPARAGUS OR CAVE FISH OR SOMETHING.
SIMPSON

HERE IT IS, MOM. MY 200-PAGE FINAL REPORT!

AS YOU CAN SEE, NOTHING IN IT IMPLICATES ME IN ANY WAY WHATSOEVER!

IT MOSTLY JUST SAYS "HELP, MILLIE IS MAKING ME WRITE 200 PAGES OF DRIVEL" OVER AND OVER.

GOOD GHOST-WRITERS ARE HARD TO FIND.

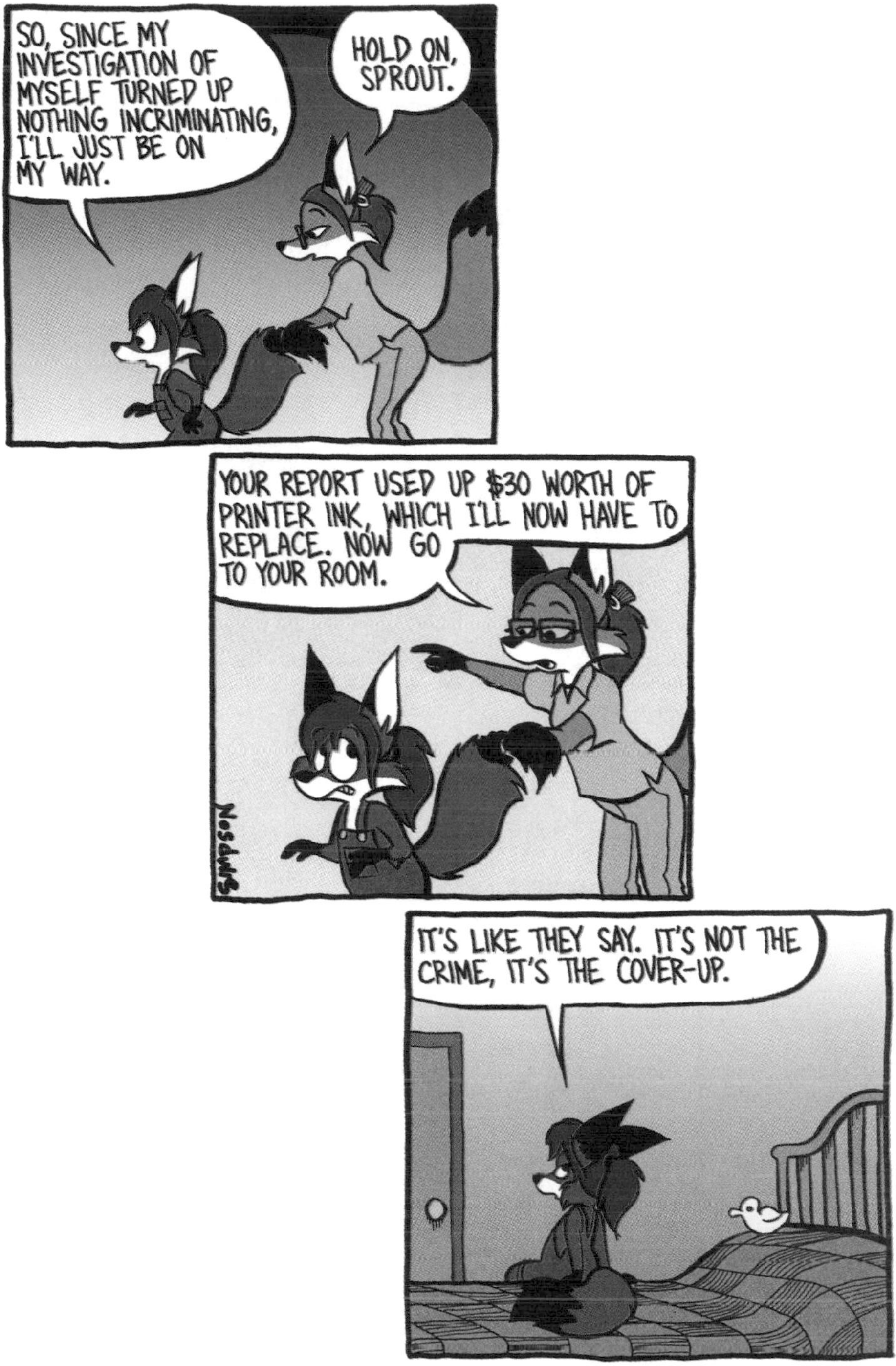
SO, SINCE MY INVESTIGATION OF MYSELF TURNED UP NOTHING INCRIMINATING, I'LL JUST BE ON MY WAY.
HOLD ON, SPROUT.
YOUR REPORT USED UP $30 WORTH OF PRINTER INK, WHICH I'LL NOW HAVE TO REPLACE. NOW GO TO YOUR ROOM.
IT'S LIKE THEY SAY. IT'S NOT THE CRIME, IT'S THE COVER-UP.

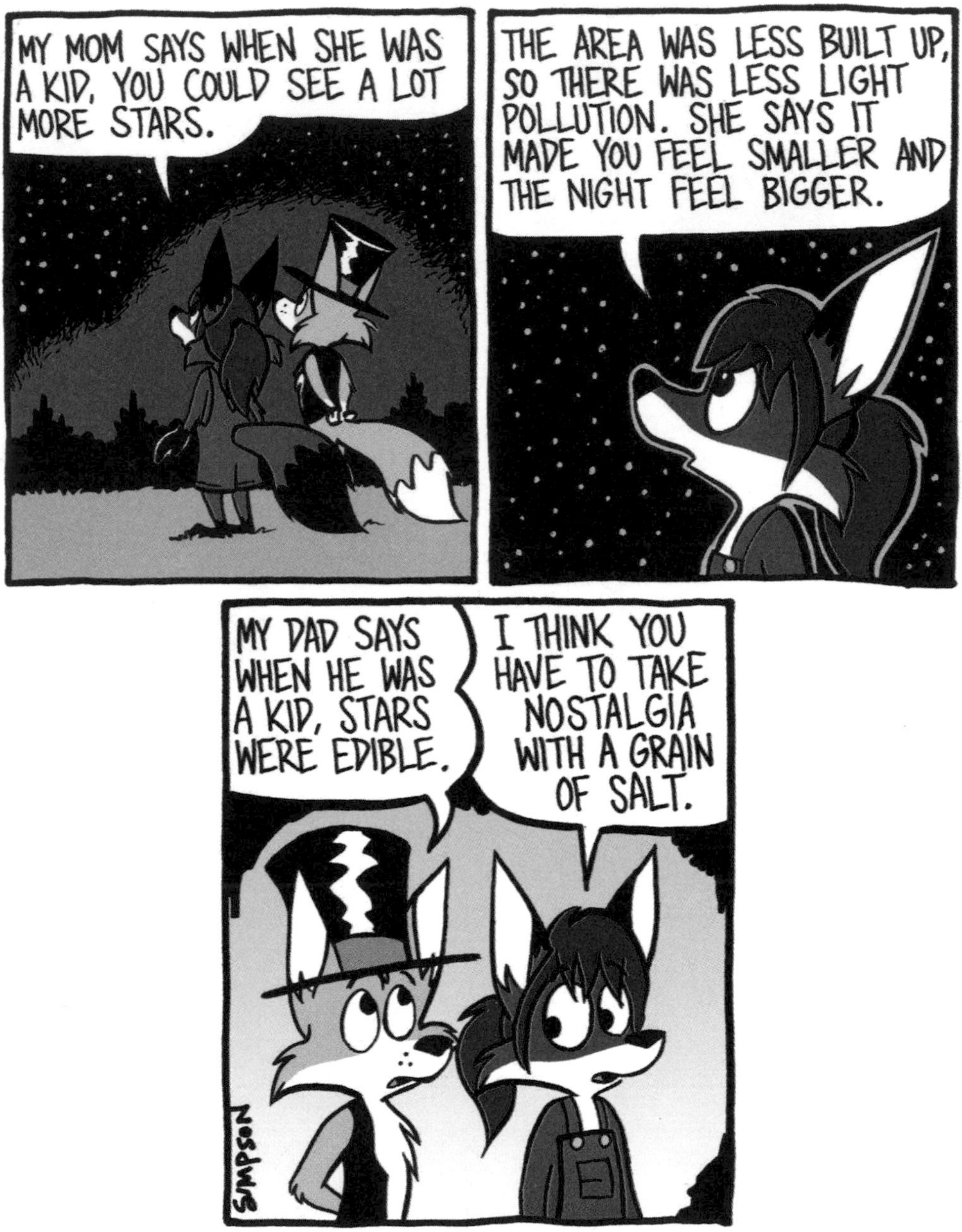
MY MOM SAYS WHEN SHE WAS A KID, YOU COULD SEE A LOT MORE STARS.
THE AREA WAS LESS BUILT UP, SO THERE WAS LESS LIGHT POLLUTION. SHE SAYS IT MADE YOU FEEL SMALLER AND THE NIGHT FEEL BIGGER.
MY DAD SAYS WHEN HE WAS A KID, STARS WERE EDIBLE.
I THINK YOU HAVE TO TAKE NOSTALGIA WITH A GRAIN OF SALT.
SIMPSON

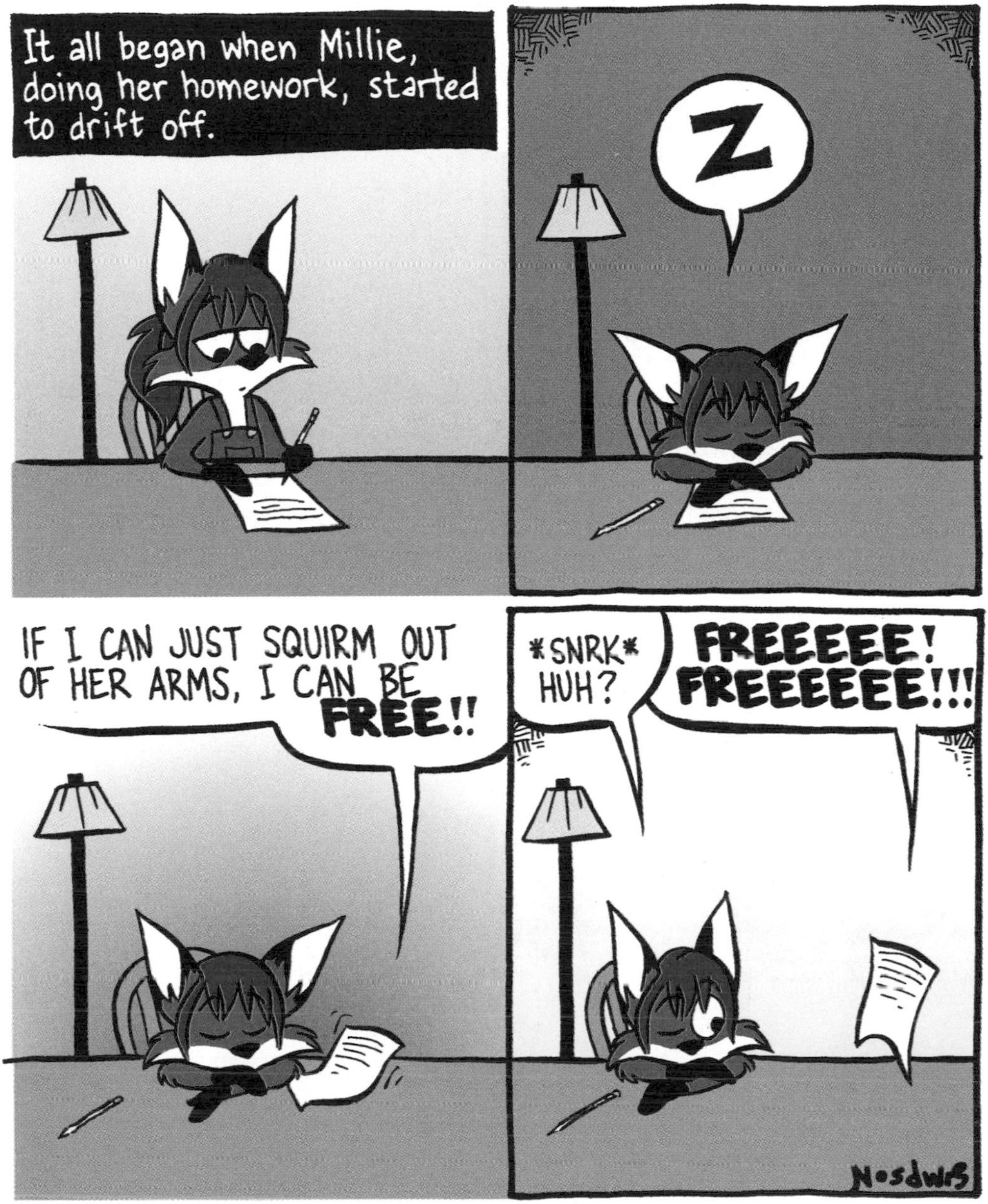
It all began when Millie, doing her homework, started to drift off.
Z
IF I CAN JUST SQUIRM OUT OF HER ARMS, I CAN BE FREE!!
SNRK HUH?
FREEEEEE! FREEEEEEE!!!
Nosdwrs

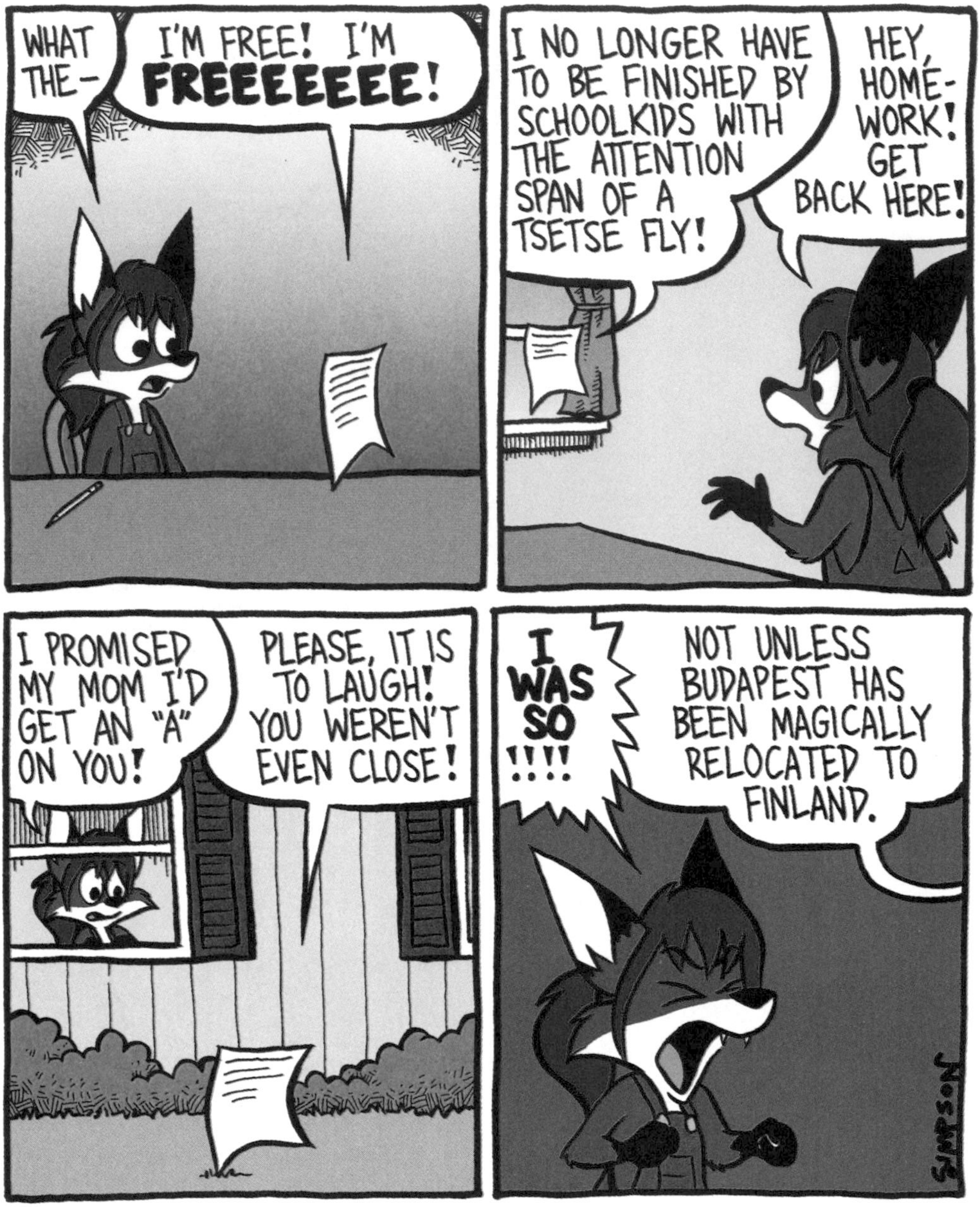
WHAT THE-
I'M FREE! I'M FREEEEEEE!
I NO LONGER HAVE TO BE FINISHED BY SCHOOLKIDS WITH THE ATTENTION SPAN OF A TSETSE FLY!
HEY, HOMEWORK! GET BACK HERE!
I PROMISED MY MOM I'D GET AN "A" ON YOU!
PLEASE, IT IS TO LAUGH! YOU WEREN'T EVEN CLOSE!
I WAS SO !!!!
NOT UNLESS BUDAPEST HAS BEEN MAGICALLY RELOCATED TO FINLAND.
SIMPSON

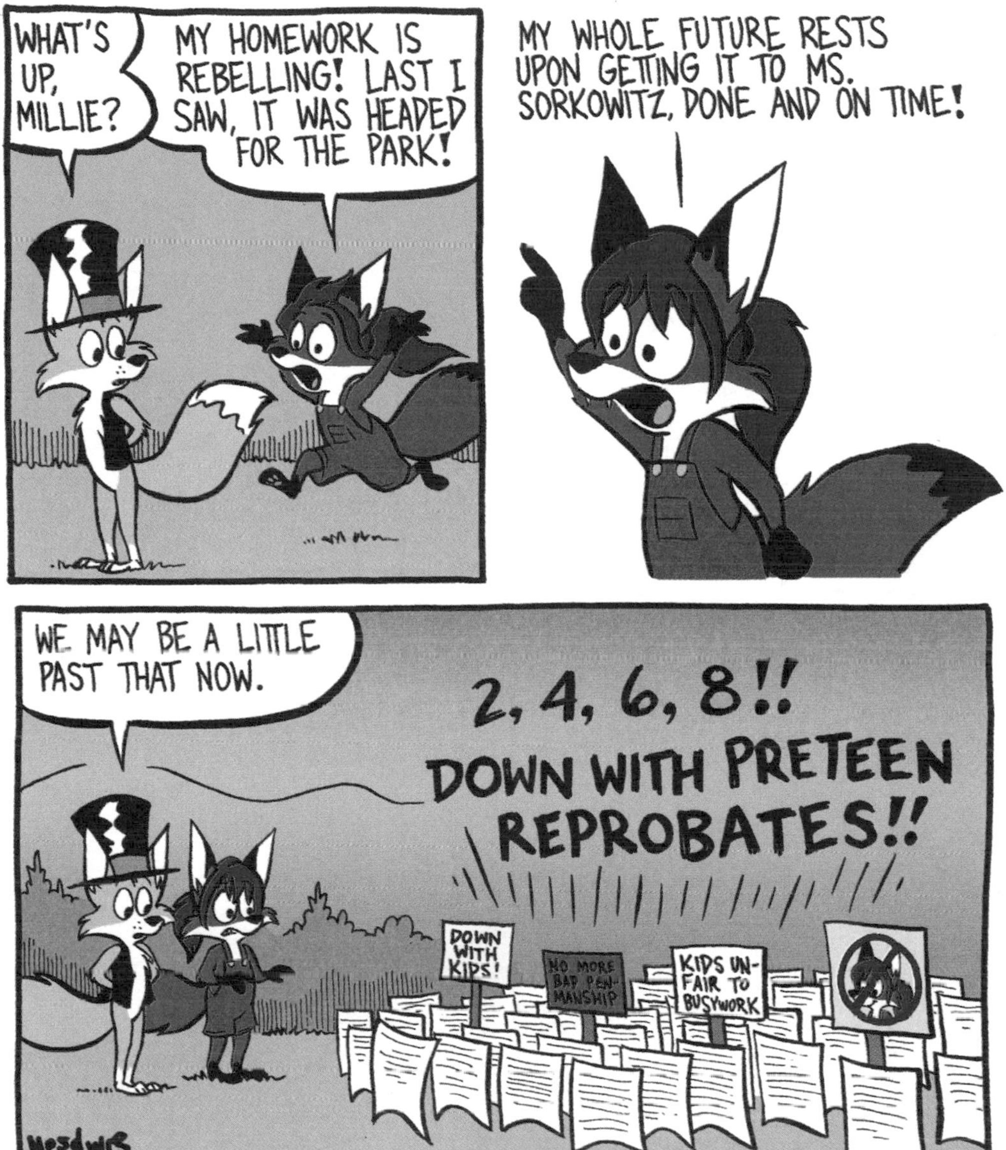
WHAT'S UP, MILLIE?
MY HOMEWORK IS REBELLING! LAST I SAW, IT WAS HEADED FOR THE PARK!
MY WHOLE FUTURE RESTS UPON GETTING IT TO MS. SORKOWITZ, DONE AND ON TIME!
WE MAY BE A LITTLE PAST THAT NOW.
2, 4, 6, 8!!
DOWN WITH PRETEEN REPROBATES!!
DOWN WITH KIDS!
NO MORE BAD PEN-MANSHIP
KIDS UN-FAIR TO BUSYWORK

MILLICENT, I MIGHT HAVE KNOWN **YOUR** HOMEWORK WOULD BE THE ONE TO LEAD THIS LITTLE INSURRECTION.

WHY AREN'T YOU STOPPING IT?

WELL, THIS COULD BE HISTORY! WE COULD BE WITNESSING THE BIRTH OF A **SOVEREIGN HOMEWORK NATION!**

THAT'S **APPEASER** TALK, MILLICENT.

I'M **NOT** AN APPEASER!

I'M A **CONSCIENTIOUS OBJECTOR!**

"CONSCIENTIOUS"?

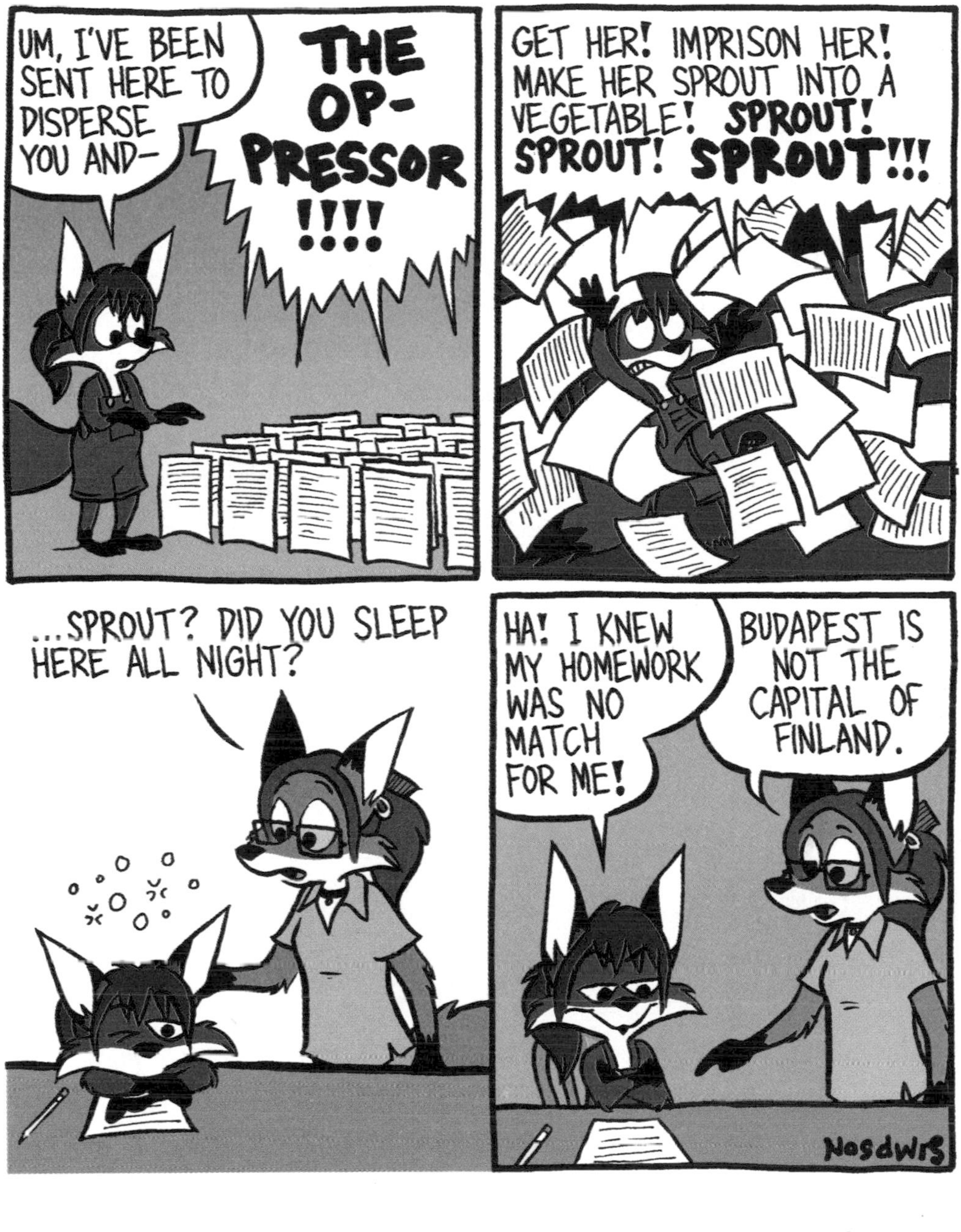
UM, I'VE BEEN SENT HERE TO DISPERSE YOU AND–
THE OP-PRESSOR!!!!
GET HER! IMPRISON HER! MAKE HER SPROUT INTO A VEGETABLE! SPROUT! SPROUT! SPROUT!!!
...SPROUT? DID YOU SLEEP HERE ALL NIGHT?
HA! I KNEW MY HOMEWORK WAS NO MATCH FOR ME!
BUDAPEST IS NOT THE CAPITAL OF FINLAND.
Nosdwrs

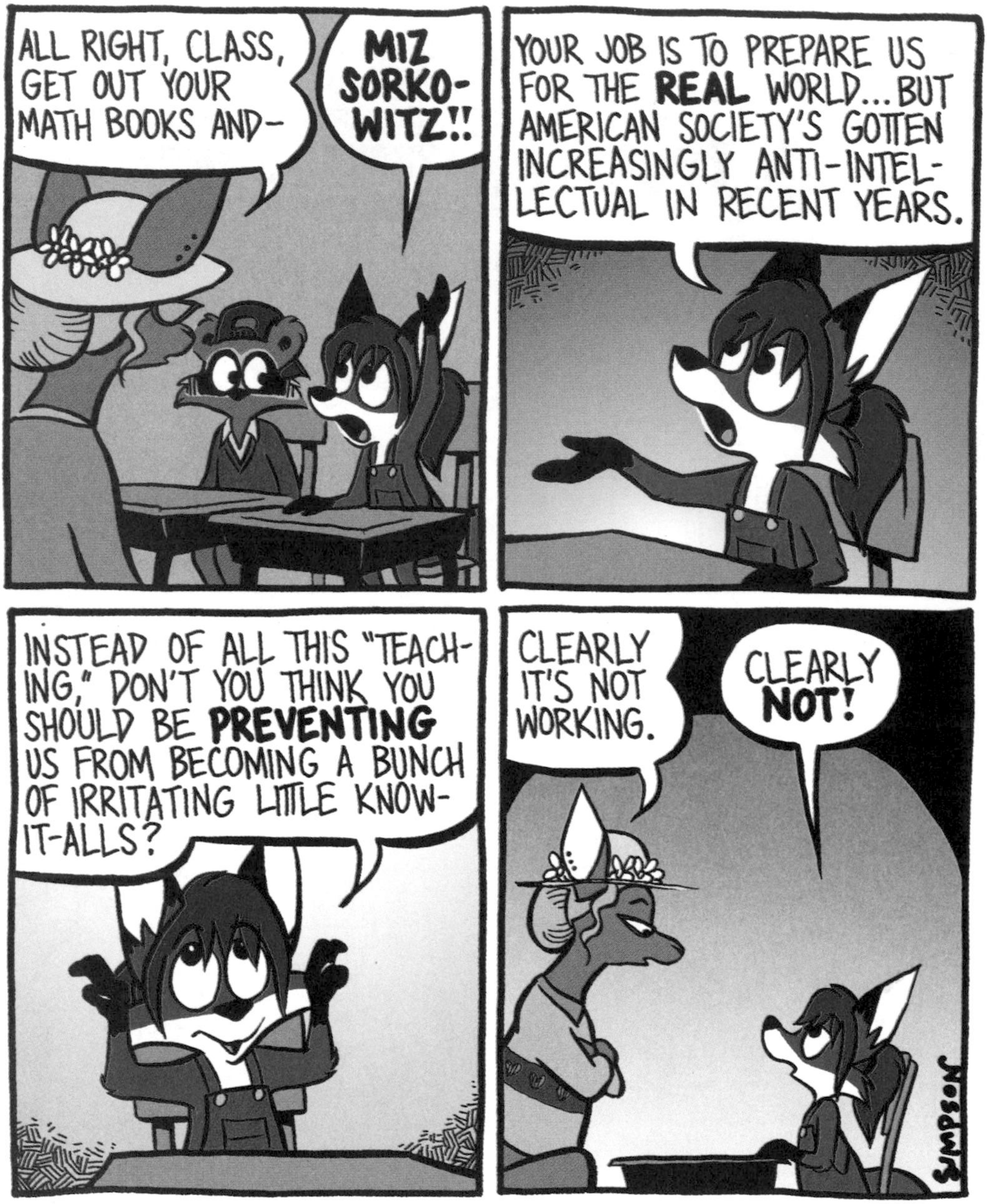
ALL RIGHT, CLASS, GET OUT YOUR MATH BOOKS AND-
MIZ SORKO-WITZ!!
YOUR JOB IS TO PREPARE US FOR THE REAL WORLD...BUT AMERICAN SOCIETY'S GOTTEN INCREASINGLY ANTI-INTEL-LECTUAL IN RECENT YEARS.
INSTEAD OF ALL THIS "TEACH-ING," DON'T YOU THINK YOU SHOULD BE PREVENTING US FROM BECOMING A BUNCH OF IRRITATING LITTLE KNOW-IT-ALLS?
CLEARLY IT'S NOT WORKING.
CLEARLY NOT!
SYMPSON

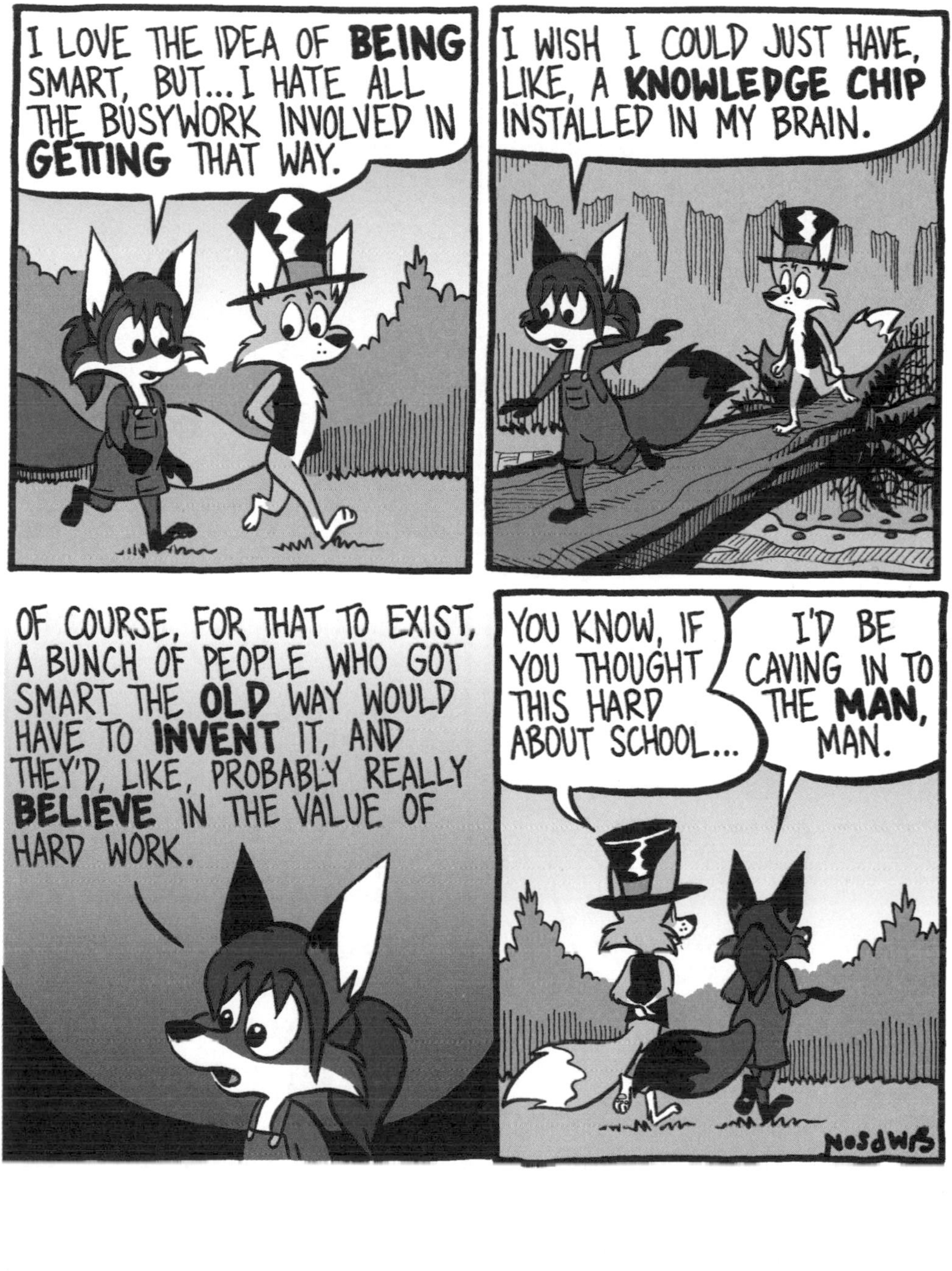
I LOVE THE IDEA OF BEING SMART, BUT... I HATE ALL THE BUSYWORK INVOLVED IN GETTING THAT WAY.
I WISH I COULD JUST HAVE, LIKE, A KNOWLEDGE CHIP INSTALLED IN MY BRAIN.
OF COURSE, FOR THAT TO EXIST, A BUNCH OF PEOPLE WHO GOT SMART THE OLD WAY WOULD HAVE TO INVENT IT, AND THEY'D, LIKE, PROBABLY REALLY BELIEVE IN THE VALUE OF HARD WORK.
YOU KNOW, IF YOU THOUGHT THIS HARD ABOUT SCHOOL...
I'D BE CAVING IN TO THE MAN, MAN.
NOSDWIS

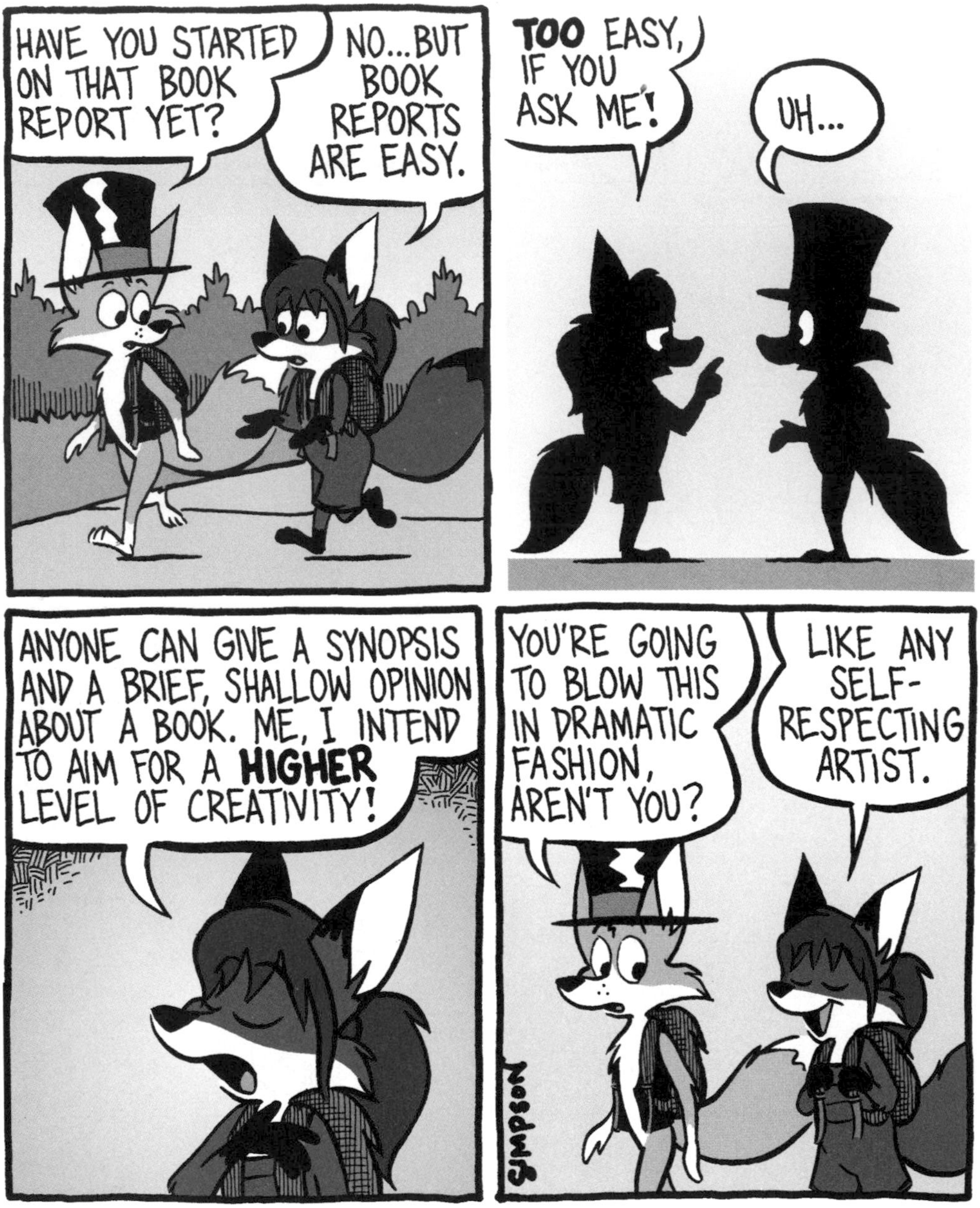

HAVE YOU STARTED ON THAT BOOK REPORT YET?
NO...BUT BOOK REPORTS ARE EASY.
TOO EASY, IF YOU ASK ME!
UH...
ANYONE CAN GIVE A SYNOPSIS AND A BRIEF, SHALLOW OPINION ABOUT A BOOK. ME, I INTEND TO AIM FOR A **HIGHER** LEVEL OF CREATIVITY!
YOU'RE GOING TO BLOW THIS IN DRAMATIC FASHION, AREN'T YOU?
LIKE ANY SELF-RESPECTING ARTIST.
SIMPSON

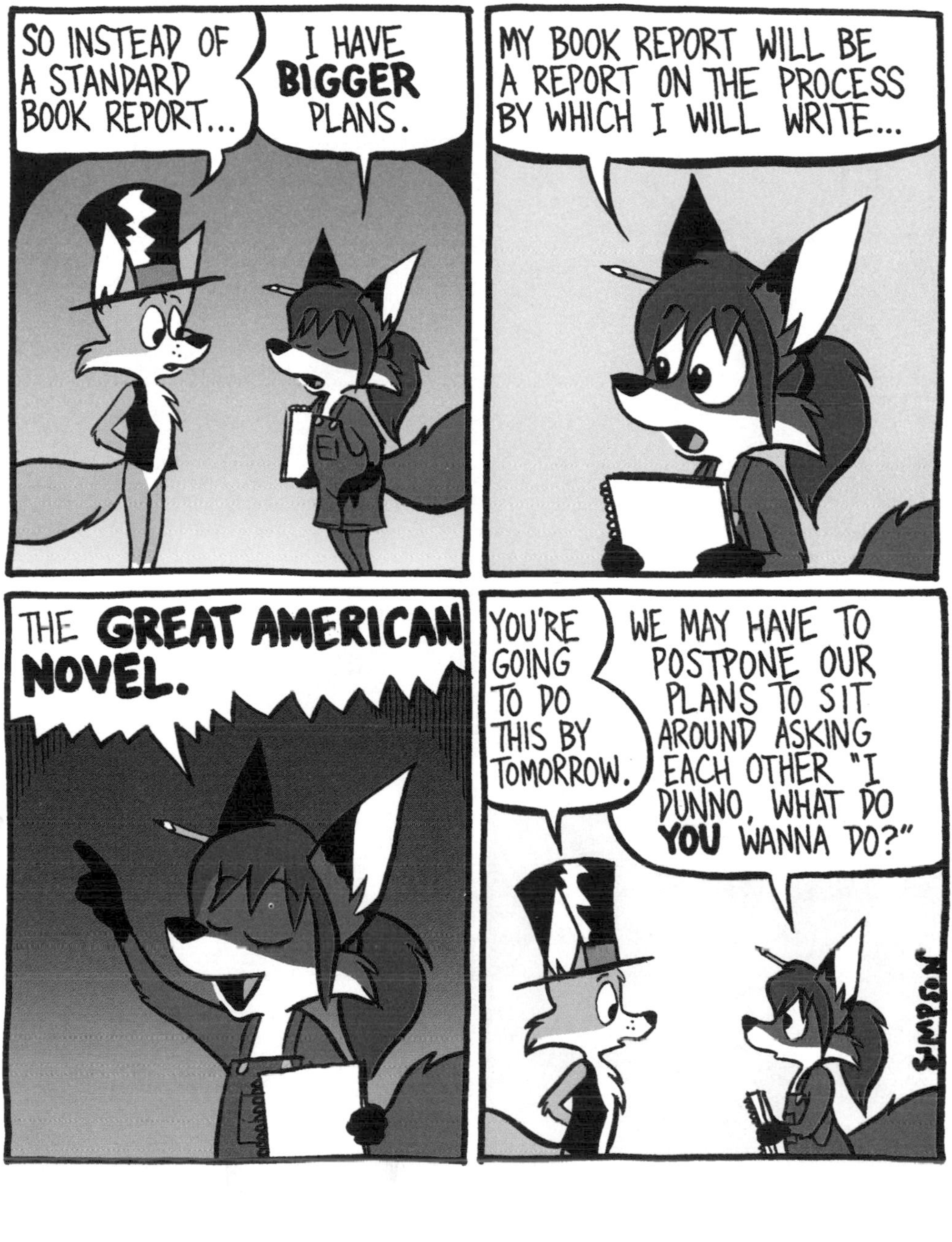
SO INSTEAD OF A STANDARD BOOK REPORT...
I HAVE **BIGGER** PLANS.
MY BOOK REPORT WILL BE A REPORT ON THE PROCESS BY WHICH I WILL WRITE...
EI
THE **GREAT AMERICAN NOVEL.**
YOU'RE GOING TO DO THIS BY TOMORROW.
WE MAY HAVE TO POSTPONE OUR PLANS TO SIT AROUND ASKING EACH OTHER "I DUNNO, WHAT DO **YOU** WANNA DO?"
SIMPSON

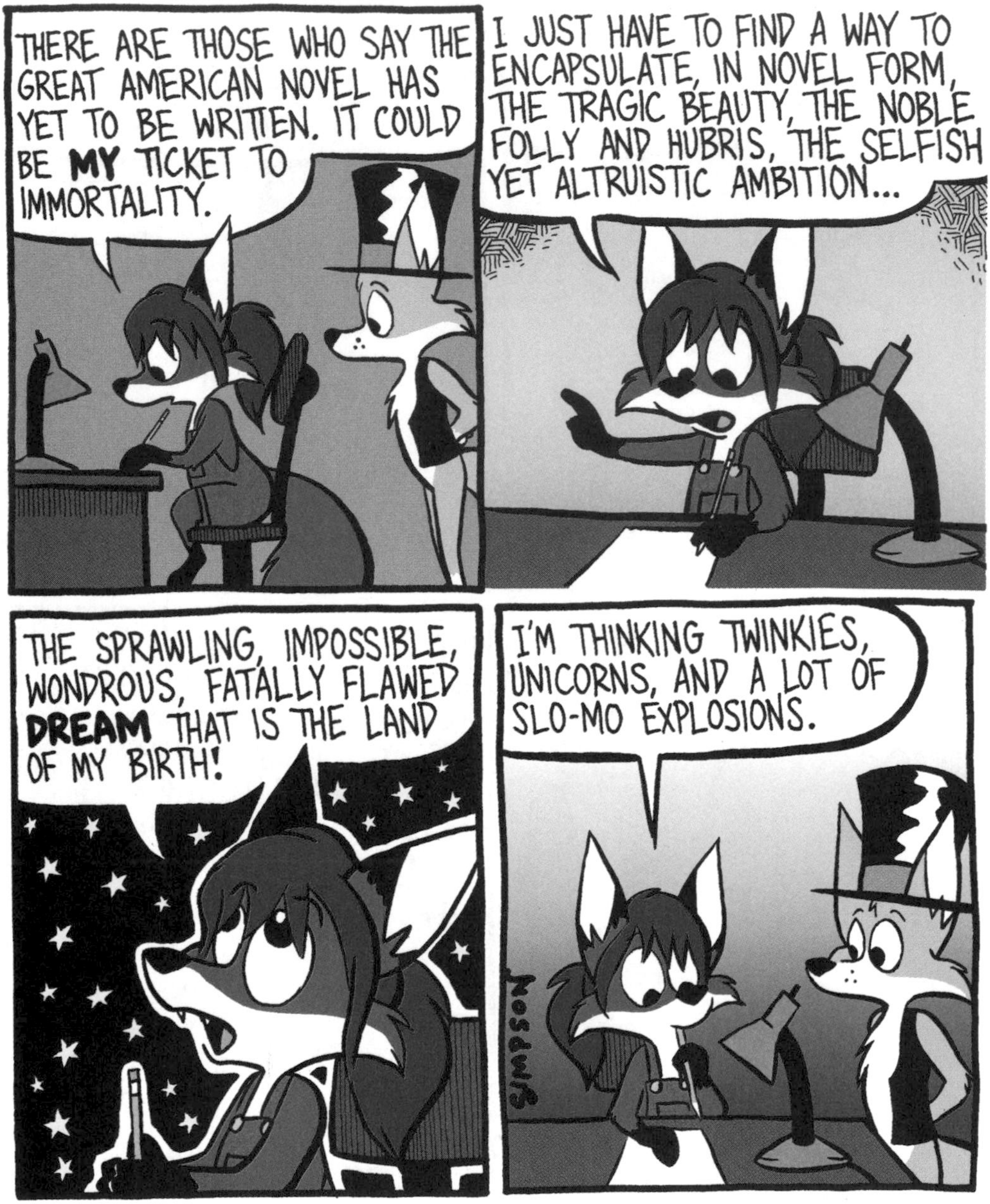
THERE ARE THOSE WHO SAY THE GREAT AMERICAN NOVEL HAS YET TO BE WRITTEN. IT COULD BE **MY** TICKET TO IMMORTALITY.
I JUST HAVE TO FIND A WAY TO ENCAPSULATE, IN NOVEL FORM, THE TRAGIC BEAUTY, THE NOBLE FOLLY AND HUBRIS, THE SELFISH YET ALTRUISTIC AMBITION...
THE SPRAWLING, IMPOSSIBLE, WONDROUS, FATALLY FLAWED **DREAM** THAT IS THE LAND OF MY BIRTH!
I'M THINKING TWINKIES, UNICORNS, AND A LOT OF SLO-MO EXPLOSIONS.
SIMPSON

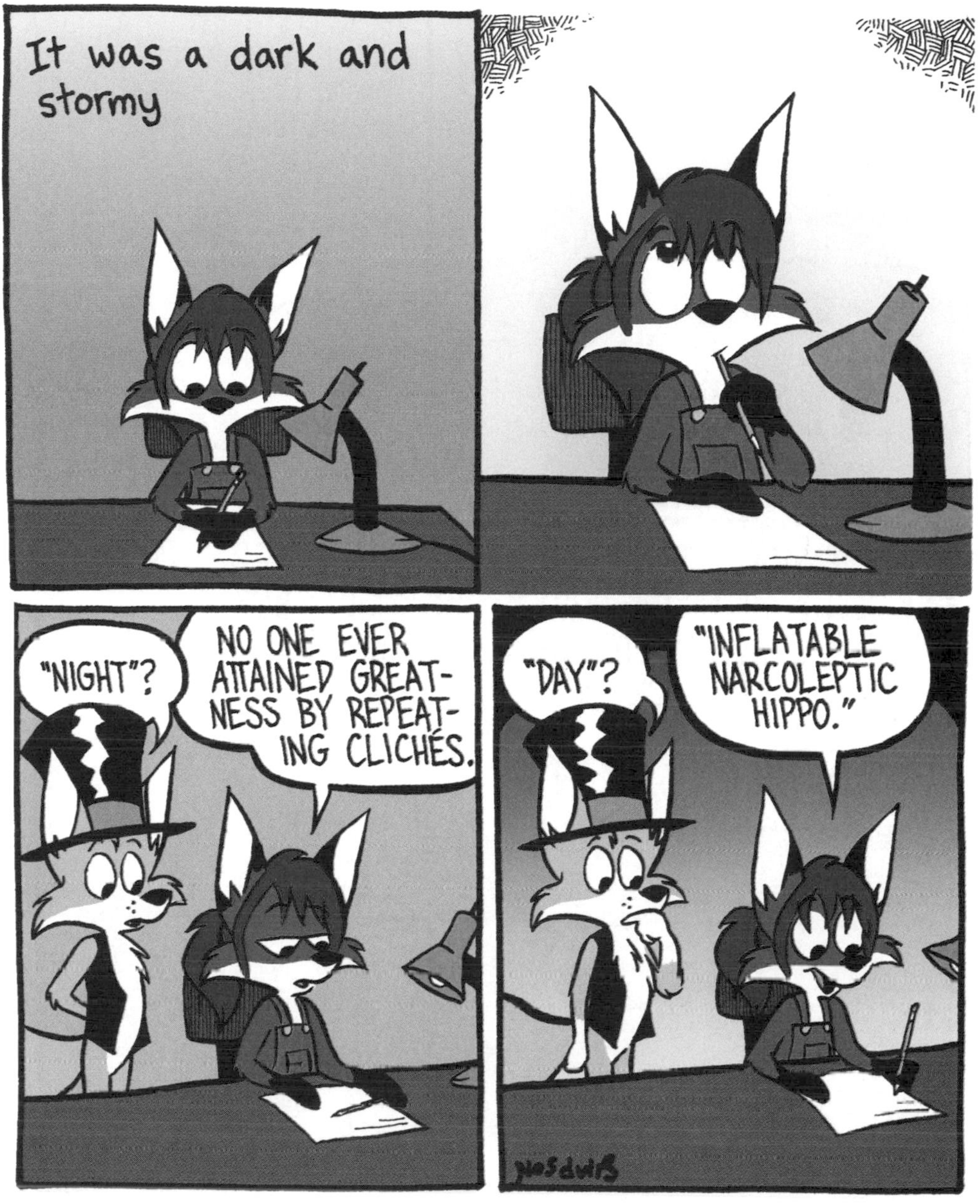
It was a dark and stormy
"NIGHT"?
NO ONE EVER ATTAINED GREATNESS BY REPEATING CLICHÉS.
"DAY"?
"INFLATABLE NARCOLEPTIC HIPPO."

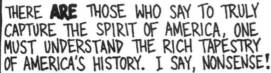 THERE **ARE** THOSE WHO SAY TO TRULY CAPTURE THE SPIRIT OF AMERICA, ONE MUST UNDERSTAND THE RICH TAPESTRY OF AMERICA'S HISTORY. I SAY, NONSENSE!

THE WHOLE POINT IS, WE'RE A NATION WITHOUT THE ATTENTION SPAN TO EVEN **LEARN** ITS OWN HISTORY.

YOU DID HAVE THE ATTENTION SPAN TO TURN THE FIRST THREE CHAPTERS OF YOUR HISTORY TEXTBOOK INTO A PILE OF ORIGAMI DUCKS.

BUT AFTER THAT, I GOT BORED AND WENT TO SEE WHAT WAS ON TELEVISION.

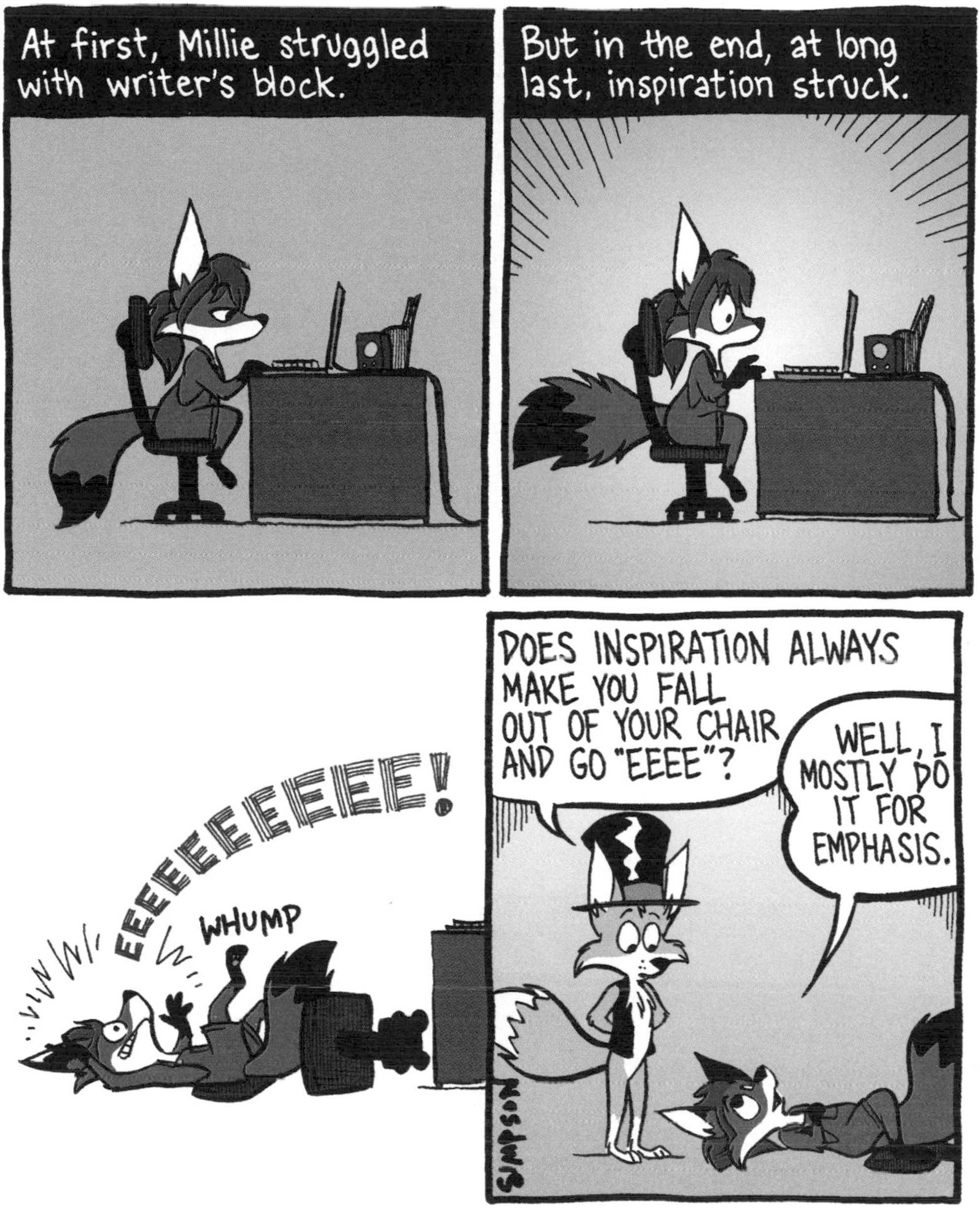
At first, Millie struggled with writer's block.
But in the end, at long last, inspiration struck.
EEEEEEEEEEEEE!
WHUMP
DOES INSPIRATION ALWAYS MAKE YOU FALL OUT OF YOUR CHAIR AND GO "EEEE"?
WELL, I MOSTLY DO IT FOR EMPHASIS.
SIMPSON

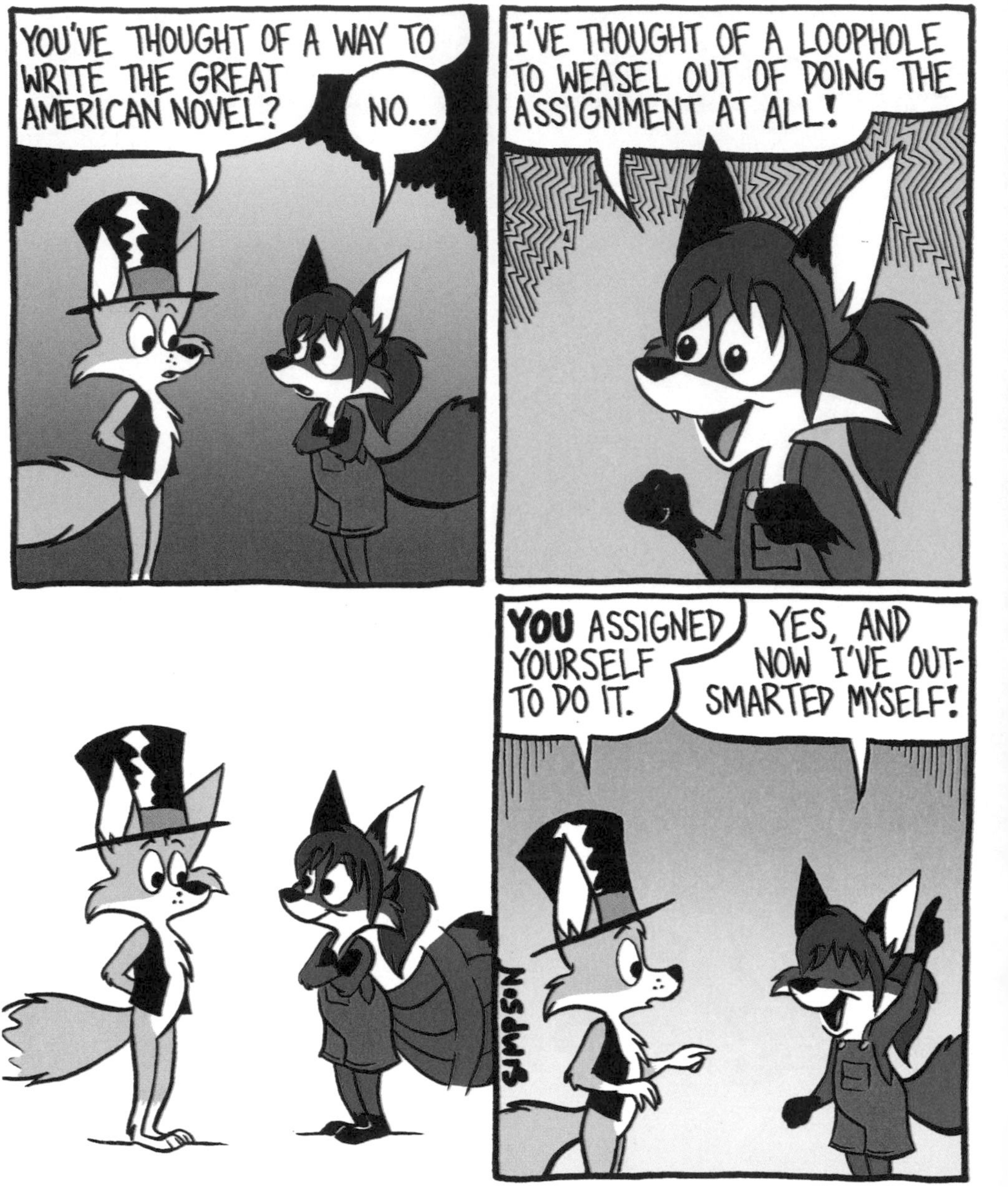
YOU'VE THOUGHT OF A WAY TO WRITE THE GREAT AMERICAN NOVEL?
NO...
I'VE THOUGHT OF A LOOPHOLE TO WEASEL OUT OF DOING THE ASSIGNMENT AT ALL!
YOU ASSIGNED YOURSELF TO DO IT.
YES, AND NOW I'VE OUT-SMARTED MYSELF!
SIMPSON

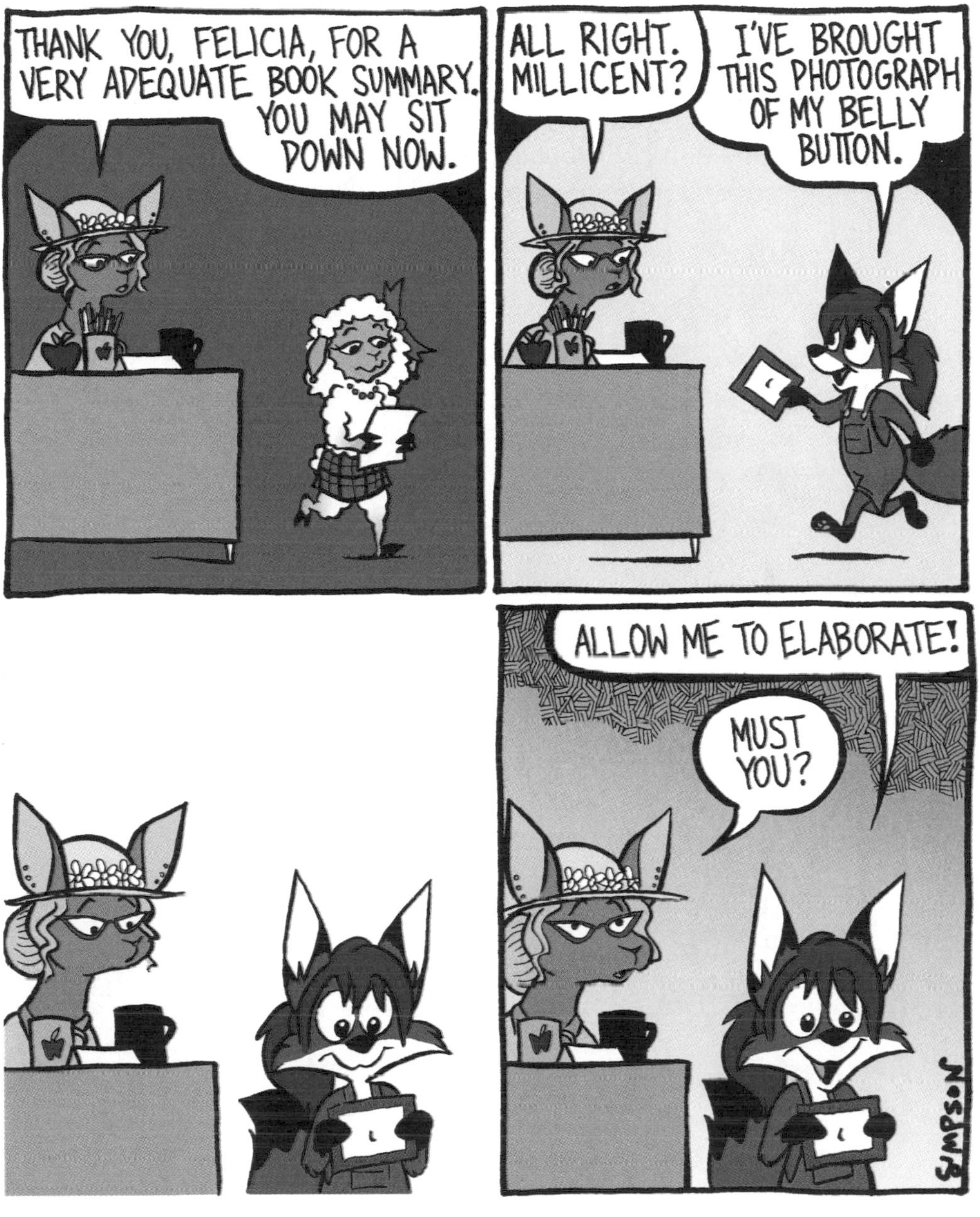
THANK YOU, FELICIA, FOR A VERY ADEQUATE BOOK SUMMARY. YOU MAY SIT DOWN NOW.
ALL RIGHT. MILLICENT?
I'VE BROUGHT THIS PHOTOGRAPH OF MY BELLY BUTTON.
ALLOW ME TO ELABORATE!
MUST YOU?
SIMPSON

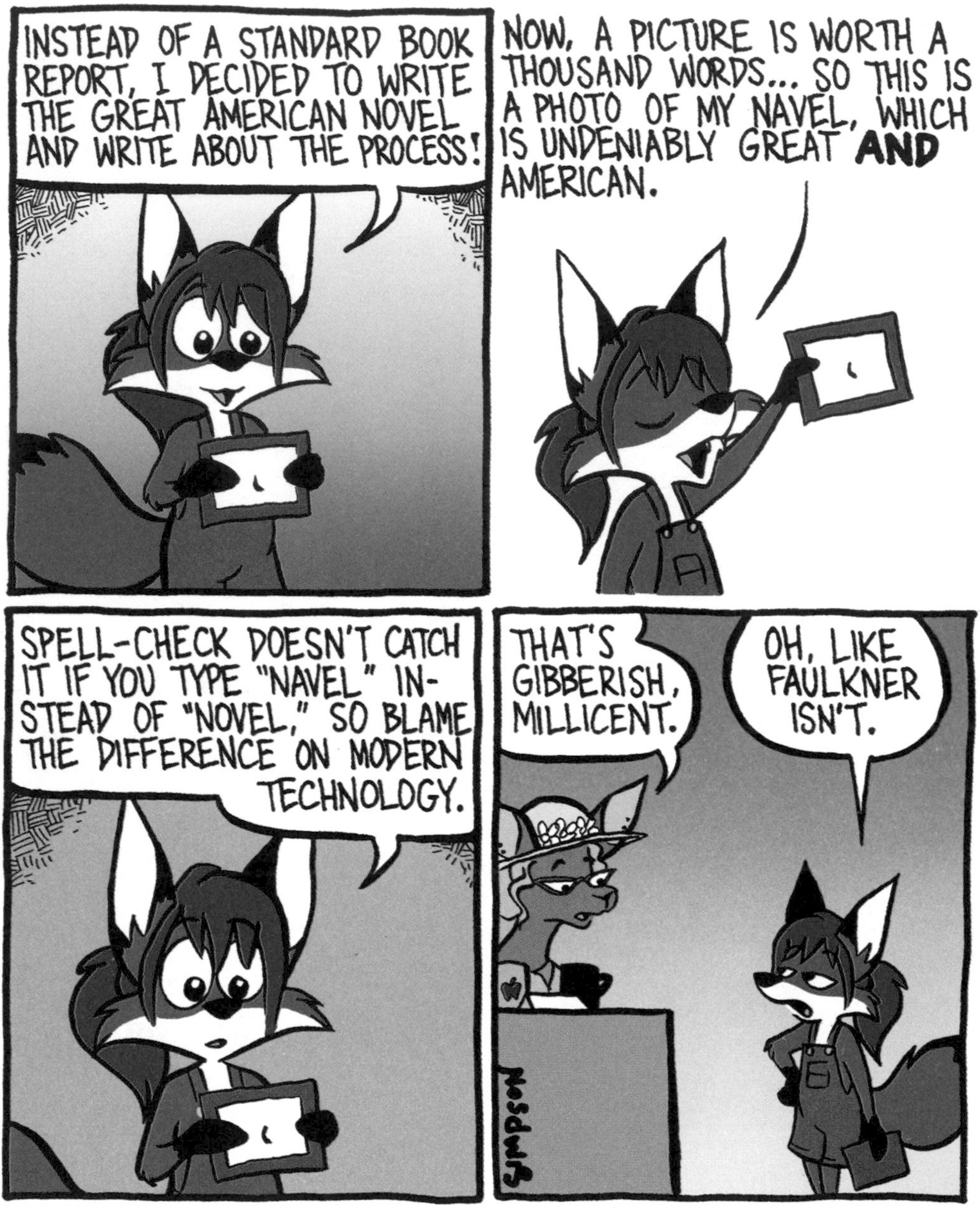
INSTEAD OF A STANDARD BOOK REPORT, I DECIDED TO WRITE THE GREAT AMERICAN NOVEL AND WRITE ABOUT THE PROCESS!
NOW, A PICTURE IS WORTH A THOUSAND WORDS... SO THIS IS A PHOTO OF MY NAVEL, WHICH IS UNDENIABLY GREAT AND AMERICAN.
SPELL-CHECK DOESN'T CATCH IT IF YOU TYPE "NAVEL" INSTEAD OF "NOVEL," SO BLAME THE DIFFERENCE ON MODERN TECHNOLOGY.
THAT'S GIBBERISH, MILLICENT.
OH, LIKE FAULKNER ISN'T.
Simpson

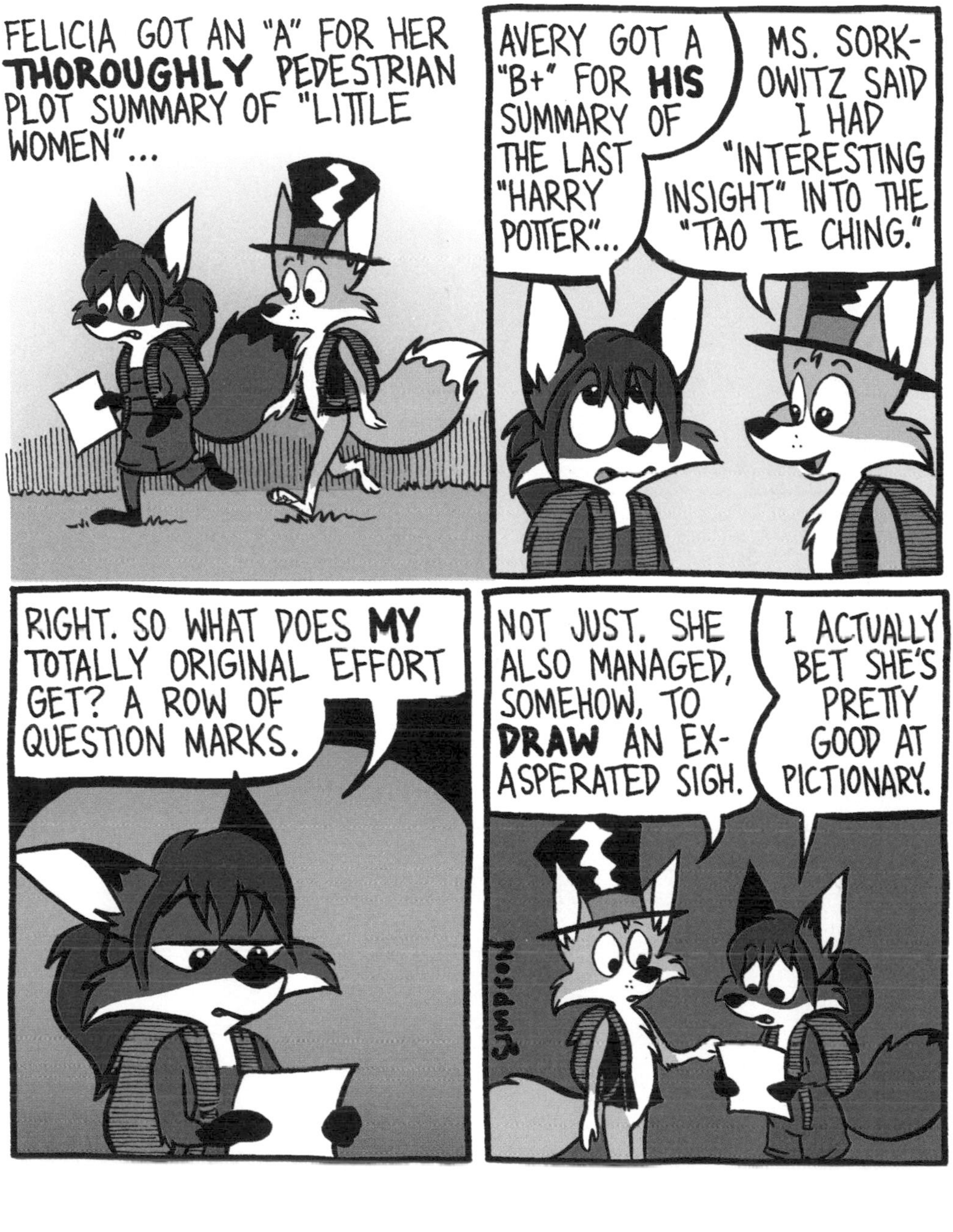
FELICIA GOT AN "A" FOR HER **THOROUGHLY** PEDESTRIAN PLOT SUMMARY OF "LITTLE WOMEN"...
AVERY GOT A "B+" FOR **HIS** SUMMARY OF THE LAST "HARRY POTTER"...
MS. SORKOWITZ SAID I HAD "INTERESTING INSIGHT" INTO THE "TAO TE CHING."
RIGHT. SO WHAT DOES **MY** TOTALLY ORIGINAL EFFORT GET? A ROW OF QUESTION MARKS.
NOT JUST. SHE ALSO MANAGED, SOMEHOW, TO **DRAW** AN EXASPERATED SIGH.
I ACTUALLY BET SHE'S PRETTY GOOD AT PICTIONARY.
SIMPSON

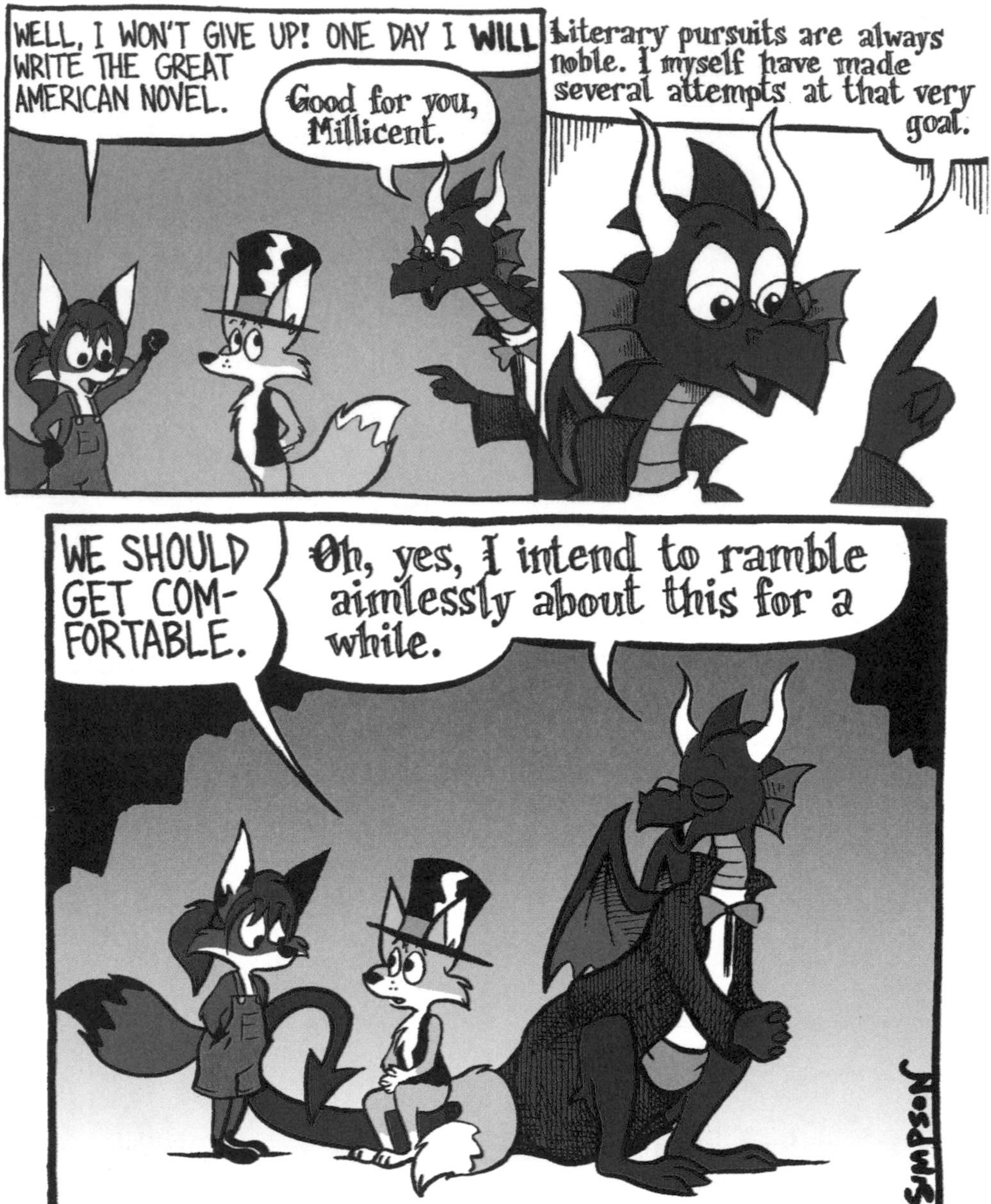
WELL, I WON'T GIVE UP! ONE DAY I WILL WRITE THE GREAT AMERICAN NOVEL.
Good for you, Millicent.
Literary pursuits are always noble. I myself have made several attempts at that very goal.
WE SHOULD GET COM-FORTABLE.
Oh, yes, I intend to ramble aimlessly about this for a while.
SIMPSON

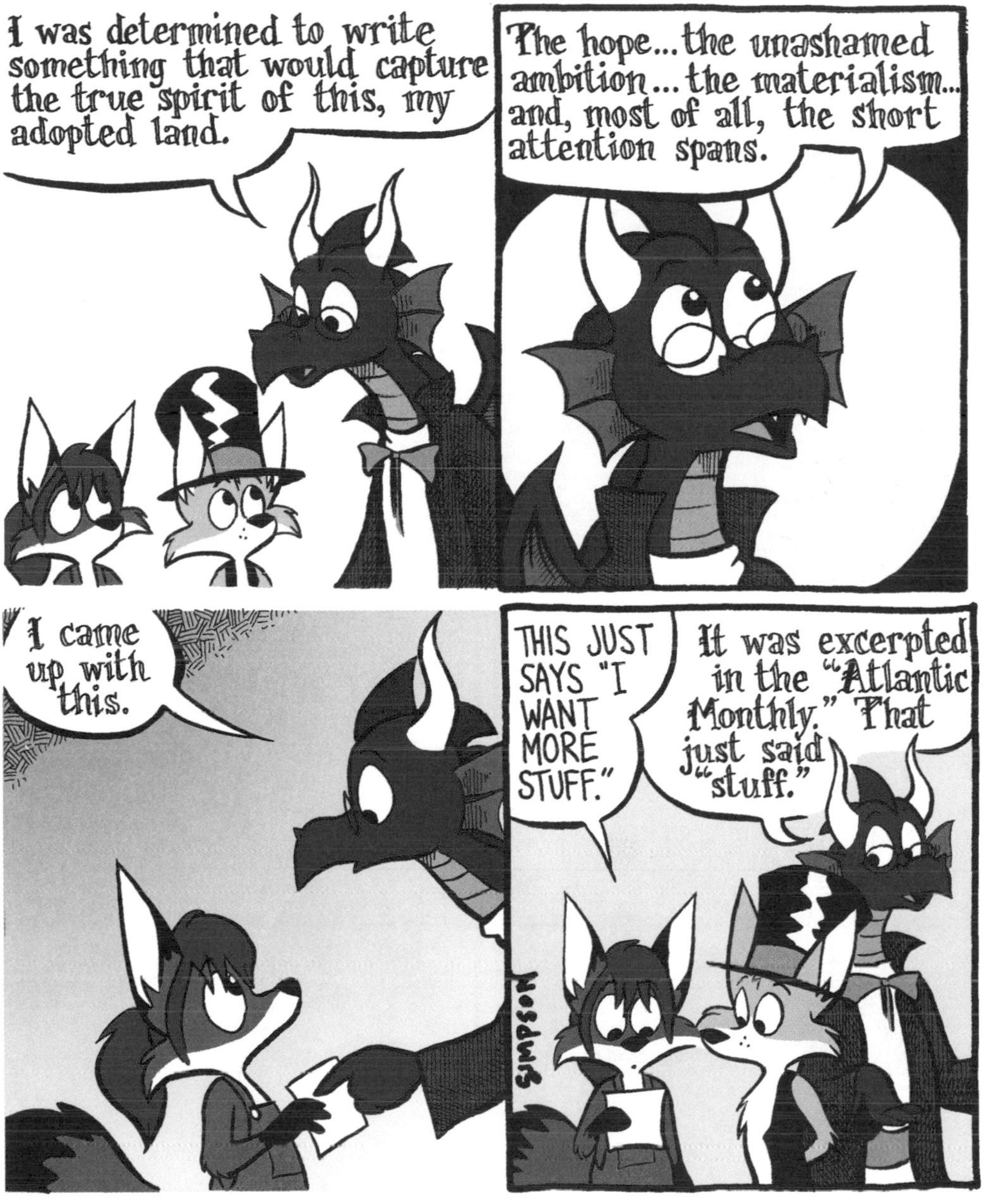
I was determined to write something that would capture the true spirit of this, my adopted land.
The hope... the unashamed ambition... the materialism... and, most of all, the short attention spans.
I came up with this.
THIS JUST SAYS "I WANT MORE STUFF."
It was excerpted in the "Atlantic Monthly." That just said "stuff."
SIMPSON

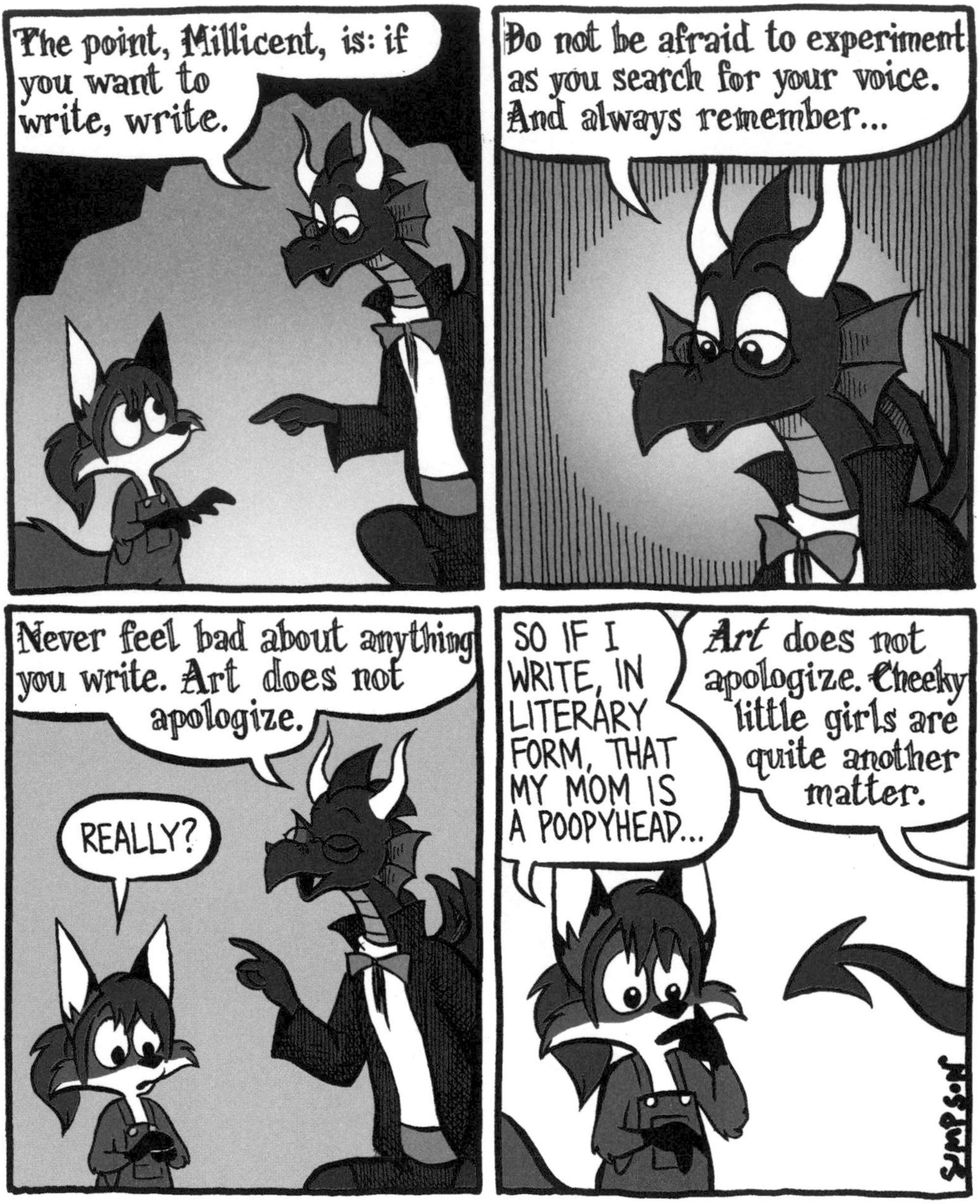
The point, Millicent, is: if you want to write, write.
Do not be afraid to experiment as you search for your voice. And always remember...
Never feel bad about anything you write. Art does not apologize.
REALLY?
SO IF I WRITE, IN LITERARY FORM, THAT MY MOM IS A POOPYHEAD...
Art does not apologize. Cheeky little girls are quite another matter.
SIMPSON

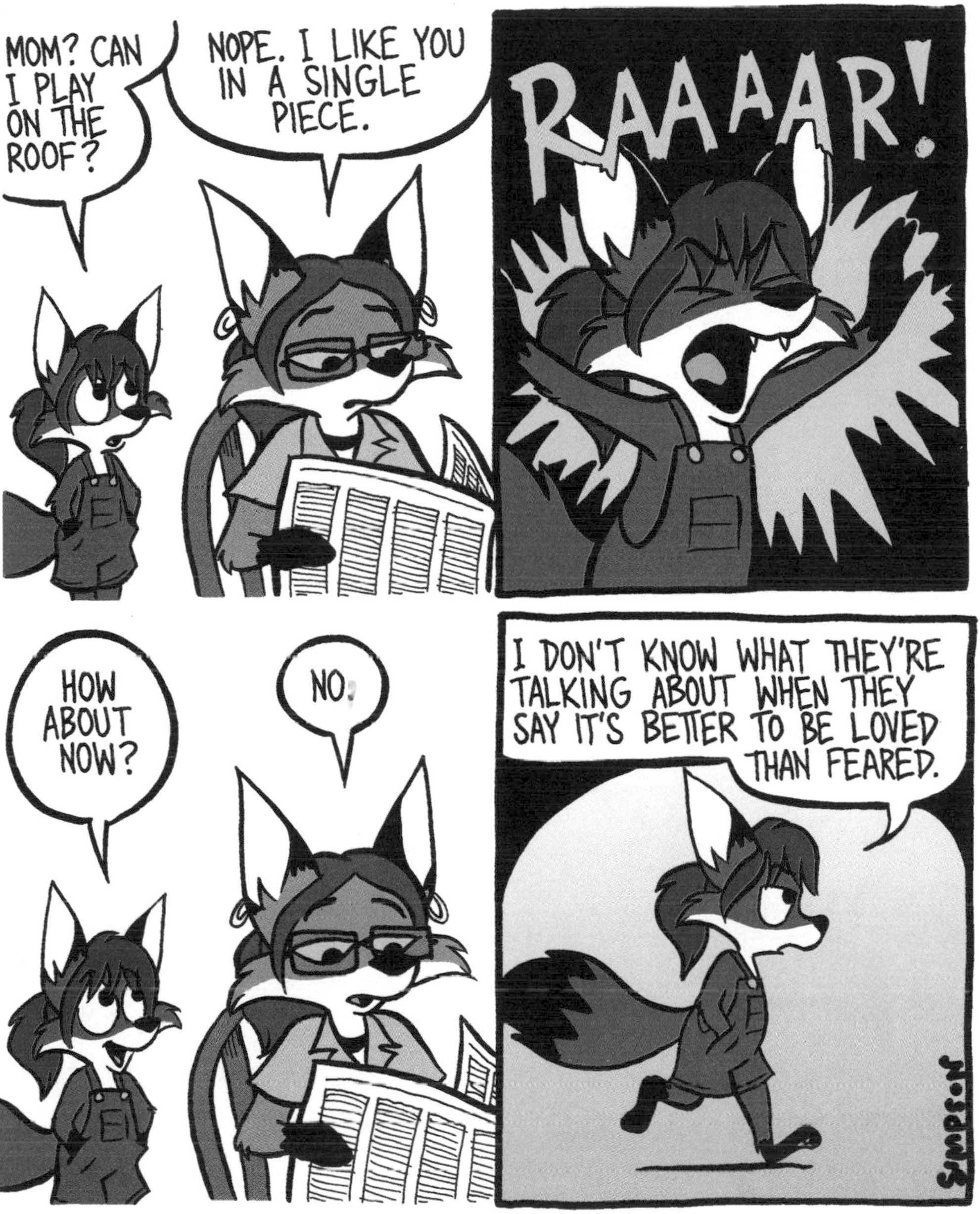
MOM? CAN I PLAY ON THE ROOF?
NOPE. I LIKE YOU IN A SINGLE PIECE.
RAAAAR!
HOW ABOUT NOW?
NO.
I DON'T KNOW WHAT THEY'RE TALKING ABOUT WHEN THEY SAY IT'S BETTER TO BE LOVED THAN FEARED.
SIMPSON

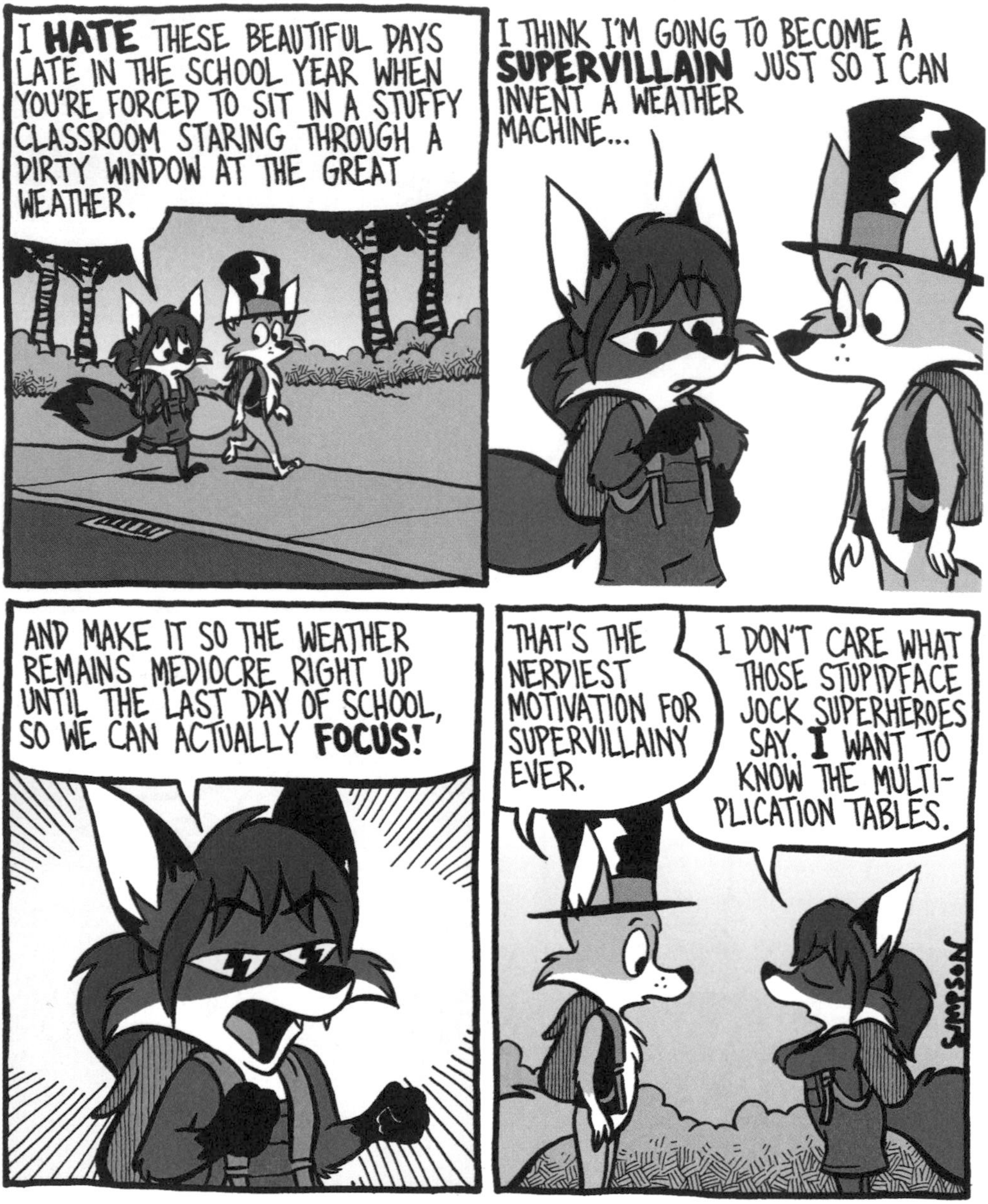
I **HATE** THESE BEAUTIFUL DAYS LATE IN THE SCHOOL YEAR WHEN YOU'RE FORCED TO SIT IN A STUFFY CLASSROOM STARING THROUGH A DIRTY WINDOW AT THE GREAT WEATHER.
I THINK I'M GOING TO BECOME A **SUPERVILLAIN** JUST SO I CAN INVENT A WEATHER MACHINE...
AND MAKE IT SO THE WEATHER REMAINS MEDIOCRE RIGHT UP UNTIL THE LAST DAY OF SCHOOL, SO WE CAN ACTUALLY **FOCUS**!
THAT'S THE NERDIEST MOTIVATION FOR SUPERVILLAINY EVER.
I DON'T CARE WHAT THOSE STUPIDFACE JOCK SUPERHEROES SAY. **I** WANT TO KNOW THE MULTI-PLICATION TABLES.
SIMPSON

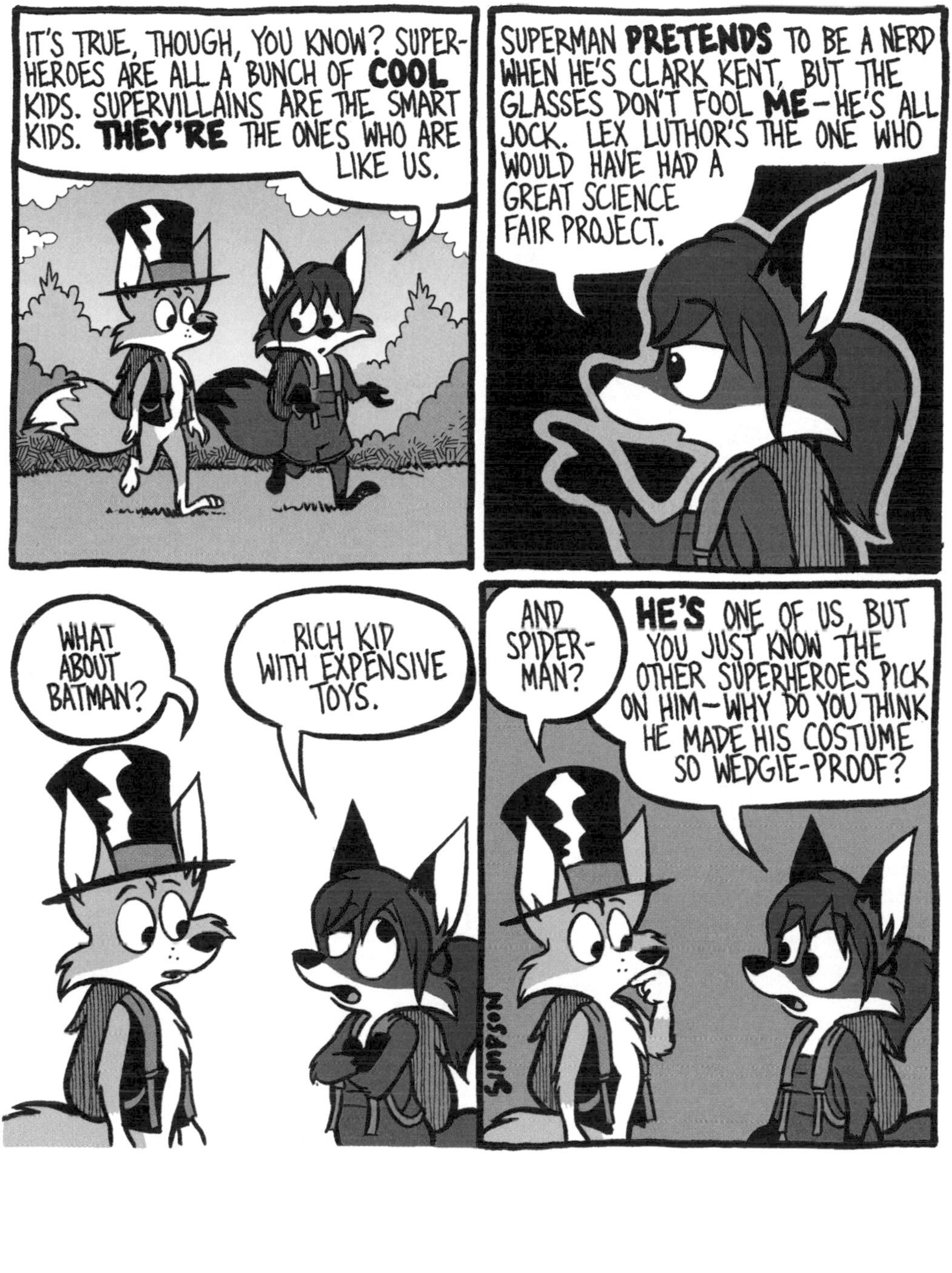
IT'S TRUE, THOUGH, YOU KNOW? SUPERHEROES ARE ALL A BUNCH OF **COOL** KIDS. SUPERVILLAINS ARE THE SMART KIDS. **THEY'RE** THE ONES WHO ARE LIKE US.
SUPERMAN **PRETENDS** TO BE A NERD WHEN HE'S CLARK KENT, BUT THE GLASSES DON'T FOOL **ME**—HE'S ALL JOCK. LEX LUTHOR'S THE ONE WHO WOULD HAVE HAD A GREAT SCIENCE FAIR PROJECT.
WHAT ABOUT BATMAN?
RICH KID WITH EXPENSIVE TOYS.
AND SPIDER-MAN?
HE'S ONE OF US, BUT YOU JUST KNOW THE OTHER SUPERHEROES PICK ON HIM—WHY DO YOU THINK HE MADE HIS COSTUME SO WEDGIE-PROOF?
SIMPSON

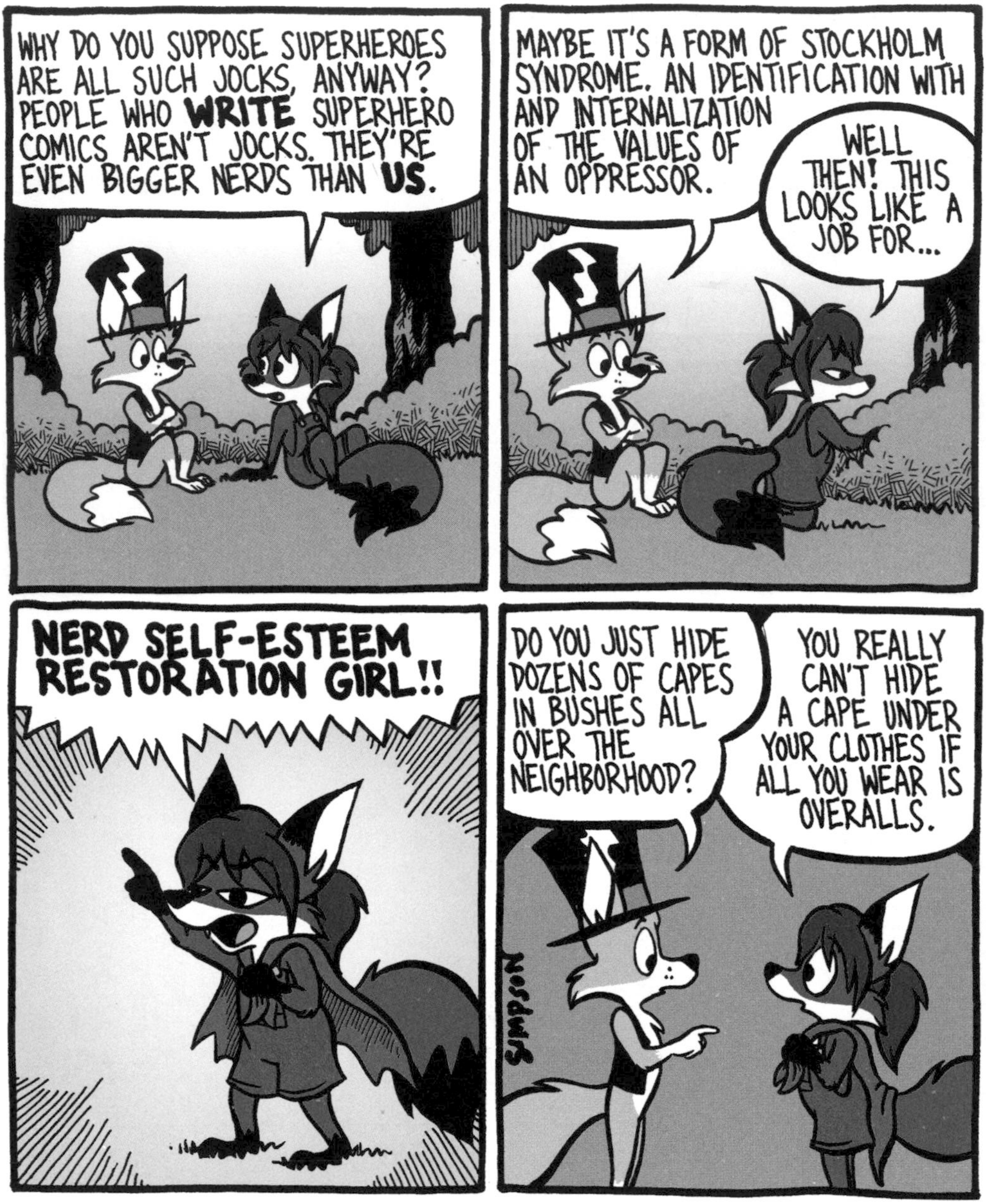
WHY DO YOU SUPPOSE SUPERHEROES ARE ALL SUCH JOCKS, ANYWAY? PEOPLE WHO **WRITE** SUPERHERO COMICS AREN'T JOCKS. THEY'RE EVEN BIGGER NERDS THAN **US**.
MAYBE IT'S A FORM OF STOCKHOLM SYNDROME. AN IDENTIFICATION WITH AND INTERNALIZATION OF THE VALUES OF AN OPPRESSOR.
WELL THEN! THIS LOOKS LIKE A JOB FOR...
NERD SELF-ESTEEM RESTORATION GIRL!!
DO YOU JUST HIDE DOZENS OF CAPES IN BUSHES ALL OVER THE NEIGHBORHOOD?
YOU REALLY CAN'T HIDE A CAPE UNDER YOUR CLOTHES IF ALL YOU WEAR IS OVERALLS.
SIMPSON

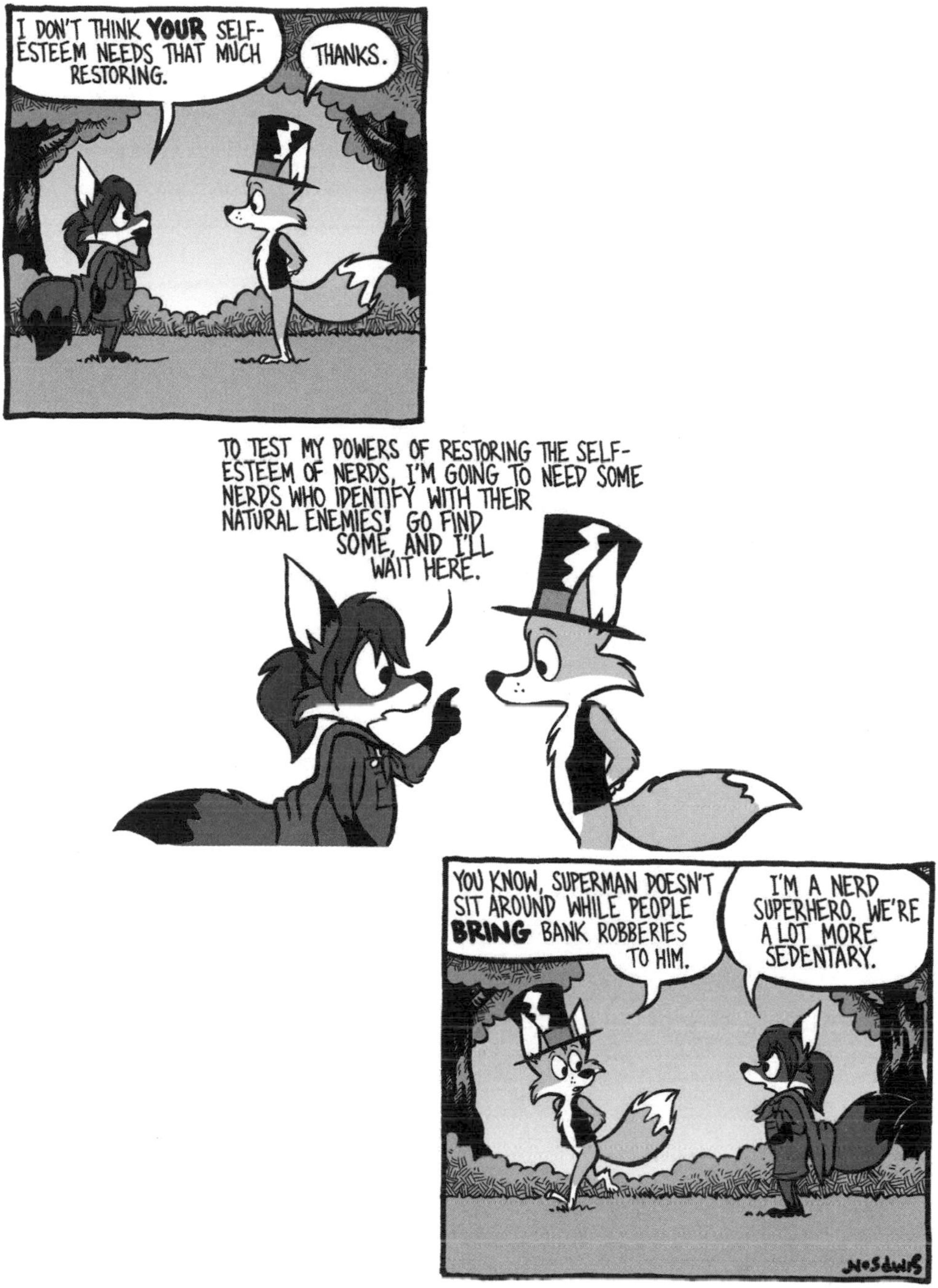
I DON'T THINK **YOUR** SELF-ESTEEM NEEDS THAT MUCH RESTORING.
THANKS.
TO TEST MY POWERS OF RESTORING THE SELF-ESTEEM OF NERDS, I'M GOING TO NEED SOME NERDS WHO IDENTIFY WITH THEIR NATURAL ENEMIES! GO FIND SOME, AND I'LL WAIT HERE.
YOU KNOW, SUPERMAN DOESN'T SIT AROUND WHILE PEOPLE **BRING** BANK ROBBERIES TO HIM.
I'M A NERD SUPERHERO. WE'RE A LOT MORE SEDENTARY.

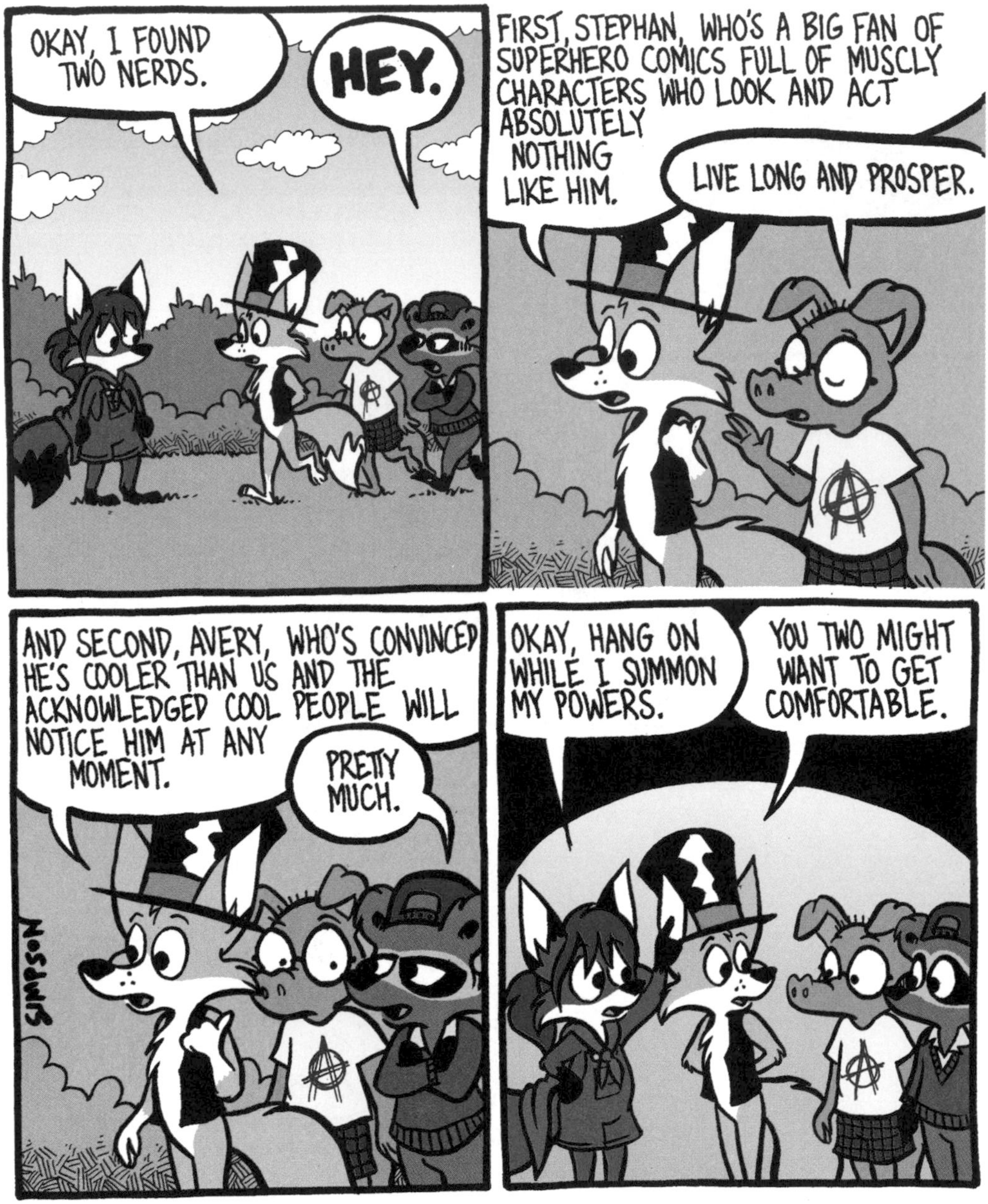
OKAY, I FOUND TWO NERDS.
HEY.
FIRST, STEPHAN, WHO'S A BIG FAN OF SUPERHERO COMICS FULL OF MUSCLY CHARACTERS WHO LOOK AND ACT ABSOLUTELY NOTHING LIKE HIM.
LIVE LONG AND PROSPER.
AND SECOND, AVERY, WHO'S CONVINCED HE'S COOLER THAN US AND THE ACKNOWLEDGED COOL PEOPLE WILL NOTICE HIM AT ANY MOMENT.
PRETTY MUCH.
SIMPSON
OKAY, HANG ON WHILE I SUMMON MY POWERS.
YOU TWO MIGHT WANT TO GET COMFORTABLE.

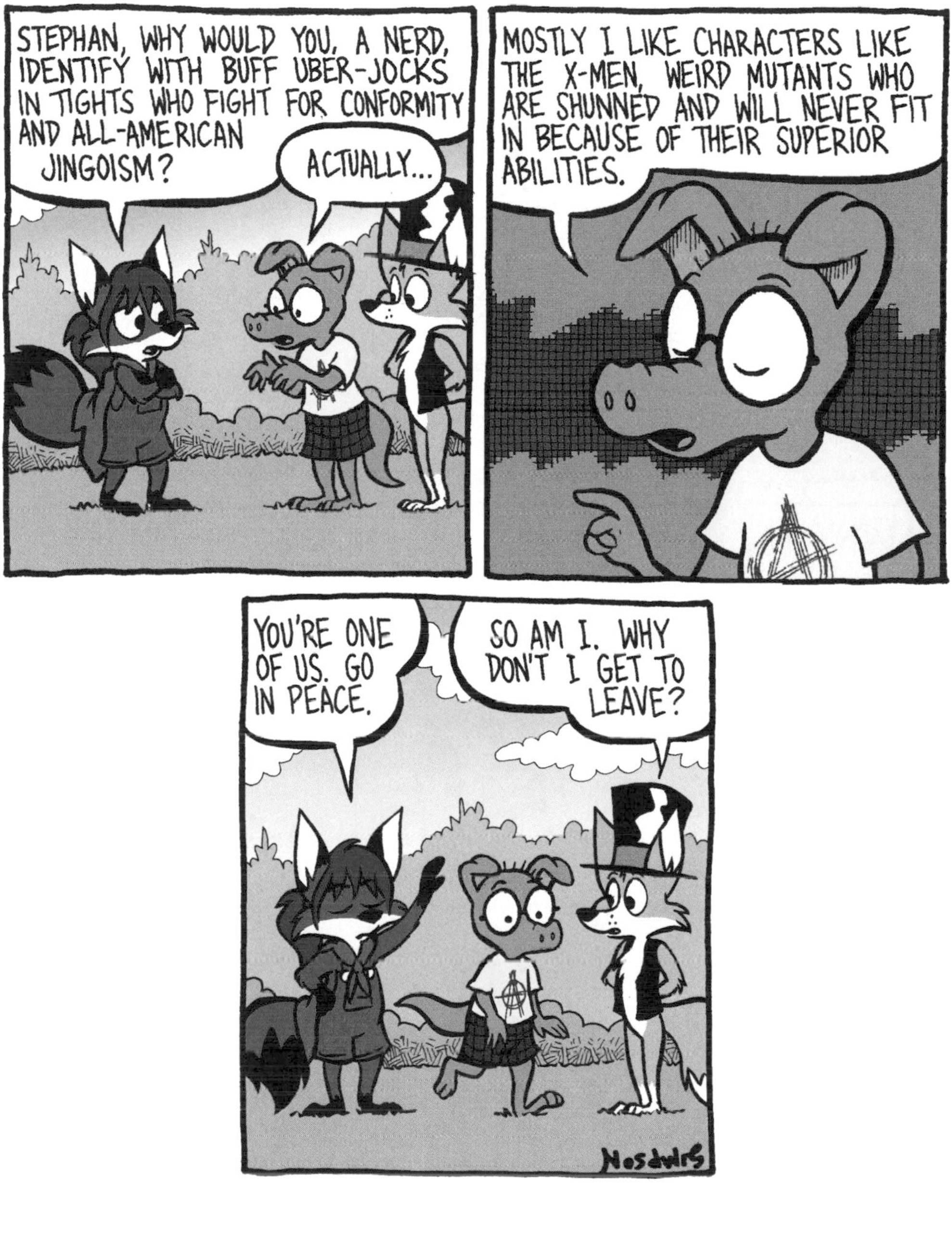
STEPHAN, WHY WOULD YOU, A NERD, IDENTIFY WITH BUFF UBER-JOCKS IN TIGHTS WHO FIGHT FOR CONFORMITY AND ALL-AMERICAN JINGOISM?
ACTUALLY...
MOSTLY I LIKE CHARACTERS LIKE THE X-MEN, WEIRD MUTANTS WHO ARE SHUNNED AND WILL NEVER FIT IN BECAUSE OF THEIR SUPERIOR ABILITIES.
YOU'RE ONE OF US. GO IN PEACE.
SO AM I. WHY DON'T I GET TO LEAVE?
Nosdwrs

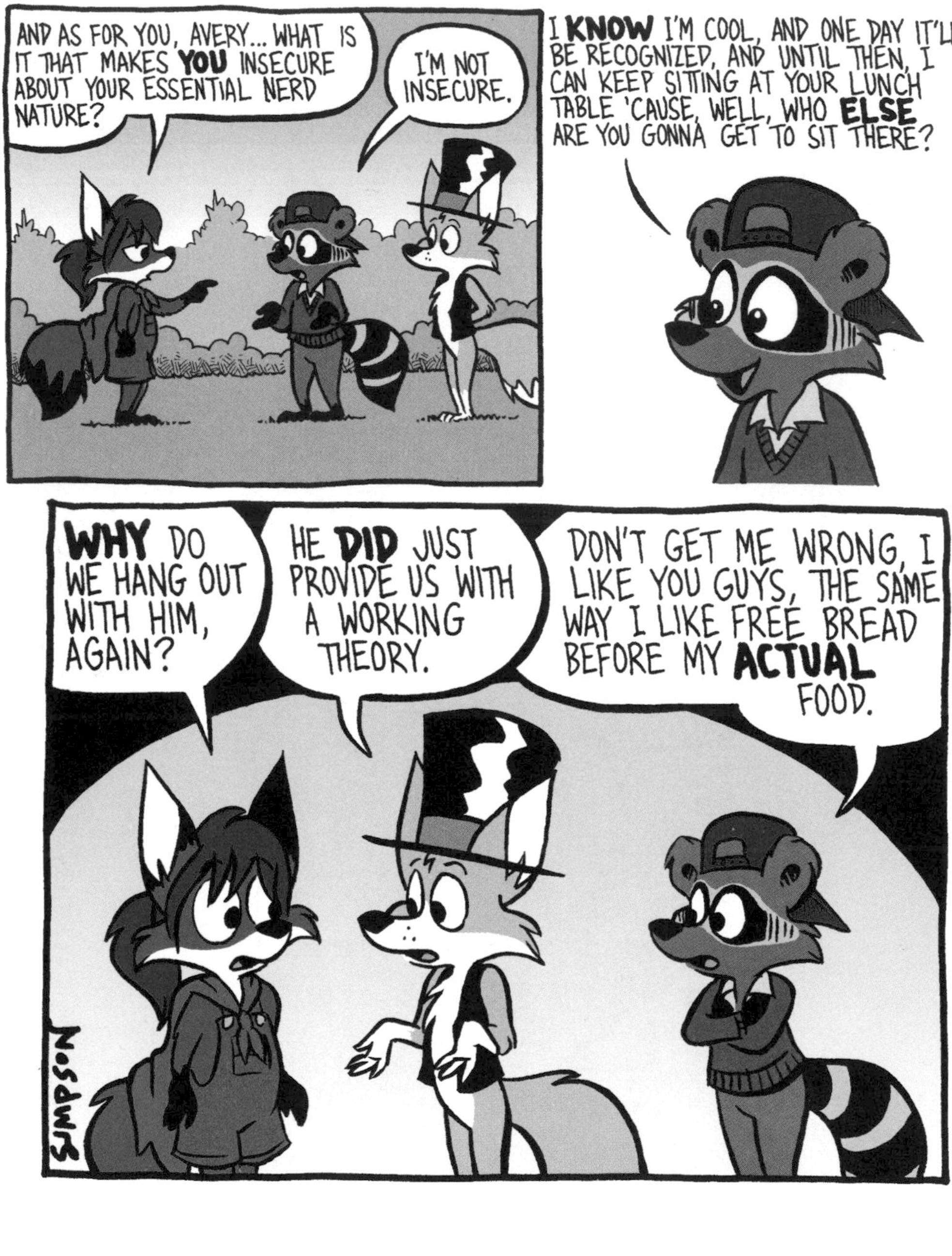
AND AS FOR YOU, AVERY... WHAT IS IT THAT MAKES YOU INSECURE ABOUT YOUR ESSENTIAL NERD NATURE?
I'M NOT INSECURE.
I KNOW I'M COOL, AND ONE DAY IT'LL BE RECOGNIZED, AND UNTIL THEN, I CAN KEEP SITTING AT YOUR LUNCH TABLE 'CAUSE, WELL, WHO ELSE ARE YOU GONNA GET TO SIT THERE?
WHY DO WE HANG OUT WITH HIM, AGAIN?
HE DID JUST PROVIDE US WITH A WORKING THEORY.
DON'T GET ME WRONG, I LIKE YOU GUYS, THE SAME WAY I LIKE FREE BREAD BEFORE MY ACTUAL FOOD.
SIMPSON

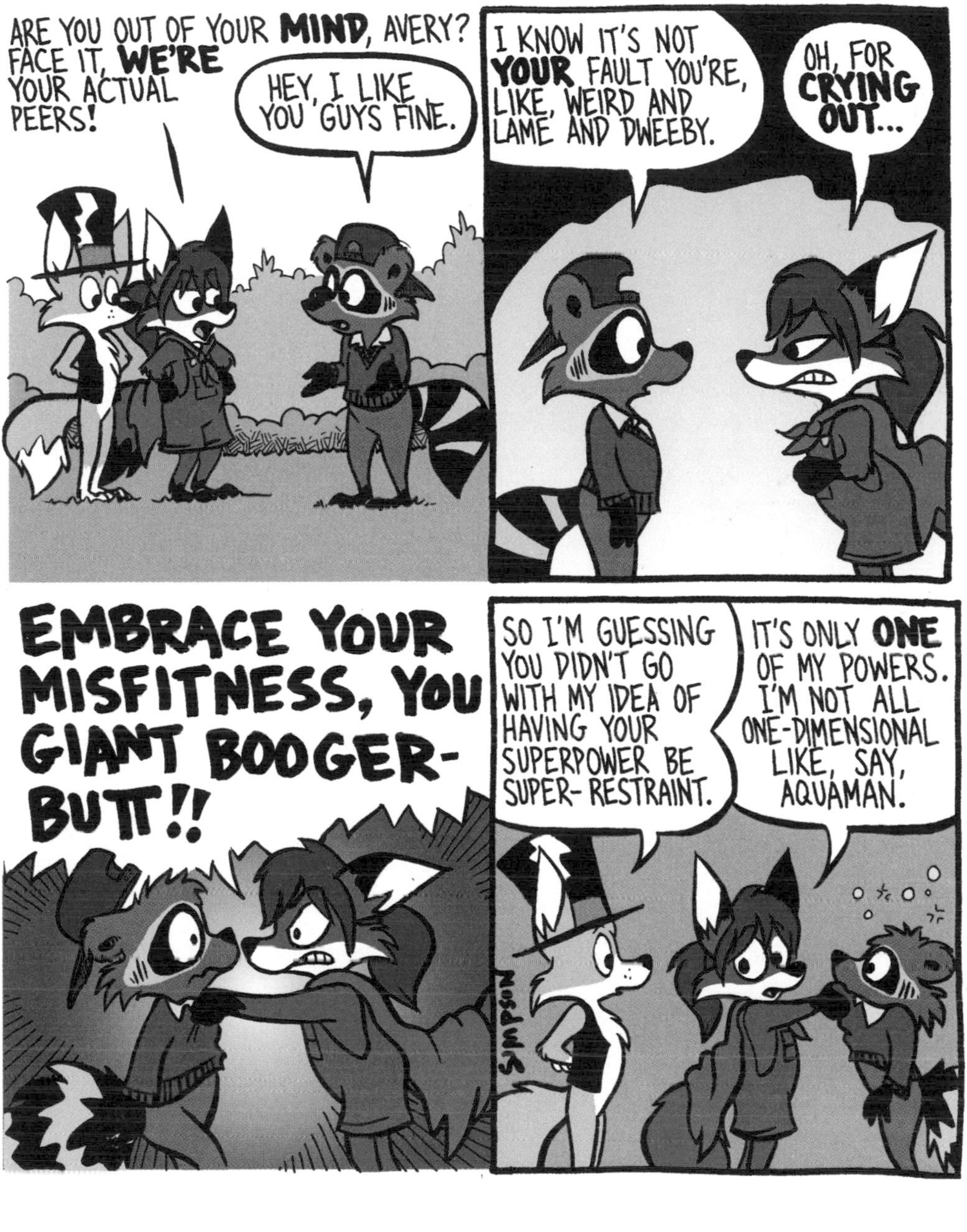
ARE YOU OUT OF YOUR **MIND**, AVERY? FACE IT, **WE'RE** YOUR ACTUAL PEERS!
HEY, I LIKE YOU GUYS FINE.
I KNOW IT'S NOT **YOUR** FAULT YOU'RE, LIKE, WEIRD AND LAME AND DWEEBY.
OH, FOR **CRYING OUT...**
EMBRACE YOUR MISFITNESS, YOU GIANT BOOGER-BUTT!!
SO I'M GUESSING YOU DIDN'T GO WITH MY IDEA OF HAVING YOUR SUPERPOWER BE SUPER-RESTRAINT.
IT'S ONLY **ONE** OF MY POWERS. I'M NOT ALL ONE-DIMENSIONAL LIKE, SAY, AQUAMAN.
SIMPSON

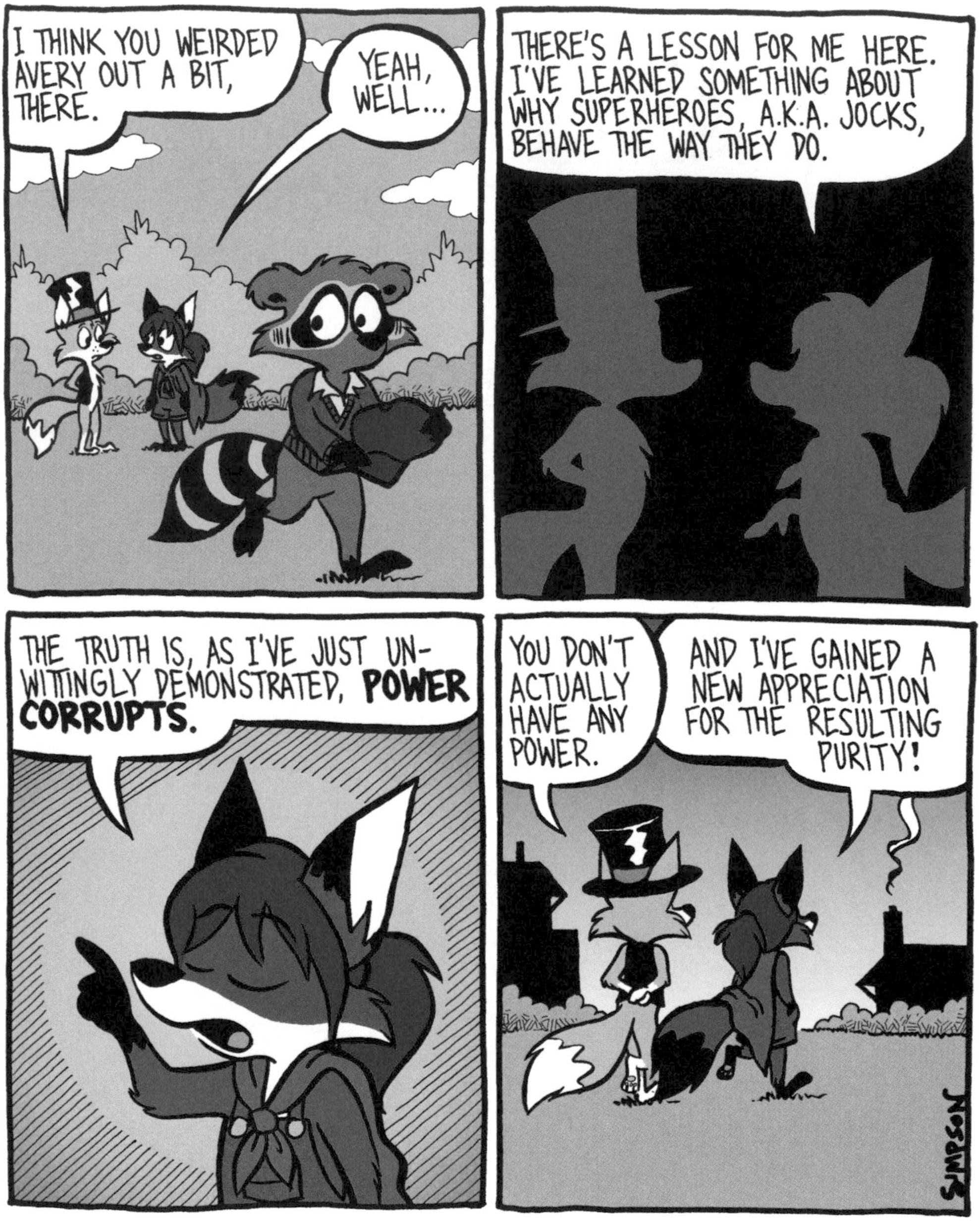
I THINK YOU WEIRDED AVERY OUT A BIT, THERE.
YEAH, WELL...
THERE'S A LESSON FOR ME HERE. I'VE LEARNED SOMETHING ABOUT WHY SUPERHEROES, A.K.A. JOCKS, BEHAVE THE WAY THEY DO.
THE TRUTH IS, AS I'VE JUST UNWITTINGLY DEMONSTRATED, **POWER CORRUPTS.**
YOU DON'T ACTUALLY HAVE ANY POWER.
AND I'VE GAINED A NEW APPRECIATION FOR THE RESULTING PURITY!
SIMPSON

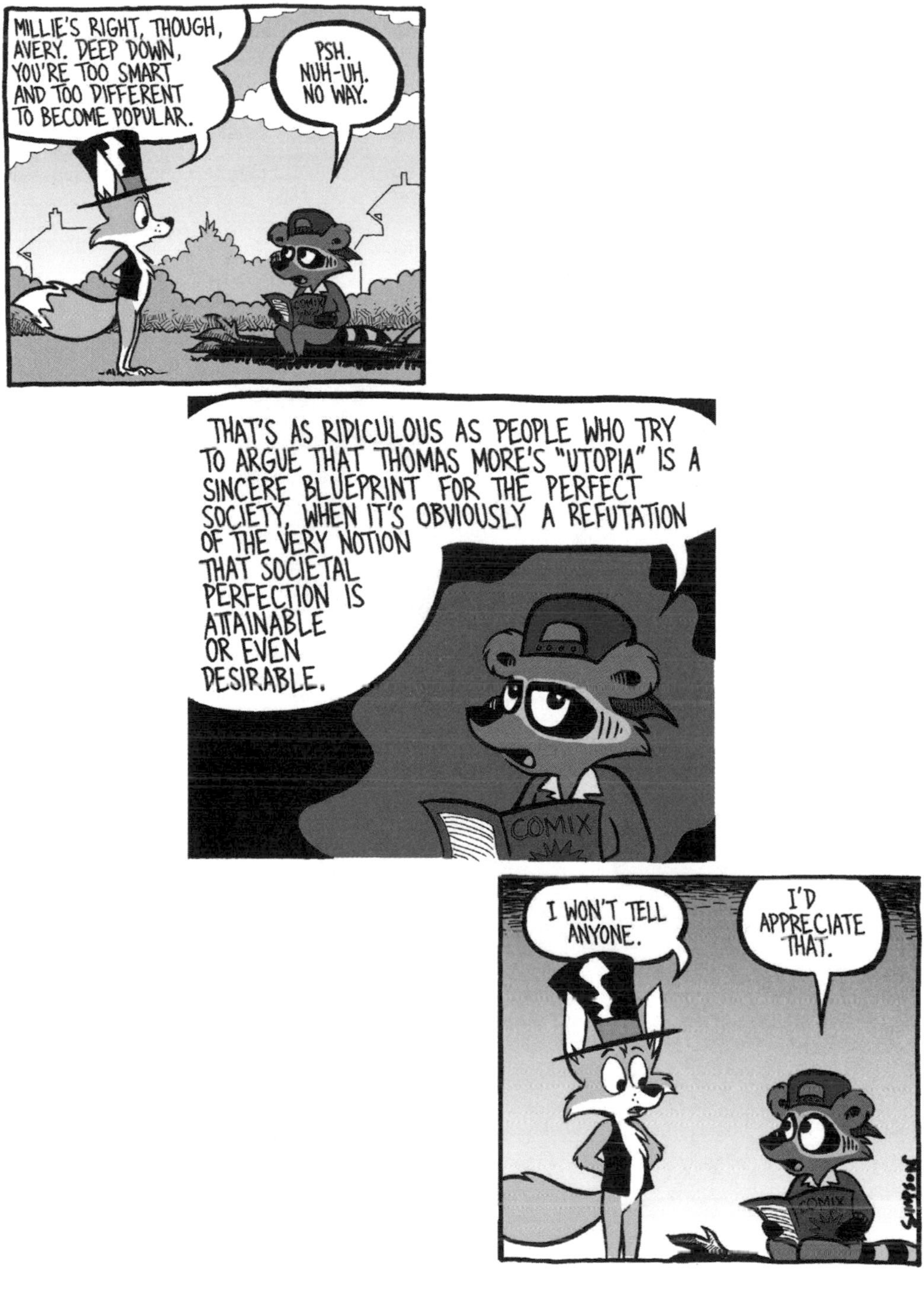
MILLIE'S RIGHT, THOUGH, AVERY. DEEP DOWN, YOU'RE TOO SMART AND TOO DIFFERENT TO BECOME POPULAR.
PSH. NUH-UH. NO WAY.
THAT'S AS RIDICULOUS AS PEOPLE WHO TRY TO ARGUE THAT THOMAS MORE'S "UTOPIA" IS A SINCERE BLUEPRINT FOR THE PERFECT SOCIETY, WHEN IT'S OBVIOUSLY A REFUTATION OF THE VERY NOTION THAT SOCIETAL PERFECTION IS ATTAINABLE OR EVEN DESIRABLE.
COMIX
I WON'T TELL ANYONE.
I'D APPRECIATE THAT.

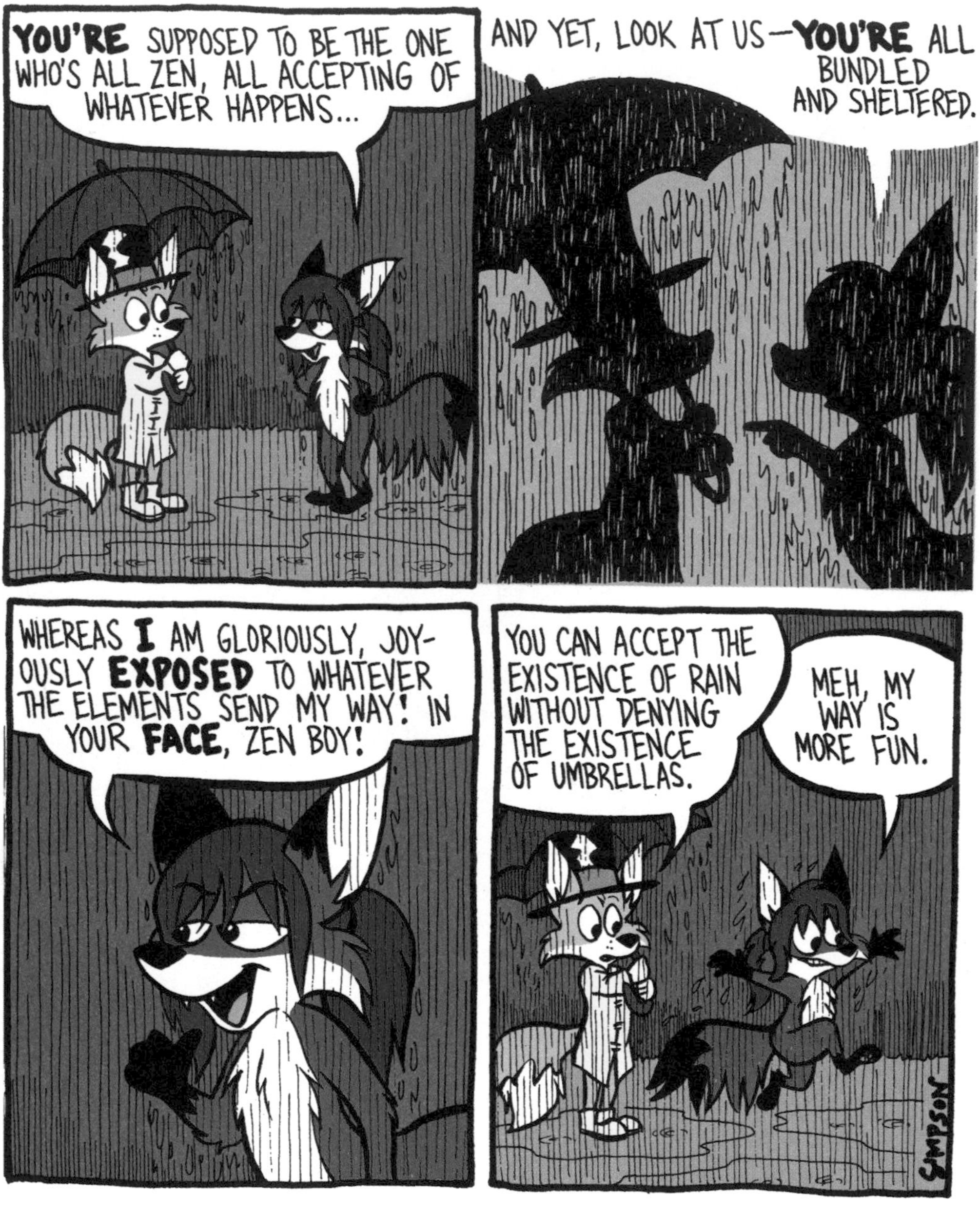
YOU'RE SUPPOSED TO BE THE ONE WHO'S ALL ZEN, ALL ACCEPTING OF WHATEVER HAPPENS...
AND YET, LOOK AT US—YOU'RE ALL BUNDLED AND SHELTERED.
WHEREAS I AM GLORIOUSLY, JOY-OUSLY EXPOSED TO WHATEVER THE ELEMENTS SEND MY WAY! IN YOUR FACE, ZEN BOY!
YOU CAN ACCEPT THE EXISTENCE OF RAIN WITHOUT DENYING THE EXISTENCE OF UMBRELLAS.
MEH, MY WAY IS MORE FUN.
SIMPSON

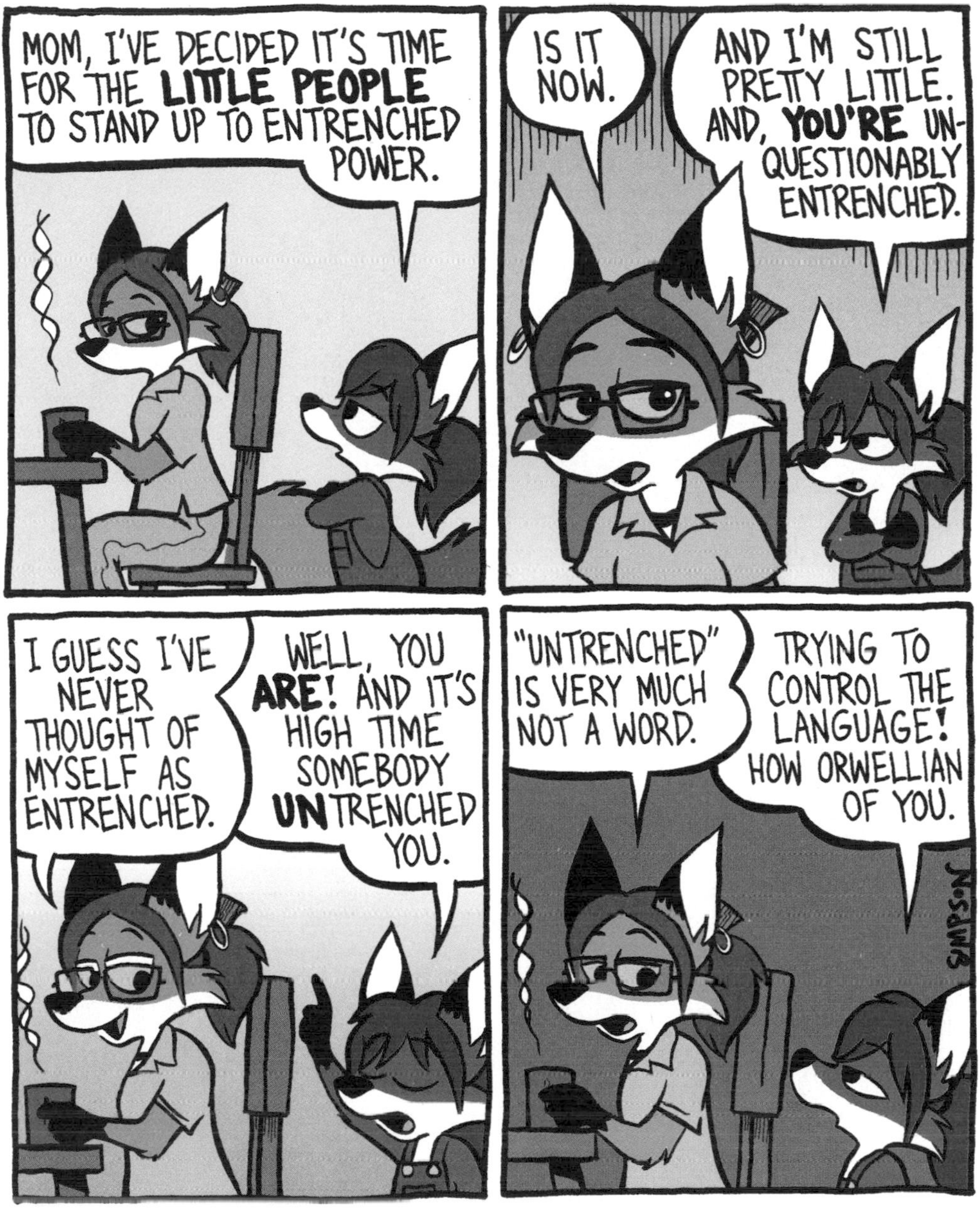
MOM, I'VE DECIDED IT'S TIME FOR THE **LITTLE PEOPLE** TO STAND UP TO ENTRENCHED POWER.
IS IT NOW.
AND I'M STILL PRETTY LITTLE. AND, **YOU'RE** UN-QUESTIONABLY ENTRENCHED.
I GUESS I'VE NEVER THOUGHT OF MYSELF AS ENTRENCHED.
WELL, YOU **ARE**! AND IT'S HIGH TIME SOMEBODY **UN**TRENCHED YOU.
"UNTRENCHED" IS VERY MUCH NOT A WORD.
TRYING TO CONTROL THE LANGUAGE! HOW ORWELLIAN OF YOU.
SIMPSON

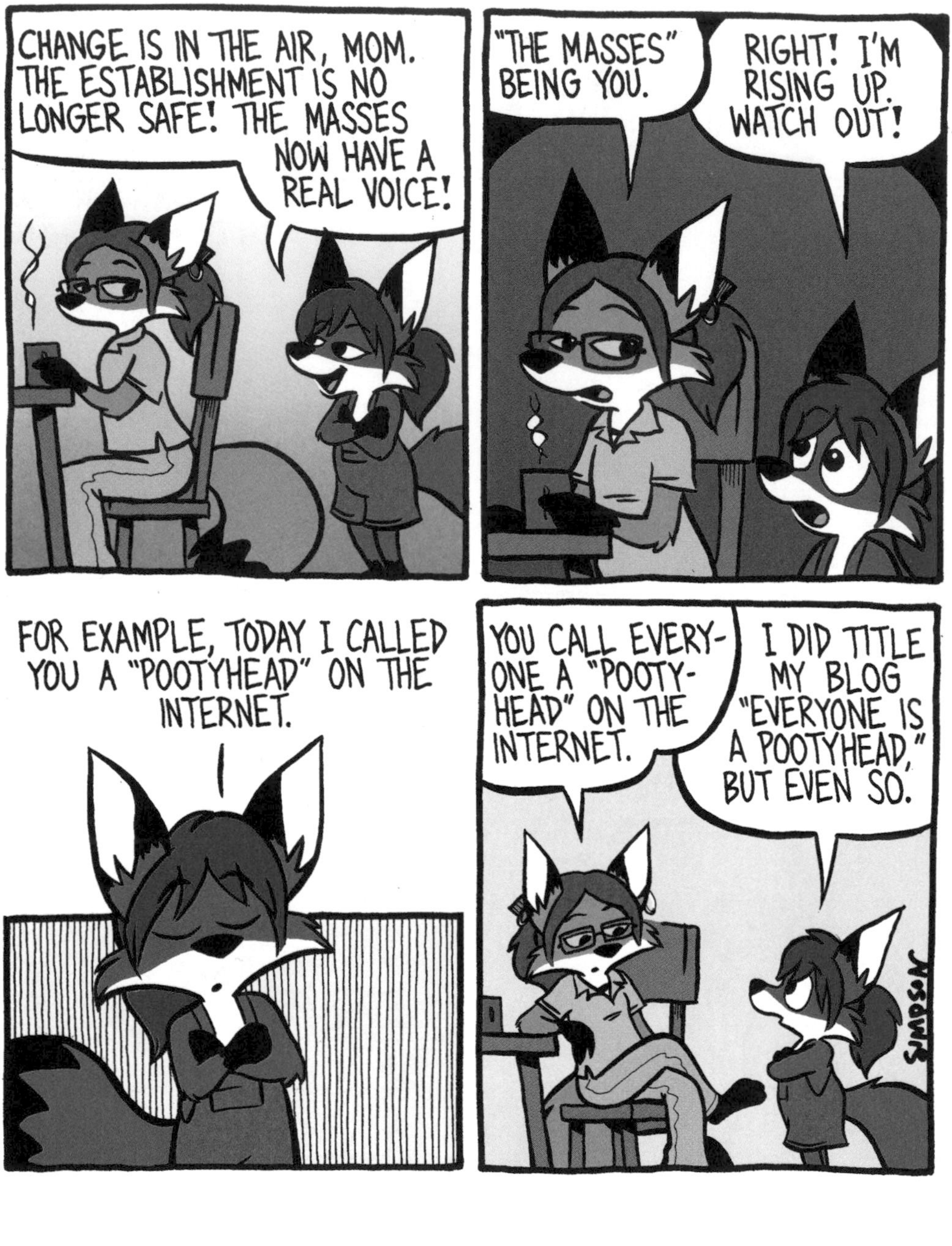
CHANGE IS IN THE AIR, MOM. THE ESTABLISHMENT IS NO LONGER SAFE! THE MASSES NOW HAVE A REAL VOICE!
"THE MASSES" BEING YOU.
RIGHT! I'M RISING UP. WATCH OUT!
FOR EXAMPLE, TODAY I CALLED YOU A "POOTYHEAD" ON THE INTERNET.
YOU CALL EVERY-ONE A "POOTY-HEAD" ON THE INTERNET.
I DID TITLE MY BLOG "EVERYONE IS A POOTYHEAD," BUT EVEN SO.
SIMPSON

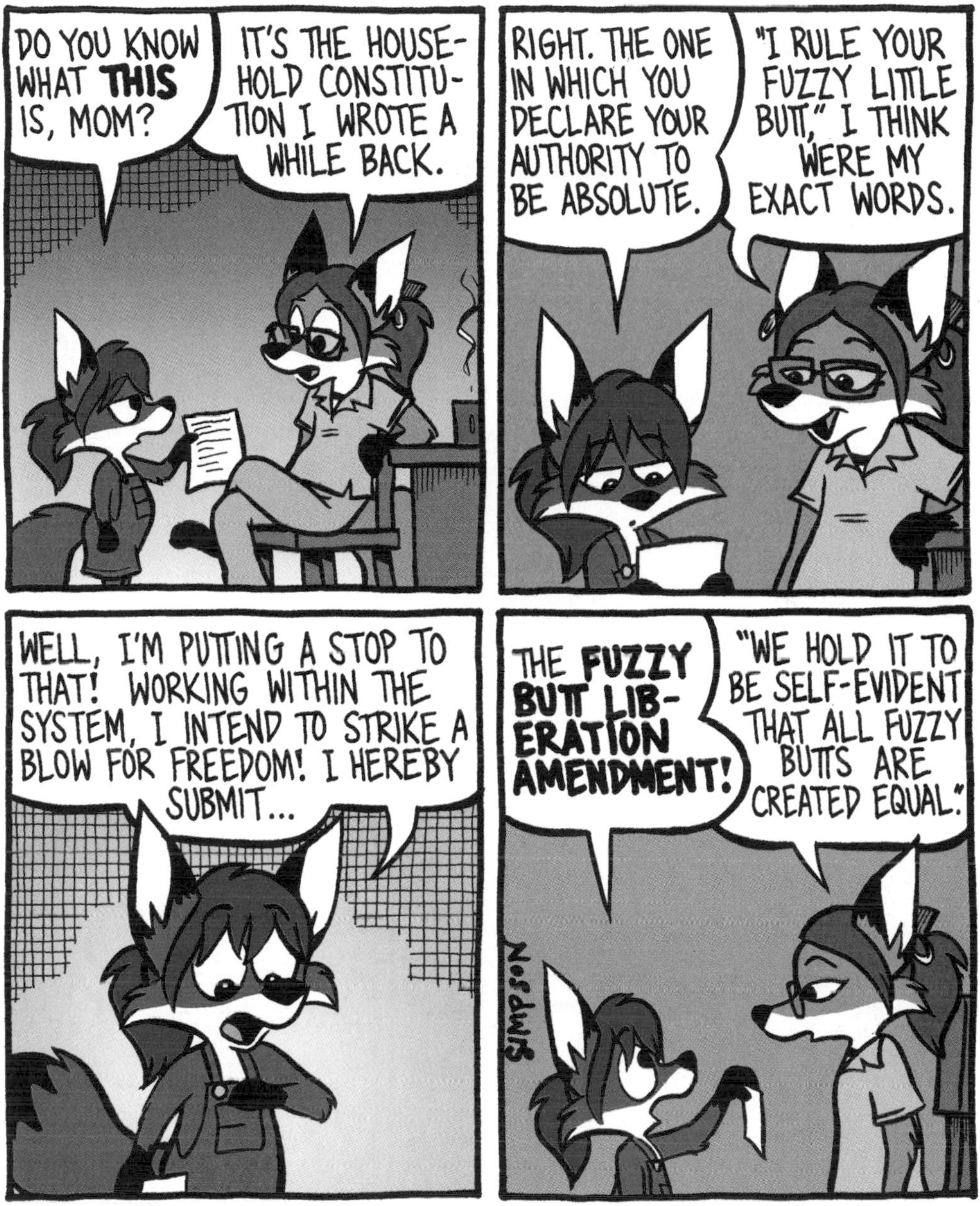
DO YOU KNOW WHAT **THIS** IS, MOM?
IT'S THE HOUSE-HOLD CONSTITU-TION I WROTE A WHILE BACK.
RIGHT. THE ONE IN WHICH YOU DECLARE YOUR AUTHORITY TO BE ABSOLUTE.
"I RULE YOUR FUZZY LITTLE BUTT," I THINK WERE MY EXACT WORDS.
WELL, I'M PUTTING A STOP TO THAT! WORKING WITHIN THE SYSTEM, I INTEND TO STRIKE A BLOW FOR FREEDOM! I HEREBY SUBMIT...
THE **FUZZY BUTT LIB-ERATION AMENDMENT!**
"WE HOLD IT TO BE SELF-EVIDENT THAT ALL FUZZY BUTTS ARE CREATED EQUAL."
SIMPSON

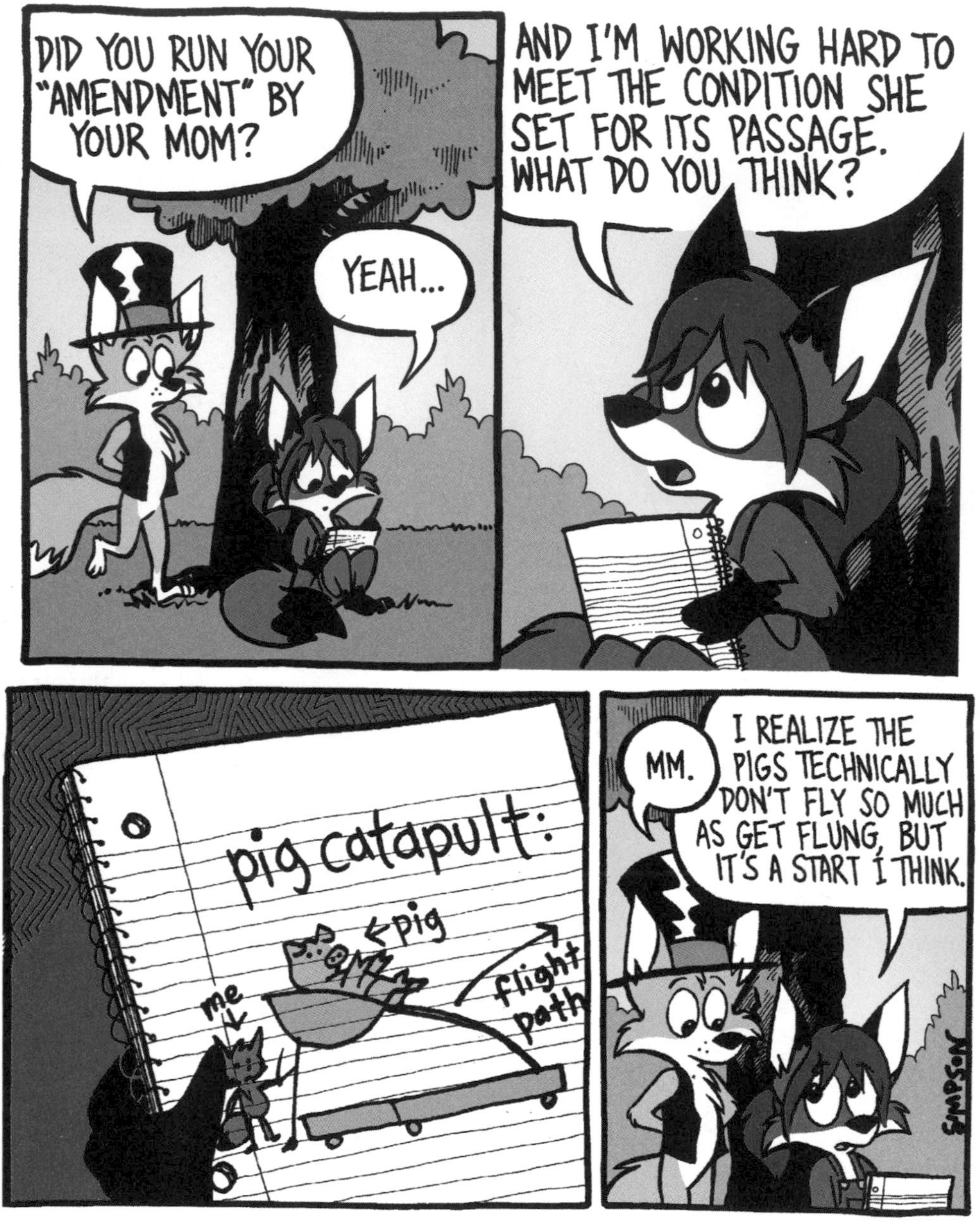
DID YOU RUN YOUR "AMENDMENT" BY YOUR MOM?
YEAH...
AND I'M WORKING HARD TO MEET THE CONDITION SHE SET FOR ITS PASSAGE. WHAT DO YOU THINK?
pig catapult:
pig
me
flight path
MM.
I REALIZE THE PIGS TECHNICALLY DON'T FLY SO MUCH AS GET FLUNG, BUT IT'S A START I THINK.
SIMPSON

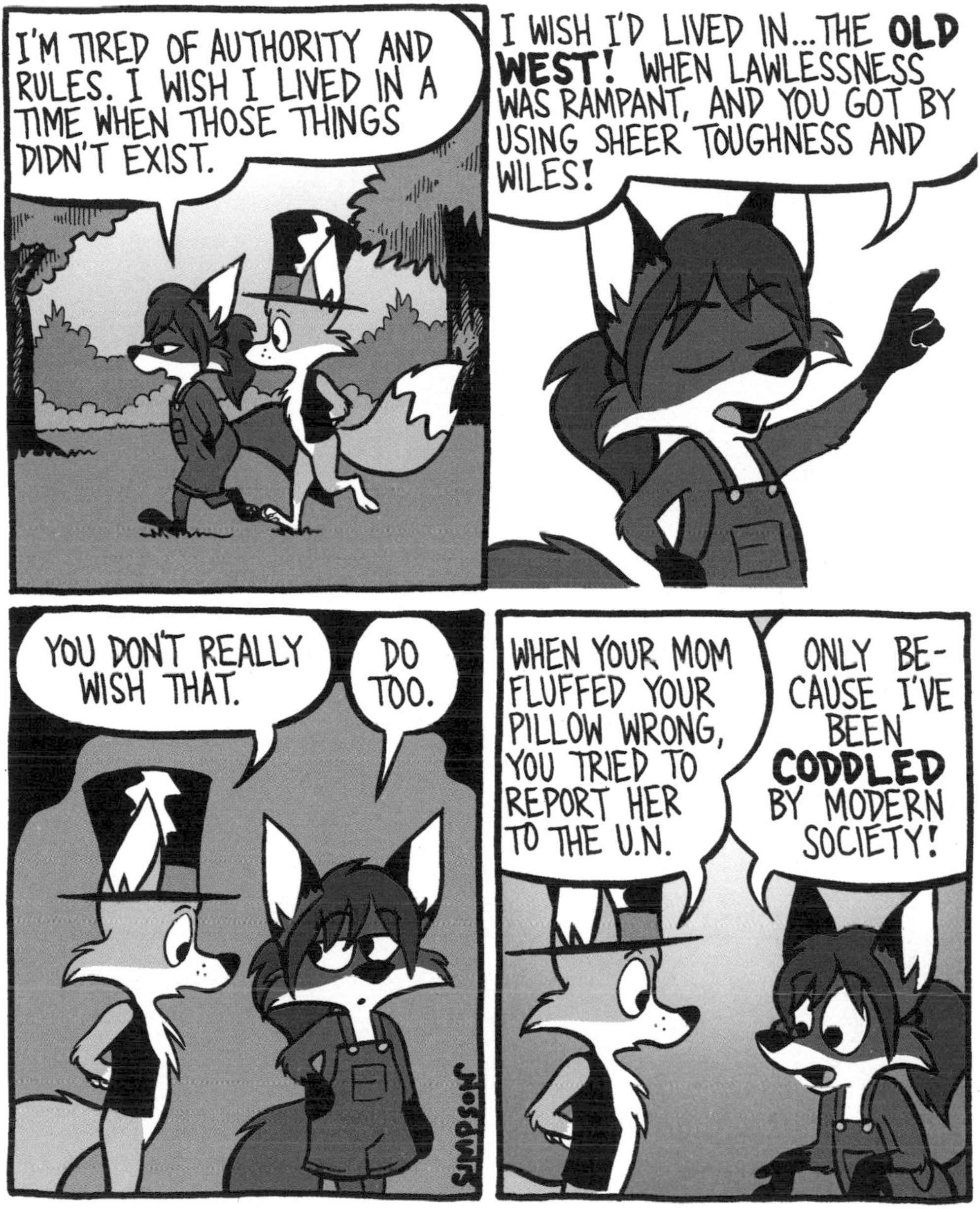
I'M TIRED OF AUTHORITY AND RULES. I WISH I LIVED IN A TIME WHEN THOSE THINGS DIDN'T EXIST.
I WISH I'D LIVED IN...THE OLD WEST! WHEN LAWLESSNESS WAS RAMPANT, AND YOU GOT BY USING SHEER TOUGHNESS AND WILES!
YOU DON'T REALLY WISH THAT.
DO TOO.
SIMPSON
WHEN YOUR MOM FLUFFED YOUR PILLOW WRONG, YOU TRIED TO REPORT HER TO THE U.N.
ONLY BE-CAUSE I'VE BEEN CODDLED BY MODERN SOCIETY!

WHY **DO** WE ROMANTICIZE FAR MORE DANGEROUS TIMES IN HISTORY, I WONDER?

THE OLD WEST...THE DAYS OF PIRATES...THE PIONEER DAYS. TIMES WHEN YOU WERE MUCH MORE LIKELY TO BE SUDDENLY STRUCK DOWN BY VIOLENCE OR DISEASE.

LIFE IS...ALMOST **UNQUESTIONABLY** BETTER NOW! BUT WE FIND OURSELVES **LONGING** FOR THE DEADLY OLD DAYS. WHY DO WE ATTACH SUCH ROMANCE TO THEM?

THEY HAD COOLER HATS?

IN ALL HONESTY, THAT **WAS** WHY I ORIGINALLY STARTED HANGING AROUND **YOU**...

160

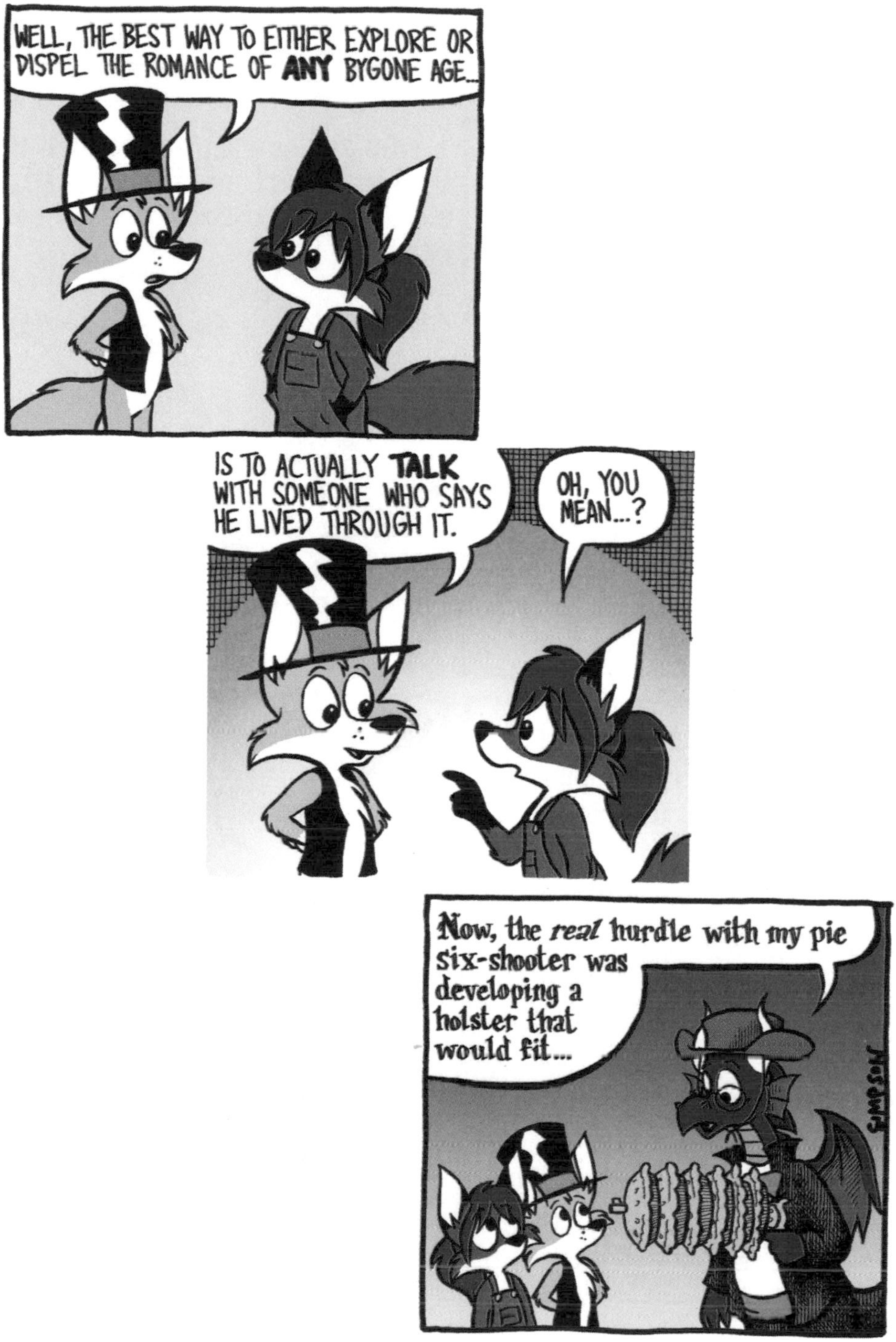
WELL, THE BEST WAY TO EITHER EXPLORE OR DISPEL THE ROMANCE OF **ANY** BYGONE AGE...
IS TO ACTUALLY **TALK** WITH SOMEONE WHO SAYS HE LIVED THROUGH IT.
OH, YOU MEAN...?
Now, the *real* hurdle with my pie six-shooter was developing a holster that would fit...
SIMPSON

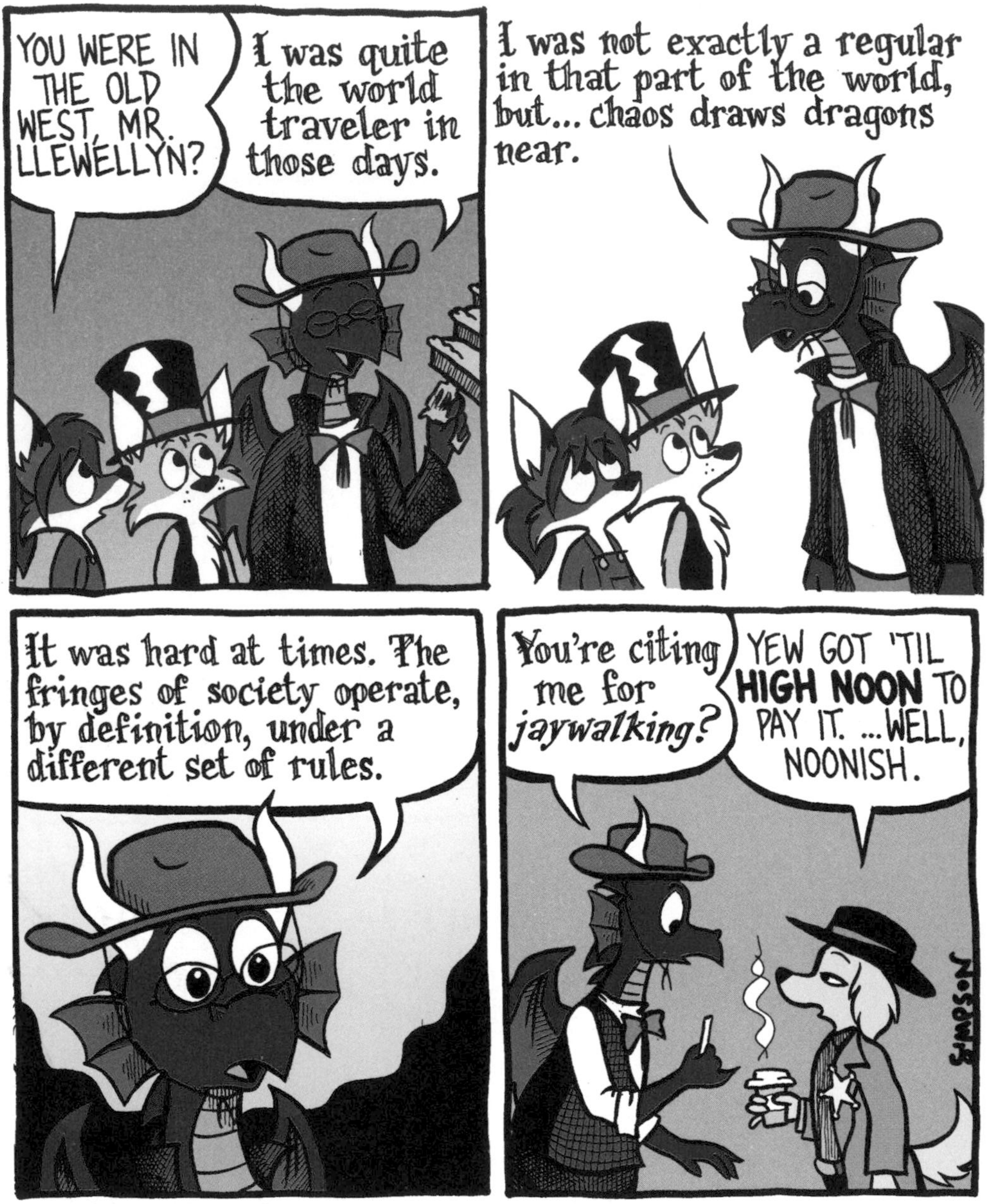
YOU WERE IN THE OLD WEST, MR. LLEWELLYN?
I was quite the world traveler in those days.
I was not exactly a regular in that part of the world, but... chaos draws dragons near.
It was hard at times. The fringes of society operate, by definition, under a different set of rules.
You're citing me for *jaywalking?*
YEW GOT 'TIL **HIGH NOON** TO PAY IT. ...WELL, NOONISH.
SIMPSON

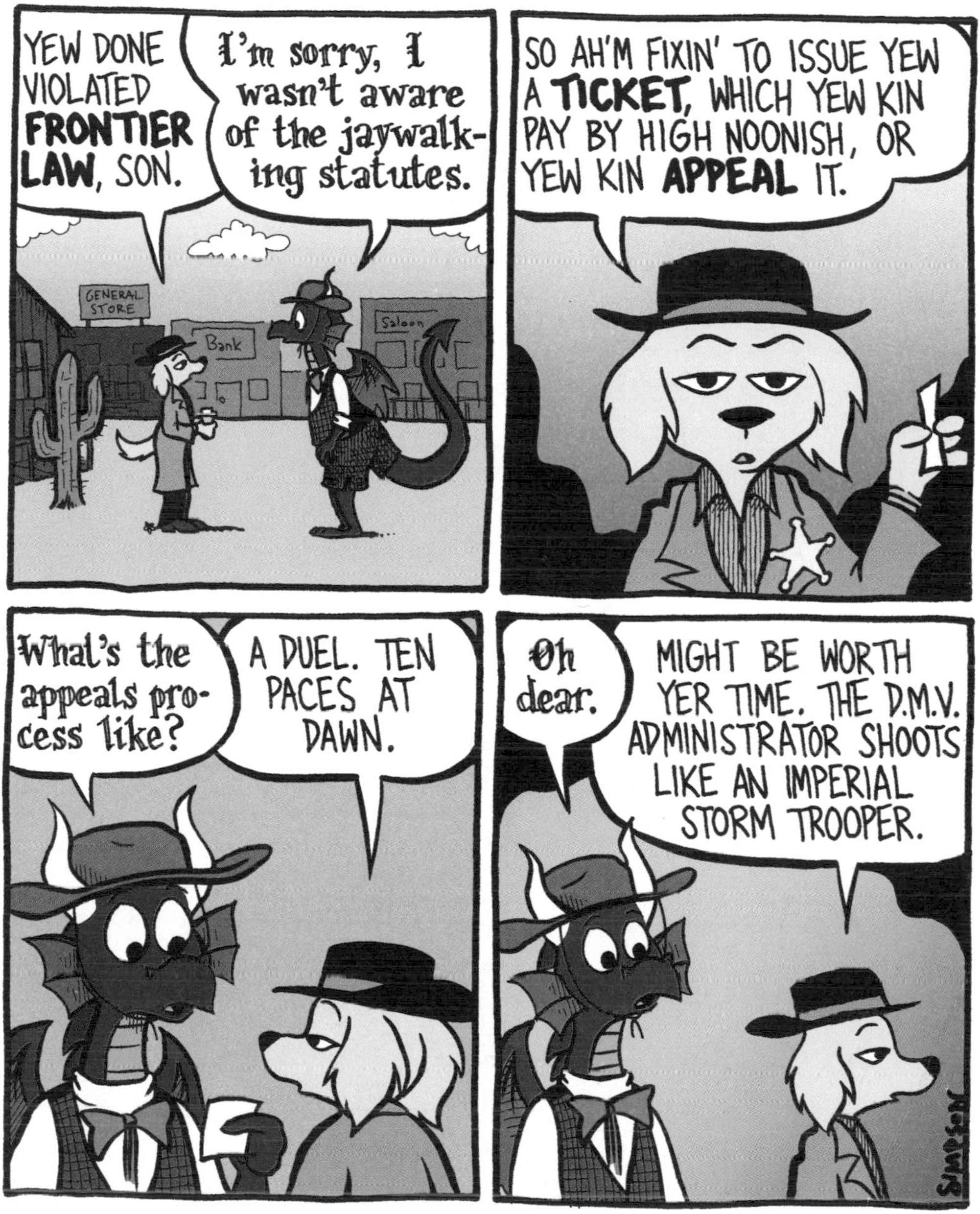
YEW DONE VIOLATED **FRONTIER LAW**, SON.
I'm sorry, I wasn't aware of the jaywalking statutes.
GENERAL STORE
Bank
Saloon
SO AH'M FIXIN' TO ISSUE YEW A **TICKET**, WHICH YEW KIN PAY BY HIGH NOONISH, OR YEW KIN **APPEAL** IT.
What's the appeals process like?
A DUEL. TEN PACES AT DAWN.
Oh dear.
MIGHT BE WORTH YER TIME. THE D.M.V. ADMINISTRATOR SHOOTS LIKE AN IMPERIAL STORM TROOPER.
SIMPSON

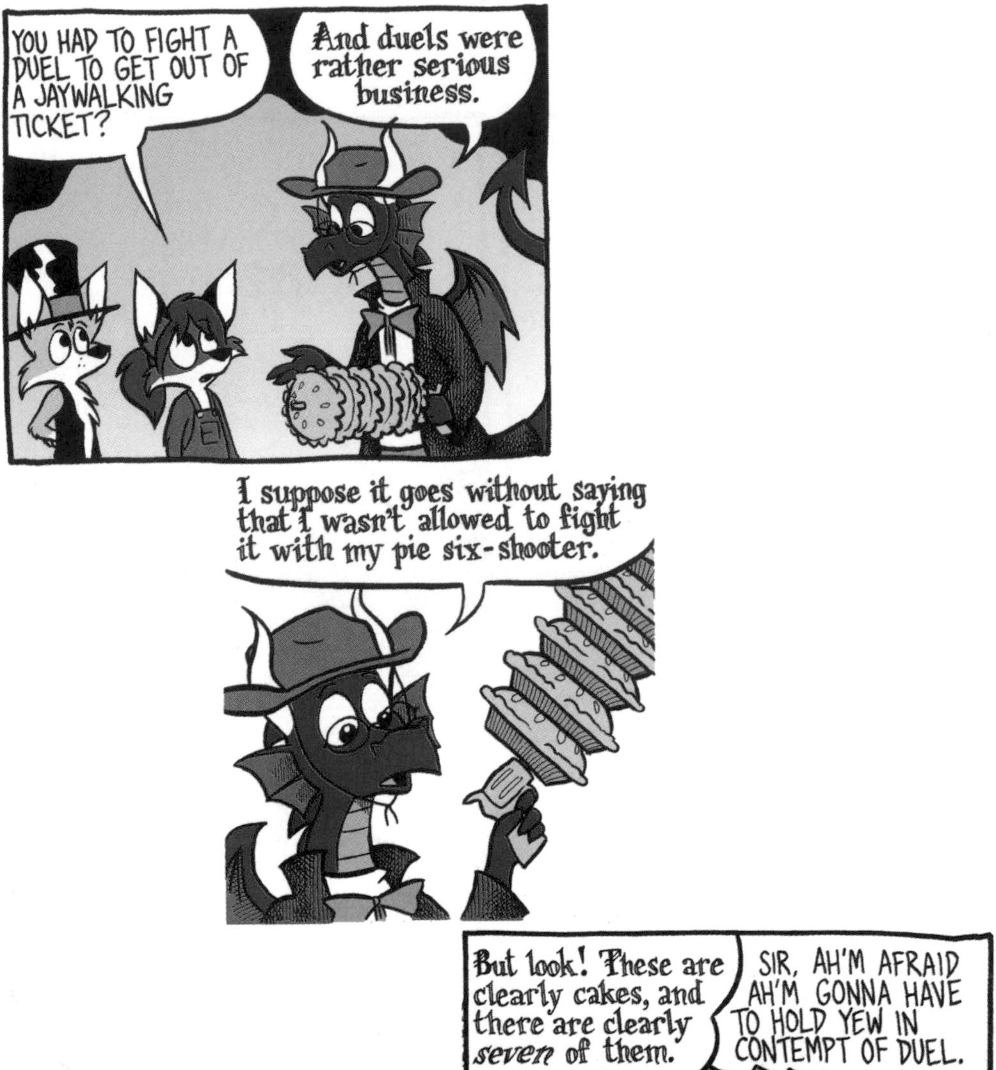
YOU HAD TO FIGHT A DUEL TO GET OUT OF A JAYWALKING TICKET?
And duels were rather serious business.
I suppose it goes without saying that I wasn't allowed to fight it with my pie six-shooter.
But look! These are clearly cakes, and there are clearly *seven* of them.
SIR, AH'M AFRAID AH'M GONNA HAVE TO HOLD YEW IN CONTEMPT OF DUEL.

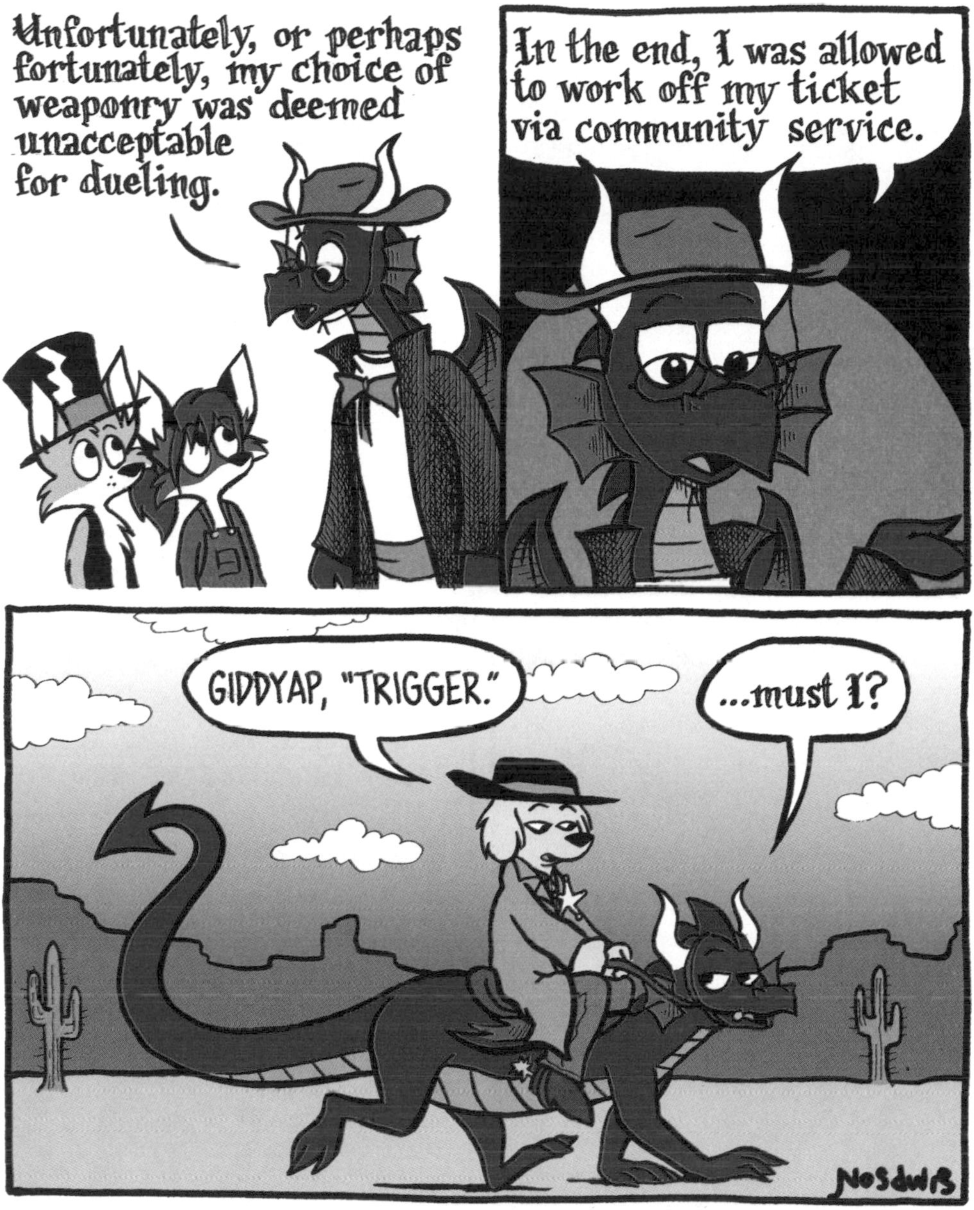
Unfortunately, or perhaps fortunately, my choice of weaponry was deemed unacceptable for dueling.
In the end, I was allowed to work off my ticket via community service.
GIDDYAP, "TRIGGER."
...must I?
NOSDWIS

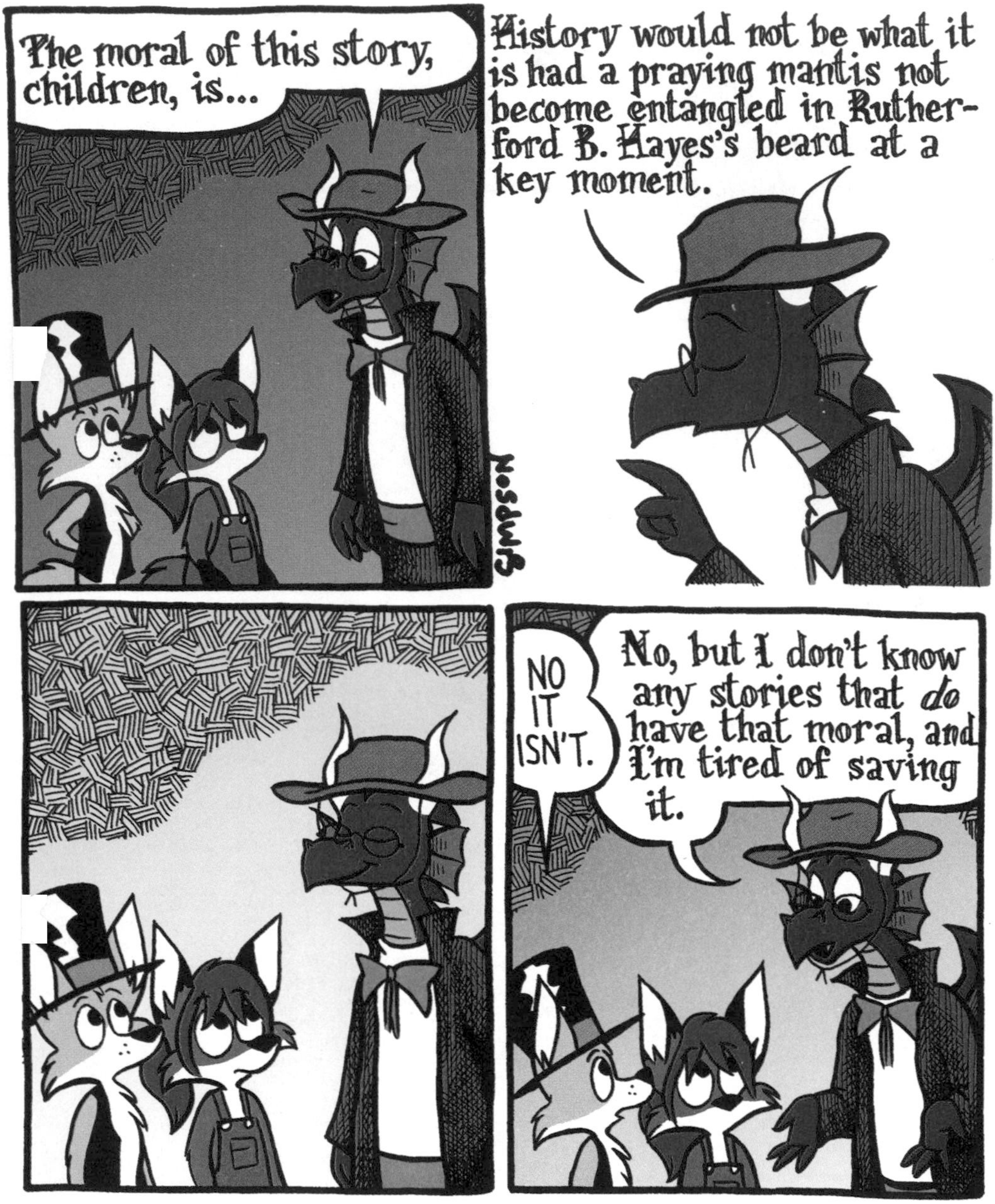
The moral of this story, children, is...
History would not be what it is had a praying mantis not become entangled in Rutherford B. Hayes's beard at a key moment.
SIMPSON
NO IT ISN'T.
No, but I don't know any stories that *do* have that moral, and I'm tired of saving it.

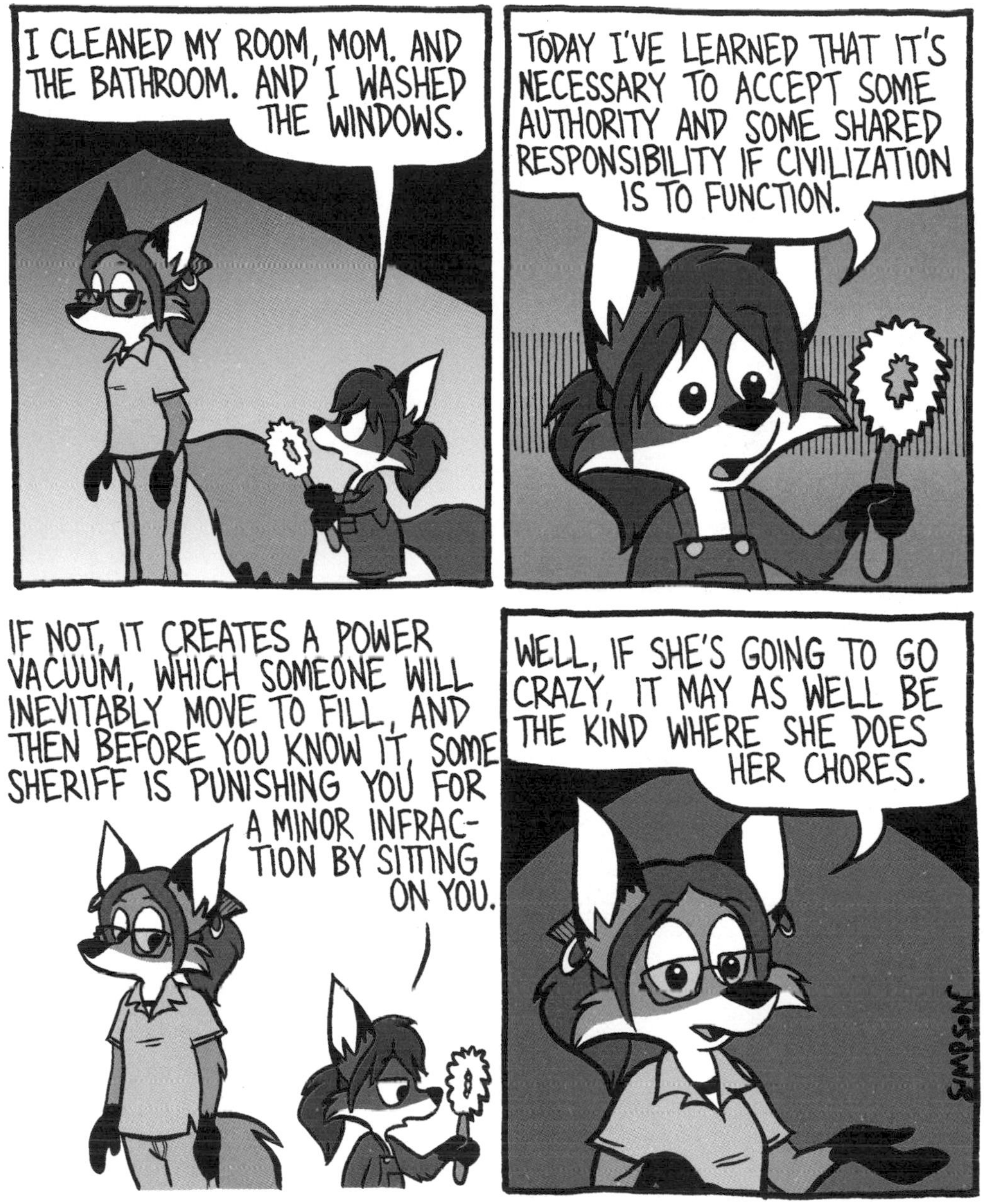
I CLEANED MY ROOM, MOM. AND THE BATHROOM. AND I WASHED THE WINDOWS.
TODAY I'VE LEARNED THAT IT'S NECESSARY TO ACCEPT SOME AUTHORITY AND SOME SHARED RESPONSIBILITY IF CIVILIZATION IS TO FUNCTION.
IF NOT, IT CREATES A POWER VACUUM, WHICH SOMEONE WILL INEVITABLY MOVE TO FILL, AND THEN BEFORE YOU KNOW IT, SOME SHERIFF IS PUNISHING YOU FOR A MINOR INFRACTION BY SITTING ON YOU.
WELL, IF SHE'S GOING TO GO CRAZY, IT MAY AS WELL BE THE KIND WHERE SHE DOES HER CHORES.
SIMPSON

MORE TO EXPLORE! A special section featuring fun activities and words to learn!

SOME TIPS ON DRAWING
OZY AND MILLIE

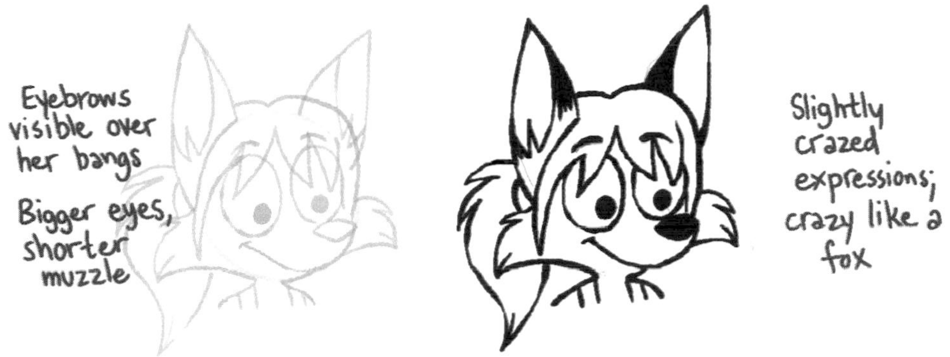
Eyebrows visible over her bangs
Bigger eyes, shorter muzzle
Slightly crazed expressions; crazy like a fox

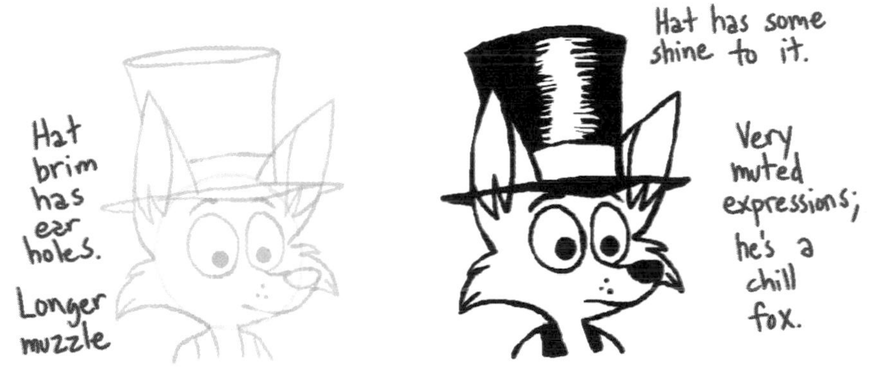
Hat has some shine to it.
Hat brim has ear holes.
Longer muzzle
Very muted expressions; he's a chill fox.

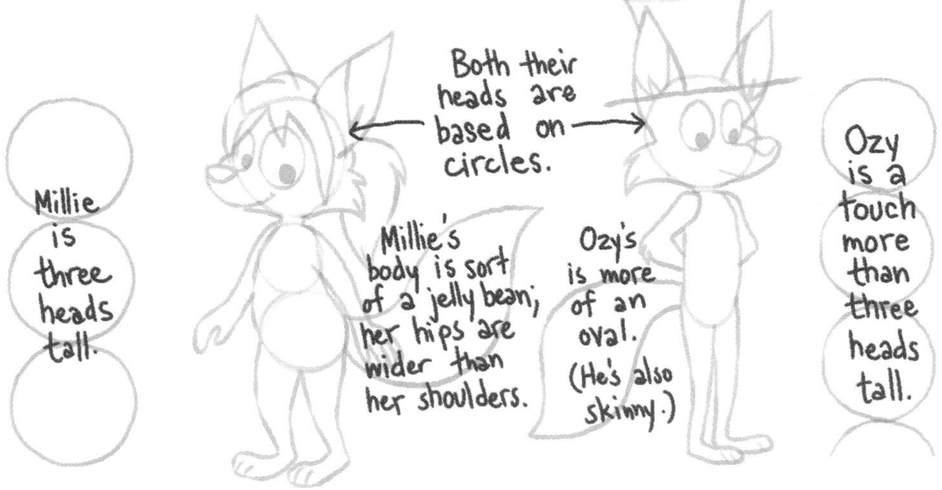

Millie is three heads tall.

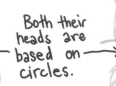

Both their heads are based on circles.

Millie's body is sort of a jelly bean; her hips are wider than her shoulders.

Ozy's is more of an oval. (He's also skinny.)

Ozy is a touch more than three heads tall.

Overalls with no shirt

Black tailtip

White tailtip

Fluffy chest

Often stands with hands behind his back

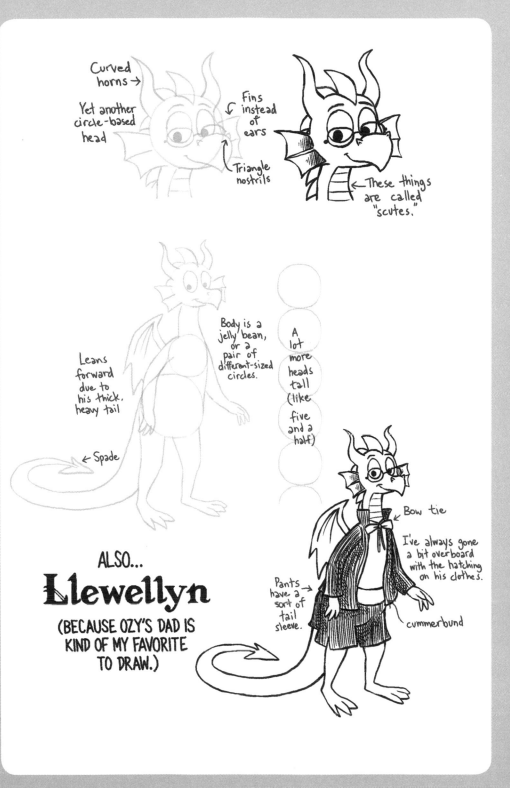

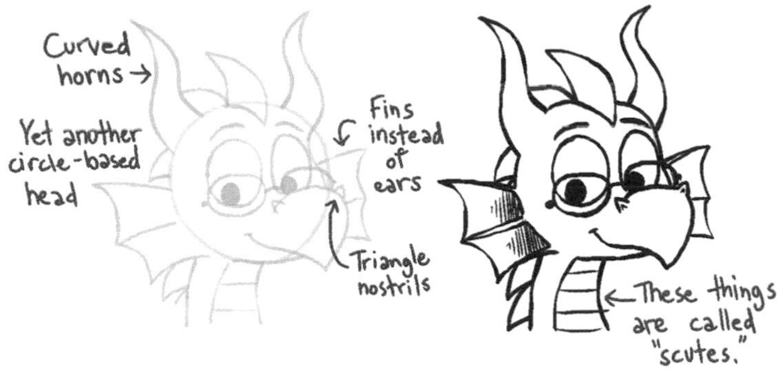
Curved horns →
Yet another circle-based head
Fins instead of ears
Triangle nostrils
← These things are called "scutes."

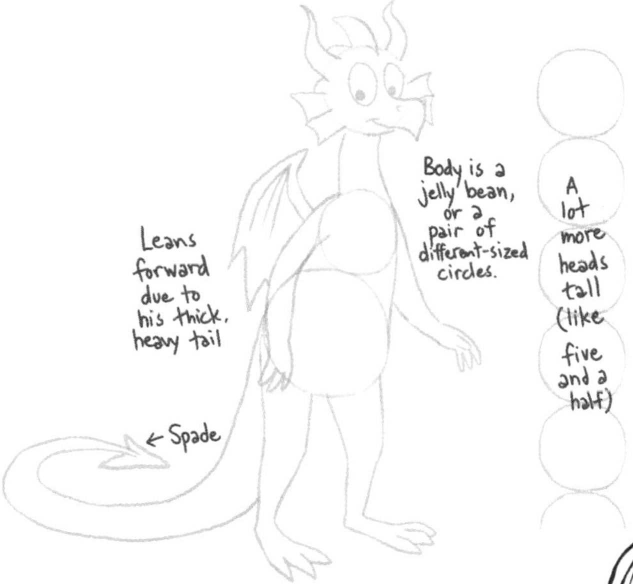
Leans forward due to his thick, heavy tail
Body is a jelly bean, or a pair of different-sized circles.
A lot more heads tall (like five and a half)
← Spade

ALSO...

Llewellyn

(BECAUSE OZY'S DAD IS KIND OF MY FAVORITE TO DRAW.)

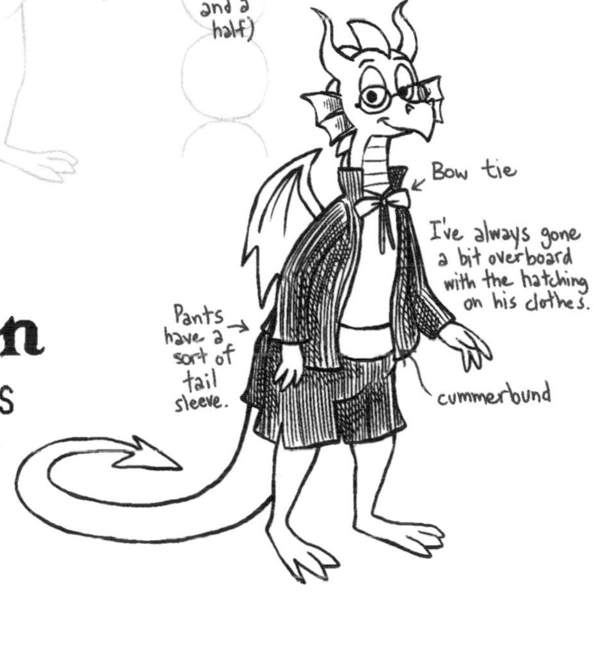
Bow tie
I've always gone a bit overboard with the hatching on his clothes.
Pants have a sort of tail sleeve.
cummerbund

GLOSSARY

ALTRUISTIC (AHL-TROO-IS-TIK): pg. 132 – adjective / showing care and concern for the well-being of other people

CAPITALISM (KAH-PI-TEL-IZM): pg. 100 – noun / an economic and political system in which a country's trade and industry are controlled by private owners for profit

CARPAL TUNNEL (KAR-PEL TUN-EL): pg. 117 – noun / a nerve condition that causes weakness and pain in the hand and fingers

CARPE DIEM (KAR-PAY DEE-EM): pg. 52 – exclamation / used to urge someone to "seize the day" by making the most of the present time and giving little thought to the future

COMPLACENT (KUM-PLAY-SENT): pg. 12 – adjective / self-satisfied and pleased with oneself in spite of possible dangers or shortcomings

CONSCIENTIOUS OBJECTOR (KAHN-SHEE-EN-SHUS AB-JEK-TER): pg. 126 – noun / a person who refuses to serve in the armed forces because of their moral or religious beliefs

COPYRIGHT (KAH-PEE-RAIT): pg. 44 – noun / the legal right to copy, publish, sell, or distribute something, such as an invention, design, or work of art

EQUILIBRIUM (EE-KWI-LI-BREE-UM): pg. 69 – noun / a state in which opposing forces or influences are balanced

GHOSTWRITTEN (GOHST-RI-TEN): pg. 117 – verb, past participle / written for and in the name of someone else

HIPPIE (HIH-PEE): pg. 36 – noun / someone who rejects the normal standards of society, often by growing their hair long, wearing unusual clothing, and promoting a peaceful, communal way of life

HUBRIS (HYOO-BRES): pg. 132 – noun / exaggerated pride or self-confidence

JINGOISM (JING-GO-IZM): pg. 149 – noun / extreme nationalism, especially in the form of militant foreign policy

MOGUL (MOW-GUHL): pg. 100 – noun / an important or powerful person, especially in the motion picture or media industry

NARCOLEPTIC (NAR-KE-LEP-TIK): pg. 133 – adjective / affected with narcolepsy, a condition characterized by an extreme tendency to fall asleep whenever in relaxing surroundings

NOSTALGIA (NAH-STAHL-JYAH): pg. 122 – noun / a longing for the past

PLEDGE DRIVE (PLEHDJ DRAIV): pg. 95 – noun / fundraising campaign that encourages people to promise to make donations to a specific cause

PREDETERMINISM (PREE-DEE-TER-MIN-IZM): pg. 38 – noun / the belief that all events, including human actions, are decided in advance

PYROMANIAC (PIE-ROW-MAY-NEE-AK): pg. 44 – noun / a person with an irresistible impulse to start fires

REVERSE PSYCHOLOGY (REE-VERS SAI-KAH-LO-JEE): pg. 104 – noun / a method of getting someone to do what one wants by pretending to want the opposite

STRATOSPHERE (STRA-TES-FEER): pg. 114 – noun / the second layer of the earth's atmosphere, extending from eleven miles (18 km) to about thirty-one miles (50 km) above the earth's surface

ZEN (ZEN): pg. 154 – adjective / showing an attitude of calmness and acceptance, often associated with the followers of Zen Buddhism

Important People, Places, and Things

HOBBESIAN SOCIAL CONTRACT THEORY: pg. 71 – proper noun / the belief of English philosopher Thomas Hobbes (1588–1679) that people can live more safely if they agree to give up individual freedoms in exchange for obeying a common authority or government

MACHIAVELLI (MACK-EE-UH-VELL-EE): pg. 71 – proper noun / Niccolò Machiavelli (1469–1527), an Italian politician, writer, and philosopher who believed that deceit and selfish behavior were OK if it led to personal gain

NAPOLEON (NA-POH-LEE-IN): pg. 111 – proper noun / Napoleon Bonaparte or Napoleon I (1769–1821), emperor of the French (1804–1815)

ORWELLIAN (OR-WEL-EE-IN): pg. 155 – adjective / resembling the totalitarian political methods warned about in the works of writer George Orwell, particularly in the classic novel *Nineteen Eighty-Four*

TAO TE CHING (DOW DAY JING): pg. 139 – proper noun / a fundamental text for both philosophical and religious Taoism, believed to date from the sixth century BC

TEDDY ROOSEVELT (TEH-DEE ROW-ZEH-VELT): pg. 110 – proper noun / Theodore Roosevelt (1858–1919), twenty-sixth president of the United States (1901–09)

THOMAS MORE (TAHM-ES MOR): pg. 153 – proper noun / Sir Thomas More (1478–1535), an English lawyer, social philosopher, author, statesman, and noted Renaissance humanist

WILLIAM FAULKNER (WIL-YEM FAUK-NER): pg. 138 – proper noun / an American writer (1897–1962) from Oxford, Mississippi, who was awarded the Nobel Prize in Literature

Andrews McMeel Publishing
a division of Andrews McMeel Universal
1130 Walnut Street, Kansas City, Missouri 64106

www.andrewsmcmeel.com

18 19 20 21 22 RR2 10 9 8 7 6 5 4 3 2 1

ISBN: 978-1-4494-9595-4

Library of Congress Control Number: 2018938006

Made by:
LSC Communications US, LLC
Address and location of manufacturer:
1009 Sloan Street
Crawfordsville, IN 47933
1st Printing—7/20/18

ATTENTION: SCHOOLS AND BUSINESSES
Andrews McMeel books are available at quantity discounts with bulk purchase for educational, business, or sales promotional use. For information, please e-mail the Andrews McMeel Publishing Special Sales Department: specialsales@amuniversal.com.

Check out more from Dana Simpson

Unicorn on a Roll
Another Phoebe and Her Unicorn Adventure
Dana Simpson

Unicorn vs. Goblins
Another Phoebe and Her Unicorn Adventure
Dana Simpson

Razzle Dazzle Unicorn
Another Phoebe and Her Unicorn Adventure
Dana Simpson

Unicorn Crossing
Another Phoebe and Her Unicorn Adventure
Dana Simpson

Phoebe and Her Unicorn in
The Magic Storm
Dana Simpson

Rainy Day Unicorn Fun
140 Magical Puzzles
A Phoebe and Her Unicorn Activity Book
Dana Simpson

If you like *Ozy and Millie*, look for these books!

Anne of Green Gables
a graphic novel

the Pinkaboos
BITTERLY AND THE GIANT PROBLEM
FRIGHT SCHOOL
Jake and Laura Gosselin

Wallace the Brave
Will Henry

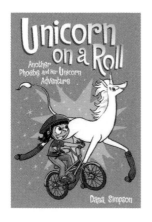

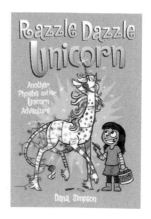

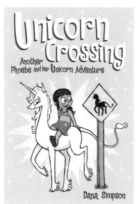

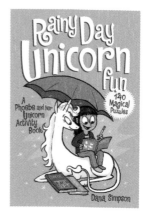

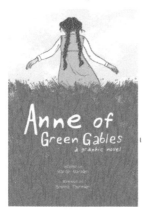

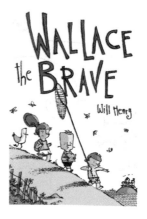